Andy McDermott is the bestselling ... Eddie Chase adventure thrillers, w... countries and 20 languages. His deb... was his first of several *New York Times* bestseller... written the explosive spy thriller *The Persona Protocol* and the action-packed *Alex Reeve* thriller series.

A former journalist and movie critic, Andy is now a full-time novelist. Born in Halifax, he lives in Bournemouth with his partner and son.

Praise for Andy McDermott:

'Adventure stories don't get much more epic than this' *Daily Mirror*

'*Operative 66* is an action-packed thrill ride . . . twists and turns that will keep you guessing at a blistering pace that never lets up' Adam Hamdy

'A writer of rare, almost cinematic talent. Where others' action scenes limp along unconvincingly, his explode off the page in Technicolor' *Daily Express*

'If Wilbur Smith and Clive Cussler collaborated, they might have come up with a thundering big adventure blockbuster like this . . . a widescreen, thrill-a-minute ride' *Peterborough Evening Telegraph*

'True Indiana Jones stuff with terrific pace' *Bookseller*

'Fast-moving, this is a pulse-racing adventure with action right down the line' *Northern Echo*

'For readers who like hundred mile an hour plots' Huddersfield *Daily Examiner*

'An all-action cracker from one of Britain's most talented adventure writers' *Lancashire Evening Post*

'A rip-roaring read and one which looks set to cement McDermott's place in the bestsellers list for years to come' *Bolton Evening News*

ROGUE ASSET

ANDY McDERMOTT

HEADLINE

First published in 2021 by
HEADLINE PUBLISHING GROUP

First published in paperback in 2022

1

Cataloguing in Publication Data is available from the British Library

ISBN 978 1 4722 6385 8

Typeset in Sabon by Avon DataSet Ltd, Alcester, Warwickshire

Printed and bound in Great Britain by Clays Ltd, Elcograf S.p.A.

Headline's policy is to use papers that are natural, renewable and
recyclable products and made from wood grown in well-managed forests
and other controlled sources. The logging and manufacturing processes
are expected to conform to the environmental regulations of the
country of origin.

HEADLINE PUBLISHING GROUP
An Hachette UK Company
Carmelite House
50 Victoria Embankment
London EC4Y 0DZ

www.headline.co.uk
www.hachette.co.uk

For Kat and Sebastian

CHAPTER 1

Konstantin Nesterov didn't spot his killers until it was too late.

Walking his dog was one of the Russian's few opportunities for tranquillity. Today was especially peaceful. The damp ground in the thick woods smothered noise. The constant rumble of London-bound traffic was barely audible.

London. His shoulders sagged at the thought of the city. It had once been a prime diplomatic posting; glamorous, cultured, exciting. But things had changed. Relations between Russia and Britain, frosty at best, had tipped towards hostility. And since Brexit, the capital itself felt distinctly unfriendly to foreigners. He was looking forward to returning home.

Not least because if the British knew his *real* job, they wouldn't let him leave. That was, not until the next exchange of spies between London and Moscow.

Nesterov was no James Bond, he readily admitted. In his fifties, overweight, divorced, he was hardly the physical type. But his purpose was still espionage. Officially he was a member of the Trade Delegation of the Russian Federation. Which was true. But he had another mission beyond expediting business deals and smoothing import-export paperwork.

His speciality was finding the weak links in corporate chains. People who might be persuaded to put their own interests above company, and country. Their interests being best served by aligning with Russia's.

Such people were generally easy to deal with, once identified. Flatter and befriend – then bribe and, if necessary, blackmail. But that last was rarely needed. People could be surprisingly easy to buy. One of Nesterov's best contacts willingly leaked critical financial secrets in exchange for Wimbledon tickets. The information he and others gave benefited Russian businesses internationally, at the expense of British ones.

In the UK, Nesterov's actions were considered a crime. One for which he didn't have the shield of diplomatic immunity. He'd always been careful; he wouldn't have lasted this long otherwise. But . . .

Things were changing in Britain. Not for the better. Since the collateral nerve-agent poisoning of civilians in Salisbury, Russians were under increased scrutiny. It was the kind of attention Nesterov could do without. He was almost certainly on MI5, GCHQ and Special Branch's watch lists. Every move had to be made with increased caution.

But something else was going on. What had started as rumours months earlier was now an open secret. Several Russians attached to the diplomatic service in the UK had met with accidents. Or 'accidents'. Falls, car crashes, fires, drug overdoses. Bad luck and coincidence perhaps, but so many, so close together? It wasn't the usual British way of playing the spy game – which made Nesterov nervous. Either someone else was involved, or the Brits were dropping their traditional cautiousness. Both possibilities were unnerving. Another good reason to return home . . .

A bark brought him back to the moment. Mischa, his Labrador, had been twenty metres ahead, exploring the trees. The reddish-brown dog was now stationary, looking off to one side. Nesterov followed her gaze. Someone else was in the woods. A man, approaching through the morning mist.

The figure called out. 'Jimbo! Come!'

Nesterov halted, listening. No sounds of another dog nearby. Mischa barked again. 'Here, girl,' he said. She trotted obediently back to him.

The man shouted again. Still no response. He continued towards Nesterov.

The Russian took him in as he neared. Late thirties, black hair, tall. Something about his bearing suggested a military background: a confident authority. He smiled as he approached, giving Mischa an admiring look.

'I say, beautiful dog,' said the new arrival. His voice was smooth, well-educated.

'Thank you,' Nesterov replied.

'I seem to have misplaced my own. You haven't seen a collie, have you? He ran off after a squirrel a few minutes ago.'

'I'm afraid not.'

The man sighed. 'Looks like I'll have to resort to bribery to bring him back.' He dug into a coat pocket, producing a large bag of dog treats. 'Jimbo! Here!' He shook the bag, rustling its contents. Mischa sat in anticipation, wagging her tail. He leaned towards her, then paused. 'You don't mind, do you?'

'No. It is fine.'

'Always polite to check.' He tossed the Labrador a treat. She snapped it out of the air. 'Good – boy or girl?'

'Girl.'

'Good girl.' He shook the bag again, keeping Mischa's attention. 'Hopefully mine will—' He turned his head. 'Oh, there he is.'

Nesterov looked for himself. No sign of any dog through the trees—

A noise behind, quiet footfalls – and a shard of fire tore upwards into his back.

The black-haired man, John Blake, watched dispassionately as his partner stabbed Nesterov from behind. Harrison Locke had slipped stealthily closer while Blake kept their target distracted. In his former life, Locke had been a military surgeon. He was also, Blake had come to realise, a cold-blooded psychopath. His black carbon-fibre blade struck with unerring precision, puncturing the liver.

The dog reacted in alarm. She barked at Locke, teeth bared. Blake was prepared. 'Hey, hey!' he called, shaking out the bag. Meaty treats scattered across the ground. The Lab was torn between protecting her master and the prospect of food.

By now, Locke had clamped a gloved hand over Nesterov's mouth, choking off his scream. He twisted his knife before withdrawing the weapon. Blood sluiced down the Russian's coat. Another couple of jabs, catching Nesterov's flailing arm. These were as carefully aimed as the first. They would create the impression of defensive wounds. The attack couldn't appear too one-sided. The assassination had to look like a mugging gone wrong.

The dog kept barking, but was too afraid to attack. Locke maintained his hold as Nesterov's movements weakened. He stabbed the other man again, this time in the side. The strike was almost half-hearted. All part of the show. The precise, lethal wound would be surrounded by ones that appeared amateurish.

Finally, Nesterov slumped. Locke released his grip. His victim crumpled to the damp ground. Blake surveyed their surroundings, opening his coat to access the gun inside. If another dog-walker had heard the commotion, they would have to die too . . .

But there was nobody in sight.

'Get his phone and wallet,' said Blake over the dog's distressed barks.

Locke gave him an icy look. 'I do remember the plan, John.' He crouched beside the twitching body. The Labrador made a move towards him. He snapped up the knife as if about to stab it.

'Hey,' said Blake as the dog flinched back. 'No need to be cruel.'

'Very amusing,' Locke replied, without the slightest hint of a smile. He rooted through Nesterov's belongings, pocketing his wallet and phone. 'Got them.'

Blake made another check of the woods. Still clear. He moved to examine the corpse.

'I assure you, he's quite dead,' said Locke.

'Just confirming the kill.' Satisfied, he stepped back. One benefit of operating on home soil was that less clean-up was needed. Arrangements could be made for DNA or other forensic evidence to be contaminated, or 'lost'. Both men were Operatives, members of an elite British covert intelligence agency: SC9. Officially, it did not exist. Outside SC9, only a handful of highly placed people knew of it. Despite this, it wielded subtle, yet powerful influence within the apparatus of state security. Its purpose, however, was blunt.

Eliminate enemies of the British state. By any means necessary.

Even knowing they would be protected, the Operatives wanted to avoid needless errors. Once Locke had cleaned and sheathed the murder weapon, they both checked the scene. Anything that might incriminate them would be microscopic in nature. All they'd left were footprints. No matter: their shoes were brand-new, bought the previous day. Before the end of this one, they would be incinerated. 'We're clean,' Blake finally announced. 'Let's go.'

Locke stared at the barking dog. 'It's a witness. We should eliminate it.'

'You know they can't talk, right?' Blake kicked a couple of treats towards the animal before walking off. 'That's a nice dog, actually. Fox red.'

'Ironic.' Again, there was no trace of humour behind Locke's reply.

Blake nodded. 'Yeah.' A brief smile. *Fox Red* was the SC9 code for an internal threat: a traitor. The agency's head was also a breeder of pedigree Labradors. He had very strong negative views about the lineage and worth of 'fox red' dogs.

The smile vanished. Anyone declared Fox Red by SC9 was to be killed, immediately. But one traitor had escaped his death sentence. Even after a year and a half, the thought still rankled Blake. Alex Reeve's survival was almost a personal insult. 'Another spy down, then. Maybe the Russians will finally get the message. Hit at SC9, we hit back ten times harder.'

The two Operatives disappeared into the mist, leaving the dog to cry over her owner.

CHAPTER 2

Alex Reeve was living his third life.

In his first, he was Dominic Finch. The son of a violent father – the man who murdered his mother. After his father was imprisoned, he was alone. He drifted through foster homes before eventually joining the army. That finally gave the young man a goal: to be the best.

It was a goal he pursued arduously. And he succeeded. His single-minded focus, determination and skill drew the attention of the special forces. He was recruited into the elite Special Reconnaissance Regiment. His task: work undercover to protect the realm. He mostly operated alone, adopting new roles, new identities. Despite the danger, he'd enjoyed it. The more time he spent as someone else, the less he had to be himself.

His second life began when he was recruited by a higher elite. SC9 took only the best of the best. Then made them even better. He adopted another new identity. Dominic Finch was gone; Alex Reeve was born. His old life was abandoned, and he was more than happy to let it go.

SC9 was the very tip of the nation's spear. Britain's enemies, at home and abroad, were not bound by the law. So neither were SC9's members – the Operatives. They fought fire with fire, taking any actions required, up to and including assassination. Such acts were necessary to protect the country.

Or so Reeve had been told.

It was all a lie.

He'd completed his training, become an Operative – then been immediately targeted for elimination. By his own side. SC9 had declared him Fox Red: a traitor. But Reeve was innocent. Why had he been marked for death? He didn't know. So he used all his skills to survive, escape – and run.

Alone, hunted by his former colleagues, he nevertheless eventually uncovered the truth. Another Operative, Craig Parker, had framed him to cover his own treachery. Reeve confronted him to learn *why*. Both Parker's parents had died; his mother in an underfunded hospital, his father in prison. The British state was, he insisted, culpable in their deaths. So he was taking his revenge by attacking it from within. Reeve had been framed simply because he was the most convenient patsy.

While SC9 hunted Reeve, Parker was free to embark on his own plan. He had been ordered to eliminate a progressive politician whom SC9's boss considered troublesome. The intent of the assignment was subtlety: to arrange an 'accident'. Parker, however, planned a very public murder. After which he would expose SC9 to the world's media. The agency had killed civilians and officials in friendly nations as well as hostile ones. It would be a diplomatic catastrophe, making Britain a pariah, tearing apart alliances. The damage to the country would be incalculable.

Reeve had stopped him, killing Parker in the process. But

his own death sentence had not been lifted. All he could do was run again, and hide.

Which was where his third life began.

He still thought of himself as Alex Reeve. Officially, though, he was now Angelo Moretti. That was the name on his fake IDs. They'd cost him thousands of euros. Money well spent; they'd held up to scrutiny. SC9 hadn't found him, and nobody else had questioned his identity.

Now he lived in Italy. And he was no longer alone. He had Connie.

Connie . . .

Just the thought of her made him smile. He'd met her by fluke while on the run. Wounded, desperate, he reached a London hospital with the intention of stealing medical supplies. Instead, he found her. A nurse, she had helped him recover, given him shelter.

Why, was a question he'd asked her more than once. She'd had nothing to gain by taking an injured stranger into her home. 'Because I'm a nurse, and it's my job to help people,' was her stock answer. But she had once given him a more personal reason. *Waifs and strays*, as she put it. As a child, she had often brought home lost or hurt animals. Selfless caring was ingrained in her. She was a healer, kind and gentle, compassionate, open.

The diametric opposite of the man Alex Reeve had once been. Yet now they were together. And he couldn't imagine being without her.

He heard the car outside and went to meet her. The heat of late summer swaddled him as he left the apartment. Rolling green and yellow hills spread to the horizon all around. The

Villa di Luna, a farmhouse converted into holiday flats, was in western Umbria. In the four months they had been here, Reeve had never stopped admiring his surroundings. He'd grown up in an impoverished part of Manchester. Beauty was hard to find there. Yet here, it was inescapable.

Feeling the sun on his face, he descended the slope at the building's side. Their old Fiat Panda stopped on the gravel drive behind it. The boxy little car was dented, green paint faded. Reeve had chosen it for several reasons, though. Both model and colour were common in rural Italy; it was anonymous. It was cheap to run, reliable enough, and easy to maintain with basic tools. And it had four-wheel drive. Many local roads, whatever online maps claimed, were little more than farm tracks. Even the relatively well-maintained route past the villa was unsurfaced. Approaching vehicles announced themselves with dusty rooster-tails long before becoming visible.

Connie smiled at him as she got out. 'Hi,' he said. 'Good day?'

'Pretty good,' she replied. 'I'm glad to be back, though. A lot of running around today.' Her qualifications had found her work at a nursing home. The job in turn had helped her hugely improve her Italian.

'Well, you can relax now. I've made pansotti for dinner. And there's still a bottle of wine in the fridge.'

She wrapped her arms around his waist. Summer in Italy had been good for her. She was tanned, long brown hair lightened by the sun. 'Aren't you just the perfect man?'

'I try.' They kissed. 'Let's go in.'

They headed back up around the farmhouse. As they

reached their apartment, the door of another opened. 'Oh hi, there you are,' said Gina Trentini, in Italian. Their landlady owned the villa. She and her late husband had renovated and divided it into flats. It was currently in a rare lull, the three people the only residents. Reeve and Connie were in the smallest flat. In exchange for a reduced cash rent, Reeve acted as handyman. Manual labour in summer had been hard work, but he'd found it surprisingly engaging.

'Hi, Gina,' Connie answered. 'How are you?'

'Good, thank you. And you? How was work? It's definitely helping you improve your Italian.'

'Yes, it's much better than when I first arrived. I only had to repeat myself once today.'

'You'll get there. Your Italian is far better than my English!' Gina turned to Reeve. 'Angelo, I'm buying the bricks for the new wall tomorrow morning. Can you help me with them?'

Reeve glanced towards his most recent handiwork. He'd laid flagstones for a sun porch. Making room for it had required him to dig out part of a sloping lawn. The exposed bare earth needed to be bricked in before the autumn rains arrived. 'Yeah, of course,' he replied. 'What time do you want to go?' He was fluent in Italian, one of the languages learned during his SC9 training.

'The place opens at nine, so eight-thirty?'

'That's fine.'

'And could you start building it tomorrow as well?'

Connie pursed her lips. 'Oh. I have the day off tomorrow. I was hoping to spend it with him.'

'I promised Gina I'd do it,' Reeve reminded her.

A faint sigh. 'You did, didn't you?'

'I won't be working on it all day,' he said. 'All I can do tomorrow is finish the foundation trench, then pour the concrete. Should be done by lunchtime. We'll still have the afternoon.'

'I suppose,' she said, in English. He could tell she was disappointed.

'I'll make it up to you,' Gina assured her. 'I can do more pansotti, if you like the first batch.'

Connie gave Reeve a quizzical look. 'I'm sure we will,' he said. 'That'd be great, thanks.'

'See you tomorrow morning, then. Ciao!' The Italian returned to her flat.

Reeve and Connie went to their own. 'So,' she said, 'I thought *you* made dinner?'

'I chopped the onions. That's the hard part. It counts.'

'Yeah, right.' She gave him a smile, but it was only thin.

Until he met Connie, Reeve had kept his emotional shields permanently raised. As a result, he wasn't skilled at reading the feelings of others. But after nine months together, he could tell something was troubling her. 'What's wrong? You're not mad I agreed to help Gina tomorrow, are you?'

'No, it's not that,' she said. 'I'm fine. Just a bit . . . homesick.'

'You're homesick?' The admission surprised him.

'One of my residents lived in London in the eighties. We got chatting about it.' She sat heavily on the sofa. 'It made me realise how much I missed it.'

'I thought you hated your flat.'

'I don't mean the flat, Alex. I mean London, in general.

England. I was born there, I grew up there. I might have an Italian passport now, but it still feels like a foreign country.' Connie's mother had been Italian, granting her dual nationality. 'I don't know the politics, the social quirks, the . . . *backstory*. I don't have much common ground when I'm talking to people. I miss that.'

'You want to go back to London?'

She shook her head. 'Not really. But I feel . . . cut off, if that makes sense?'

'We *are* a bit isolated out here.' The nearest town was Castiglione del Lago, almost ten kilometres away.

'Yeah. And I'm a city girl! I love it here, it's beautiful. But I feel like I'm missing out on things I used to take for granted.'

'Like what?'

'Silly stuff. Going out to a club. Music, meeting friends, bitching about politics. Just . . . *gossip*, you know? Finding out what's going on.'

'Right.' Reeve nodded in what he hoped seemed like understanding agreement. He didn't miss the social banalities at all.

She saw right through him, he realised. But she didn't hold it against him, or try to score points. 'I know, that's not your thing,' Connie said instead. 'It'd just be nice to do something a bit more lively.'

'We could go to Venice,' he suggested. 'We've been talking about it for ages. We should actually do it.'

The idea visibly perked her up. 'Really?'

'It's, what, four hundred kilometres away? We could drive there in a morning. Or get the train. There must be a connection to Venice from Florence.'

'There is. I looked it up a while ago.'

'You did?'

She gave him a small, sly smile. 'Might have looked up places to visit as well.'

'Advance recon, eh? You've learned something from me.'

A flicker of emotion in her eyes, quickly covered. He had turned his back on SC9, but she still knew its purpose. 'Just basic Girl Guides stuff,' she said. 'Be prepared.'

'I always am.' Both their gazes went to something near the front door: the 'bug-out bag'. It contained everything they might need if they had to leave in a hurry. The pack had been their constant companion for nine months. The first five, travelling through France and Italy, it had rarely left Reeve's side. He'd gradually relaxed as it became clear SC9's Operatives weren't right behind them. Lately, he'd even started going out without it. Was he getting lax – or just feeling secure? He'd chided himself over it, but . . .

Well, he *did* feel secure. He'd successfully evaded his pursuers for almost eighteen months. And the last person he'd seen from SC9 had let him go. As thanks for stopping Parker, Reeve's former mentor Tony Maxwell gave him a head start. Only three minutes, but that was enough to disappear into London.

After that, he recovered, regrouped, re-equipped. He'd already acquired money from a drug dealer stupid enough to tangle with him. That let him buy new identities. He'd burned one of them to leave the country; it was too risky to use again. But he had others in the bag, if needed.

Which hopefully they now wouldn't be. Eighteen months. SC9 hadn't caught him in that time, with almost limitless resources. The agency could call upon all of British Intelligence – MI5, MI6, GCHQ and more. If they hadn't found him by now, they probably never would. As long as he kept his head down.

Reeve certainly wasn't planning to raise it. His new life made him happy. *Connie* made him happy.

And he wanted to make her happy in return. 'Maybe we could go next week,' he said. 'If you can take a few days off?'

'I'm sure I can,' Connie replied. 'Okay, then. It's set. We're going to Venice!' Her smile returned, wider. 'I'll check for hotels after dinner.'

'Nothing too fancy,' he jokingly cautioned. 'We don't want to blow all our money.'

'Aw. I had my heart set on the penthouse at the Gritti Palace.'

Reeve laughed, then started to cook dinner.

CHAPTER 3

The reddening sun lay fat on the western horizon. Reeve ran towards it, eyes narrowed against the glare.

Gina's pansotti had been as delicious as he'd hoped. Connie was now relaxing with a glass of post-dinner wine. Reeve, though, had headed out on a 5K run. It was probably too soon after eating. But he might not have time next morning – and he'd also been slacking.

A run had long been part of his daily routine. But as with the bug-out bag, recently he'd started letting it slide. He needed to watch that. Just because he'd found a comfortable life didn't mean he could turn into a blob . . .

His route took him on a loop. It wasn't a precise five thousand metres, but he could live with it. He would once have been far more anal about the discrepancy, he thought with amusement. Out from the villa, up into the village of Sanfatucchio. Past the second church, back downhill to the hamlet of Bracacci. West along the track, cut up through the fields, then back on the unpaved road.

From here, the only house ahead was the villa. There was another landmark, though: the haystack. It wasn't like the little rotund ones of childhood stories, however. This was larger than some of the area's farmhouses. Forklift-equipped tractors had built it up over summer, bale by hulking bale. He'd occasionally seen local kids climbing on top of it.

Reeve ran past it, descending back towards the villa. A car was heading towards him from Sanfatucchio, a pale cloud swirling behind. He wouldn't reach home before it passed. A faceful of dust awaited. Still, he needed a shower anyway.

Round the next bend, the hill steepening. The track to the villa branched off a hairpin. As he'd expected, the car, a Volkswagen, came around it first. He moved to let it pass. He'd seen the Golf before, but still checked the driver as it approached. Car and face – an overweight Italian man in his fifties – matched in his mental database. Definitely not Operative material. He waited for the dust to subside, then ran again.

The last leg was down a rutted track. It weaved through trees to Bracacci, but his destination was only a hundred metres on. He turned up the villa's drive, rounding the farm-house to reach the flat.

He checked his time. Just over twenty-five minutes. Far from his best, but he hadn't been pushing. He stood in the golden sunlight to regain his breath, then went inside.

Reeve knew at once that something was wrong. Connie was on their laptop, hurriedly looking around as he entered. Her expression was . . . guilty? No, worried, as if she'd seen something she shouldn't. 'Alex. Oh. Hi.'

He went to her. 'You okay?'

'Yeah, I'm fine.' She wasn't.

He glanced at the computer. An English newspaper's website. 'So what's the matter?'

'I, ah . . .' She hesitated. Reeve grew concerned himself.

Had she done something to give them away? He doubted it – she knew the dangers, the precautions they had to take. The laptop was as secure as he could make it, microphone and camera removed. It also ran a security-enhanced Linux operating system to restrict hacks and malware. Their online footprints were as light as they could be. So what was troubling her?

'I was looking at the news from home,' she continued. 'All kinds of stuff, just catching up. There was a story about Elektra Curtis.' Connie admired the young progressive politician – who had been Parker's assassination target.

'Something's happened to her?' said Reeve, alarmed.

'No, she's fine. But – well, I'll show you.' She clicked back to the previous page. An image of Curtis appeared. She looked older, more serious, than when she and Reeve had briefly locked eyes. Her political star had risen; she was now Shadow Minister for Security. 'There was one of those "also in the news" sidebars. And I saw . . . this.'

She indicated the link. Reeve looked more closely.

And froze.

It was a picture of his father.

Like Curtis, he looked older. Understandable; Reeve hadn't seen him since childhood. But his expression wasn't the cruel anger he remembered. He was smiling: a smug smirk of triumph.

The accompanying headline explained why. *Wrongfully convicted man freed after 16 years.*

'I saw his name,' Connie went on. 'Jude Finch. I remembered you'd said that was your dad's name. So I checked the story, and . . . it's him. They let him go.'

19

'They . . .' A feeling from the past rose inside Reeve, one he'd hoped would never return. A cold, paralysing fear, gripping his heart. He forcefully overcame it. 'Let me see.'

Connie moved so he could sit at the laptop. He read on. *Jude Finch released after son's testimony revealed as lie.*

He clicked the link. The page Connie had been reading reloaded. *Murder sentence quashed.* He speed-read the story. Anger grew alongside the inner chill.

His father had indeed been released from his life sentence. The reason was Reeve himself. His own testimony, key to the conviction, had been struck down. Without it, only circumstantial evidence remained – Jude Finch had carefully covered his tracks. That had not been enough to keep him in prison.

But the story had a frustrating lack of detail. The newspaper was a tabloid, dealing in short sentences and snappy soundbites. The human-interest summary was all its journalists cared about. '*It took a long time, but justice was finally done,*' said Finch. *What will he do first now he's free?* '*I'm going to the pub!*'

The story had a final, brief paragraph. *Finch's son, Dominic (29), is wanted for questioning on perjury charges. His whereabouts are unknown.*

Reeve stared at the words, then called up a search engine. 'What are you doing?' asked Connie.

'I need to know more,' was his brusque reply. He typed in search terms: *jude finch released*. Links appeared. He clicked on one. Another picture of his father, triumphant. Reeve's anger surged again.

The new story had more details. Not only had his father been released; he'd received compensation for wrongful conviction. That in itself confirmed a dawning suspicion. When it came to paying for its mistakes, the British government *never* moved quickly. Yet Finch had got his money immediately. 'It's them,' he growled as he clicked back. 'SC9.'

Connie stiffened in alarm. 'What do you mean?'

'They got him out.' The next story told him his father had returned to his home city of Manchester. 'They're using him to find me.' Another shock on the following link: a picture of himself. The mugshot was a few years old, from his military ID. *Liar: Dominic Finch was dishonourably discharged from the Army*, read the caption. 'It's an excuse for them to put my face all over the news. If anyone sees me, SC9 can send Operatives after me again.'

'But that'll only work back in England,' said Connie. 'Nobody'll see it in Italy. And besides, this was eight months ago.' She indicated the story's dateline.

In his rush to read the facts, he hadn't noticed. He checked the other stories. All were months old. 'You see?' she said. 'If anyone had seen you, they would have come looking by now.'

She was probably right. But the sickening sense of fear wasn't subsiding. He realised why as he looked at the screen again. Jude Finch smirked back at him. The man who had beaten him as a child. Murdered his mother. The person he hated most in all the world.

And now he was free.

'They let him go,' he said, struggling to control his fury. 'The bastards let him fucking *go*!' He slammed both fists on the table. Connie flinched. 'And it's my fault.'

'How is it your fault?'

'Because I told Scott what I did at Dad's trial.' Sir Simon Scott was the reclusive head of SC9. Reeve had found and confronted him, wanting to know why he'd been declared Fox Red. The encounter went badly. 'I had a polygraph test during training. I thought it was just an exercise, but it was to find the mole. Scott said it showed I was hiding something. He thought it was because I was a Russian spy. I had to tell him the truth to explain what it *really* was.'

'The truth about the lie.'

He gave her a sharp look. 'Yeah. The lie I told in court. That I saw Dad murder Mum.' Connie had overheard part of his discussion with Scott. Her immediate reaction to the confession had been appalled shock. 'If I hadn't, he would have got away with it. And he *did* kill her,' he snapped before she could say anything. 'He showed me her body. And he said I'd wind up alongside her if I said anything.' Awful memories flooded back. Damp desolation, cold wind cutting through him as he was forced up a trail. A ragged, muddy hole awaited him. And in the brown water at the bottom, wrapped in plastic . . .

'I know.' Sympathy in Connie's voice. She held his hand; he flinched, as if surprised by the touch. 'Alex, I've never seen you like this before. I've never seen you this . . .'

'Angry? Yes, I'm fucking angry! They let him go!'

'No. It's not that. You sound . . . *scared*. And I never imagined that could happen.'

'Everyone gets scared,' he said. 'I was just trained not to show it.'

'But you're showing it now. Why?' Her gaze went to the

laptop. 'It's not because of SC9, is it? It's about *him*.'

Reeve's father was still on the screen. 'Yeah. He . . .' A moment to control his churning feelings. 'You didn't know him. He was *terrifying*. I was a kid, and he was this . . . monster. Big, always angry, always had to get his own way. And he got violent whenever he didn't.' He had turned to Connie while speaking; he made himself look back at the image. 'My whole life as a kid, I always had the same feeling. It wasn't only fear, it was . . . *dread*. Just from knowing he was around. Because I never knew what might set him off. And if he was drunk, he didn't even need a reason. He'd do it just because he could.'

'My God,' Connie said softly. 'You told me about him before, but I never knew it was that bad.'

'I couldn't fight him, so I'd hide. But he always found me, and when he did he was even angrier. There was only one place in the house he never found me. I was in it for hours. But I had to come out eventually. I'd hoped he'd calmed down.' A grim look. 'He was worse. I never dared hide in there again.'

Connie held his hand more firmly. 'I'm so sorry . . .'

'And now he's out.' He stared at the laptop. 'He's free, he even got compensation. So now he's walking around Manchester laughing it up. And my mum's still dead.' A slow, hissing exhalation. 'I should find him. I'm not scared of him *now*. I could break every bone in his fucking body and make him confess. Put him back in prison where he belongs.'

Connie's reaction wasn't what he expected. A small laugh, but not one of humour. Rather, startled dismay. 'You can't seriously be thinking about going back to England? It's *obviously* a trap! SC9 let your dad go so you *would* try to find him. They're probably watching him, waiting for you.'

'I beat them before. I can do it again.'

'You're sure of that?' He didn't answer. 'And even if you beat a confession out of him, then what? It wouldn't be accepted in court. And you sure as hell can't stand as a witness. Never mind the perjury charge; SC9 would kill you before you even reached the door.' Her expression changed, darkening. 'Or were you just planning to kill *him?*'

'He deserves it.' His reply was cold, the feelings behind it anything but.

She let go of his hand, folding her arms. 'Alex, I love you, but . . .' She shook her head. 'I'm a nurse. I help people – it's what I do. And a lot of the time, that involves giving people comfort. But sometimes, you have to give them the truth. Even if it hurts.'

'What truth is that?' He already knew he wouldn't like the answer.

'Like I said, I love you, Alex. So I'm not saying this to attack you in any way, please believe me. But everything you've been through in life has made you . . . how can I put it? Emotionally closed.'

Reeve forced himself to remain blank-faced. Then he realised his reaction to the accusation only proved it. He listened in stiff silence as Connie continued. 'And I know, I *understand*, that you did it to protect yourself. But what that means is that . . .' She paused, reluctant to hurt him. 'Part of you is still a thirteen-year-old boy whose mother was murdered. That part hasn't been able to move on. But right now, it's also doing the thinking. It wants revenge. It wants to *kill* your dad for what he did. And you could do it; I know that. But so does SC9.' She moved closer, beseeching. 'They're manipulating you. They *want* you to go after your father. They *want* you to get angry. Because if you're angry, you'll make mistakes. Then they'll catch you.' She took his hands again. 'And kill you.'

He knew she was right. The only other person who knew he'd lied on the stand was Sir Simon Scott. And few but the head of SC9 had enough power to overturn a murder conviction. He had probably also influenced the media. Not directly, but through other security agencies, compliant editors. Everything said about Reeve in the news stories was calculated to enrage him.

'You're right,' he said at last. 'And I knew it was a trap, but . . .'

'You were angry,' she said, managing a relieved smile. 'I get that. I'm sure I would be in the same situation.'

'I don't think so. You're not the angry type.'

'Oh, you've never seen me when they're out of Pinot.'

His own smile was small – but genuine. 'Thank you.'

'For what?'

'You just saved me. Again.'

She was surprised. 'What, you really would have gone back to England?'

'I was definitely considering it.' He squeezed her hands. 'But I prefer the weather here. And the company.'

'I'm very glad to hear that.' She kissed him. 'It's hard, but sometimes you have to let the past go. If you don't, it can wreck your future. And you're not even thirty yet. You've got a lot of future ahead.'

'*We've* got a lot of future,' he corrected, returning the kiss. A glance at the laptop. 'Get that off the screen. Show me what you want to see in Venice.'

Connie closed the tab. The picture of Jude Finch vanished. 'So we're definitely going?'

He smiled, this time broadly. 'We're definitely going.'

CHAPTER 4

Tony Maxwell put down his phone with deep ambivalence.

The caller had been Sir Simon Scott. SC9's boss had given him some unexpected news. GCHQ had a possible lead on the location of Alex Reeve.

Had it been anyone else, Maxwell would have simply got on with the job. SC9 had a target: they had to be found. But Reeve's case was different. Twice, Maxwell had been face to face with the fugitive. Both times, he'd lied to Scott about the circumstances. Both times, he'd let Reeve get away.

He'd had his reasons: for a start, he never believed Reeve was a traitor. And he'd been proven right. Craig Parker had framed Reeve, right under everyone's noses. Embarrassing for all concerned. Only Scott's declaring Reeve as Fox Red over Maxwell's objections had saved him from punishment. The boss had also fallen for the trap.

So Maxwell survived the fiasco, however narrowly. Even with other operations on his plate, hunting Reeve was still his responsibility. Now, the rogue asset might have resurfaced.

He opened his laptop and checked the secure file that had just arrived. Rural Italy? Nice place to lie low. He was tempted to check the lead in person.

But he had other matters to deal with. And the art of leadership was delegation. If his career progressed as he intended, at some point he would delegate *everything*.

He raised the phone again and made a call. 'Deirdre? It's Tony.' Deirdre Flynn was, like him, an Operative: one he had trained, and trusted.

'What is it?' Alertness in the Northern Irelander's tone, already expecting action. While her senior preferred informality, he wasn't one for casual chats.

'The boss just called. We have a possible lead on Alex Reeve, in Italy. How soon can you move?'

'Give me ten minutes. Which airport?'

'Heathrow. I'll provide the flight details as soon as I have them. I'll get Six to arrange a car at the other end.'

'Fully stocked?'

'Of course.' The MI6 station in Rome would be called upon to provide a vehicle – and weapons.

'Just me, or will I have company?'

'Probably Mark.'

Flynn's professionalism was briefly overcome by dismay. 'Stone? For fuck's sake.'

'He's available. John and Harrison just finished an assignment, and you know the downtime rules.' After missions on home soil, Operatives were required to lie low.

'Isn't there anyone else?'

'Yes. But I wanted to keep this in the family, so to speak. Alex got away from us before. It's our responsibility to close the file.'

'Okay, okay. I'll go with Stone.'

'I'll be in touch soon.'

28

Maxwell ended the call, and made another. This took longer to answer. 'Yeah?' came the irate reply.

He put more steel into his voice than with Flynn. 'Mark, it's Tony. I have a job for you. How soon can you be at Heathrow?'

'Heathrow? Fuck, I don't know. I'm on the other side of London. And I'm in the middle of something.' From the background noise, Stone was in a bar or restaurant.

'Then get to the end of it, now. We have a lead on Alex Reeve.'

Stone's attitude instantly changed. 'Reeve? Okay, I'll be there soon as I can. Where am I going?'

'Italy. You're flying with Deirdre.'

The Londoner made a dismissive sound, but didn't otherwise express his antipathy towards Flynn. 'Right. Flight details?'

'You'll have them soon. Ground transport'll be ready on arrival.'

'Great. How solid's the lead?'

'Enough for the boss to demand action. GCHQ had a standing watch on online news stories about Reeve's father. Someone in Italy read several different ones in a short time. That tripped a flag.'

'That's it? Nothing more definite?' Before joining SC9, Stone had been a cop. His scepticism about the lack of concrete evidence was clear. 'Might be another wild goose chase.'

'The boss wants it done. That's all that counts. Besides, you're getting a free trip to Italy. It's beautiful at this time of year.'

'Yeah, a nice romantic holiday with that bogtrotter is just what I need.' A mocking laugh. 'I'm on my way.'

Maxwell rang off, then sat back. His flat was near Crystal Palace, with a view northward towards central London. The city was shrouded in grey clouds, colours muted by drizzle. He gazed out across it, deep in thought. He could have assigned other Operatives; it might even have been preferable. Reeve had trained for nearly a year with Flynn and Stone. He knew their abilities – and would recognise them instantly. An Operative he'd never met would have the advantage of surprise.

But Reeve had evaded detection for a year and a half. That required caution, suspicion to the point of paranoia. And even an unrecognised Operative might give away their true nature without realising it. Subtle clues could reveal the lurking predator to their prey. Especially to prey with identical skills.

Besides, Flynn and Stone knew Reeve – and his weaknesses. Their visibility might even work to SC9's advantage. The moment Reeve saw them, he would run.

The prey would be flushed out.

If it *was* their prey. As Stone said, the lead might be nothing.

Boots on the ground were the only way to know for sure. Another benefit of sending Flynn and Stone. They were both highly motivated to bring Reeve down. If they found him, they would go above and beyond to eliminate him.

You had a good run, Alex, Maxwell mused. But it was for the best that it ended. Reeve's survival had been a distraction, a splinter in SC9's flesh. Scott had dedicated excessive time and resources to hunting him. Better for everyone that the case was closed.

And Reeve's death would also protect Maxwell. The truth about their two encounters would never come out. In the end, it came down to priorities.

Right now, his top priority was himself.

CHAPTER 5

Reeve lay with Connie, enjoying the warmth of her body. She wriggled gently against him. 'Last night was good,' she said.

'It was,' he replied, smiling. 'Want to do it again?'

'I'd love to, but we won't have time. You're supposed to be getting those bricks with Gina.'

He checked his watch. A little after eight o'clock. 'Oh. Yeah. Damn.'

'Maybe tonight?'

He kissed her neck. 'I like your thinking.'

'And *definitely* in Venice.'

'Oh, absolutely.'

She rolled to face him. 'I can't think of anything more romantic. I'm really looking forward to it.'

They kissed. Reeve slid his hands down past her hips. 'Sure there isn't time?'

Connie grinned – then reacted at a knock from outside. 'Oh, you're kidding. She's early!'

'And I haven't even brushed my teeth yet,' Reeve groused as he sat up. 'I'll be there in a minute,' he called out in Italian. A muffled apology reached him. 'That's my morning, then. Lifting bricks, digging ditches and mixing concrete. You?'

'I've been talking about it for a while, so I might actually try making bread. I'll have to get some ingredients from town, though.'

'Gina bakes her own bread as well. Just ask her. I'm sure she'll let you have some.'

'Good point. You know, I think it'll be fun.' A faint shift in her tone. 'I'd rather spend my day off with you, though.'

'We've still got the afternoon,' he reminded her as he found fresh clothes.

'If you finish on time.'

'I'll work my arse off to do that.'

'And it's such a nice arse.'

Amused, Reeve dressed and went to the door. 'Ah, good morning!' chirped Gina. 'Sorry I'm early.'

'It's no problem,' he assured her.

'I had a text from the builders' merchant. They opened early because they're getting a delivery. So we can pick up the bricks as soon as you're ready. If that's all right?'

'Just give me five minutes to brush my teeth.'

'Make it ten. Don't rush. Have a coffee!'

Reeve smiled, then went back inside. 'Did someone say coffee?' said Connie, emerging from the bedroom.

'I'll make it,' he replied, filling the kettle. 'Then I've got to go.'

'Well, at least I got to spend a *little* of my day with you. We're going to do something together this afternoon, though?'

He gave her a smile. 'Definitely. I promise.'

*

A while later, he was hard at work.

The bricks and other materials had been collected. It took some heavy lifting and both the Panda and Gina's Renault MPV. The suspensions of both were strained, especially on the final stretch of track. But now everything was unloaded, and Reeve stood knee-deep in a trench, digging.

'How's it going?'

He turned to see Connie in their doorway. 'All right,' he said. 'Nearly finished the trench. Then I'll start mixing the concrete.'

She nodded. 'Do you need any water? It's getting hot.'

'Yeah, thanks.' She brought him a sports bottle. He took a drink with relief. 'How's the bread-making going?' Gina had happily donated ingredients.

A slightly forced smile. 'You like pitta bread, don't you?'

'Yes. Why?'

'I don't think I put in enough yeast. It might be a bit flat.'

'It'll taste the same.'

'Let's hope.' She kissed his cheek. 'I'll see you in a bit. Love you.'

'See you soon.' Smiling, Reeve watched her go, then turned back to his work.

Connie had been right. The temperature was already into the high twenties. It would keep going well into the thirties. The sky was deep blue, cloudless, intense sun baking the fields.

He paused to wipe away sweat. On the crest of the hill, he saw a moving dust cloud. A car was coming along the road, nearing the tarpaulin-covered haystack. A minute, he estimated, and it would reach the hairpin. He resumed digging as

34

it dropped out of sight, subconsciously counting down the seconds. A sustained crunch of gravel at six. The car was speeding, braking hard. *Benvenuti in Italia!* The driver made it around, though. The dust cloud reappeared between trees, heading for Sanfatucchio.

He kept working. Half an hour, and the trench was finished. He placed marker stakes in it, then made the concrete. Another dust plume on the road. He barely registered it, focused on creating the perfect mix.

'That's it, down there.'

Mark Stone pointed to the left. Deirdre Flynn, driving their Peugeot 508, looked for herself. A few hundred metres downhill, beyond a field of cropped wheat stubble, was a farmhouse. Warm stone walls, red tile roof, shutters covering most windows. It disappeared from view as the road started to descend.

There were no other buildings nearby. As little as she trusted Stone's judgement, he was probably right. 'Did you see anyone?'

'No.'

A large haystack stood near the roadside. 'Let's have a better look before we get too close.' She pulled over beside the great block of bales. They both got out. Flynn went to the boot. Several dark cases were inside. The longest contained her weapon of choice, an AX308 sniper rifle.

She opened a smaller case, though, finding binoculars. Stone frowned. 'You're not taking your gun?'

Flynn shut the boot. 'What, you think Reeve's going to be standing right outside?' She started around the haystack.

Stone muttered an insult, then followed.

The stack's end formed ragged steps. It was easy enough to scale. The tarp covering it radiated a sickly heat. The pair dropped low and crawled to the end nearest the road.

The landscape opened out before them. The farmhouse was in clear view. Beyond it were trees, a road weaving towards a tiny village. Bracacci, Flynn remembered from her research on the flight. The house itself was called the Villa di Luna. Holiday flats; was Reeve hiding out in one?

First things first. They needed to properly reconnoitre their surroundings. Online maps and satellite photos could only reveal so much. The road they were on had already taken them aback. It was marked as a main thoroughfare, but in reality was merely unsealed gravel. Neither Operative wanted any further surprises.

Stone stared down the slope. 'Can't see any cars. They might be round the back, though.'

Flynn raised the binoculars. 'Quite a few doors. Must be the separate flats.'

'How many are occupied? We don't need witnesses.'

'Most of the shutters are closed, but that doesn't – holy *shit*!'

Stone dropped flat, instantly on alert. 'What is it?'

'It's Reeve,' she hissed, as if afraid her target might hear. 'It's fucking Reeve, right there!'

He had been out of sight behind a rise – then stepped back into view. He stood with hands on hips, contemplating something at ground level. His appearance had changed since Flynn last saw him. His hair was longer and lighter, skin tanned, a few days' beard on his jaw.

But it was him. The traitor. Alex Reeve.

Stone squinted at the distant figure. 'You sure?'

'Course I'm fucking sure. I'm looking right at him!'

'And you didn't bring your fucking gun,' he reminded her sarcastically. They both hurriedly crawled back along the haystack and descended.

Flynn threw the boot open again, pulling out the largest case. Stone checked no cars were coming and extracted another. He took out his weapon, a compact UMP submachine gun. A magazine was snapped into place in a rapid, practised move. 'I'm going after him.'

'Wait for me to get into position first, for Christ's sake.' She quickly attached a suppressor to her rifle, then locked the telescopic sight into place. No time to zero it in. Reeve was only two hundred metres away, though. If her first shot was off-target, she could immediately compensate with the second.

Flynn loaded the mag, then ran back and ascended the haystack. She scurried to the end and lay down. The tarp's heat was almost unbearable. She grimaced, but brought herself into firing position.

The scene below appeared in the scope. Reeve was still outside the farmhouse. Whatever he was doing, there was no urgency to it.

She slid the crosshairs over his head. Her finger curled around the trigger.

Ready to fire.

CHAPTER 6

Reeve stood in the sun, staring at the trench. He suspected he'd underestimated how much concrete he would need. The foundation had to be at least forty centimetres deep. Would he have enough?

He regarded the wheelbarrow in which he'd mixed it. No; he needed more. Connie would be annoyed. Their afternoon together would have to start later than planned.

A sigh, then he looked up. The dust trail on the road had gone. He hadn't registered the sound of the car rounding the hairpin. Odd – where was it? There were no other houses, so no reason for it to stop. He glanced towards the haystack. Maybe the driver was having a pee behind it . . .

Movement on the stack's top. Someone had climbed on to it. Not kids. He saw a person lying flat at its end, facing him.

Warning signals clamoured in his mind. Sunlight caught facets of dark metal. A rifle.

Aimed right at him—

Trained instinct kicked in. He dropped. An instant later, something whipped overhead. It hit the farmhouse's wall with a sharp *crack*.

He scrambled into the cover of the dug-out embankment. 'Connie!' he yelled. 'It's SC9! They've found us!'

*

Flynn saw Reeve look straight at her. She pulled the trigger – as he ducked. The round impacted a wall behind him.

The suppressor had muffled the rifle's bark, but Stone heard it clearly. The hulking straw-blond man was already haring across the road, gun in hand. 'I missed him!' Flynn shouted after him.

'I fucking won't!' Stone yelled back. He hurdled the verge and ran through the field of bleached straw. 'Cover me!'

Flynn cycled the bolt, then looked back through her scope. Reeve was still in hiding. She swept the crosshairs from side to side, hunting for targets.

Reeve heard Connie call out, but couldn't tell what she said. He looked at the flat's open door. Movement inside, approaching. 'No, go back!' he shouted. 'Grab the bug-out bag, and go through the bedroom window.'

To his relief, Connie retreated. 'But it's a fifteen-foot drop,' she objected.

'If you come through the front door, you'll die.' The sniper – had it been Deirdre Flynn? – wouldn't have given up after one miss. 'Get to the car!'

He glimpsed her as she hurried through the flat. She had the bag. The bedroom was on the farmhouse's other side; she would be shielded. Unless there was another Operative covering the drive . . .

No time for hypotheticals. Immediate survival was his priority. Right now, he was pinned down. He had to reach better cover. He crawled along the trench's edge and risked a glance up the hill.

A figure charged through the field. Mark Stone. The Operative was a hundred and fifty metres away, holding a suppressed UMP. Beyond him was the haystack, a huddled shape on its top. Reeve pulled back. A moment later, another rifle round smacked off the flagstones just behind him.

Stone would reach him in under thirty seconds. He had to move. But he would be shot the moment he entered the open—

A noise nearby. A door opening. Reeve whirled. Gina stepped out of her flat, drawn by his shouts. 'No, get back!' he cried – realising too late his warning was in English.

A muffled clatter of gunfire. The UMP, on full-auto. The wall around Gina's doorway erupted with bullet impacts. Gina flew backwards, bloody wounds bursting open across her chest.

Reeve was already moving. There was nothing he could do for her. He sprinted towards his own flat. Stone would need a moment to acquire the new target—

He dived through the doorway. Stone sprayed more fire, bullets hitting the door frame. Reeve rolled sideways. A split-second later, a sniper round shattered a tile where he had just been.

He jumped up. The farmhouse's thick stone wall gave him cover – but Stone was still coming. The laptop sat on the table. He grabbed it and ran for the bedroom.

The window was open. He looked out at the drive below. Connie had landed heavily on the gravel, only just recovering. 'Get in the car!' he ordered as he climbed through the window. Laptop under one arm, he turned and dropped. His other hand caught the sill. Tendons strained, but his grip held. He let go and fell the remaining distance to the ground. He rolled to absorb the impact, then jumped up.

His car keys were in his pocket, always carried. Connie had used her own keys to enter the Fiat. The passenger side; she knew he would be driving. In their early days in Europe, they had run escape drills many times. He took his seat. 'Hold this,' he said, passing her the laptop. She had her own handbag as well as the larger bug-out bag. Reeve started the car and reversed, fast.

A jerk on the wheel and he threw the Panda into a J-turn. Gravel sprayed up from the front wheels. He slammed the car into first as it came about, speeding down the drive.

Through her scope, Flynn saw Stone reach the farmhouse. He ran to the doorway and stopped with his back against the wall. A moment to ready his weapon, then he whipped around into the opening—

And stopped. He didn't fire. Reeve wasn't there.

Flynn knew he wouldn't be hiding. That would be a death sentence. He was running. There must be another way out – an escape route.

She jumped up and hurried back along the haystack, returning to the car.

Gun raised, Stone surveyed the room. Reeve wasn't there.

A doorway at the back. He ran to it. A small hallway beyond. Two more doors. Bathroom, empty. Bedroom—

The window was wide open, curtains wafting in the wind. Engine noise from outside. Stone raced to the opening. An old green Fiat Panda charged away down the driveway beyond, kicking up dust. Two people were inside.

He leaned through the window and opened fire. Several hits, one of the car's lamp clusters shattering – but it kept going. It swung around an outbuilding and disappeared from sight.

'Shit!' Stone shouldered his gun and climbed through the window. He dropped down and ran in pursuit.

The Panda reached the bottom of the drive. Reeve turned sharply left on to the dirt track. The movement threw Connie sideways.

'Fasten your belt,' said Reeve. 'It'll get bumpy.'

She did so, looking ahead in alarm. The rutted track weaved through trees towards Bracacci, half a kilometre distant. 'Why are you going this way?'

'Their car's on the main road. They'd catch up.' He weaved to guide the Fiat through deep ruts. It lurched violently, suspension banging, but cleared the obstacle. 'We've got four-wheel drive, and they don't. They'll have a job following us. And the trees'll give us cover.'

She looked back towards the villa. 'What about Gina?'

'She's dead.'

Connie gasped. 'Oh . . . oh, my God.'

Reeve gave her a glance, but there was no time for sympathy. He was now totally focused on survival. Another harsh jolt as the Panda bounded through a furrow, then he rounded a bend. One more turn, and Bracacci would be visible ahead.

Stone reached the foot of the drive. A dirt track led left and right. Which way had Reeve gone?

Drifting dust to the left. He rounded the corner, gun raised. The narrow lane was flanked by bushes and trees. The Fiat was out of sight behind them. Another curse.

A car braked hard on gravel behind him. He turned and ran towards it. Around a slight bend, and he saw the Peugeot gingerly approaching. He hurried to it and got in. Flynn immediately put the car into reverse. 'What're you fucking doing?' Stone demanded. 'He's ahead of us – go forward!'

'Have you seen the state of this fucking track?' she snapped. The car was lurching, even at low speed. 'We can't get down it in this.' She jabbed a finger at the console's screen. 'Find another way around on a proper road.'

Stone scowled, but brought up the satnav. 'Keep going down the main road. About half a klick, there's a road to the left. It joins up with the one leading to where he's going.'

'Okay.' She backed on to the road and accelerated away in a cloud of dust.

Reeve finally reached Bracacci. His running route branched off to the left, but he continued through the hamlet. 'Where are we going?' asked Connie.

'We need to get clear. Not just of the villa, but the whole area.' They were out of the trees. He rapidly scanned the landscape. No cars speeding towards him. If SC9 were here in force, they would have covered all escape routes. Were Stone and Flynn the only hunters?

If they were, their chances of survival had risen. After four months, he knew the area intimately. The Operatives didn't; they would be relying on satnav maps. And he'd made a point of finding where such maps were unreliable.

A loose dog barked angrily as he swept past the little cluster of houses. Paved road ahead at last. It was narrow, poorly maintained, but at least he could now build up speed. He looked across the fields to his right. The villa stood on the hillside beyond. Where were his pursuers?

There. He couldn't see their car, but a dust trail betrayed its position. It was speeding along the road towards Sanfatucchio.

The village was strung out along the crest of the hill ahead. Church towers marked each end. His own route would take him to one, SC9's the other. Once they reached the main road, they could easily outpace the old Panda.

But he was gambling that they wouldn't stay on their present course.

'He's there!' shouted Stone, looking to the left across farmland. The little green Fiat had just come into sight, heading out of Bracacci.

It was going in the same direction as the Peugeot, on a parallel route. A glance at the satnav. The road he had told Flynn to follow cut across to meet it.

'We can get behind him,' he told her. 'Maybe even in front, if you put your fucking foot down.'

Flynn held in a biting retort, concentrating on driving. Over a narrow hump-backed bridge, the car briefly leaving the ground. She swung the 508 into a drift around a right-angled bend. The junction with the connecting road was ahead. She poured on the power along a straight, then slowed for the turn.

The Panda entered her line of sight ahead. If she kept up her speed, they would catch it.

A hundred metres down the new road, they realised that wasn't going to happen.

'They're coming down the side road,' warned Connie.

'Good,' Reeve replied, to her surprise. 'I'd hoped they would.'

'Why?'

'They're using their satnav. That road's marked as a normal one – but it's just a dirt track. Once you pass the farmhouse, it's hard enough to drive in a 4x4. And they're in a regular car.'

Connie looked again. There was a building alongside the road. The car briefly disappeared behind it, then re-emerged . . . moving more slowly. 'How did you know? We've never been down that road.'

'I have.'

'When?'

'Every time I drove into town on my own, I went a different way. I wanted to find all the possible escape routes.'

His own road was clear. He accelerated, speeding towards Sanfatuccio.

Stone gripped the door handle as the 508 jolted sideways. 'Jesus Christ! Keep the fucking thing on the road.'

'You think you can do better, drive it your fucking self,' Flynn shot back. Even before her intensive SC9 training, she'd had years of off-road driving experience. Her parents' farm had been in an equally rural part of County Tyrone.

This track was tough going even for her, though. Tractors had deeply rutted the winter mud . . . then the summer sun baked it hard. It took all her effort to keep the car out of a ditch.

Stone swore, then lowered his window and leaned out with the UMP. The Panda shot past the end of the track. He tracked it as best he could and fired a burst. The Fiat continued uphill, apparently unharmed. 'Shit! We're losing him!'

It took another sea-sickening minute to reach the intersection. Flynn pulled out and jammed her foot to the floor. The car surged up the hill, sweeping through curves past the red-towered church.

The road ended at a junction, a wider route heading left and right. 'Which way?' snapped Stone.

'Fucked if I know.' Flynn slowed to check both ways. Another road branched off fifty metres to the left. None of the routes showed signs of recent traffic. Reeve could have taken any of them. She stopped at the intersection. 'Which do you think?'

Stone nodded to the right. 'That goes to the village. He could double back past where we found him.'

'Or he might be trying to open up as much distance as he can.' Flynn indicated the left-hand road.

'Well, we can't sit here with our thumbs up our arses. Just go right, for fuck's sake.'

She gave him a dirty look, but complied. 'Remember, you chose this way.'

Less than a minute later, they were in Sanfatucchio. The village was quiet. Both Operatives stared down each side street. No sign of the little Fiat. They reached the road to the villa. No dust in the air.

'He didn't double back, then,' said Flynn.

'Fuck off,' was Stone's irritated reply. They rounded the second church. Italian flags marked the village square. Cars were parked around it—

A green Panda amongst them.

Stone whipped up his gun. Flynn brought the Peugeot closer . . .

'Fuck!' the Londoner growled, lowering the UMP. 'It's not him. His car didn't have a roof rack.'

Flynn nevertheless scrutinised the empty Fiat as she drove past. Stone had said he'd hit Reeve's car – but this had no bullet damage. 'Well, shite,' she said, pulling away. 'We've lost him.'

CHAPTER 7

Reeve stopped the Panda. 'We're getting out here.'

He had headed for Castiglione del Lago using the back roads. An industrial estate sat on the edge of town, beside the railway line. Garages, small factories, a cement works – mundane stuff. But his reconnoitring had found an empty plot used for parking. The Fiat was now out of sight from nearby roads.

Connie didn't react at first, in a state of dull shock. After a moment, she looked at him. 'What? We're leaving the car?'

'It's got bullet holes in it. It'll draw police attention.'

'So what are we doing?'

He gestured towards the railway. 'The station's not far. Wherever the first long-distance train's heading, that's where we go. Probably Rome or Florence.'

'It sounds like you've planned for this.'

'I have. Come on. The longer we stay here, the more chance SC9 will find us.'

She hurriedly exited the car. Reeve took the bug-out bag and laptop from her. 'So it was definitely SC9?' Connie asked as they headed through the industrial estate.

'Stone and Flynn. Stone killed Gina.'

He knew as he spoke that he shouldn't have said it. Connie stayed silent until they neared the estate's perimeter. 'Was . . . was it quick?' she finally said.

'Yes.' He didn't elaborate. Gina had been hit several times in the chest. Death could have been instant . . . or taken minutes as she bled out. He didn't know. But he was sure Connie didn't *want* to know.

'Why did you bring the laptop?' she asked. Changing the subject. 'I thought it was secure.'

'It is, as much as it can be. But I didn't want SC9 to get it. I'll run the secure erase program when we're somewhere safe, then dump it.'

'You're leaving it behind?'

'We need to leave *everything* behind. We can't go back. And that includes to your work. I'm sorry.'

Connie fell silent again. Reeve tried to read her expression as they walked. Sadness, fear – guilt? All three? It was hard for him to tell.

They crossed a main road and headed down the Via della Stazione. It ran alongside the railway, fields and – incongruously – a boatyard opposite. Reeve felt exposed in the open. Every sound of an approaching car put him on heart-pounding alert. But traffic was thankfully light, and none were their pursuers.

They soon reached the station. Reeve checked the timetable. The next train was to *Firenze*: Florence. Twelve minutes to wait. Checking nobody was watching, he took a wad of cash from the bug-out bag. There was considerably more inside, in various currencies. He bought two single tickets. The low fares of Italian trains compared to British never failed to impress him. He led Connie through a subway to their platform, validating the tickets at a machine. Then they waited.

Seven minutes. The station road was visible beyond a fence. He watched it intently. Six minutes. A couple of cars drove by. He'd only seen the Operatives' vehicle from a distance, but it was silver. Probably a Peugeot, but he wasn't certain. Five minutes, four. Even in the shade, the heat was rising. It was late morning, the intense sun high overhead—

Silver car. He stared at it, unconsciously holding his breath . . .

A hatchback, not a saloon. He relaxed, slightly. The minutes crawled by. He looked southwards down the railway line. Were those headlights in the distance? It was hard to tell through the shimmering haze.

Another silver car. Saloon. Reeve stiffened, readying himself to fight – or run . . .

Four people inside, not two. One had a bouffant mane of hair. He eased again. He doubted either Operative had brought their grandmother.

They *were* headlights to the south. 'Hey,' he said to Connie, who was staring blankly across the tracks. 'Train's coming.'

'Okay.' Her reply was flat, tired.

He put an arm around her. 'We'll get clear of here, come up with a plan, then move on.'

'To where?'

'I don't know yet. But we'll have to leave the country.'

Her eyes widened in dismay. 'What?'

'There'll be an investigation into Gina's death. The

police'll be looking for us. If they arrest me, I'm dead. SC9 will find me.'

'What about me?' she asked.

'I'll do everything I can to keep you safe. Don't worry. I'm not going to leave you.'

'Just everything we had together,' was the quiet reply.

He didn't have a response. All he could do was wait until the train arrived. They boarded, and it soon set off.

Carrying them away from the life they'd started to build, for ever.

Stone and Flynn swept the area around Sanfatucchio, then returned to the Villa di Luna. But their faint hopes that Reeve had doubled back were quickly squashed. Nobody was there except the dead woman, sprawled inside her doorway. 'Fucking *balls*,' Stone growled as he emerged from Reeve's residence. 'Found some paperwork; Reeve's using the name Angelo Moretti. But there's nothing in there that might help us find him.'

'No phones or laptops?' Flynn asked.

'Chargers, but nothing connected to them.'

She took a deep breath. 'I'd better call in. Give Tony the bad news.'

He pointed a thick forefinger at her. 'I don't want to hear one fucking *word* blaming me for losing him, all right?'

'Ah, fuck off.' She put her phone on speaker and made a call.

Tony Maxwell was quick to answer. 'Well?'

Another breath before Flynn replied. 'Our old friend Angelo Moretti *was* here. Got himself a comfy little home.

We tried to give him his present, but we just missed him.' On an unsecured line, codes and euphemisms were the order of the day. 'He's gone away with his girlfriend, but we don't know where.'

'That's . . . a shame.' Maxwell's voice was as calm as always, but he couldn't hide an edge of aggravation. 'What's his place like? Messy?'

She glanced at the corpse. 'Yeah, there's some mess.'

'Enough to cause problems with the landlord?' More code: would the authorities get involved?

Stone let out a grunt of grim amusement. 'I think it *was* the landlord.'

'Then you should clean it up before anyone sees it. We'll have to catch up with him later. And his girlfriend.'

'Right.'

'Talk again soon. Bye.' Maxwell disconnected.

'Well, you heard the man,' Flynn told Stone. 'We need to clean up the scene.' Another look at the dead woman.

He made his impatience clear. 'Or we could just go, and let the Italian cops deal with it. They'd be looking for Reeve, not us.'

'And what if they arrest him and he tells them all about SC9? That's just what we want on the record, isn't it? A British assassination team gunning down Italian civilians. You dumb bastard.' She started back towards their car. As well as weapons, it contained cleaning supplies – of the kind used on crime scenes. 'Let's get this over with.'

Maxwell lowered his phone, gazing across London. His expression was placid; his mind anything but. So it *had* been

Reeve. That in itself was troubling enough. His escape only made matters vastly more complicated . . .

He made a call, waiting for the secure connection to be confirmed. 'What is it, Maxwell?' demanded Sir Simon Scott.

'Operatives 63 and 64 just reported in from Italy, sir.'

'And?' Tense anticipation filled the single word.

'They found Reeve.'

'Did they get him?'

'No.'

'*What?*' Maxwell twitched at the explosive bark in his ear. 'How the hell did they miss him?'

'We were on an unsecured line, so I haven't had a full report yet. But he'd been there for a while. He had the advantage of local knowledge while escaping.'

Scott was silent for a long moment. Then: 'Get more Operatives over there. Find Reeve, and finish the job. 61 and 62 are available – send them out, immediately.'

'Sir, Blake and Locke just finished an assignment. They're supposed to be lying low—'

'Don't tell me the rules,' Scott snapped. 'I wrote the bloody rules. Your team screwed this up, Maxwell. They can finish it. They'd *better* finish it.'

'Reeve won't stay in Italy. He'll be—'

'Then they'd damn well better catch him before he leaves!'

Maxwell controlled his own anger more successfully than his superior. 'Yes, sir. I'll send them,' he said in a placatory tone. 'Do you want me to go as well?'

'No,' Scott decided. 'I need the preliminaries finished on this German job. But stay in close contact with your Operatives on the ground. I want Reeve found and killed.'

'He's with someone,' Maxwell told him. 'Probably Connie Jones – the nurse who helped him in London.'

'Then kill her as well.' The order was as dispassionate as an instruction to swat a fly. 'Why wasn't she under observation?'

'She was. Total electronic surveillance for six months after Reeve was last seen. No evidence of contact between them. GCHQ queried the cost of continuing to monitor her. You approved ending the surveillance.'

The point was not taken with good grace. 'I know full well what I approved, Maxwell. Get on with it, then. And this time, make sure Reeve's dead.' The call abruptly terminated.

Maxwell shook his head. Scott was letting anger drive his decision-making. Reeve would try to leave Italy as soon as possible. That was what Maxwell himself would do – and Reeve had learned the trade from him.

But Scott was the boss. For now, he had to be obeyed – even if he was wrong.

More calls to make. One to Harrison Locke, Operative 61, was first. 'Are you sure that's wise?' Locke replied. His voice was as level as always, but Maxwell didn't miss the implied criticism. 'Surely Reeve won't stay in the country.'

'The boss's direct orders,' said Maxwell. 'You go to Rome. We'll liaise with MI6 to get more eyes on the airport. I'm sending John to Milan.'

'And what if Reeve flies out of Florence? Or Venice, or Pisa, or Bologna?'

'Let's hope he doesn't,' was the curt response. Maxwell ended the call, then made another. This was to Operative 62:

John Blake. 'John, we've found Alex Reeve.'

Blake had sounded bored on answering. That attitude instantly vanished; now he was keen, predatory. 'Are we going after him?'

'Yes. He's in Italy. I need you to go to Milan.'

'Is that his location?'

'No, he's in Umbria. But I need the major airports covered. Harrison's going to Rome.'

'Wait, you're sending us on a fishing expedition?'

'Direct orders from the boss. Deirdre and Mark checked out a lead, which turned out to be real. But Alex got away from them.'

'What – Flynn and Stone cocked up, so we're casting a dragnet over the whole country? That's hardly the best use of our resources, Tony. We should leave the flatfoot work to Six.'

'Take it up with the boss,' Maxwell told him firmly. 'Those are your orders. I'll give you flight details at Heathrow.'

'Understood.' The confirmation wasn't quite delivered with petulance, but Blake's irritation was plain.

Maxwell hung up. Two jobs on his plate, then. The German operation was complex, with potentially serious political and diplomatic blowback. Maxwell didn't approve of the approach Scott had mandated, but again, orders were orders. It was the mission that should demand most of his attention.

But finding Alex Reeve was also a *personal* mission. Mistakes could land squarely upon Maxwell's own head. And Operatives who screwed up that badly wouldn't remain Operatives for long.

Or remain alive for long, either.

So Reeve took priority. Maxwell opened his laptop and called up a map of Italy. His former student couldn't have left the country yet.

He had to find him before he did.

CHAPTER 8

The train from Castiglione del Lago pulled into a station. Not Florence's Santa Maria Novella terminus, but an earlier stop. Campo di Marte was farther from the city's centre, less busy.

Reeve was disembarking there for exactly that reason. The journey had only taken a little over ninety minutes. SC9 might have guessed where he was heading. If so, they wouldn't have had time to cover every point of entry.

Despite that, he was still wary as he led Connie from the train. Rather than exit through the station building, he went down the platform. Stairs led to a footbridge spanning the tracks. He looked back as they ascended. Nobody following. Brief tension as a man approached ahead, but he passed without a glance. Another check in both directions at the top. Nothing triggered his warning radar. Reeve turned right. The bridge led down to street level. He surveyed his new surroundings. Dozens of bikes and scooters parked nearby, people bustling around the station's entrance. His training, in both SC9 and the SRR, had attuned him to potential watchers. He saw none.

'I think we're clear,' he said, starting westwards. The sun was high overhead, heat rising from the pavement.

'Where are we going?' Connie asked. Conversation on the train had been stilted, numbed.

'There's an internet café near Santa Croce. I need to find somewhere to hide out for a few hours.'

'How do you know about the internet café? We didn't go to any when we came here.'

'I came on my own.'

She was surprised. 'What? When?'

'When you visited your grandma after we first arrived in Umbria. I needed to reconnoitre in case we had to run here.'

'You came here without me?'

'Sorry. I went to Rome as well. I wasn't playing tourist, if that's what you're bothered about.'

'It's not,' came the curt reply. Reeve gave her an apologetic look, but survival trumped sympathy.

They continued onwards. Trees provided blessed shade from the beating sun. Across a main road, and they headed into the narrower streets of the old city. On their previous visit, they'd taken their time, soaking up the atmosphere. Now, Reeve moved with purpose. It only took a few minutes to reach their destination.

The internet café was small, more scooters outside. Its customers were young and almost entirely non-Italian. Reeve heard Turkish, Arabic, Farsi. Most screens showed video chats, with a few online games as well.

Nobody paid him or Connie any attention. He spoke to the bored man at the counter. Two euros would buy thirty minutes of internet access. Reeve doubted he would need that much. He paid, and was pointed to an empty seat.

Two tasks before he began. The first was to turn the

computer's webcam away from him. The second was to set the browser's preferences to private. Then he started a search. 'Airbnb?' Connie asked, watching. 'You're going to rent somewhere?'

Reeve shook his head. 'They'd want a credit card. I'm just finding somewhere to borrow for a couple of hours.'

'How?'

He searched for flats in central Florence. Listings appeared. He clicked through them. 'If anything's available today, that means it's not occupied right now.' He soon found one with potential. Rather than read the descriptive text, though, he checked the photos. One showed the exterior door. A shake of his head, and he went back to the main list.

'What were you looking for?' Connie asked, intrigued despite herself.

'A key lockbox outside. That didn't have one.' More pictures flicked by. 'This one does, though.'

He quickly read the apartment's details. It mentioned a particular street. Then he opened a second tab and brought up Google Maps. 'Rental sites don't give the exact address or the owner's details,' he explained, typing. 'They want you to go through them so you can't cut out the middleman.' The map loaded. He went to Street View and panned around the scene. A quick comparison of the first tab, then he moved the viewpoint along the road. 'But if the owner puts up a photo of their front door . . .'

Another sweeping stride down the virtual street. 'That's it,' said Connie.

'And it's got a lockbox.' There was a small metal cabinet beside the entrance. He entered the precise address. The map of Florence reappeared, zooming in on a street not far to their southwest. 'People put way too much information on the internet. Okay, let's go.' He closed the tabs, checking that the browser history was clear, then they left.

They angled towards the Arno, the river bisecting the city. It didn't take long to reach the address. Reeve regarded the building. A handsome terrace, centuries old. Four main floors with a balcony visible at the roof's lip. The interior pictures had shown a vaulted ceiling, so the flat was probably the topmost. 'Give me some cover,' he said, going to the doorway.

'What're you doing?'

'Getting the key.' He took a small leather wallet from the bug-out bag. Inside was a collection of shining steel lockpicks.

Connie's eyes widened. 'You're breaking in?' He gave her a sarcastic look. 'Well, obviously,' she said, frowning. 'I meant you're doing it in broad daylight?'

'Just block people's view,' he said, examining the lock. He'd defeated far tougher ones in training. 'Give me thirty seconds . . .'

The lock yielded in under ten. Reeve spirited the picks away, then opened the box. There were only two key hooks; not every apartment was available for short-term rent. The hook with the highest number was probably the top flat. He took a keyring from it and closed the box.

The largest key fitted the old door's keyhole. The tiled hall within was dark and cool. Stairs led upwards. He checked the numeral on a door near their foot: *1*. The highest numbers were indeed at the top.

He went up, Connie following. The stairs ended on the third floor. One door matched the number from the key hook. He went to it and knocked. No answer. Another key fitted the lock. He opened it.

The building was old, but the flat was ultra-modern. Despite her tension, Connie made an admiring sound. 'This is *nice*.' The original flat had been expensively gutted to create a large open space. The room before them was a lounge and kitchen area. Stairs led up to a glass-sided mezzanine in what had been empty loft space. The rooftop balcony was accessible from the upper level. 'What do we do if someone comes?'

'We're not staying long,' Reeve told her. 'I just needed somewhere safe while I figure out what to do next.'

'So what *are* we doing next?'

'I don't know.' He'd spent much of the train journey inwardly cursing himself. Their time in the peace and calm of the villa had made him feel settled. Now he knew it was just complacency. SC9 hadn't stopped their hunt. Somehow, they had found him.

He put down the laptop. The assassins arrived right after he read the news stories about his father. That couldn't be a coincidence. The machine was no longer safe to use. 'First thing, I need to run the laptop's kill program.' He had deliberately chosen a model with a physical wireless switch. He made sure the Wi-Fi was off, then booted the machine.

Connie smacked dry lips. The flat was hot, sunlight beaming through the south-facing windows. 'I need a drink.' She started for the kitchen, then hesitated. 'Will it be okay to use their glasses? In case we leave fingerprints, or anything.'

'So long as everything goes back exactly as we found it, we'll be fine.' Even if they did, it wouldn't matter. He intended to escape the reach of Italian law enforcement as soon as possible.

She filled a glass from the tap. 'Do you want any?' she asked after drinking.

'Yes, please.' She refilled it and brought it to him. 'Thanks.'

She regarded the laptop. 'How did they find us? Was it because I found that story about your dad?'

'If they did, it wasn't your fault,' he assured her. 'One person looking at an old story wouldn't have raised any alarms. It was because I looked at several different ones.' He brought up the command line and started typing. 'I should've thought of it. GCHQ can track where a website's traffic comes from, even through a VPN.'

She frowned. 'I thought VPNs can't be traced.' The couple had used a Virtual Private Network to further anonymise their online footprints.

'Normally, yes. But GCHQ can do it – it just takes a lot of computer power. So they don't do it routinely, only for specific jobs.'

'Like when anyone takes an interest in stories about Jude Finch.'

He gave her a downcast look. 'Yeah. SC9 put a lot of effort into setting up their trap. I didn't think they'd go that far, not after so long. I got careless. And now . . .' He could tell she was thinking about Gina. 'I'm sorry.'

'So what can we do? Can we get away from SC9?'

'For now.' He set the eraser program running. It would overwrite the hard drive with random data. Even if SC9 recovered the machine, it would reveal nothing. 'But that's only in the short term. Now they definitely know I'm alive, they'll be looking a lot harder.'

'That *we're* alive,' Connie corrected, grim-faced.

He faced her. 'There's only two ways we can keep them from catching us. Run, and never stop. Or threaten them.'

She mulled over the options. Neither appealed. 'I don't want to spend the rest of my life running scared. We had a life, Alex!' she said, suddenly emotional. 'We were settled. We were *happy*.'

'I know,' he said. 'But if we run, that's something we can't have.'

'So the alternative is threatening them. How?' Her eyes widened at an idea. 'Scott! You went to his second home in France. You could go after him—'

'He'll have sold it,' Reeve cut in. 'His location – his security – was compromised. He might not have wanted to, but he'll have done it.'

Her brief excitement was instantly crushed. 'Oh. So how *can* you threaten them?'

Reeve searched the bug-out bag, producing a smartphone. 'With this.'

Connie peered at it. The screen was cracked, the case dented as if dropped hard. 'I haven't seen that before.'

'It was Craig Parker's.' A flicker across her face, and she unthinkingly touched her upper left arm. Parker had shot her there. 'He used it to email encrypted SC9 files to the media. I stopped the decryption password from being sent. But,' he went on, 'it should still be queued in his mail app.'

'So the emails are still on his phone? The *files* are still on there?'

'There's a good chance.'

'So you tell Scott, "Back off, or we release the files"?'

'Basically, yes. That is . . . if I can unlock the phone.'

'You don't know the PIN?'

He shook his head. 'It'll erase everything after so many wrong login attempts. Ten's the standard number. But I only know the first two digits.'

'Leaving a hundred possibilities.'

'Probably more. The PIN might be six digits, or eight, or twenty. All I know is that the first two digits are zero, and two. It might be the start of a date. Or it might not.' He stared at his dark reflection in the damaged screen. 'If I get it wrong, I'll never access what's on there.'

Connie regarded the phone thoughtfully. 'Do you know anything about Parker himself? If it's a date, it might be something personal.'

'When I caught him, he told me how his parents died,' said Reeve. 'He was still a kid. It was his justification for what he was about to do. He blamed the British establishment for everything. People who went to Oxbridge, judges, lawyers, politicians – that lot. "Posh bastards", as he called them. He thought exposing SC9 to the world would bring down the establishment. Which it might well have done. Britain would be an absolute pariah internationally. But he didn't care that would hurt ordinary people too – probably more than rich people.'

He turned the phone over in his hand, thinking. 'I did some detective work while I was hiding out in London. Parker said the papers used a photo of his dad on their front pages. He had a fight with their landlord, accidentally killed him. Was convicted of murder – and got stabbed in prison.'

Connie reacted with shock. 'That happened when Parker was just a child? God. No wonder he was so angry at the system. I'm not saying it justifies what he did, but I understand why he did it.'

Reeve nodded. 'So I found the papers, then did some research. Got Parker's real name: David Laurence. Once I had that, I found out more about him and his family.'

'But nothing that might be the PIN?'

'No. I thought it might have been his mum's birthday. She was born on July 2nd, 1971.'

'Or in numbers, oh-two-oh-seven-seven-one.'

'Yeah. But I tried it with six and eight digits. Neither worked – and it cost me two attempts. So I didn't try again.'

'But you might have to now.'

'I know. I need to charge this up. Problem is, that might bring SC9 to us.'

'How? Do they even know you have it?'

'They know Parker *didn't* have it. GCHQ would have found out Parker sent his emails from a phone. They'd probably be able to ID *which* phone. So if I charge it up . . .'

'. . . they might find us,' Connie finished. 'Great.'

'They might not,' said Reeve. 'It's a risk, though. But I'll have to take it. Because if I can't access the files, I've got no leverage against SC9.'

'And then all we can do is run.'

'Yeah.'

A long silent moment. Finally, Reeve took a charger from the bag. 'Well. No choice. I've got to power the thing up. Then try to figure out Parker's code.'

She let out an unhappy breath. 'If SC9 *can* trace it, how long will we have?'

'If they're here in Florence, maybe just minutes. But,' he went on, seeing her alarm, 'I doubt they'll be that close. They might still be searching Castiglione del Lago. So they'd have to drive here, get into the city and find the exact apartment. That'll take at least two hours.'

'They won't know exactly where we are?'

'GCHQ'll be able to triangulate which building we're in. But not which floor.' He glanced up at the mezzanine. 'We can watch the street from the balcony.'

Connie followed his gaze. 'At least it'll be cooler with those doors open,' she said. Then: 'Suppose you do get into those files. Would you actually release them to the media?'

'Whatever Scott thinks, I'm not a traitor,' Reeve replied firmly. He started for the stairs. 'Come on. Let's find a plug.'

CHAPTER 9

Garald Kazimirovich Morozov sipped a cappuccino while he decided how the Englishman would die.

It was nothing personal. Morozov knew little about the man besides his name and profession. His *real* profession, not the non-official cover he worked under. If asked, Bryan Roach would claim he was employed by an import-export company. Since Britain left the EU, many had sprung up to handle paperwork, for a fee.

In reality, Roach was an officer of the Secret Intelligence Service – MI6. He operated undercover to further his country's interests abroad. A wry smile made a rare and brief appearance on Morozov's face. The Russian could describe his own work in exactly the same way. The difference was in the details. Roach was a glorified accountant, obtaining financial intelligence on Italian businesses.

Morozov, though, was a killer.

His employer was the SVR – *Sluzhba Vneshney Razvedki*. Russia's Foreign Intelligence Service, successor to the feared Soviet-era KGB. He worked for Directorate S: the Illegal Intelligence department. His job description was simple.

Eliminate enemies of the Russian state.

All major nations had such a unit, Morozov mused as he

watched Roach. The difference between Russia and the United Kingdom was that Russia admitted hers existed. Like Israel's Mossad, knowledge of its purpose helped act as a deterrent. *Fuck with us, and we will kill you.*

At least, that was how things were supposed to work. The British, normally cautious to the point of fearfulness, had recently changed tack.

Morozov knew why. They had thought SC9, their covert kill-unit, was completely secret and secure. But the SVR had learned of it some years earlier. One of SC9's so-called Operatives had been captured on assignment in Ukraine. He'd made the mistake of not killing himself. A few months of intensive torture, and he revealed everything he knew.

Which was surprisingly little. Grudging admiration for the Brits' skill at compartmentalising information. The name of SC9's boss, even the location of its headquarters, remained unknown. But there had been enough to start the SVR on the agency's trail.

And when they found David Laurence, later known as Craig Parker, it all paid off.

Almost. But at the last moment, everything fell apart.

Realising it had been compromised by Russian intelligence, SC9 then struck back. Several Russian agents and assets had been killed over the past year. There was only one possible response from the SVR. The British wanted a war?

They would have one.

Morozov had observed Roach for a few days. The Englishman had a routine. Accountants usually did. After lunch, he stopped at a coffee shop before returning to work. His office was on Rome's Via dei Capocci. An unremarkable business on an unremarkable street. The kind of anonymity MI6 liked.

They were about to get some attention. Morozov could have killed Roach at his apartment, or on the Metro. But doing so right on his employer's doorstep would send the British an unmistakeable message. Again: *fuck with us, and we* will *kill you*.

What method? The garrotte was almost a signature of the SVR, and the KGB before it. But in broad daylight on a city street? Not fast enough; too risky. Shooting Roach would be quick and simple. But it lacked . . . *terror*. The British needed to be made afraid of Russia again.

A stabbing, then. He'd already located local CCTV cameras, planned how to avoid them. Walk up behind Roach as he reaches the door. One hand clamped over his mouth, the other driving the blade into his neck. Slash the carotid artery, rupture the trachea, then push forward. The move would tear open his entire throat. Death would be rapid, bloody, and horrific. Morozov knew that from practised experience. He would be gone in moments. Out of the city in twenty minutes. Out of the *country* in an hour. The Italian authorities wouldn't react fast enough to catch him. More knowledge from experience.

Roach drained his cup and stood. Morozov put down his own drink. His knife was sheathed inside his jacket. His gun was also concealed under his clothing. A fallback, in case anyone tried to interfere. He rose—

His phone rang.

In the circumstances, he would normally have ignored it. But he knew the ringtone. His superior was calling.

He would only interrupt an active mission on a matter of extreme importance.

Hesitation – then he sat again. Roach could wait. Routine would bring him back here tomorrow. Instead he answered the phone. 'Go.'

'Garald Kazimirovich.' He knew the voice. Pyotr Viktorovich Grishin, head of Directorate S. 'Are you enjoying the weather in Rome?'

'It's entirely agreeable,' Morozov replied. A basic call-and-response code. If either man had varied from the script, the call would have ended. Deviation meant they had been compromised or were under duress.

'Good, good. And your business?'

'I was about to go to our meeting when you called.' More mundanities, euphemisms. You never knew who was listening.

'You need to postpone it.'

He was surprised. 'Oh?'

'We just learned the British acquisition we discussed last year is now in Florence. You need to obtain it.'

'Understood,' Morozov replied. The 'acquisition' was a phone belonging to Craig Parker. Morozov had person-ally recruited him as an SVR asset. Parker's hatred of the British establishment meant his goals aligned precisely with Moscow's. He had been moulded into a perfect candidate for the British assassination unit. Once in, Parker operated successfully as a mole. Russian knowledge of SC9 grew enormously.

Despite that, Morozov hadn't trusted him. Even when they ostensibly worked for you, you could never trust the

British. *Perfidious Albion*, as the saying went. His concerns had been justified. Parker was supposed to hack into SC9's servers and obtain their assassination files. He had done so – but hadn't handed them over to his controller. Instead he'd embarked on a high-risk mission to release them to the global media.

It failed. Parker died. His phone, containing copies of the files, had presumably been recovered by British Intelligence.

Except . . . perhaps it hadn't.

'Do we know who has it?' he asked.

'We haven't identified them yet. You'll be informed as soon as we do. For now, get to da Vinci airport. We've hired a helicopter for you.'

More surprise. A helicopter? The SVR rarely took such extravagant measures. His new mission really was top priority. 'I'll get a taxi. I should be at the airport in about thirty minutes.'

'Good. We'll send more details on the way. Remember, Garald Kazimirovich – this acquisition is extremely important. Do whatever is necessary to obtain it.'

The call ended. Morozov lowered his phone. Grishin's final instruction was plain. No limits. Anyone who might prevent him from getting the phone was to die.

The thought didn't trouble him. It wasn't his first no-limits mission. He left the coffee shop and looked for a cab.

Flynn's phone rang. She answered, putting the call on speaker. 'Yes?'

'It's me,' said Maxwell. 'Where are you?'

'In a car park at a supermarket in the town.' The windows

were down, she and Stone drinking water in the breeze. 'We finished things at our friend's.'

'Did you clean everything up?'

'Yeah. We've got some rubbish in the boot we need to get rid of.'

'It'll have to wait. Our friend's gone to Florence. You need to meet him.'

The pair both sat up. 'What's he doing there?' Stone asked.

'How did you find him?' was Flynn's more pertinent question.

Maxwell was silent for a moment. 'Can anyone hear you?'

'No,' she told him. They had parked at the lot's far end, shaded by trees. Nobody was nearby.

'Okay, I'm going to violate protocol by telling you on an unsecured line. We don't have time to beat around the bush with codes. Craig Parker sent out his emails from a phone. GCHQ later identified the particular one. It was never found. But,' he went on, 'it just came back online in central Florence.'

'Reeve had it all the time?' said Flynn.

'So it seems. He can't have ever powered it up until now – GCHQ would have pinged it. They had a standing trace watching for it.'

'So we know exactly where he is?' said Stone.

'To within fifty metres. If he doesn't move, that'll be five metres by the time you get there. So get going.'

Flynn ended the call and started the car. She set the satnav, then headed for the autostrada. 'Come on, then,' growled Stone after a few minutes. 'Put your fucking foot down.' The Peugeot was sticking firmly to the speed limit.

'You want to get stopped by the police?' she shot back. 'We've got a corpse in the boot, you stupid shite.'

Eventually, they reached the motorway. They passed through the tollgate, then Flynn accelerated, heading north towards Florence.

CHAPTER 10

Reeve sat inside the balcony's open doors, letting the breeze cool him. The apartment's rental rates, he'd noticed, were high. Now he knew why. The building was not directly on the riverside, but from the rooftop provided a view. The world-famous Ponte Vecchio bridge, spanning the Arno, was – partially – visible.

Connie couldn't help going back out to admire their surroundings. Reeve, though, had more important concerns. One item in the bag was a notebook. He'd recorded every scrap of information he could find about Craig Parker. Background, family details, important dates, his military career. Anything that might help him unlock the phone. Reaching a dead end, he'd stopped working on the puzzle months earlier.

Now, it might be the only way to keep himself and Connie alive.

Zero, two. The first two digits of Parker's passcode. Reeve had forced him to enter them at gunpoint. They could be fake. But Parker had known a deliberately failed attempt would end his life. He had thumbed them in as a delaying tactic rather than use facial recognition.

The only number Reeve had found beginning zero-two

was Parker's mother's birthdate. It hadn't worked. Eight attempts remaining – maybe.

What else could the code be?

A reversal of something? He went back through the notes, certain he would have checked that before. He had. Nothing ended in two-zero.

Two-zero. Twenty. Would any date from that year have been significant to Parker?

Reeve realised there was one significant to both of them. The day they started training to join SC9.

Could that be it? He mentally reversed the numbers. The trailing twenty became a zero-two prefix. Six digits, or eight? He would have to try both.

He picked up the phone. It was charging – *very* slowly, the percentage still only in single figures. The battery might have been damaged by the long period without use. It had also taken a six-metre drop on to stone. That it worked at all was a minor miracle.

It was also a danger. It would reveal his position to GCHQ, even with the SIM removed. Or while switched off. As long as its battery had power, any smartphone was still technically active. GCHQ had ways to reach this electronic subconsciousness. And the phone's user would never know.

The thought spurred him on. If he had a possible answer, he had to try it. Before it was too late.

He brought up the keypad. A pause, knowing the risk – then he tapped in the eight-digit code.

It didn't work.

The six-digit version—

Was also rejected. 'Shit!' Two more attempts gone.

Connie came in from the balcony. 'What's wrong?'

'I thought I'd worked out the passcode,' he said. 'I hadn't.'

'What did you think it was?'

'Does it matter?'

'Go on, tell me,' she said. 'Maybe I can help. I'm quite good at number puzzles, remember.'

'This isn't exactly a Sudoku.' But he said it with humour. 'I reversed the date when he joined SC9. That way, twenty became the two numbers I know – zero and two. But, I tried it with six and eight digits. Neither worked.'

'What about *four* digits?' He gave her a questioning look. 'If there are zeroes before the day and month, take them out. So, say, the seventh of April – oh-seven-oh-four – just becomes seven-four.'

Reeve nodded. 'Clever.'

He tapped in the four numbers. The result was as he'd feared. 'Shit,' he said again. Half his attempts gone, if not more.

Connie winced. 'Oh. I'm sorry – I thought it might—'

'It's okay. Not your fault. It was a good idea, though. So if you have any more good ideas, tell me.'

She held up her hands. 'I'm not sure I can handle the responsibility.'

'You were a nurse!' he scoffed with a grin.

Her own expression was more serious. 'Life and death in a hospital is one thing. When it's *our* life and death . . . I really don't want to make any more mistakes.' She returned to the balcony. 'Tell me if you think of anything else.'

'However long that takes,' Reeve said after her. Time was an increasingly pressing issue. How much longer could they risk staying here? He'd plugged in the phone an hour ago. If he was no closer in forty minutes, he decided, they would leave. He was about to tell Connie—

Realisation brushed his mind, a mental connection almost but not quite made. *Tell me* – the words were somehow important. It wasn't about Connie. Tell who?

It felt as if the answer was staring him in the face. He read his notes again. Those on this page were mostly about Parker's parents. Numbers stood out. Birth dates, death dates. He'd already ruled them out. What else had he just been thinking about? Time, how long certain things took. Tell someone about time? Something had taken time to tell? He juggled the possibilities—

Parker. He'd said something, on the roof in London. About . . .

His father. His father's death. Reeve flicked through his notebook, but his mind was already on the rooftop. Parker stood before him in the rain and darkness. What had he said?

He died, and they didn't even fucking tell *me!* Parker's shout was filled with pain and years of pent-up rage. His father had been killed in a prison brawl. Reeve had found details in a newspaper story. He'd made notes: where were they?

There. His summary was brief and blunt. *Darren Laurence stabbed in fight, died in prison hospital, Sat Sep 30th.* The story itself, he recalled, wasn't much longer. To the press, murderers who died in prison had got what they deserved. More lines were spent eulogising Laurence's victim, his landlord.

Parker had said more. *I got pulled out of class on the*

Monday. That was when he learned of his father's death . . .

Which had been on the Saturday. Two days earlier. In date form, 30-09. Move the clock forward to Monday—

That was it.

Not the official date of Darren Laurence's death. The date that mattered to Parker – when he had been *told*. When everything changed. When his long journey towards vengeance began.

Zero-two, one-zero. The first four digits, they *had* to be. But how many followed?

Only one way to know.

Reeve snapped up the phone. He entered the four numbers. Hesitation, then: two digits for the year. He tapped them in—

Another failed attempt. He froze, half-expecting the phone to warn that it was deleting everything. But the lock screen reappeared.

He carefully typed the numbers again. Zero-two-one-zero. Another fractional pause, then he continued. Four more digits. Time seemed to slow. He waited, the phone considering its response . . .

A grid of icons appeared.

Reeve exhaled sharply. He hadn't even realised he was holding his breath. 'I'm in.'

Connie hurried through the doorway. 'What?'

'I worked out his passcode. The day he was *told* his father died – which was two days after it happened.'

'They didn't even tell—' Her instinctive sympathy was overridden by more pressing matters. 'So now what are you going to do?'

'Find a way to save our lives.' The phone hadn't been used in almost eighteen months, but its memory was still intact. A swipe brought up the app switcher. He went to the email program. The decryption password was set to be sent to the media on a timer. He'd stopped it. The email containing the password was still there, undelivered. He opened it.

Two lines of text. *This password decrypts the files listing assassinations carried out by the British government.* It was followed by a string of characters: *andnowismytime!*

That was the key. Where was the lock?

He checked the only other email in the app. An attachment contained the encrypted files. Parker had sent it a few minutes before the attempted assassination. The second mail was his backup plan. He'd intended to reveal the password to the stunned press after Curtis's death.

The attachment was called, mundanely, *Classified Documents*. Reeve brought up the search bar, entering the name. The original file was located. He tapped on it. A password request appeared.

He typed in *andnowismytime!* An exchange of worried looks with Connie . . .

Then a message appeared. *Decrypting*. A progress bar began to fill.

'How long do you think it'll take?' Connie asked.

'I don't know.' He watched the bar's sluggish movement. 'A while.'

The decryption went slowly but steadily. Reeve checked his watch. Still over thirty minutes before his self-imposed departure deadline. Unless the progress bar was drastically inaccurate, there was time to complete the job.

And hopefully time to see what secrets the files held.

Five minutes passed. He took the opportunity to disable the passcode lock. Another five. His frustration grew. Progress seemed to be slowing. Maybe the individual files were getting larger. He wondered how many there were. The maximum size for an email attachment was typically around twenty-five megabytes. Enough for hundreds, even thousands of text files.

SC9 had existed for thirty years now. How many people had its Operatives killed? How many were on Sir Simon Scott's death list? They were questions he had been neither encouraged nor inclined to ask during training.

The bar gradually neared its end. Twenty minutes. He was pacing, he belatedly realised, going back and forth along the mezzanine. He ended another pass on the balcony, looking down at the street. Vehicle access to central Florence was restricted; there were few parked cars. None were silver Peugeots. He doubted that Flynn and Stone would have changed their vehicle. Their pursuers hadn't caught up – yet.

An incongruously cheerful chime from the phone. He darted back to it. 'Is it finished?' asked Connie.

'Yeah.'

New documents had appeared. A *lot* of new documents. Over four hundred and fifty. The filenames were dates followed by codenames: FLOTILLA ORPHAN, TRUCULENT BLUE, EVEN EAGLE. They told Reeve nothing about their contents – which was the point. They were randomly generated by a computer to be utterly meaningless.

He opened one at random. REINDEER FIREWORK was dated from 1996. He skimmed the text. The target was one

Amad Al-Ajmi, an Omani. Married, father of three. A lawyer, acting for a group of Omani expatriates. He'd brought a lawsuit in London against British oil and gas interests. The case reached the High Court. It seemed likely to go in the plaintiffs' favour.

Until Al-Ajmi fell under a Tube train in rush hour.

Operative 17, Michael Pierce, had carried out the killing. He'd shadowed Al-Ajmi for days, waiting for the perfect moment. When it came, he shoved the lawyer over the platform's edge. Before anyone could react, he disappeared into the crowd. He was out of the station before police arrived. Afterwards, he remained in a safehouse until SC9 confirmed he was not a wanted man. Witness statements were 'lost' and CCTV recordings 'accidentally' erased to ensure it.

Without its chief lawyer, the court case crumbled. The defendants won. All legal costs – in the millions of pounds – were dumped upon the plaintiffs. Corporate and personal bankruptcies followed.

The final paragraph was attributed to Scott himself. *All objectives achieved. Operative uncompromised. Outcome satisfactory.*

Reeve stared at the last words. Cold, bureaucratic, impersonal. Yet behind them a man was dead, a family destroyed, livelihoods ruined. All for a simple, mundane summary: *satisfactory*.

That was what he had been trained to achieve. He felt a sick sense of revelation: this would have been his life. Killing without remorse, bringing pain and anguish to the victim's loved ones. And for what? Scott's curt approval: *outcome satisfactory*. One target down, on to the next. And the next.

And over four hundred more nexts – at least. Parker might merely have crammed as many files into the attachment as would fit. There could be many more. Michael Pierce was SC9's seventeenth successful recruit. Reeve himself would have been Operative 66, twenty-five years later. Scott had a lot of assassins on his payroll.

The only reason to have so many was to use them.

Scott had declared himself the sole judge of threats to the British establishment. Maybe it was once a task taken on out of duty, with a heavy heart. If so – which Reeve doubted – it certainly wasn't now. Scott was *proud* of his position, relishing it. The power of life or death, on his decision. On his whim. Accountable to nobody . . .

'What is it?' Connie was looking at him, curious – concerned.

'They're exactly what Parker said they were,' he told her. 'SC9's assassination files.'

'Oh, my God. How many are there?'

'Hundreds.' He scrolled through the list, looking for more recent entries. Operative 17 was active in 1996. Tony Maxwell was Operative 45 . . .

'SC9 have killed *hundreds* of people?'

He nodded as he opened another file. TAPESTRY SILVER, dated 2014. Target: Peter Collings, British. Operative assigned: 53, James West. Collings claimed to have been sexually abused as a child by a now-senior politician. That Scott had ordered his death to silence him suggested the accusation was true. Disgusted, Reeve returned to the directory. 'What are you looking for?' asked Connie.

'One of Tony's files.'

'Why?'

'Because I know how to find him. He's the only Operative who might listen to me. Rather than try to kill me on sight.'

He continued his search, looking for anything he could use against his hunters.

CHAPTER 11

Morozov's helicopter flight to Florence took just under an hour. He approved. Maybe next time, the SVR would pay for a private jet . . .

Brief amusement at the ridiculous thought, then he headed through the terminal. His people had done their jobs quickly and well. Contacts had prepared back routes through each airport, bypassing security. A good thing: he was still armed.

His phone rang. 'Yes?'

'It's Pervak.' One of Morozov's support team in Moscow. A pasty, skinny nerd, but he was excellent at his work. To the field agent, ability was worth infinitely more than appearance. 'How was the flight?'

'Good. Quick.'

'Glad you enjoyed it. You don't want to know how much it cost. But listen, we've pinpointed the acquisition. Parker planted a honeytrap on it. It was just triggered – someone opened the files. We've connected to live streams from the phone's microphone and cameras.'

'I know about the honeytrap,' said Morozov, with mild irritation. Another of the Englishman's time-wasting displays of independence. Parker's justification had been that SC9 would take the phone following his arrest. When they checked its files, the SVR would then see and hear whoever was there. Faces and names would be revealed – perhaps even SC9's elusive and as yet anonymous director. Morozov had disapproved, thinking the plan overcomplicated, but was unable to force the issue. His asset was operating beyond his direct reach. 'If Parker had just *given* us the files, we wouldn't be in this situation.'

'But then you wouldn't have got a helicopter ride, would you?' Pervak chuckled, then became serious again. 'We've identified the man with the phone. Parker's patsy had it all along. Alex Reeve.'

'Reeve.' The name flashed up a mental file for Morozov. Parker's assessment, delivered piecemeal on the rare occasions when contact was possible. Reeve was highly capable – but then, the Russian expected nothing less. SC9's Operatives were as good as the best SVR agent. On a personal level, Parker considered him cold, detached, borderline autistic. In many ways, the perfect trained killer. Once given a task, Reeve would carry it out with robotic efficiency.

Yet he wasn't unimaginative or inflexible. His escape and survival proved that. And in the end, he had killed Parker himself. The victim of the frame had taken his revenge. Then, he'd disappeared.

But now he had resurfaced, nearly eighteen months later, in another country. Why? What had changed – and why had he powered up the phone?

Morozov put the question aside. He was there to kill Reeve, not question him. Then he would take the phone. The files it contained would be a treasure-trove for the SVR.

They might even allow a direct strike against SC9 itself, instead of MI6 accountants . . .

'He's with someone else,' Pervak continued. 'A woman, British. No ID yet, but we're still listening.'

'It doesn't matter,' said Morozov dismissively. 'She'll get the same treatment as Reeve.'

'Ah . . . about that.' Pervak's shift of tone suggested an unwelcome change of plan. 'Grishin wants you to capture him.'

'What? Why?'

'Parker told us he's met SC9's boss, face to face. At his vacation home in France. We can use that information to track him down.'

'He won't go back there.' Morozov didn't doubt even for a moment that the information would be extracted from Reeve.

'Probably not. But there'll be records in France. Legal documents, financial transactions. If we have those, we can track them to their source in England.'

'Hmm.' Morozov's doubt was plain in the little sound. But Grishin had ordered it, so . . . 'All right. I'll hold him.'

'Backup's just set off from Milan. They'll help with Reeve's transfer. The woman, we don't care about.'

'Well, obviously.' Though she could still be useful. She was probably Reeve's girlfriend. In which case, a gun to her head should persuade him to surrender.

Bright sunlight ahead as he reached the terminal's exit. 'All right. I'm getting a taxi. Give me Reeve's exact location.'

*

'Have you got his exact location?' asked Stone.

'Not quite,' replied Maxwell over the speaker. 'GCHQ has pinned it down to one apartment block. They can't identify the specific flat.'

Flynn had just brought the car off the autostrada south of Florence. 'What's the address?'

The senior Operative gave a number on the Via dei Vagellai. Stone entered it into the satnav. 'Ten minutes away,' he reported. 'Right in the centre.'

'Traffic's restricted in central Florence,' Maxwell warned. 'If you park without a permit, the cops will be all over your car.'

'If we piss about for too long, Reeve might leave,' replied the Londoner.

'You're on the ground – your decision.'

The two Operatives exchanged a look. 'It's not our car anyway,' decided Stone. 'It's Six's problem; fuck 'em.'

Flynn was less blasé. 'And what if we walk out covered in blood and the police are right there? With a corpse in our boot, at that. Besides, I'm driving. Find the nearest car park to Reeve's location.'

Stone was about to argue, but Maxwell spoke first. 'You're in luck – there's one at the end of the street. The Piazza Mentana. You'll get fined for entering the restricted zone, but as Mark said, that's MI6's problem.'

'We'll put on earpieces, give you updates,' said Flynn.

'Good. If Reeve moves, I'll tell you.'

'Can GCHQ track his phone in real time?' asked Stone.

'Real-ish,' said Maxwell. 'It's updated every thirty seconds. I'm following their track on my laptop, so I'll relay it to you.'

'All right,' said Stone. He clenched his fists, psyching himself up. 'Let's go and kill that little bastard.'

'Got him,' Reeve said at last.

Connie came in from the balcony. 'You found something about Tony?'

'Yeah.' Picking files at random had eventually yielded a result. BARRIER STRATOS, 2015. Maxwell had eliminated a Nigerian union activist. Perhaps predictably, the justification was connected to British oil interests. Scott's definition of threats to the UK was extremely broad.

'So . . . he assassinated someone? Murdered them?' Reeve nodded. 'God. And I met him, that time on the roof. He seemed so . . . *normal*. He was just some guy. You'd never think he was a trained killer.'

'That's the point. The best Operatives are the ones who don't get noticed.'

'Like you.'

'I'm not an Operative any more,' he assured her. 'But now I've got proof that Tony killed someone, I can use that against him.'

'As blackmail?'

'More to show that I've got Parker's stolen files. Parker was right, you know,' he went on. 'If this information went public, it would be *disastrous* for the British government. SC9 hasn't just assassinated targets from hostile countries. They've killed people from our closest allies. America, France, Germany – and that's just in the files I've flicked through. Some were government officials, even politicians. If they opposed British interests, in Scott's view, they became targets.'

'Like Elektra Curtis,' said Connie gloomily.

Another nod. 'There are as many targets at home as abroad. *That* would blow up the British establishment, just like Parker wanted. SC9 was created to be totally deniable. But this,' he indicated the text on the screen, 'proves it's funded by the government. Linked to the other intelligence services, and run by a senior civil servant. The files have names, dates, places, money. Any decent journalist could tie everything together – and blow things wide open.'

'Couldn't the government suppress it?'

'They could use super-injunctions and DSMA notices. But Parker sent the encrypted files to news organisations all over the world. If he'd managed to send the password as well, everyone would have this information. There'd be no way to hide it.'

Connie said nothing, taking everything in. 'So . . . what happens when you find Tony?' she eventually asked.

'I prove that I've seen the files, including ones incriminating him,' he said. 'Then I offer him a deal. Convince SC9 to stop hunting us, or I'll release them. I don't even need to send the files – they're already out there. They just need the decryption password. That I've seen one of his files proves I've got it. Tony knows I'm not a traitor. I'm sure he'd take the deal.'

'But he's not in charge, is he?' she pointed out.

'I know. If they call my bluff, SC9 might go all-out to kill me.'

'And me,' was Connie's unhappy rejoinder.

'Yeah.' Reeve sighed, then checked his watch. His deadline was nearly up. A glance at the laptop. It had rebooted, flashing an error message. The hard drive had been wiped.

One task completed, at least. 'We need to go soon. Let's clean everything up.'

The taxi dropped Morozov on the Via dei Vagellai. He got out before the target building to survey it from a distance.

Pervak had reported what the phone's hacked camera revealed. The apartment had two levels and a vaulted ceiling. That almost certainly meant it was on the top floor. Morozov regarded the rooftop. A balcony, doors open, matched the description.

He crossed the street and headed for his destination. There was a lockbox beside the ornate doorway. Morozov considered picking it – then saw someone had beaten him to it. Fresh scrapes around the keyhole. Reeve had broken in. It was a hideout of opportunity rather than a prepared bolthole. Was the Englishman on the run?

No point trying to open the lockbox himself. Reeve would have taken the keys. Instead he went to the door buzzer. Twelve buttons. How many flats on the top floor? The building had four main floors, so assume a quarter. The highest numbers. He pushed the lower nine one by one. A woman's voice soon crackled through the speaker grille.

'Hi, I've got a delivery for you,' Morozov replied in fluent Italian.

'Oh, okay,' she replied. 'Come on up.' The buzzer sounded.

Morozov darted inside. Stairs led upwards. He quickly ascended, rubber soles near-silent on the marble. A door opened on the first floor, the woman awaiting her delivery. But he was already past.

He stopped just below the top landing and listened. No sounds from above. Three apartment doors were visible. Which was his target behind? He phoned Pervak. 'I'm here. Which apartment is he in?'

'Hold on, I'll overlay your position . . . got him,' Pervak replied. 'The flat to your right.'

Morozov's gaze locked on to the relevant door. 'What's he doing?'

'Talking to the woman.'

'Is he armed?'

'No weapon in his hands. Doesn't mean there isn't one close by, though. Watch yourself.'

Morozov drew his silenced automatic and moved carefully to the door. 'What's his exact position?'

'On the upper level. We've got access to the phone's GPS and compass. He's facing the balcony, so his back's to you.'

'The woman?'

'From where he's looking, in front of him.'

'Okay. I'm going in.' He ended the call. Three deep breaths, muscles tensing in readiness . . .

Then he kicked open the door.

Reeve had just unplugged the phone when a loud bang came from behind him. Behind and below – the door. He whirled. *SC9—*

But it wasn't Stone or Flynn. The man who burst in was older, tight-faced, broad-jawed. His gun was already aimed up at the mezzanine. 'Don't move!' he barked. The order was in English, but the accent was Russian. He advanced, pushing the door shut. It didn't close fully, damaged wood catching the frame.

Connie gasped in shock. She instinctively started to retreat towards the balcony. 'Stay still,' Reeve told her urgently. The intruder's eyes were ice-cold. He would kill her without a qualm. All he needed was a reason – or an excuse. She froze.

The man rapidly climbed the stairs. His line of fire was briefly obstructed. Reeve used the moment to look for a weapon – but found nothing useable. The apartment was tidy to the point of spartan.

The Russian reached the upper floor. His gun reacquired Reeve. 'Where is the phone?'

'Here.' Reeve slowly raised his hand to show him. 'Let her go, and you can have it.' He moved to put himself in front of Connie.

A mordant chuckle. 'I will have it anyway.'

'Who are you?' asked Connie fearfully.

'That is not important. But,' he said to Reeve, 'we have a mutual . . . friend, is not the right word. Acquaintance. Craig Parker.'

'You're his control?' said Reeve.

'I recruited him, yes. But if I had truly been in control, we would not be here now. We wanted the SC9 files. But he wanted revenge. Foolishly, we permitted it. But now, I am here.' He advanced on the couple. 'Give me the phone.'

Connie moved closer to Reeve. 'What are you going to do with us?'

'He,' the intruder indicated the Englishman, 'is coming back to Moscow with me. You? That depends on whether he cooperates.'

'Why do you need me?' Reeve demanded.

'You have met the man who runs SC9, been to his house in France. You know his name, his face.' The Russian's expression hardened. 'You will tell us everything you know about him, and SC9.'

'I won't.'

'Oh, you will.' He shifted his aim towards Connie. 'You, we need. Her? We do not.' She retreated behind Reeve. The man simply moved to retarget her. 'It is up to—'

The door was kicked open again.

CHAPTER 12

Flynn and Stone heard voices as they reached the top floor. They immediately identified Reeve's. One apartment's door was ajar, the wood splintered. Surprise from both Operatives; they'd expected him to be more subtle.

But now they had him. They drew their weapons and flanked the door. Stone raised his foot. Three, two, one—

He booted it open and rushed in. Flynn was right behind him. They split up to cover each side of the room beyond.

Reeve wasn't there.

But his voice had been close. So where—

They both registered the upper level at the same moment. Stone looked up, but his view was obstructed by the stairs. Flynn, though, saw Reeve, Connie – and an unknown man.

He spun towards her. *Gun!* She whipped up her own weapon—

Too late.

The mystery man's round hit her chest like a hammer. She crashed backwards against a bookcase. It collapsed, its contents spilling over her.

Stone saw her fall. He couldn't see how many enemies he was facing. Footsteps told him at least two.

One set broke into a run. Someone was coming for him.

He needed cover. There was a kitchen counter at the room's far end. He ran for it.

Reeve saw Flynn go down. The Russian rushed towards the stairs, gun raised. Going after Stone.

Whoever came out on top, Reeve didn't care. What mattered was that they had a chance to escape.

He grabbed Connie. 'Go!' He propelled her towards the balcony, snatching up the bug-out bag as he went.

'Where?' Connie protested.

'On to the roof!' They rushed into sunlight. The balcony was three metres wide, barely one deep. Low railings surrounded it. He moved an open wooden shutter to reach the nearest side. 'Go up over the top.' He waited for her to clear the obstacle before starting to follow.

Stone had no idea who he was facing as well as Reeve. He didn't care. All that mattered was taking them down.

He dropped behind the counter. One enemy was descending the staircase. The Londoner popped up, weapon readied—

He'd expected his opponent to open fire on him. Instead, a man leapt from the stairs and dived for the open door. Stone tracked him and fired. Missed! His target made it through the opening. Scrambling footsteps outside, then he ran down the stairwell.

One threat gone, but where was Reeve? Stone backed across the room to see more of the upper level. Nobody there. He must have gone on to the balcony.

Trying to escape over the roof.

Gun covering the mezzanine, Stone hurried to its stairs.

A moan; Flynn moved under the wrecked bookshelves. Not knowing if Reeve was armed, both Operatives had donned ballistic vests under their clothing. 'Jesus,' she groaned. 'Get me up.'

'Get yourself up, you fucking idiot,' Stone snapped as he ran upwards. 'Maybe don't walk into some cunt's bullets next time.'

The balcony doors were open. He charged through them—

And was sent reeling back as a heavy wooden shutter slammed into him.

Reeve kicked the shutter closed, hard. A pained grunt told him he'd hit Stone, knocking the big man down.

He ran up the roof after Connie. Florence opened out before him as he reached the red-tiled crown. His immediate surroundings were a multi-layered hotchpotch of old buildings. Rooftops stepped down to a central courtyard like a volcanic caldera.

Connie waited at the edge of their building. 'Which way?'

Reeve didn't know. 'Over there,' he said, pointing across the crater. 'Go around the middle.'

'Can we get down there?'

He had no answer. They ran, old tiles clattering underfoot.

Flynn staggered upright. Her life had now been saved twice by a bulletproof vest. The experience was no less unpleasant eighteen months on. Dull pain roiled through her bruised chest.

No sign of the man who had caused it. Or her partner. 'Stone! Where are you?'

'Here,' came an irate growl. She looked at the mezzanine to see Stone getting up. 'That fucker just kicked a door shut in my face.'

'The guy who shot me?'

'No, Reeve. He went on to the roof.' Stone returned to the balcony doors. 'He's gone. I'm going after him.' He disappeared from sight.

Flynn found her gun amongst the fallen books. A faint buzzing noise reached her. Her radio earpiece, dislodged in the fall. She put it back in.

'Deirdre!' Maxwell, sounding concerned. 'Can you hear me?'

'I'm here, I'm here,' she said into the microphone concealed in her collar. 'I'm okay.'

'What the hell happened?'

'I don't know. Reeve was here – with someone else. No idea who. The bastard shot me,' she added, in brief outrage.

'If there's another player, we need to find out who,' said Maxwell. 'Can you pursue?'

Flynn raised the gun. 'Fucking right I can.' She checked the landing. Nobody there. Faint echoes of running feet from below. She hurried after them. 'You want him dead or alive?'

'Your call. Try not to shoot him in the face, though. We might be able to ID him.'

'I'll bear that in mind.' She continued her descent.

A flare of sunlight in the lobby told her the man had reached the street.

Morozov ran out on to the Via dei Vagellai. His heart raced with the rush of the unexpected battle. His attackers must have been SC9: they'd tracked the phone too. Britain's GCHQ had done a good job.

Not good enough, though. The Operatives hadn't expected him to be there. Which meant they didn't have access to the phone's mic and camera, only its location. That gave Morozov an advantage. Cell tower pings alone couldn't triangulate a phone's position in real-time. The updates were too slow. But the SVR had a direct link to its GPS. Pervak could guide him after it, second by second.

He holstered his gun and ran west, looking for somewhere to get out of sight. A mini-market provided the opportunity. He ducked into the shop, trying to appear calm. The woman at the till glanced up, then looked away again, bored. Morozov took out his phone. 'Pervak,' he said. 'There was a complication.'

Relief filled Pervak's voice. 'You had us worried! We knew something had happened, but didn't know what.'

'Two SC9 Operatives came for Reeve. He's running – he's still got the phone.'

'I know. The woman's with him. We're tracking them. What about the Brits?'

'I shot one of them. Don't know if she's dead or not – hold on.' Movement outside, someone running past. A flash of reddish-brown hair. 'Damn. She survived. She's pursuing Reeve.'

'You can't let them get him. Or the phone.'

'I won't.' Morozov returned to the doorway. The woman was gone. 'If Reeve tells his girlfriend where they're going, you tell me.' He stepped back outside. 'I'll find them.'

CHAPTER 13

'We can't get down from here!' Connie cried.

Reeve saw for himself as they reached the edge of the far rooftops. He'd thought they stepped downwards towards ground level. But it was an illusion. A narrow street sliced between the buildings, cutting off the apparent escape route. They were three floors up; a fatal drop.

None of the nearby roofs were any lower. He looked back. Stone appeared over the crown of the building where they had sheltered—

He saw them. His weapon came up.

Reeve grabbed Connie's arm, ducking as they ran along the edge. A gunshot – and a bullet cracked past. Connie gasped.

Chimney stacks blocked Stone's line of fire as they hurried along. 'Over there,' said Reeve. On the opposite rooftop was a large dormer window, one pane open outwards. 'We've got to jump across.'

'It's too far!' The gap was five metres, the building across the street slightly lower.

'We don't have a choice.' He angled back up the roof. Stone was rounding the angular crater in pursuit. 'Now, quick!'

A couple of metres' run-up was all they had. It would have to do. Two rapid strides, and the street reappeared below. He jumped—

Connie was still with him. But she had mistimed her leap. He lost his grip on her wrist as they sailed over the gap. Red tiles rushed at Reeve—

One shattered underfoot as he hit it. It suddenly felt as if he was on ice. He clawed at the roof as he slipped, dislodging dirt, moss, bird droppings. Then his fingers found purchase. He jerked to a halt.

Connie hit the roof on her side. Neither of her hands found grip. She slithered towards the drop with a scream—

Reeve lunged sideways to catch her. His hand found her forearm – but couldn't close around it.

Her legs went over the edge—

His fingers hooked around hers. He gripped them as hard as he could. She cried out as bones ground against each other – but her fall stopped.

Reeve strained to pull her back. The extra weight made his position even more precarious. 'Get your feet up!'

Connie swung her legs. One foot caught the roof's edge. She forced herself higher. The pressure on Reeve's fingers eased. He dragged himself upwards. 'Climb over me,' he rasped. 'Get hold of the dormer.'

Panting, she did so. 'Open the window and go inside,' he told her. She hesitantly sidestepped to the front of the dormer.

Reeve secured himself. The most immediate danger was over—

But there was still another.

He looked across the street. Stone had halted his scramble over the rooftops, taking aim.

Connie tugged at the open window. Metal rattled. 'It won't move!'

Stone's gun locked on to Reeve. He fired—

As Reeve let go.

He slid down the roof. The round smacked into the tiles just above him. Someone inside the building screamed. He grabbed the dormer's base, abruptly stopping his descent. The jolt strained his shoulder muscles. A tile broke loose beneath him and fell, exploding on the street below.

Reeve knew he would join it if he didn't find cover. Connie was still trying to open the window. A metal stay held it in place. She couldn't reach far enough around the frame to unlatch it.

He moved up beside her and smashed the glass with his elbow. 'Go in!'

Connie squeezed through, crystalline debris tinkling around her. He moved to follow. Another glance back. Stone had moved closer, taking aim again. Reeve gripped the window frame and propelled himself inside.

He tumbled over a sink and fell heavily to the floor beyond. A second bullet whipped over him. A picture on the kitchen wall shattered.

Another scream. The flat's occupant was a middle-aged woman, regarding the two intruders in horrified disbelief. 'Get back! Keep your head down!' Reeve shouted in Italian. She retreated, hands flapping in fear.

Connie helped him rise to a crouch. 'Are you okay?' he asked.

'Yeah,' she replied, wide-eyed. 'But you've been cut!'

His arm was bloodied, lacerations slicing out from his elbow. One palm also stung. Glass fragments were embedded in the skin. Neither injury was dangerous in the short-term. 'I'm all right. We've got to go.'

Reeve rapidly scanned the room. A wooden knife-block on the counter. He moved towards it, checking the window. If Stone was on the rooftop opposite, he would have line of fire on him—

A loud *bang* from outside told him otherwise. The Operative had made a flying leap across the gap. Reeve snatched the largest knife from the block. 'He's coming. Go!'

They ran through the flat. The woman cowered behind a chair. The door was on a bolt and a chain. Reeve fumbled with both locks. Precious seconds lost. More glass broke behind. Stone was at the window.

The chain finally came free. Reeve threw the door open and rushed Connie out on to a confined landing. A small skylight illuminated a narrow old staircase winding downwards. They ran to its top, about to run down—

Reeve halted. The landing was L-shaped, branching to reach another flat. The corner was at the top of the stairs. 'Get down to the ground,' he told Connie. 'I'll follow you. Run!' She hurried downwards.

He took cover around the corner, gripping the knife. Stone would be here in seconds. Connie's descending footsteps would catch his attention, drawing him to the stairs.

Should catch his attention. He might anticipate an ambush . . .

Another shriek from the flat. The thud of running feet grew louder—

Reeve whirled out from his hiding place. Stone was right there. The knife lanced at his chest.

Stone snapped up a hand to deflect the strike – his *gun* hand. The blade's edge slashed through the heel of his palm. A choked snarl of pain.

Both men crashed together. The impact jolted the gun from Stone's wounded hand. It spun into the stairwell.

But Reeve was unable to seize the advantage. The collision with the bigger man knocked him backwards – towards the stairs. He barely caught the banister, teetering on the edge.

Stone lunged. Before Reeve could react, the Operative body-slammed him.

He overbalanced, falling—

Reeve snatched at Stone's clothing as he went. He caught his jacket. The sharp tug brought the other man over the edge with him.

They both tumbled down the stairs. Reeve took the brunt, Stone on top of him. The knife struck one of the banister's metal stanchions. Its tip barely missed Reeve's face as it was knocked loose. It clattered down the steps ahead of them.

The two men thumped against the wall at the staircase's first turn. Reeve was pinned under the larger man. He tried to pull free. Stone drove a couple of punches at his stomach. Reeve gasped, winded. The other man jumped up. A brutal kick slammed into Reeve's side. He cried out, writhing. Stone pulled back, turning to aim another kick at his head—

Reeve's heel slammed against Stone's kneecap. The

Operative staggered, falling against the wall. Reeve rolled to his knees, trying to stand.

Stone's boot pounded into Reeve's ribcage. The impact bowled him down the next leg of the staircase. He landed hard on the landing below. Stone took the steps two at a time after him.

Reeve opened pain-clenched eyes. Metal glinted on the dimly lit floor. The knife. He grabbed it. Stone was upon him, foot rushing at his head—

He threw himself backwards, arm sweeping up to intercept the incoming attack. Stone roared as the knife stabbed into his left thigh. Reeve twisted the blade. Stone screamed – and his other leg gave way with the pain.

He collapsed. The knife was wrenched from Reeve's grip. He had to scramble sideways to keep the Operative from landing on top of him.

Reeve stood. Stone glared up at him. A snarl of rage through clenched teeth. 'You fucking little—'

Anything else was cut off as Reeve kicked him full-force in the balls. Stone let out a breathless shriek. He folded, convulsing helplessly.

Reeve was about to recover the knife when an apartment door opened. An elderly man gawped at the scene. Reeve cursed. He couldn't kill Stone now; not in front of a witness. An Operative would have simply killed the witness too – but he no longer was one. Instead he bolted down the stairs.

Connie waited in the lobby. 'Are you okay?'

'Yeah,' was his pained reply. 'Come on.' He opened the door.

'Where?'

'Santa Croce. It's the nearest taxi rank,' he explained as they hurried out. 'You can't just flag down a cab in Florence. You have to get them from specific places.'

'And where are we going after that?'

'I don't know yet.' They were on the narrow street they had jumped across. He got his bearings. The Piazza di Santa Croce was to the northeast. 'This way.' They both ran.

Morozov's phone rang. 'We know where Reeve's going,' said Pervak. 'Santa Croce. He's getting a taxi.'

'I know the place.' Morozov had visited Florence several times, not solely on business. It was one of his favourite cities. 'Where are they now?'

'A hundred metres west of you. Heading north.'

The Russian looked up the street he had just entered. The Via dei Benci led directly to the piazza's western end. The taxi rank was at its corner – about two hundred metres away. 'I can beat them there.' He pocketed the phone, then headed briskly towards the piazza.

To hell with Grishin's orders. With SC9 involved, he didn't have time to capture Reeve. He would simply kill him and the woman when they reached Santa Croce.

CHAPTER 14

Stone hobbled down the stairs, one hand pressed against his leg wound. The old man from the flat called frantically after him, gesticulating. 'Yeah, I'm fine, grandad,' the Operative growled back. Italian was not one of the languages he'd learned during training. 'Just fuck off back inside and eat your Dolmio.'

A voice in his earpiece: Flynn. 'Stone. Where are you?'

'Haven't a fucking clue. Reeve jumped to another building and went into a flat. I followed him.'

Maxwell joined the conversation. 'Did you get him?'

'No, and the cunt stabbed me in the leg.' His balls hurt almost as much as his thigh. Stone opted not to mention his more humiliating injury. He reached the ground floor. The exterior door was open, daylight flooding in. A glint of metal caught his attention. His gun. He collected it, staggering as he bent down. A quick check that the weapon wasn't damaged, then he holstered it and limped outside. A narrow street. No sign of his prey. 'I've lost them,' he reluctantly conceded. 'Where are you, Flynn?'

'Near the car. I went after the guy who shot me. I've lost him, though.'

'We can still find Alex,' said Maxwell. 'GCHQ's trace should update in a moment . . .' A pause, then: 'Okay. He's north of you. Seems to be heading east. Mark, do you need medical help?'

'I'll manage,' Stone said through his teeth. He started up the street, wounded leg dragging. 'Just let me know when I'm close to him.'

'I'll try to direct you both to box him in. You'll need to be on the ball, though. All these narrow streets interfere with the signal. GCHQ can't guarantee locational accuracy beyond thirty metres.'

'That's within gunshot range,' Stone replied. 'It's all we need.'

Reeve and Connie hurried along the Via dei Neri, heading east. A side street angled north. She was about to pass it, but he turned up the narrower alley. 'Santa Croce's this way,' she said. A sign had pointed the way towards the piazza – straight ahead.

'The phone must be being tracked,' Reeve replied. 'That's how they found us. But the buildings should mess with the signal. They won't get an accurate fix until we're in the open. By then, we'll be in a cab.'

'And then what?'

'Once we're far enough clear, I'll work that out.'

They entered a little piazza, people strolling through it. Connie looked eastwards; an archway led to a wider street. 'That way?'

Reeve went in the opposite direction. 'This leads round to the same place. We'll keep them guessing.'

She was already breathless, tiring. 'This isn't how I wanted to explore Florence.'

'Sorry. Not far now.'

They followed the curving Via de'Bentaccordi to the Via Torta. Reeve turned east; Santa Croce was now directly ahead. They hurried past clutches of tourists. The street opened out. There was the great Basilica, sunlit white marble gleaming at the piazza's far end. The taxi rank was to their right, at the square's southwestern corner. Several cabs stood waiting. They headed for them—

Reeve stopped sharply. Connie almost stumbled into him. 'Jesus, Alex!' She realised he wouldn't have halted without a good reason. 'What's wrong?'

'Get back,' he said, reversing at walking pace so as not to draw attention. 'The Russian's already here.' The broad-jawed man stood against a wall near the taxis. The direct route would have brought them into the piazza just metres from their hunter.

'Oh, shit,' she gasped. They retreated. Reeve kept his eyes fixed on the Russian. 'How did he know where we were going?'

Realisation struck him. 'The phone's microphone,' he whispered. 'They can hear us – probably see through the camera too.'

Her eyes widened in alarm. 'You've got to get rid of it.'

'If I do, I lose any chance of stopping SC9—'

The Russian turned his head. A routine sweep of his surroundings, watching as much for police as his targets . . .

His eyes locked on to Reeve's.

Reeve muttered a curse. 'Run.' They both raced back down the Via Torta.

'Is he following us?' Connie asked fearfully.

Reeve hadn't seen him move. But he knew the answer. 'Yes.'

'Oh, God. What do we do now?'

Two choices of taxi rank in this direction. The one near the majestic Santa Maria cathedral, Florence's centre-piece, was closer. The obvious destination – so he wouldn't use it. 'Keep moving. And I'll do something about the phone.'

He took it out and set the screen brightness to maximum. Connie glanced at it as they ran. 'You're *filming* this?'

'It's not for YouTube,' he replied, starting to record a video. He then switched on the phone's Wi-Fi and Bluetooth. 'HD video uses a lot of processing power. It'll burn through the battery. So will having everything else switched on.' A check of the battery level. Seven per cent. 'That's why it was charging so slowly. It was streaming everything to the bloody Russians!'

A look back. One particular Russian was fifty metres behind them. He was running, but not at full pelt. He knew he could track them. That would change when his controllers told him what his target had just done. Reeve pocketed the phone. 'Down here.'

He and Connie weaved through the streets, angling southwest. The other cab rank was past the Ponte Vecchio. If their pursuer were tracking them only by sight, Reeve knew he could lose him. But while the phone was still active, he might as well yell his position. How long before the battery ran down?

Another turn, on to the Via dei Leoni behind the towering

Palazzo Vecchio. They were nearing the river. If they kept far enough ahead of the Russian to reach a taxi—

Flynn appeared ahead of them.

The Operative was thirty metres away. The moment she saw Reeve, she burst into a sprint. Her hand went into her jacket.

Reeve instantly changed direction, swerving Connie into an entrance to the Palazzo. They raced up steps into a high-walled courtyard. Tourists looked around in surprise as they tore past. An arched entrance led deeper into the ancient building. They ran through, Reeve glancing back. Flynn was coming up the steps.

Of the Russian, there was no sign.

Morozov reached the Via dei Leoni. No sign of Reeve or the woman – but he *did* see the female SC9 Operative. She didn't spot him, though. Instead she hurried through a tall archway, presumably pursuing the same quarry. Her partner was following, but some way behind. The big man was limping, badly. Had Reeve injured him?

One less problem to worry about. The Russian reversed course and continued west on the Via dei Gondi. He had visited the Palazzo Vecchio several times, exploring its art collection. He knew how to get in – and out. From here, Reeve's exit options were limited. Emerging from the Palazzo's north side would put him right in front of Morozov. Every other option would bring him to the Piazza della Signoria. The great statue-lined plaza was always packed with visitors. They would give Reeve cover from his pursuer.

But the reverse was also true. With the phone transmitting his position, Morozov could remain hidden as he homed in.

And then kill him.

No time to admire Florence's artistic wonders. Reeve and Connie hurried through the Palazzo. Their pell-mell rush through the echoing chambers drew attention. A blue-shirted security guard called out a warning in their wake. If he alerted his comrades, they might block the exits—

Another courtyard. Bright sky above. Reeve glanced up, seeing the great tower at the Palazzo's western end. Almost out: the Piazza della Signoria was beyond. It would be bustling with tourists, providing them cover.

It would also, he knew, be bustling with cops. That was both a boon and a curse. Boon, because it would deter his pursuers from shooting. Curse, because the police might take an interest in *him*. His arm was bloodied, and he was sure his face was too. A running man who had clearly been in a fight was catnip for cops.

That worry could wait. They were almost out. Another guard moved to intercept, but they were already past. Through the great wooden doors into the piazza—

It was crowded, as he'd hoped. A replica of Michelangelo's David just beyond the exit drew the most gawkers. Several tour groups clashed before it, the guides' flags like the standards of rival armies. Reeve drew Connie through the midst of the sightseeing battle. Where were the police?

A glimpse of white cars across the plaza. There would be others. He had to locate them – he couldn't risk running right past a patrol—

Connie unexpectedly pulled at his arm. 'Alex, this way!'

She took the lead, head low. He glanced back at the Palazzo. Flynn emerged, searching for them. He ducked and followed Connie through the crowd.

A man had a little stall near the statue gallery on the Piazza's southern side. Connie rooted in her handbag as they reached him. She thrust a ten-euro note into his hands. '*Acqua, per favore, grazie!*' she said, snatching up a water bottle. They were gone before the startled man could react.

She hurriedly splashed the bottle's contents over her hands. 'Here,' she said, washing his face. 'You've got blood on you. We don't need the police after us as well.'

He managed to smile. 'You always take care of me. How does it look?'

She wiped his cheek. 'You've got a cut, but it's only small. Should stop bleeding pretty quickly.'

He took the bottle and washed his arm. The blood sluiced away, but more bloomed almost instantly from the lacerations. 'Those are deeper.'

'Nothing I can do without dressings. We need to find a pharmacy.'

'It'll have to wait.' He led again, curving northwards across the Piazza. More police were in sight at its edge.

They weaved to stay amongst the thickest clusters of tourists. 'Where are we going?' asked Connie.

He put a finger to his lips, then indicated the phone in his pocket. The plan had changed: Flynn was too close to risk getting a taxi. The Russian wasn't in sight, which if anything felt even more dangerous. 'We'll get a cab out of town by the Ponte Vecchio,' he said.

To his relief, she knew immediately what he was doing, and nodded. They continued north, away from the river. He doubted the ruse would trick the Russians for long. But an extra thirty seconds could mean the difference between escape and death.

He took out the phone. It was still filming. The battery indicator had fallen to five per cent. He pocketed it again and looked back. Flynn was hidden amongst the crowd.

Still no sign of the Russian.

Morozov stopped and surveyed the Piazza della Signoria. The lack of commotion told him the Operative hadn't made her kill. So where was she – and where was Reeve?

He concentrated his attention around the statue of David. It was the most likely exit point from the Palazzo. Nobody was in a rush, that he could see. He looked for secondary indicators: people reacting in annoyance or alarm to being jostled. Still nothing.

He took out his phone. The call was quickly answered. 'Where is he?' Morozov demanded.

'I was about to call you,' Pervak replied. 'Reeve's figured out that we're monitoring him.'

'Has he dumped the phone?'

'No – but he's doing everything he can to drain the battery. Once it dies, we can't track it.'

Morozov set off again. 'Tell me where he is.'

'He said he was heading for the Ponte Vecchio – but he's actually going north.' The Russian immediately changed direction to put the sun at his back. 'He's a hundred metres from you. Just entered one of the side streets.'

'I'm following. Stay on the line; I need real-time updates.'

'We're with you.'

'Good. And so are SC9,' he added.

'Will they be a problem?' asked Pervak.

Morozov felt the weight of his weapons beneath his clothing. 'No.'

Flynn turned in place, frustration rising. She was not tall, and the surrounding crowds blocked her view. 'Bollocks,' she finally snapped. 'I can't see them. Tony, I need an update.'

'Hold on,' Maxwell said in her earpiece. 'Should have one any second . . . there. He's changed direction, now going north.'

She was instantly suspicious. When she first reacquired her target, he'd been heading south. 'You think he's palmed off the phone on some tourist?'

'No.' His reply was immediate, and firm. 'It's the only leverage he has against us. He kept it for this long, he won't dump it now.'

Another voice cut in: Stone. 'Flynn! Where are you? I've just come out of the big building, by some statues.'

She looked towards the Palazzo. Stone was on the stairs, visible even over the crowd. 'I'm at your one o'clock, twenty metres away.' She raised her free arm. 'My hand's up.'

'I see you. Wait for me.'

'Reeve's getting away,' she objected.

'Just fucking wait!' he snapped. Flynn stood in annoyance as he limped towards her. 'Have you seen that arsehole you lost track of?'

'Oh, get to fuck,' she growled. 'You lost *Reeve*!'

114

'The bastard stabbed me,' he said. 'I'm not exactly fucking Usain Bolt right now.'

'And sure he's glad about that.' She regarded the other Operative's legs. His left thigh was wet with blood. Luckily, he was wearing dark trousers; it wouldn't show at a casual glance. 'You're not running anywhere like that. We'll lose Reeve if I have to wait for you.' She turned, about to set off again.

'Hey!' Stone barked. 'You're not fucking leaving me behind.'

She gave him a mocking look. 'If it's a choice between completing the mission or saving another Operative? You complete the mission.' It was a direct quote of Maxwell's words to her at the end of training. She tossed him a two-euro coin. 'Here. Buy yourself a fucking Elastoplast.'

She ran off, leaving the seething Stone behind.

CHAPTER 15

Reeve and Connie followed a crooked route through Florence, zigzagging up narrow side streets. Not so much to confuse their pursuers; Reeve knew the phone was still being tracked.

It was to keep them from getting a bullet in the back.

Every path soon became noticeably more crowded. 'We're nearly at the Duomo,' Reeve told Connie.

'Are we getting a taxi there?' she asked.

'Yes,' he replied – while shaking his head. She got the message. A quick check on the phone. Still recording: four per cent charge. He shoved it back into his pocket.

Another turn – and the Duomo rose beyond the end of the narrow street.

The Cathedral of Santa Maria dominated the city. The white-and-green marble walls shone as if aglow. Atop them stood the huge red dome that gave the building its more familiar name. It was not just one of Florence's most iconic attractions, but of all Italy's.

Which was exactly why Reeve had come to it.

The streets near the Palazzo Vecchio had been busy. Around the Duomo, they were packed. In tourist season, the wait to enter was usually at least two hours. The line could run halfway around the vast building.

So many tourists in one place were a prime draw for hawkers. And criminals. And terrorists. The Italian government was well aware of this. As a result, security around the Duomo was handled by multiple forces. The area was patrolled by Florence's *Polizia Municipale*, the national *Polizia* and *Carabinieri* . . .

And the army.

The military's presence had drawn Reeve's attention on his recce visit. He'd stored the information as potentially useful. It was about to pay off.

He hoped.

They reached the end of the Via dello Studio, emerging on the cathedral's southern side. Reeve turned west, rounding a large tour group. Ahead, the Campanile di Giotto thrust into the blue sky. The bell tower stood apart from the Duomo, cutting into the long piazza alongside it. It created a bottleneck, people flowing through in both directions. He looked back as they reached it.

The Russian was following at a run. He had come out of the street beyond the Via dello Studio. His jacket was now draped over his right arm, covering his hand. Reeve knew his gun was concealed beneath it. He held a phone in the other hand. The tour group was in his way; he skirted around them.

Flynn emerged from the Via dello Studio – on the other side of the group.

The two assassins were practically level, mere metres apart. But they didn't see each other through the tourists. By the time they passed the group, they were in the bottleneck. The crowd closed around them.

Reeve and Connie were already on the far side. They turned north to run past the cathedral's front. The scene was visual chaos. Hundreds of people, horse-drawn carriages, souvenir stalls, an ambulance attending to a fainter. They weaved through it, heads low. Reeve looked ahead, searching for—

There.

Camouflage colours amongst the bright bustle. An Italian army Iveco LMV: an armoured 4x4, parked at the cathedral's northwestern corner. Two soldiers stood at its front. There would probably be another two at the rear.

The line to enter the Duomo ran right past the LMV. Maximum visibility for maximum deterrence. The soldiers were armed, holding Beretta assault rifles. Reeve angled towards them.

Connie saw them too. 'That's the army!' she hissed in alarm.

'I know.' The street to the cathedral's north was narrower than its southern counterpart. The LMV acted as another bottleneck, outdoor seating for cafés further narrowing the way. Reeve brought them through the middle of the crowd. Behind, he glimpsed the Russian, closing. He couldn't see Flynn, but she would be no further away. 'Give me the bottle.'

She handed it to him. They passed the jeep. As Reeve had expected, two more soldiers were stationed at its rear. 'What for?'

'I'm going to chase you with it. When I do, run. But pretend we're having fun.'

She was confused, but he had no time to explain further. The crush eased. Another look back. The Russian was nearing the LMV. His eyes were locked upon Reeve.

'We're having fun,' Reeve reminded Connie – before splashing her back with water. 'Run!'

She gasped, then broke into a sprint through the thinning crowd. Reeve followed. 'C'mere, c'mere!' he whooped. 'I'm gonna get you!'

She finally cottoned on and laughed. To Reeve it sounded painfully forced, but it had the desired result. People moved aside, smiling or tutting depending on their temperament. 'No, don't get me wet!' Connie cried.

He chased her, waving the bottle over her head. Water slopped out, producing a genuine shriek of protest. A check behind. One of the soldiers watched with a half-smile.

The Russian emerged from the crowd not far from him.

As did Flynn.

Flynn's hand was inside her jacket, on her automatic's grip. She was about to draw it when she spotted the soldiers—

And the mystery man.

He was less than ten feet away. Both assassins froze.

Flynn made out the form of his gun beneath his draped jacket. Her own weapon was still holstered. He had the advantage . . .

But the soldiers were right beside him. Even a suppressed gun made noise. They would recognise it instantly. If he fired, they would take him down. They were not the only threat. A pair of carabinieri were approaching, one checking out Connie as she passed.

Neither the Operative nor the SVR agent could act against the other. A standoff.

People moved around them as they stared each other down. Flynn broke the deadlock. 'Well, well,' she said. 'If it isn't our friend from the flat.' She was speaking to Maxwell as much as her opponent.

The man gave her a cold smile. 'I did not expect to see you again so soon.' His accent was Russian.

'You can't keep a good woman down.'

His gaze went to her chest. Not lecherously, but professionally, seeing the hole in her clothing. 'I will set my sights higher next time.'

'There won't be a next time. Word of advice: mind your own fucking business. We'll take care of our problems.'

'But he *is* a problem, isn't he? Reeve, I mean. Alex Reeve. He has caused a lot of trouble for SC9.'

Flynn kept her expression neutral. Inside, she controlled her shock. How the hell did he know about SC9?

Maxwell voiced her thoughts through the earpiece. 'Deirdre, Mark's on the way. Keep him talking.'

'Okay,' she said, blending the acknowledgement into her next words. 'So what's your interest in Reeve?'

'He has something we want. The phone. It has the password to the files Craig Parker stole from you.'

'Which means they *don't* have the password,' Maxwell noted with relief.

'He also knows the name of SC9's director.' The malevolent smile widened, yellow teeth exposed. 'We are very keen to learn it. He has caused some . . . *unpleasantness* for us recently.' A brief glance at the soldiers. 'Several deaths were involved.'

'That's a shame,' Flynn said sarcastically. 'My condolences. Be too bad if there were any more.'

'It would.' He briefly looked along the street. Flynn did the same. The two carabinieri drew closer. Reeve and Connie, though, passed out of sight around a corner.

The Russian frowned, then turned slightly more towards Flynn. In return, she slipped her gun upwards in the holster. She was painfully aware that the soldiers might recognise her stance at any moment. Only passing people kept them from getting a clear view. 'You should turn around and walk away,' he continued.

'No, I'll let you do that.' Both knew it would be a death sentence. The first to retreat would be followed by the other. Two steps into the crowd, and a bullet would hit them in the back.

Another standoff. This time, Maxwell broke the silence. 'Deirdre,' he said, voice urgent. 'Alex has turned west. He's doubling back.'

Flynn realised what Reeve had done. He'd deliberately come this way to force his pursuers to face each other. He was a clever bastard, if nothing else . . . 'We can't stand here all fucking day glaring at each other,' she said. 'I'm from Ireland, I'll get sunburn.'

Genuine amusement on her opponent's face. 'Then you should do as I tell you.'

'I'm not turning my back on you.'

'Then walk backwards. I will do the same.' He took a couple of steps, still facing her. His gun arm lowered. Flynn considered shooting him, but the risk was too great. She released her weapon, hand hovering as if scratching an itch on her chest. 'Goodbye,' he said. 'If I see you again, I will make it a permanent one.'

Flynn gave him an empty smile. 'You're welcome to try. Now piss off.'

She backed into the crowd. The Russian also retreated, their eyes never leaving each other. Then people moved between them. By the time they were clear, the man was gone.

Flynn immediately hurried westwards. 'Tony, I'm clear. Guide me to Reeve.'

Morozov checked the woman wasn't following, then continued down the street. The phone was still in his hand. He raised it. Pervak's worried voice was audible even before it reached his ear. 'Morozov! Garald! Can you hear me?'

'I'm here,' Morozov replied. He reached the corner where the street rounded the cathedral's transept. No sign of Reeve. 'I ran into one of the SC9 Operatives.'

'Did you kill them? Are you all right?'

'I couldn't do anything. Reeve set us up to meet right in front of some soldiers.' The rogue agent was clever, quick to adapt. 'Where is he now?'

'North of you – but he's doubled back, going west. Looks like he's heading for the railway station.'

'Shit.' Realisation: the SC9 woman had already known. *That* was why she'd given in. Someone was guiding her through a hidden earpiece, no doubt. He broke into a run, turning up the next street. 'Direct me to him.'

Connie and Reeve ran out from the Piazza dell'Unità Italiana. 'There's the station,' she gasped. The pale brick slab of the

Santa Maria Novella terminus was two hundred metres away.

Reeve checked the phone. It was down to one per cent charge – but still clung to life. In front of the station was a tram stop. A sleek modern tram stood at the platform. 'Over there, quick.'

'We're getting the—' She stopped, remembering that they were being monitored. 'The train?' He gave her a brief smile of approval.

They raced across the road. Ahead, the last couple of passengers boarded the tram. It would leave at any moment. Reeve ran faster, aware Connie was struggling. He took her hand. 'Come on, nearly there.'

Another glance at the phone. The screen showed the pavement blurring beneath him—

Then it went blank. The phone's logo appeared, a *busy* icon spinning below it for a moment . . .

The display finally went dark.

Reeve still didn't trust that it was completely dead. But that worry could wait. He had more immediate concerns. He looked back as they reached the tram stop.

Flynn was running across the road after them.

A hydraulic hiss from the tram. He practically dragged Connie through the narrowing doors. They clapped shut behind her. A young Italian man inside said 'Woo!' and gave them a thumbs-up.

Reeve shot him a weary, humourless grin as the tram moved off. He looked through the rear window. Flynn pounded towards the platform, hand inside her jacket. He pulled Connie down on to a seat, positioning himself to shield her. The tram accelerated away from their pursuer. Would Flynn open fire? He tensed—

No shots came. Too many witnesses – and there was a police car outside the station.

Flynn fell away behind. Even from a distance, he could tell she'd yelled an obscenity. The tram snaked around a bend, picking up speed. The Operative disappeared from sight.

'It's okay,' he told Connie. 'We're clear.'

He was only lightly winded from the dash, but she was panting. 'Oh, God. Where are we going?'

'Wherever this takes us.' He hadn't ridden the trams on his recce, merely memorised the network's map. This route went to the airport. 'Are you okay?'

'Yeah, I'm, I'm . . .' She was practically hyperventilating. 'No,' she eventually gasped. She slumped against him, clutching him tightly.

Reeve held on to her. 'We're okay. We made it.' The attempt at reassurance was as much for himself as her.

'Fucking *shite*!' Flynn yelled after the tram. She halted, glaring as it passed from view. If the doors had shut one second earlier, she would have had them!

Maxwell's voice came through the earpiece. 'That sounds like you missed Alex.'

'He got on a fucking tram,' was her angry reply. 'Are you still tracking him?'

'Afraid not. GCHQ just lost the trace. The battery might have gone flat.'

'So we don't know where he's going?'

'No. He could ride it to the end of the line – or get off at the next stop. No way to know.'

'Well, that's just fucking marvellous.' She turned in frustration—

The Russian had caught up.

His concealed gun was aimed at her head. 'We meet again,' he said, with a lupine smile. 'I told you what would happen.'

Flynn remained still. 'You're going to shoot me in broad daylight?' A flick of her eyes towards the station. 'There are cops right over there.'

'Somewhere more private, I think.' He looked around. The area before the station was large and open. 'Down there.' Not far away, a concrete spiral led a cycle path underground. 'Move. Or I *will* shoot you. By the time the police realise you didn't faint, I will be gone.'

'Do what he says,' Maxwell said in her ear. 'Find an opportunity. You can do it, Deirdre.'

Flynn reluctantly started towards the ramp. The Russian angled after her, maintaining a safe distance. She neared the circular opening in the ground. Maybe she could vault the railing, drop down—

A noise from behind. The sputtering growl of a moped, a ubiquitous sound in Italy. So common the brain tuned it out.

But this was getting louder—

Flynn and the Russian both realised at the same moment. They spun – to see Stone abruptly stop a moped behind them. He supported it on his uninjured leg, gun aimed beneath the handlebars. The weapon was hidden from the police by the front fairing. 'All right, cunt-chops,' he snapped. 'Drop your gun or I drop you.'

The other man remained still. 'As your friend said, there are cops over there.'

'Maybe they'll think you just fainted,' said Flynn cuttingly. She drew her own gun, shielding it with her jacket.

The Russian looked between them. Finally, he lowered his gun hand. 'We have all lost Reeve. The phone's battery is dead – none of us can track him now. Perhaps we should all go our own ways.'

'Or we could kill you, *then* go our own ways,' Stone suggested.

Maxwell spoke again. 'No, he's right. Stand down. The more time we waste with this guy, the further away Alex gets.'

'Okay,' Flynn told the Russian. 'You, go down there.' She indicated the spiral. 'Don't put your fucking head back up, or we'll blow it off.'

A mocking chuckle as he started towards the opening. 'And I thought the English were supposed to be polite.'

'I told you, I'm not fucking English,' she replied. Both Operatives kept their guns poised as the man descended. Then he was gone.

Stone leaned back, holstering his gun. 'Aren't you going to thank me for saving your arse? A blow-job'd be nice.' Flynn's expression was pure disgust.

'Mark, enough,' snapped Maxwell. 'We have to find Alex again. And we have to do it before the Russians.'

'Shooting him would've helped with that,' was Stone's sardonic riposte.

Maxwell ignored him. 'They know about us – about SC9. That's a major problem. Craig Parker must have told them. The question is, how much?'

'They don't know the boss's name,' said Flynn. 'That's something.'

'Which is why they're so keen to grab Alex – because he *does* know.' His voice became more determined. 'We've *got* to get him before they do.'

CHAPTER 16

'We've got to get off,' warned Reeve.

Connie raised her head. 'Why?'

'Ticket inspector.' A uniformed man stood a couple of coaches along, arguing with a woman. 'We don't need any extra attention.'

Luckily, the tram soon halted. Reeve and Connie disembarked before the inspector reached them. 'Where are we?' she asked. Signs read *Roselli*.

'Not far enough away.' They were barely beyond the railway terminus. 'Let's get moving.' The journey had hardly given Connie time to recover her breath. Reeve held her hand; she was shaking. 'We'll find a pharmacy, then somewhere to eat. Then, we'll figure out what to do next.'

'I'm not hungry right now,' she said, voice tremulous.

'You will be soon. And you need to eat. We both do. Can't run without fuel.'

'That's all we're going to be doing from now, isn't it? Running?' He had no answer.

The restaurant they found turned out, incongruously, to be Indian. Reeve shrugged. 'Well, it's been a while since we had a curry.' They went in. He surveyed the interior. Daylight was visible through a doorway beyond the bar at the rear.

'Can we sit back there?' he asked the waiter. The request proved no problem. 'So we're near another way out,' he told Connie after they sat.

'You know what you're doing,' was her tired reply.

They ordered, then Reeve went through the bug-out bag. They had everything needed for the immediate future. Money, burner phones, survival gear, passports. In his case, more than one. He could adopt a new identity easily enough. Connie, less so. He mentally cursed himself. He should have insisted she get a fake ID. Why hadn't he got one for her when he became Angelo Moretti?

Because she'd resisted. She didn't *want* to become someone else. She didn't want to run – or think she might have to. And she didn't want to believe that he might have to, either.

All that was over. Survival was now his imperative. And he had two different enemies hunting him.

He thought more about both threats as they ate. The Russians, he wasn't yet sure how to deal with. He remembered what the new player had said. He'd been Craig Parker's controller. On the rooftop in London, Parker had mentioned a name – what was it? Reeve couldn't quite recall. Had it begun with 'M'? It would come to him.

They wanted the phone – and him. For information, inter-rogation . . . but he would end up as dead as if SC9 caught him. What to do?

Evasion was the best option for now. With the phone's battery dead, they could no longer track him. He couldn't be one of the SVR's highest priorities. If he were, they would have sent more than one man.

SC9 was another matter. They would use every possible

resource to find him again. Sir Simon Scott would be terrified that he might expose the agency to the world. That Reeve wouldn't did not matter. The *threat* of exposure was enough. The Operatives had to kill him. And SC9 would co-opt every other British intelligence agency to do so.

If he ran, they would find him. It might take weeks, or months. But they would never give up.

Unless they were *made* to give up.

His mind was now in full operational mode: analytical, planning. The idea he'd started to form at the flat returned. It didn't take long to develop further. He had the phone; he had the stolen files.

He had leverage.

The decision was made by the time they finished the food. 'I'm going back to England,' he said.

Connie stared at him. 'It's too dangerous.'

'It's the only way to get SC9 off our backs.'

'But what about the Russians?'

'They'll be looking for me here, in Italy. SC9 will as well. None of them would expect me to go back home.' He held up one of his fake passports: it was British. 'This'll get me through customs.'

'But they'll be looking for me too,' she protested.

'Which is why you're not coming with me.'

'*What?*'

'I don't want to leave you, believe me. But like you said, they'll be looking for you. SC9 will have flagged your British and Italian passports with the Border Force. You'd be arrested at immigration. And SC9,' he went on, grim-faced, 'would use you to get to me.'

'I wouldn't give you up,' Connie insisted.

She would, he knew. But he didn't want to break her illusion of resistance. 'That's not what I mean,' he said instead. 'They know *I'd* come for *you*. And they'd be ready.'

'You've got past them before. Like when you found Tony Maxwell at that football match.'

'A crowd situation's one thing. A secure government facility's something else. But,' he said, 'it won't happen. Because you're not going back to England.'

'But—'

'Connie.' He gripped her hands across the table, looking into her eyes. 'I don't want you to get hurt. If you were . . .' He didn't want to think about it. 'I'm doing this to protect you. Right now, I'm a target. If you're too close to me, you'll be hit as well. So you need to be somewhere else – just for a while.' He thought for a moment. 'When we talked about Venice, did you actually look up hotels?' It had been yesterday, but felt like weeks ago.

She shook her head. 'I thought about it, but got sidetracked with looking at the news.' Her face fell. 'God, this is all my fault. If I hadn't found that story—'

'It's not your fault.' He squeezed her hands again in reassurance. 'It's SC9's. But if you didn't look anything up, they can't know we meant to go there. So you go to an internet café – there's one back near the station.'

Connie let out a faint *huh*. 'I'd ask how you know, but, well.'

Reeve gave her a small smile. 'Find a hotel in Venice. Pick one at random, and don't tell me.' He rummaged in the bag. 'Take one of the burners. Keep it charged, but don't use it for anything.' He passed her the boxed phone. 'I'll call you when it's safe for us to meet again. Duress code is "How are you feeling?" If I say that, hang up, chuck the phone, and leave.'

She nodded. 'And what if I don't hear from you?'

He couldn't quite meet her gaze. 'Let's hope you do.'

'Alex . . .'

His eyes met hers again. 'I'll call you. I promise.'

'When?'

'When I've forced SC9 to call off the dogs.'

'And how will you do that?'

'I'll find Scott again. And I'll *make* him back off.'

She looked sceptical. 'How?'

'I've got something in mind.'

'But you're not going to tell me. Why?' An undercurrent of fear behind her words. 'So I can't tell them if they catch me?'

'Just do as I tell you, and they won't,' he said firmly.

After nine months together, he should have expected her reaction. 'I'm not your *subordinate*, Alex,' she said, bristling.

'That's – that's not what I meant.' He held back his exasperation. 'Connie, I'm doing this to *protect* you. You're the most important person in the world to me. You saved me – you've *changed* me. For the better.' That softened her attitude. 'But I'm trained in this, and you're not. I can help you stay alive. But you have to trust me.'

It was her turn to squeeze his hands. 'You *know* I do.'

'I do.' A shared smile. 'There's money in the bag – at least five thousand euros. You take it. Wait for me in Venice.'

'How long should I wait?'

'I don't know. It might be a couple of weeks.'

'That long?' she said in alarm.

'Hopefully less – it depends what I need to do.'

'And you can't tell me what that is.' There was no rancour in the statement this time. 'I *do* trust you, Alex. I'll be there. Just make sure you are too.'

He smiled. 'I will. Okay, I'll give you what you'll need.'

Making sure the staff didn't see, he passed Connie most of the euros. He would need some for himself. She put them in her handbag with the burner phone. 'Alex,' she said. 'You're *only* going to England to deal with SC9, aren't you?' Her tone was unexpectedly pointed. 'Not to see your father as well?'

'What I care about right now is keeping us both alive,' he said. It was the truth, if not its entirety. 'Okay, we need to go.'

Connie managed a weak smile. 'I'll pay,' she said, taking money from her bag.

They took a different, circuitous route back to Santa Maria Novella. Nobody tripped Reeve's mental alarms. 'That's the internet café,' he said, pointing out a shop east of the station. 'Find a hotel in Venice. You can take a train from here.'

'And you?' she said unhappily.

'Airport. I'll get a flight home.'

'Oh, my God.' She looked miserably at the pavement. 'This is really happening, isn't it?'

Reeve held her for a long moment. 'I'll see you again soon.' He kissed her.

She raised her eyes to him. 'I love you, Alex.'

Another kiss. 'And you.' He released her. 'Stay safe, okay? Remember what I taught you about escape and evasion. If you think someone might be suspicious, treat them as if they are.'

Tears glistened in her eyes. 'I remember. Go on, then. Bye.'

'See you in Venice.' He turned and walked away, leaving Connie behind.

A tram ride – with a ticket this time – took him to Florence's airport. He dumped the other burner phones in a bin. They would be no use in the UK, and draw questions at the security check. Some of his equipment, like the lockpicks, had to go too. They would show up on the X-ray. A shame, but he had no choice.

He also disposed of all Angelo Moretti's paperwork. His Italian identity had been blown. The remaining IDs were stuffed into a tabloid in the bag. Paper would blend with paper on the X-ray. It was unlikely to catch the security staff's attention.

The money was more of a concern. Most of the euros had gone on a plane ticket. Airlines didn't like dealing in cash, but wouldn't turn it down, either. He had a few thousand pounds in mixed notes. The total was below the amount that legally had to be declared at customs. But it might still alert an officious or nosy officer . . .

It went through the checkpoint without comment, however. Luck was on his side. He was clear.

He headed for his gate. The flight was not direct, requiring a change in Amsterdam. But he would reach his final destination by morning.

It was not London. When Reeve told Connie he was going home, he was being completely truthful.

He was going to Manchester.

CHAPTER 17

Sir Simon Scott was in a foul mood.

Part of his ire was aimed at his own people. Several ongoing operations were not proceeding to his satisfaction. Germany, for instance; the planning was taking too long. Maybe it was time to put a different Operative in charge.

There was also Alex Reeve. A frown at the thought of the rogue asset. He had escaped from the Operatives sent to kill him – twice. Four times, counting the botched attempts eighteen months earlier. The man led a charmed life.

Not for much longer, Scott had already decided. But he had other matters to address first.

His car descended into an underground parking lot. The London headquarters of SIS – the Secret Intelligence Service, or MI6 – was the meeting's location. Even though Scott was a former SIS officer, he had never worked here. The post-modern green-glass ziggurat was completed in 1994, after SC9's creation. His MI6 posting had been at the considerably more mundane Century House, a mile away. Dull and drab – but an architectural wonder compared to SC9's home.

No matter. The wrapping wasn't important, only what was inside. SC9 was, in Scott's eyes, the nation's most crucial line of defence.

The others needed to be reminded of that.

His driver – an Operative – stopped at the barrier. Multiple cameras stared at the car. Scott knew there were other sensors examining it. Millimetre-wave scanners to see through the metal, explosive sniffers, and more. SIS took its security extremely seriously. Even tourists taking photos of the building would be approached by armed police patrols. A mocking shake of his head. Spies and terrorists would be imbeciles to be so obvious nowadays. Anyone with Google Maps could view the entire exterior in 3D. SIS even had a high-resolution aerial photo on their website, for God's sake. The agency had gone downhill since its existence was officially acknowledged.

Security through obscurity was his approach, and it served him well. SC9 had remained the deepest secret of British Intelligence for thirty years. He intended to keep it that way. But being *summoned* – he rankled at the idea – to a meeting here would not help. It only took one chance encounter with a former colleague to start gossip, raise questions . . .

The gate guards were finally satisfied, handing Scott and his driver their day passes. Their parking space was in a reserved section near a lift – with restricted access. At least *someone* had their head screwed on.

'Wait for me here,' Scott ordered as the driver opened his door. He went to the lift. More cameras scrutinised him. The pass featured a QR code; he placed it against a scanner. A screen confirmed his presence was authorised. If it hadn't been, he would be greeted by a SWAT team.

But the lift that turned up was empty. He didn't need

to push a button; it was programmed with his destination. Up to the seventh floor, and out.

An officer in an off-the-peg suit awaited him. His jacket's cut didn't fully conceal the gun holstered beneath. Scott's dark look warned the man not to attempt small talk. Instead he escorted the new arrival to a meeting room.

The others were already there, seated at an oval table.

Scott immediately noticed their blunt attempt at intimidation. The heads of Britain's intelligence agencies sat facing him as he entered. The only empty chair was on its own opposite them, closest to the entrance. He took it without a word, cold gaze sweeping each man in turn.

A nod from Aubrey Ryford-Croft, the Chief of SIS, and Scott's escort departed. 'Good morning, Simon,' said Ryford-Croft after the soundproofed door closed. 'Glad you could join us.'

Scott had no time for pleasantries. 'What's this about, Aubrey? I don't appreciate being hauled from my office on short notice. I'm a busy man.'

'You were hardly dragged here by wild horses,' came the amiable reply. 'And we're sure you *are* busy. That's why we wanted to see you.'

Scott was instantly on guard. SC9's business was its own; total deniability was the entire point of its existence. The other agencies were accountable to Parliament – to politicians. SC9 very specifically was not. 'You have something to say to me?'

'We do.' The speaker was Justin Stockley, Director General of the Security Service: MI5. 'I'll get straight to the point. Have you authorised the killing of Russian agents and assets?'

'I have no comment to make regarding SC9's operations,' Scott replied, face studiously blank. 'You know full well that's the only answer you'll get from me on that, Justin.'

'Of course.' Stockley was far younger than Scott, still in his thirties. A political operator, a lightweight whose professional balls had barely dropped. Scott held him in utter contempt. 'I ask because a surprising number have suffered sudden and violent deaths. Eight in the past six months alone, I believe. In the UK as well as abroad. Which is a matter of some concern.'

'For me in particular,' said Ryford-Croft. 'Because two SIS officers have been murdered in reprisal. A number of British assets in other countries, as well. The Russians are not subtle. If they kill one of ours, they generally make sure we know who did it. The thing is,' he leaned forward, eyes fixed on Scott, 'we don't know *why*. None of us have taken any actions that would prompt such reprisals.'

Scott's gaze was equally unflinching. 'I have no comment to make regarding SC9's operations. I'll merely point out it has full remit to act against enemies of the state. That remit also guarantees no interference from other agencies. *Any* other agencies.'

'Duly noted,' said Stockley with a dry edge of sarcasm.

One of the other men spoke for the first time. Michael Barwell was the Director of GCHQ – Government Communications Headquarters. Britain's electronic spy agency, surveilling the entire world – at home as well as abroad. 'Now, the next matter we need to discuss . . .' He made a show of turning a page in the papers before him. 'Well, two matters, but they seem closely connected. Dominic Finch, also known as Alex Reeve.'

A chill struck Scott. How the hell had they found out about Reeve? He kept his voice level. 'I don't know the name.'

'No?' Barwell made an irritating clicking sound with his tongue as he paged through documents. 'A year and a half ago, SC9 requested we run a broad sweep. Phone, email, social media, even backdoor access through encryption apps. We don't like doing the latter unless we absolutely have to. Too much risk of exposing that we *have* a backdoor. The name we were searching for was Dominic Finch. You don't remember?' he added, looking pointedly at Scott. 'I can give you the exact dates and times if you like.'

Scott silently cursed himself. He had indeed ordered the electronic dragnet following Reeve's escape from his execution in Scotland. The search had been for any family or friends he might contact for help. Nothing came of it; Reeve had always been a loner. But GCHQ had not only kept everything they trawled up, but investigated further. That was a clear breach of protocol. 'At the risk of boring you with repetition, I have no comment to make regarding—'

'Regarding SC9's operations, yes,' Stockley cut in.

Scott shot him an angry glance. How *dare* this little bastard interrupt him! He turned back to Barwell. 'Might I ask, who is Alex Reeve, and how is he connected to Dominic Finch?'

'Alex Reeve would appear to be the new identity of Dominic Finch,' came the reply. 'The name came up while cross-checking the sweep's results. We put the pieces together and found the link.' His voice became patronising. 'We *are* an intelligence agency, Simon.'

'Which brings us to the second matter – Dominic Finch's father, Jude.' Timothy Kent was Director-General of the National Crime Agency. Scott had wondered why he was here; the NCA's intelligence role was in counter-terrorism. 'You requested his release from prison eight months ago. Part of an ongoing operation, you said. So he was released – to a fair bit of uproar at Justice. The man was a convicted murderer. Cost a lot of political capital to arrange, you know. Some people, myself included, are quite keen to know why.'

'GCHQ also established an IP address trace on news stories concerning Jude Finch,' added Barwell. Glances between the other men at the table. It was clearly a matter they had already discussed. 'It received enough hits to be flagged to SC9, per your instructions, two days ago.'

No way to deny anything here; Scott had made the demands himself. 'It was necessary for national security purposes,' he said. 'Beyond that? I have no comment.' He glowered at Stockley, daring him to complete the sentence, but the bait wasn't taken.

'And the granting of over a million pounds in compensation for wrongful imprisonment?'

'Again, no comment.'

'Is Alex Reeve, formerly Dominic Finch, a rogue SC9 Operative?' Ryford-Croft's question was asked in a raised voice. Only slightly, but in the quiet room it stood out like a shout.

Scott could no longer contain his irritation. 'I have no comment to make regarding SC9's operations,' he said. Each word was distinct, *bang, bang*, bullets across the table. 'If you've nothing worthwhile to add, I'll be on my way.'

'There is one more matter, Simon,' said Stockley. 'Craig Parker. The man who tried to assassinate a Member of Parliament in front of TV cameras.'

'I'm aware of who he is,' said Scott.

'And I'm sure you're also aware of what he claimed to be? A member of an unnamed British intelligence agency responsible for extrajudicial assassinations?'

'What he claimed to be is irrelevant. The man was obviously insane.'

'But his description of this agency's function exactly matches SC9's. And Parker himself – real name David Laurence – was a former member of the SAS. He left under dubious circumstances ten months before the assassination attempt.'

'Which,' added Ryford-Croft, 'is the stock in trade for recruits to SC9. The old identities leave their former jobs officially under a cloud. All for deniability should they ever be identified. They can be dismissed as embittered washouts with a grudge. Or am I mistaken?'

Scott narrowed his eyes. 'I have no comment.' Ryford-Croft was, of course, correct.

'Now,' Stockley went on, 'Parker sent out encrypted files that he claimed were stolen from SC9. My apologies,' a mocking glance at Scott, 'this *unnamed agency*. As yet, nobody has cracked the encryption, so his veracity can't be confirmed.'

'Or denied,' said Scott pointedly. 'But I can assure you that no such files have been stolen from SC9. Our security is uncompromised. Parker was a crank, nothing more. His files will be full of rubbish, the usual paranoid conspiracy theories.'

Barwell shifted in his chair. 'Perhaps if you would allow GCHQ to audit your servers, we could confirm that.'

'Absolutely not,' was the snapped reply. 'SC9's charter guarantees total independence from the other intelligence agencies. Full deniability must be maintained. Your role is to service us, and that is all.' The last few words were again delivered with machine-gun sharpness.

Stockley was first to break the silence that followed. 'One *could* argue that this independence and deniability amounts to a total lack of oversight.'

Scott bristled. 'Are you challenging my competence? And my results?'

'Merely an observation,' said the younger man insouciantly.

His laconic dismissal served only to increase Scott's anger. 'Let me tell you something, Justin,' he growled. 'SC9 exists to protect the country. Under my command, it has done so, for thirty years now.'

'Which is rather the point,' said Stockley. 'That's a long period for one man to stay in charge. Times are changing. And so is the country. Fail to see the moving tides, and you'll end up like King Canute. Killing a popular progressive like Elektra Curtis could have had consequences. For all of us.'

'Credit me with *some* competence,' Scott said. 'If I had ordered her removal, it wouldn't have been in such a public way.'

Barwell leafed through his papers. 'I have Parker's email

to the press. It could easily be interpreted to say he was acting contrary to his orders. He intended to expose SC9 by making a spectacle of the assassination.'

'That's one interpretation,' Scott countered. 'One of many. But it certainly doesn't implicate SC9. He could just as easily mean MI6. Or MI5,' he added, giving Stockley a cold look. 'Occam's Razor applies here, though. Parker wasn't the first lone nut to target a female progressive politician. As for his alleged stolen files, they'll turn out to be exactly what I said. Rubbish.'

'The truth will come out eventually,' said Barwell. 'Every intelligence agency in the world will be trying to crack the encryption. We certainly are. Sooner or later, someone will find the password.'

'And then we'll all be able to breathe a sigh of relief, won't we?' Scott stood. 'Because, as I said, SC9 is completely secure. There *are* no stolen files; there *are* no rogue Operatives. Alex Reeve – Dominic Finch – was a person of interest, nothing more.'

'*Was* a person of interest?' asked Stockley. 'Is he still?'

Scott gave him a thin smile. 'For the last time, I have no comment to make regarding SC9's operations.' He turned away from the other men. 'Now, if you'll excuse me, I have real work to do.' With that, he exited.

Scott maintained his expression of calm confidence until he was back in his car. Behind the tinted glass, it became a tight, angry snarl.

Who did those bastards think they were? Summoning him like some underling, questioning him like barristers. As if he was accountable to them! They needed reminding of how things were supposed to work. Especially that little shit Stockley . . .

It could wait, though. Alex Reeve was his top priority. That other agencies were sniffing around made eliminating him more critical than ever. He had apparently killed Craig Parker; the details were still murky. One fact was certain, though. Parker, it was later determined, sent his emails from a phone. There had been no phone on his body. There was therefore a strong probability that Reeve had taken possession. That supposition had now been confirmed.

Which meant Reeve had Parker's files. Despite Scott's assertion, SC9's security *had* been breached. An attempt to hack into the servers using Russian software had been easily blocked. However, that now seemed like a distraction from a more subtle intrusion. There was no way to know what had been accessed – or copied – in the process.

As an intelligence officer, Scott abided by certain rules. One was: *When in doubt, assume the worst.* That worst case? Reeve had the files – and planned to release them to the media. Or to the Russians.

Under no circumstances could either be allowed to happen. The consequences would be devastating. For the country, for the government, for SC9 . . . and for Scott himself.

Once the car was clear of SIS, he made a secure phone call. 'Maxwell.'

'Sir,' Tony Maxwell replied.

'Any word?'

'Not yet. Flynn is still searching for Reeve and his girlfriend in Florence. Stone had to be pulled for medical treatment;

Reeve stabbed him. Blake and Locke are covering Milan and Rome. Sir . . .' A note of caution. 'The odds of them finding them in Italy are slim. They'll almost certainly have left the country by now. But from what was found at their flat, Connie Jones was still using her real name. If you get GCHQ to do a sweep—'

'I don't want other agencies involved,' Scott interrupted. 'Reeve is *our* problem. Call upon all necessary resources. I want Craig Parker's phone in my hands. And I want Alex Reeve and his girlfriend *dead*.'

CHAPTER 18

'Welcome home,' said the Border Force officer.

'Thanks,' Reeve replied.

His fake passport had held up. Nobody challenged its authenticity, and no computers triggered alarms. He didn't relax his guard, though. As long as he was in the airport's confines, he was at risk. He left passport control at a quick but steady pace. Just somebody in a hurry to get their train, nothing to see here . . .

It worked. He cleared the terminal, then entered the elevated tube of the Skylink walkway. The railway station was a brisk stroll away. He'd intended to catch a train to central Manchester. The discovery that a tram line now served it was a pleasant surprise. He hadn't set foot in his home city for over a decade; things had changed.

The journey took half an hour. He took in the rain-washed city as the tram rolled through it. Some areas were familiar from his youth; others were unrecognisable. New tower blocks had sprung up around the centre. He guessed most were flats – expensive flats. Manchester was following the same gentrification path as London.

He left the tram a stop before Victoria station. His caution seemed unfounded; nobody was following him. But it had kept him alive this long. No point breaking the streak.

His first objective was to find a hotel. No chains, nothing fancy; they would want ID, credit cards. He instead found the Tourist Information Centre. From there, he got a list of hotels. A few candidates in the east of the city, where he wanted to be. Next: buy a phone. There were plenty of phone shops in the main retail areas. A cheap handset with credit and a removable battery was all he needed. He bought two, from separate stores. One went into his bag as a reserve. The other, he used to make calls.

He soon had a room. It was small and too warm, the mattress uncomfortably soft. But it would do. He had a base of operations.

Now he needed a plan.

Two objectives. One was in London: finding Maxwell. But he wouldn't get the opportunity until Saturday. It was now Wednesday. Two and a half days to kill. Literally? He hoped not. Connie wouldn't approve.

The thought of her brought a pang of longing. He picked up the phone, about to re-insert the battery. But he put it down again. It wasn't safe to call her. Not yet. He had to complete his mission first.

Missions, plural. The second was here in Manchester.

He was going to find his father. And make him regret leaving the safety of prison.

Clayton, Reeve's old home, was two miles east of Manchester's centre. He could have taken public transport. But he decided to walk, despite the drizzle. Partly for the exercise, but also to get a feel for the area.

Some things had changed. Manchester City's football stadium was now emblazoned with Etihad sponsorship. Colourful new tower blocks dotted the horizon. The tram line had even found its way to Clayton, or at least its edge.

Other things, though, looked exactly the same. The heart of Clayton was a tight grid of small red-brick terraced houses. Reeve had grown up in one. He hadn't intended to go to it, but somehow found himself drawn to the street.

When he'd lived here, several houses had been boarded up. One's roof had even collapsed, a tree poking out of it. He and his friends had broken into the derelict properties many times. Now, money had found its way even to the poorest areas. Dirty old brickwork had been cleaned, new windows installed. In Reeve's day, hardly anyone owned a car. There were now enough to make finding a space troublesome.

One house stood out, however.

Its bricks had been cleaned, but half-heartedly. The door and windows were blocked by heavy wooden panels. Weeds were visible in the rotted guttering. The house had fallen into decay, unoccupied for sixteen years.

That told him something. His father still owned it. He had used his legal right to buy the former council property when Reeve was young. Even in prison, it remained in his possession. Until recently, it would have been more trouble to sell than it was worth. The area was now being gentrified, but Jude Finch still hadn't sold it. With over a million pounds to his name, the value of his old home was chickenfeed.

Reeve stared at the house. It brought back many memories. Few were good. He tried to focus on those he could catch. His mother helping him make a collage, cooking with him . . .

But his father was always there, never involved but lurking nearby. Angry, belittling, violent. Nothing was ever good enough. His son, an annoyance to be tolerated at best.

Reeve realised the mere idea was producing a fear response. Unthinking, a knot of stress and nausea in the pit of his stomach. He took a breath, controlling it. There was no reason to be afraid of his father. He wasn't a scared kid any more. He had fought and beaten – killed – far more dangerous men.

The fear subsided. Reeve turned away and headed back to the main road. His father once had certain haunts nearby; he needed to check them out.

He passed more terraced rows. A woman pushed a young child in a buggy towards him. He moved to the roadside to let her pass. She gave him a nod of thanks, their eyes meeting—

Recognition spurred Reeve to do a double-take. The woman reacted with equal surprise. They both stopped, staring at each other.

She was first to speak. 'Dominic?'

'Ally?' he replied. More memories rushed back. Alison Marks had been his first girlfriend, at the age of thirteen. Then, she'd been a freckle-cheeked, curly-haired tomboy. The freckles were now gone, her hair in a shoulder-length bob.

She gave him a delighted smile. 'Oh, my God, it *is* you! I haven't seen you for years! How are you?'

'I'm fine, thanks,' Reeve replied. 'How about you?' He indicated the buggy. 'You're a mum, then.'

'Yeah. This is Daisy. Say hi to my friend, Daisy.' The little girl said nothing, concerned only with her toy horse. 'Oh well, I tried. She's like that with anybody she doesn't know.'

'I won't take it personally,' he said. 'So, are you married?'

The question produced a scathing response. 'Yeah. Right.' It was only then he noticed she didn't have a wedding ring. 'He freaked out when I told him I was pregnant and ran off. I would have gone after him for child support, except he's in prison. Got caught dealing.'

'I'm sorry.'

'That's okay. He was an idiot. I was an idiot for seeing anything in him in the first place. But I've got Daisy, so something good came from it.' She looked him over. Her expression suggested she approved. 'Wow. You've changed a lot since I last saw you. It must be, what? Fifteen, sixteen years?'

'Something like that.' They'd lost contact as he was shuffled between foster homes.

'What have you been up to? You're looking well.'

'Thanks. I was in the army for a while, then went into business.'

'What kind of business?'

'Nothing exciting.' He knew she would press further, so continued: 'I work for a paper towel company.' It was the dullest thing he could think of.

It worked. 'Oh, okay,' she said, all interest in his profession quashed. 'What are you doing here?'

'Got some meetings in town. Heard they'd done this place up, so thought I'd take a look.'

'Well, yes, it's changed.' She indicated the terraced rows. 'Some of these are going for insane money now. Well over a hundred grand.'

He couldn't imagine his small childhood home being worth even half that much. 'Somebody's cashing in nicely.'

'Yeah, it's great if you're selling. You're screwed if you're buying, though. Not that I can even think about that.'

'Where are you living?'

'Same place I always did.'

'You're still in the same house?' Her home had been one street over from his.

A sardonic nod. 'Yep. Sixteen years, and I haven't moved an inch. I'm on my way back – come on, I'll make you a cuppa.'

Reeve was about to politely decline, but she was already moving. He smiled. Ally had always been one to act immediately on her decisions. He followed. 'Let me take those bags.'

Two carriers of shopping dangled from the buggy's handles. She hesitated, then accepted the offer. 'Thanks.'

'No problem.' He took the bags and walked with her. 'Are you still living with your parents?'

'Not now. They're in a better place.'

'Oh. Sorry.'

An awkward pause – then she grinned. 'On holiday. They're in Tenerife.' He let out an exasperated sigh. Ally cackled. 'You *still* can't tell when someone's taking the piss, can you? Oh, my God. It must have been hell for you. I couldn't help winding you up.'

'But you've got it under control now, I see.'

Another smile. 'Yeah. Sorry.'

They turned on to her street. Like Reeve's, a clean-up crew had been at work. Her home had received new windows and front door. Otherwise, it was much as he remembered. 'Here we are,' she said. 'Are you coming in?'

'I'd love to, but I have to go.' She was a little disappointed. 'Maybe we can meet up again while I'm in town.'

'Well, I'm a stay-at-home mum, so it's not like I'm going anywhere.' Her shoulders dropped as she spoke, dispirited.

He brought the bags into the house. 'Where shall I put them?'

'Just pop them on the floor. I'll unpack.'

'Okay.' He did so, then turned to leave. 'Great seeing you again, Ally.'

She gave him a slightly bashful smile. 'It's been years since anyone called me that.'

'Oh, I'm sorry. Alison.'

'But it's okay. I like it. Reminds me of some fun times when we were kids.'

He smiled back. 'Yeah. They were good, weren't they?'

Ally nodded, her expression becoming pensive. Reeve knew what she was thinking. *Until . . .* 'Anyway,' he said, 'I've got to go.'

She came to him. 'You can't leave without at least giving me a hug.' She wrapped her arms around him. 'It was really, really good seeing you again, Dominic.'

He returned the gesture. 'And you too.' He was first to let go; she held on for a few seconds before withdrawing.

What she said next caught him off-guard. 'I can't believe they let your dad out of prison.' The smile had gone, her words quiet and sombre.

'You know about that?' Reeve felt a sudden concern. Did she know the 'official' story behind his father's release?

152

He – Dominic Finch, at least – was wanted for perjury. No statute of limitation applied to that offence. It would give the police cast-iron cause to arrest him if he was found. And once they did, SC9 would soon catch up. Was she planning to turn him in? Adrenalin rose. He needed to get out, now—

But her attitude was nothing except sympathetic. 'I've seen him around. Cruising about in a Range Rover like he's a footballer or something. After what he did to your mum? It's . . . unbelievable.'

'Yeah,' he replied, voice level. 'Do you know where he lives?'

The question surprised her. 'No. Why? You don't want to see him, surely?'

'I want to know where to avoid while I'm in town.'

She seemed to accept the excuse. 'I don't know. Don't really want to, to be honest.' She cocked her head at a thought. 'Mickey probably does, though.'

'Mickey's still here?' Mickey Rowland, his childhood best friend. Until he was set adrift after his mother's murder, at least.

'Yeah. I see him around quite a lot. More than I'd like, to be honest.' Her tone became disparaging. 'My having a baby hasn't stopped him trying it on. But I don't want him around Daisy. He's another one who did time. Dealing.' The word came out with a snort of disgust.

Reeve tried to cheer her up. 'He's harmless, surely,' he said jokingly. 'He always was annoyed that I got you as a girlfriend, not him.'

Her smile returned, though not for the reason he expected.

'You didn't *get* me, Dominic,' she said, eyes twinkling. 'I *chose* you.'

'Same end result.'

'You keep telling yourself that.' A broad grin. 'Okay, I've got to unpack. But I expect to see you again while you're in town, okay?'

'You will.'

'Good. See you later.'

Reeve stepped outside – then paused. Ally looked at him expectantly. 'I might look in on Mickey. Where can I find him?'

She covered her disappointment. 'He usually hangs around Crispy's Chicken on the New Road. He's a bike courier – does food deliveries.'

'Okay. Thanks.' He hesitated, then gave her another hug. 'Glad you're okay, Ally.'

She held him, then kissed his cheek before releasing him. 'See you again soon, yes?'

'Definitely.' This time he departed, but not before waving goodbye.

CHAPTER 19

Parts of Clayton might have seen new money arrive, but some things never changed.

Reeve returned to the main road from central Manchester. One section was home to a cluster of takeaway food shops. Also there were several young men, standing on street corners despite the rain.

They wore similar clothing – sports gear and baseball caps. All had drawn, pallid faces, cheekbones prominent beneath taut, greasy skin. Reeve knew who they were, and what they were doing. 'Scallies': these were either selling drugs or working for a dealer nearby. The smart ones were lookouts. The stupid ones ended up in police cells.

Mickey Rowland had apparently been one of the latter. That didn't surprise Reeve. Mickey had never been too bright, squeaking by on brass neck and bullshit. His luck had eventually run out. Judges didn't appreciate scally swagger.

There was Crispy's Chicken, gaudy neon alight even in the daytime. A sign told him there was a car park behind it. He went down a litter-strewn alley. The space beyond was hemmed in by buildings. The stench of marijuana hung in the air.

The source was obvious. A small group of men, mostly in their twenties, huddled near the takeaway's rear door. Several bikes were lined up nearby. All heads turned towards him, suspicious. He knew why. Someone unknown, walking rather than driving – police? Scally hatred of cops outweighed any other rivalries. Hands hurriedly whipped joints out of sight.

Reeve quickly assessed them as he approached. None displayed the cocky overconfidence of a nobody with a gun. That didn't mean they were unarmed. Knives or sharpened screwdrivers were the most likely threat. 'A'right, lads,' he said, letting his natural Mancunian accent return. 'Mickey Rowland here?'

Hurried glances between them. They knew Mickey. 'Who's askin'?' said the oldest man. He brought one hand to his chest as if scratching an itch. That told Reeve he had a weapon inside his tracksuit top.

He was in no mood for a fight. 'I'm an old mate of his, we were at school together,' he said genially. 'A friend told me he worked here. I was just seeing if he's around.'

The spokesman pursed his lips, then called into the open doorway. 'Mickey! Someone wants you.'

'If it's the cops or a bailiff, I'm not here,' came the reply. 'If it's a woman, send her in!'

'It's some bloke. Says he's an old mate.'

A head looked around the door frame. Reeve smiled at the familiar, if considerably aged, face. 'Mickeyyyyyy!' he said, the old greeting coming from the depths of his memories. 'How you doing?'

Mickey Rowland regarded the visitor in confusion – then his eyes went wide. 'Fuckin' hell!' he cried, hurrying out. 'Dommo, it's you! Fuck me. Must be twenty years since I seen you, at least.'

'About sixteen,' Reeve replied. 'Still a long time, though.'

'Too right, too fuckin' right. Shit, man, I don't believe it. What're you doing here?'

'I'm in town on business. Came to look around the old neighbourhood. Someone told me you worked here.'

'Yeah, delivery rider.' Mickey indicated the bikes. 'Fuckin' shite job, but it keeps me fit, eh? And it's better than being banged up.'

'Yeah, I'd heard you got sent down.'

Mickey reacted with surprise. 'Who from?'

'Ran into Ally.'

'Ally?' A sly grin. 'Me and her have got a thing going now, you know.'

'That right?' Reeve hid his amusement, deciding not to let Mickey know Ally's opinion of him. 'Hey, you free?'

A glance towards the door. 'Not really. I'm on call.'

Reeve regarded the other men. Now they were reassured he wasn't a cop, the joints were being puffed again. 'It doesn't look that busy at the moment.'

'They, ah, sometimes want their fastest rider on the job.'

Clear evasion – why would he lie? But Reeve didn't really care. 'I just wondered if you knew where I could find my dad.'

'Your dad?' Mickey said, surprised. 'You want to talk to him?'

'I'm thinking about patching things up.' Merely uttering the lie made him feel sick.

'Yeah? Well, now's the right time.' A cunning smile crossed Mickey's face. 'Seeing as he's loaded. But I bet you know that already.'

'Yeah, I know.'

The smile widened. 'Just remember your old mate, eh? He's got a nice place out towards Ashton. Flash Range Rover, too. And fuckin' hell, his girlfriend's hot. Blonde, big tits, short skirts. She's not even as old as us! Your dad's landed on his feet, the lucky bastard.'

'Sounds that way,' Reeve said, with a fake smile. 'Where's this house?' Mickey gave him the address; he memorised it. 'Is he just living it up on his millions, or does he do anything?'

Even before Mickey spoke, Reeve could tell he was being evasive again. 'I think he's back in the trade,' he said. 'You know, the *drugs* trade.' The word *drugs* was mimed. 'Made some friends in prison, and he's working with them now he's out. Top-league guys. And he's still mates with the Burton brothers as well. That's what I've heard, anyway.'

The Burton brothers, Reeve remembered, owned a scrapyard. His father had always described them as friends. In hindsight, though, the relationship was more businesslike. Reeve had sometimes gone with his father on debt-collecting jobs. Said debts were occasionally collected by force. The money was always brought back to the scrapyard's office. 'Right,' he said, nodding. 'Well, I'm not interested in that sort of stuff.'

'You never were any fun,' Mickey said, grinning. He looked around at a shout from the shop. One of the younger men hurriedly pinched out his joint and went indoors. He returned with an insulated food delivery box. It was on his back by the time he reached his bike. He donned a baseball cap, then whizzed out of the car park.

'You lot don't hang around,' Reeve observed.

'Got to be quick to get a good tip,' said Mickey. 'And some customers get proper arsey if you take too long. Wouldn't want to deliver late to your dad, for starters.'

'I bet,' said Reeve. 'You know if he hangs out anywhere? Does he still go to the Five Bells?'

Mickey laughed. 'They demolished it fucking years ago, mate! No, he goes to the Copper Kettle now. Seen him in there quite a lot.'

The pub in question was outside Clayton's immediate environs. 'Bit upmarket, isn't it? Or has it changed?'

'No, it's still the same. But he's rich, remember? He fits in places like that now.'

'I meant it was a bit upmarket for you. What were you doing there?'

'Cheeky cunt,' Mickey snorted. Reeve grinned. 'Are you in town for a while?'

'A few days at least, yeah.'

'We'll have to have a proper catch-up. I haven't seen you since you were like thirteen. You've grown as well, you lanky bastard.' At six feet, Reeve was three inches taller. 'I used to be bigger than you.'

'I'll give you a call.' They exchanged numbers, Reeve purposefully transposing the burner phone's final digits. He didn't need his old friend pestering him. 'See you later.'

They said their goodbyes, and Reeve started back towards the street. Then he stopped. The rider had sparked an idea. 'Mickey – those delivery boxes?'

'Yeah, what about 'em?' Mickey replied.

'Where would you buy them?'

CHAPTER 20

Reeve stopped outside the Copper Kettle's car park, watching his father enter the pub.

After meeting Mickey the previous day, he had made some purchases. He now owned a bike, helmet, several colourful jackets – and a food delivery backpack. The latter was unbranded, but similar in livery to a major online company.

One of the first things taught in the SRR was how to blend in. In an urban environment, it wasn't always enough to seem as if you belonged. Sometimes, you needed to be *invisible*. Certain professions created psychological blind spots for observers. A hi-vis jacket, paradoxically, made its wearer less memorable. Reeve had read various theories as to why. One was that the unnaturally bright colours drew attention from the wearer's face. He didn't know if it was true. He *did* know, from experience, that it worked.

Delivery rider was a new disguise for him, but it seemed effective. Even in the morning, there were plenty around. He had ridden from his hotel to his father's house.

Mickey was right. It was a nice place. One he didn't deserve. Detached, mock-Tudor, large gardens. A black Range Rover and red Mazda MX-5 were parked outside.

Reeve stored all the details, creating a mental map. Then he spent a while cycling around, passing the house every few minutes. Watching for activity.

It first came at eight-thirty. A blonde woman emerged and got into the Mazda. Reeve stopped nearby, pretending to look at his phone. The gates opened automatically. The woman drove away, heading towards the city.

Not his target. He maintained his surreptitious watch.

It was well after ten before anything else happened. Reeve was passing when he caught the front door opening. He stopped, again taking out his phone as if checking a map. His attention, though, was directed sidelong at the house.

Jude Finch stepped outside.

Reeve felt his stomach clench with instinctive fear. The last time he saw his father had been in court, sixteen years earlier. He had barely dared look at him while delivering his testimony. When he did, his father's eyes were filled with a seething rage. More than that. Not just anger – *hate*.

He forced down the feeling of panic. There was no need to be scared any more. He knew he could beat his father. To death, if necessary.

Finch's time in prison hadn't made him any less physically imposing. If anything, he looked more menacing, youthfulness knocked away. He was now bald, head shaven. He strode to the Range Rover and entered. The outer gates started to open.

Reeve gambled that he was heading into Manchester and set off again. He glanced back. The Range Rover emerged, then turned. Following him. Good. Finch soon overtook. But if he stayed on urban roads, with a thirty limit, Reeve could

161

keep up. Any faster, though, and he would lose him . . .

But his father's business had been local. Reeve followed him throughout the day. His first visit was to somewhere familiar: the Burton brothers' scrapyard. He glimpsed him talking to the two older men. All seemed to treat each other as equals. Mickey had been right. Finch's time in prison had perversely helped him climb the underworld hierarchy.

From there, he'd followed his father from place to place. Most stops were at shops or service businesses. Two launderettes, a tanning salon, an off-licence, a couple of takeaways. Crispy's Chicken was one. Almost all his stops were only for a few minutes. One place, however, he stayed at for longer. He drove to the rear, Reeve losing sight of the Range Rover. When Finch hadn't reappeared after ten minutes, he risked checking that there wasn't another exit. There wasn't; the 4x4 was parked beside a metal staircase to the upper floor. A clue to the establishment's nature was on the ground nearby. Business cards, soggy from rain. Vixen's Massage Parlour. He doubted the massages were purely therapeutic. His father was mixing business with pleasure.

The thought filled him with disgust. Finch had had several affairs while married. Even with a new girlfriend, he still couldn't stay faithful. Reeve couldn't imagine betraying Connie, but his father did it to his partners constantly. How could they put up with it? What did they see in him in the first place?

Finch eventually left after another twenty minutes. A few more short visits to other businesses, then he returned to the scrapyard. He'd been on a collection run, Reeve deduced. Everywhere he'd visited had something in common. They worked largely in cash. Easy to make under-the-counter transactions, or skim a percentage of the proceeds. A protection racket, drug deals, prostitution, whatever – his father was back at his old work.

The Range Rover emerged from the scrapyard. Reeve followed. It soon became clear Finch was returning home.

Reeve stayed with him. He needed to know his father's entire daily routine. Sooner or later, he intended to confront him. He wanted to have the advantage.

The ride back took almost half an hour through traffic. Reeve passed several genuine delivery riders. That reminded him of Mickey – in turn triggering more introspective thoughts.

They were not welcome. Hindsight had made him realise his childhood best friend was a bad influence. Mickey was unmotivated at anything except avoiding work, concerned only with his current pleasures. It was his rebellious nature that had drawn the young Dominic Finch to him. Rebellion at his own home would provoke a beating. Mickey's parents, however, didn't care what their son got up to out of sight. Mickey had introduced him to smoking, pornography, alcohol, glue-sniffing and more. Drugs would doubtless have followed when they got older.

Except . . . everything changed with his mother's murder.

His old life was quickly stripped from him. With no relatives in the UK, he was put into care. He lost contact with Mickey, Ally, his other friends. Broken, despairing, lashing out, he was labelled as 'troublesome'. Foster home after home after home, unwanted, rejected. It took joining the army to bring any kind of order to his existence.

But with it, he thrived. Found reasons to push himself, to excel. He became good enough to be approached for the Special Reconnaissance Regiment. Then after that, the secret elite of SC9 . . .

Would he have achieved any of that if his father *hadn't* murdered his mother? He didn't like his mind's emotionless answer: *no*. An alternate path revealed itself. Fear of his father, his best friend holding him back. Laziness, lack of ambition, a fear of *trying*. Menial work, drugs, trouble with the law. Ally might have had her child in her teens rather than late twenties, with him. He would have been just another scally, trapped in his small world.

But was his real world any better? He was an assassin, on the run, hunted by his own side. He had one chance to call off the dogs. If it failed, he would never be safe. Nor would Connie. All they could do was keep running. And nobody could run for ever . . .

Reeve put the depressing thoughts aside as his father reached home. He resumed his watch. The Mazda returned around six o'clock. He got a better look at Finch's girlfriend. She was attractive, but not dressed as immodestly as Mickey had implied. He guessed she worked directly with customers; her outfit had an office-uniform air.

Afternoon slipped towards evening. Lights came on in the house. Finch and the woman were probably eating. Reeve munched on another energy bar from his delivery box. His other jackets were in it as well. His bike, helmet and trousers were black; casual observers would register only the vivid colours. Even if his father had noticed him during the day, he'd now worn three separate jackets. To most people, *cyclist in yellow* was a different person from *cyclist in turquoise*. He doubted anyone had paid him any attention.

At half past seven, the front door opened again. Reeve watched from a distance. His father and the woman drove off in the Range Rover. He cycled after them. From the route they took, he soon realised their destination. The Copper Kettle.

The Range Rover's occupants got out. Reeve's father wore smart-casual clothes: jacket, shirt and black jeans. Something about his poise made Reeve suspicious. His left arm was held slightly farther from his body than the right. Did he have a concealed weapon?

His girlfriend's outfit had changed a lot more. She was now in a tight miniskirt, two-inch work heels replaced by tall stilettoes. A stylish leather jacket accentuated her shape. Finch held out his arm. Not an invitation, but an instruction. An order. She obeyed, taking hold of him. He was making it clear to everyone to whom she belonged.

They went inside. Reeve chained his bike to a railing. Even a relatively upmarket pub like this would be prone to opportunistic theft. What to do with his other gear? He looked around. Behind an outbuilding were some bushes. He put his helmet in the delivery box, then shoved it behind them. The box would be invisible once darkness fell. Satisfied, he headed for the main entrance.

Despite its upmarket reputation, the Copper Kettle was noisy, boisterous even on a weekday. Reeve moved through it, searching for his target. He found him at a corner table, facing the room. Several men were already with him. Most were younger than Finch, ranging from twenties to mid-forties. They looked like former scallies: older, better-off, but not necessarily any wiser. From the empty glasses, all were on at least their second drink.

Reeve found a small table within sight of them. He put his jacket on a chair, then went to the bar. Returning with a non-alcoholic lager, he found it still there. Maybe the pub deserved its reputation after all. He sat, sipping the drink as he observed his father.

Finch was clearly the alpha male. The others laughed at his jokes, fell silent when he spoke, bought his beer. A pecking order emerged. Three men in particular seemed to be the top of the pile. A wiry, twitchy guy with a moustache, vaguely familiar from Reeve's childhood. A tattoo-covered body-builder. The youngest of the group, who while handsome clearly considered himself even more so. They sat closest to Finch and his girlfriend, and received most of his attention.

Reeve turned his observations to the woman. Her blonde hair wasn't natural; he saw hints of darker roots. He remembered his father trying to make his mother bleach her hair. Had Finch's girlfriend chosen a preference, or been issued another order? Reeve suspected the latter. She was being attentive, but not in a loving way. More clingy, wanting Finch to know she was only interested in him. As if afraid of the consequences if he thought otherwise. His father wanted to *control* people, to dominate them. His mother, him, people whose paths he crossed. Now this woman. Many smiles, but they rarely reached her eyes. Reeve started to feel sorry for her.

His sympathies grew when she took off her jacket. One sleeve had bunched up beneath, exposing her arm. She hurriedly tugged it down. But the moment had been enough for Reeve to spot bruises. They had been made by someone's hand. A large hand – his father's.

He hadn't changed, hadn't been rehabilitated. Not one bit. The slow-burning anger deep within flared hotter.

He kept watching as the pub filled up. More rounds came to Finch's table. He was now well past the legal limit to drive, but still in control. Reeve considered leaving. He doubted he would learn anything more tonight—

Someone went past him to stand before the table. Conversation around it stopped. Finch's expression became fixed, oddly calm. Reeve tensed involuntarily. He remembered that look. The newcomer had one chance not to disappoint his father. If he did . . .

The man was agitated, fingers twitching as he spoke to Finch. Reeve strained to listen over the bar chatter and music. Something about money, needing an extension to pay it back.

Finch's expression slowly darkened. The new arrival stopped talking. A nervous laugh from one of the acolytes. Then Reeve's father spoke, jabbing a forefinger at the other man.

Reeve couldn't hear him, but was able to lip-read most of his words. 'I don't fucking care about your personal problems. You owe me money. Sell your car, your house, your kid. I do not fucking care. I want the money in my hand by five o'clock on Saturday. If it's not . . .' Finch leaned forward in his seat. Even though the man was on the far side of the table, he shrank back. 'I will fucking come and find you. And you will not fucking like what I do to you. Okay?'

The visitor bobbed his head obsequiously. 'Okay, Jude. Okay. You'll have it. I promise.'

'I'd better. Now fuck off.' The man hurriedly departed.

Finch sat back. 'Fucking hell,' he exclaimed. 'They let fucking anybody in here these days.' His companions laughed. He turned to the woman. 'Go and get us a drink, love.'

She headed for the bar. Finch watched her go. His friends seemed to be making an effort not to do the same. She came towards Reeve. He looked down at his lager, not wanting to risk his father recognising him. The woman passed, miniskirt tight over her hips. Reeve glanced back towards his father—

He was staring straight at him.

Reeve froze, lowering his eyes. Had he been spotted?

Finch stood. The other men hurriedly moved to let him past.

Adrenalin surged through Reeve. His father had recognised him. Too soon. He wasn't ready to confront him.

He pushed his chair back, but Finch was already coming for him—

No. He was looking *past* him. Reeve followed his gaze. A group of young men sat at another table. Some were shamelessly checking out Finch's girlfriend as she reached the bar. Another looked up at the approaching man – and straightened in alarm, muttering a warning. Most of his friends immediately found their drinks more interesting. One did not, keeping his eyes on the woman's backside.

Finch blocked his view. 'What the *fuck* are you doing?'

'I'm not doing anything!' the younger man said, startled. His defensiveness rapidly became aggression. 'What's your fucking problem?'

'You're staring at my girlfriend. She doesn't like that. *Nor do I*.' The threat was unmistakeable.

The man rose, filled with alcohol-fuelled bravado – only to find Finch was bigger. 'Hey, lads,' he said to his friends. None moved to back him up. Reeve realised why as some of Finch's companions filed past. They formed a wall beside their leader.

The barman hurried closer. 'Is there a problem, Jude?' he asked loudly. Finch's girlfriend looked on open-mouthed, afraid to interfere.

'No problem, Keith,' Finch replied, not looking away from the other man. 'These boys were just leaving. Weren't you, lads?' His left arm drew back, pulling his jacket open.

The young man's eyes popped wide in fear as he saw what was inside. 'Uh, yeah, yeah. We're going. Guys, come on, let's go.' He hurriedly grabbed his coat and retreated. His friends followed him to the exit.

'All sorted, Keith,' Finch called to the barman. 'You should watch who you let in here. Lowers the tone.'

The barman nodded with excessive enthusiasm. 'Right, Jude. You're right.'

Finch and the others returned to their table. Reeve kept his head down as they passed. His father *did* have a gun. It was the only thing that could have caused such a reaction. That complicated things.

He needed to even the odds. He couldn't do that here.

But there were places where he could. One last glance at his father, then he left the pub.

CHAPTER 21

Ally's surprise as she opened the door was quickly replaced by delight. 'Dominic! Hi! I didn't expect to see you again so soon.'

'I was in the neighbourhood,' Reeve replied, smiling. 'And I wanted to ask you something, but didn't have your phone number.'

'Then I'd better give it to you. And you give yours to me.' She quickly found her phone. 'Okay, you first.'

He recited the burner's number. Correctly, unlike when he'd given it to Mickey. She entered it. 'You want mine, then?'

'Yes, of course.'

She waited for him to make a move, looking puzzled when he didn't. 'Aren't you going to get your phone out?'

'Just tell me, I'll remember it.'

A small disbelieving grin. 'What, when did you become Mr Memory?'

'Trick I learned in the army. Go on.'

She gave him the number. He repeated it back to her. 'And you'll remember it now?' she asked dubiously.

'Yeah.'

'Uh-huh. What's my number again?' He recited it a second time. 'That's a fluke.'

'No, I really do remember it. But that's not why I came to see you.'

'It wasn't?' She glanced back into the house. 'Daisy's in bed. If you want to come in . . .' It was an invitation rather than a question.

'It'll have to be another time, sorry.'

A faint sigh of disappointment: at least, that was how he read it. 'So what did you want to ask?'

It wasn't a question she'd expected, or hoped for. 'What's the roughest, most horrible pub that you'd always avoid around here?'

The Northumbrian was half a mile from Ally's home. Reeve remembered the pub from his childhood. There was an old steam locomotive on its sign. His mother had always avoided it, to the point of crossing the road.

It was as he expected inside. Hard tile floor – easier to clean up spills, and blood. The décor suggested it was last refurbished in the eighties. Compared to the Copper Kettle, it was brightly lit. The security staff were on constant lookout for troublemakers. Too many fights, or open drug use, would see the place lose its licence.

Despite that, he still picked up the scent of dope. Customers had finished their joints before entering, leaving their clothes reeking. There were probably harder drugs in use as well. The atmosphere was charged, aggressive. Testosterone-laden. Over three-quarters of the drinkers were male. Mostly young, but with an older hardcore contingent. The latter sat in small groups on the fringes, daring anyone to annoy them. Scallies all, whatever their age.

Reeve felt hostile stares as he bought a drink. *Who's he? What's he doing in our place?* He feigned the glassy-eyed placidity of someone several pints into the evening. It did the trick. He still drew some suspicious looks, but nobody got in his face.

He found a spot on the sidelines and watched the other customers. Looking for any wannabe gangsters, swaggering, displaying their peacock feathers. Drug dealing had a universal hierarchy. Lookouts became runners, became dealers, became suppliers, became importers, became kingpins. Each step brought more reward – for more risk. Not just from law enforcement. The competition was literally murderous. But weapons were as much status symbol as means of self-defence. They were kept hidden from the cops, for obvious reasons. But amongst peers and potential rivals, they were flaunted.

He soon identified two potential groups. Men in their mid-twenties, flashing gold jewellery, wearing expensive brands. The pub's staff were more concerned with keeping them apart than challenging them. Reeve had been searched before being allowed into the pub. He suspected his targets had received perfunctory pat-downs at best. Security meant nothing against friendships, bribes or threats.

One guy in particular stood out. Tall, crop-haired, the drawn cheekbones and glistening skin of a junk diet. Gold chains on prominent display. A harsh, barking laugh that exposed too many teeth. When he laughed, his friends did too. Another alpha, like Jude Finch.

And like Jude Finch, he was armed.

Reeve spotted the weight in his jacket pocket even from

across the room. Too heavy for a phone, probably over half a kilogram. Not large, so metal. There was only one thing it could be.

He maintained his watch. Twenty minutes passed – then the man headed for the toilets.

Reeve slipped through the crowd after him. He kept his head down to minimise exposure to the CCTV cameras. The pub was more busy than when he'd entered. If there were too many people in the loos, he would be out of luck . . .

The men's toilets were cramped and squalid. Three urinals, one cubicle. Fortunately only two of the former were in use. Reeve's target took the remaining one. Reeve entered the cubicle, leaving the door open. The blocked toilet was brimming, the water a vile yellow-brown. He was glad he was only pretending to use it.

One of the other men zipped up and left. The other kept pissing like a horse. Reeve tensed. If the toothy guy ended first, or someone else came in . . .

A grunt, and the second man's torrent ceased. He lumbered drunkenly out. Reeve's target finished, pulling up his zip—

Reeve stepped up behind him. Two rapid kidney punches. The man fell against the tiled wall, back arched in pain. Reeve chopped his palm's edge against the base of his neck. The stunning blow to the nerve cluster there had the desired effect. His victim collapsed as if his bones had liquefied. Reeve caught him. In a quick, smooth move, he swept him into the cubicle and spun him around. The man slumped on to the toilet. Filthy water sloshed over the bowl's edge. Reeve ignored it, delving into his pocket. His fingers found metal. He'd been right: it was a gun.

He slipped it into his own jacket. A short-barrelled revolver; from the glimpse, a Colt. Then he left the cubicle, pulling the door closed. A moment later, someone else came in. Reeve turned, facing the washbasin rather than the new arrival. The man waddled to a urinal. Reeve exited, again keeping his head down.

He headed straight outside. Not in a rush – that would have looked suspicious. He didn't pick up his pace until he was past the bouncers. Around the first street corner, then he ran. His target would have recovered by now – and want revenge.

Reeve had no intention of staying around. He hurried down an alley between two darkened shops. His bike was chained to a fence behind one. To his relief it hadn't been vandalised. He unlocked it. The half-folded delivery box was hidden under some soggy cardboard nearby. A yellow jacket was inside; he switched it with the blue one he was wearing. Then the box went on his back. He turned on the bike's lights, then set off.

Up the alley, out on to the road. He looked in the direction he'd come. Someone ran around the corner, heading towards him. He started to turn away – then changed his mind. His pursuers didn't know who they were looking for. Only that he would be running from them . . .

He rode towards the approaching man. It wasn't the toothy guy, but one of his friends. He looked right at the cyclist. Reeve acted as if he hadn't seen him. Just another delivery rider, only interested in his next job . . .

It worked. The man ran on. Someone else rounded the corner as Reeve reached it. It was the man he'd mugged. 'Oi!

174

Mate!' he yelled. 'You seen someone in a blue coat?'

'No, mate, sorry,' Reeve replied. He stopped at the junction to check for traffic, then rode off. The toothy guy hadn't seen his face clearly enough to identity him. He stood on the corner, looking around in frustrated fury.

Reeve pedalled away. He felt no sympathy for his victim. Merely having a gun meant he'd committed himself to the wrong side.

But now his weapon was Reeve's. The odds were even.

He could confront his father.

CHAPTER 22

'This is a complete waste of time,' said Blake over the phone. As instructed, he had flown to Milan to hunt for Reeve.

Maxwell agreed, but kept it to himself. 'If you find Alex, it'll have been worth it,' he said instead. 'If you don't, then think of it as a free Italian holiday.'

'I'm sure Locke's already booking his opera tickets. But Reeve must have left the country by now. He could have easily reached France, Switzerland, Austria or Slovenia by the end of Wednesday. It's now Friday. He's long gone, Tony.'

'Well, let's be sure. Besides, this is on the boss's direct orders. He wants it; we do it. You know how it works.'

Blake begrudgingly accepted the situation. 'Yes. I know. But,' he went on, 'do we know anything more about this Russian?'

'Not yet. Deirdre and Mark gave good descriptions of him, though. They've been passed on to Five and Six. If he's been a person of interest to them, we should know soon.'

'So Reeve was a traitor working for the Russians all along.' A statement, not a question. 'And he keeps slipping through our fingers.' His voice hardened. 'I won't let that happen again.'

'Then you need to find him,' Maxwell pointed out.

'That *is* my intention. But I'm working blind here. I have no new information to go on, and I'm wasting my time in—'

'You have your orders,' the older man said firmly. 'As soon as we have any new info, you'll get it. Until then, keep looking.'

'Understood.' The word was edged with sarcasm. Before Maxwell could say more, the call ended.

Annoyingly, Blake was right; Reeve would surely have left Italy. But refusing a direct order from Scott could cost Maxwell his standing in SC9. He was still on thin ice following Reeve's initial escape eighteen months earlier. That two other Operatives under Scott's direct command fared worse had saved him. He was far from secure, though . . .

His position needed to be bolstered. A success – any success – would do that. He thought back to the discussion with Blake. The mystery Russian's involvement was a problem, although not for the reasons Blake thought. Maxwell was certain – *almost* certain – that Reeve was no traitor. He'd been Parker's patsy, set up as a diversion from his real objectives. He'd survived entirely because, well, he was *that* good. Maxwell had told Reeve he'd been one of the best recruits he'd ever trained. He hadn't been lying.

So who was this Russian? And what did he want from Reeve? Key questions. As yet, with no answers.

He was about to return to his computer when his phone buzzed. A text. He read it.

Tony Maxwell, please await call from 6, imminent.

He was instantly on alert. How had anyone outside SC9

got his number? The '6' suggested MI6, but they shouldn't know who he was—

The phone rang. Unknown caller, but in central London. He hesitated, then answered. 'Yes?'

'Mr Maxwell.' A languid, upper-class male voice. 'This is Aubrey Ryford-Croft. I assume you know who I am.'

The Chief of MI6. 'I do.'

'Good. I wondered if we might have a brief chat today. Face to face.'

'I'm currently unavailable,' Maxwell replied. He didn't like this. SC9 was meant to be walled off from the other agencies. Being known to them suggested one of those walls had crumbled . . .

'That's a shame. I thought your being at home might have meant otherwise.'

He whirled to face the windows, shocked. Was he being watched? Or had they triangulated his phone's position? That would mean GCHQ were involved too . . . 'What do you want?'

'As I said, a brief chat. I hope it may be of use to us. But it will most certainly be of great value to you.'

Maxwell was silent, thinking. Then: 'Where and when?'

'I do enjoy a walk along the Thames. And to pay my respects at the SOE memorial. Do you know where that is?'

'Yes.'

'Good. Meet me there in an hour.' With that, Ryford-Croft was gone.

Maxwell lowered the phone. Protocol demanded that he notify Scott immediately. But the head of MI6 calling him directly was no ordinary security breach. Something was going on – something big.

Of great value to you . . .

Another moment of calculated thought, then he collected his coat.

And his gun.

The Special Operations Executive was a wartime counterpart to MI6, an even more secret service. The memorial to its agents stood in a park alongside the Thames. A bronze bust of a young woman topped the plinth. Her name, Maxwell knew, was Violet Szabo. She was executed by the Nazis at the age of just twenty-three. Despite that, she had fought fascism more directly than many older male agents.

Any modern-day Violet Szabos, he mused, would be prime candidates for SC9. Scott liked to portray it as the SOE's direct successor. It was far smaller than the mainstream agencies: faster, more agile. More capable of taking immediate and decisive action against the nation's enemies. Not mired in bureaucracy and politics. It existed in a deliberate blindspot within the intelligence community specifically to avoid interference. SC9 wasn't touched, because nobody wanted to get their hands dirty.

But now, someone was poking at it.

Maxwell had looked up Ryford-Croft on his phone during the journey. He recognised him approaching from the south. Mid-fifties, greying hair in a carefully styled swoop across his forehead. MI6's headquarters were not far downriver. A glance around the park. He had already picked out three watchers nearby. They were good at looking unobtrusive. He was better at spotting them. He let them continue to believe they hadn't been seen as he calculated firing angles.

Ryford-Croft ignored him at first, standing before the memorial. Maxwell could have believed he was genuinely paying his respects. Then he turned and started northwards. 'Walk with me,' he said as he passed.

Maxwell flanked him, on his right. That would give him the fastest shot if he had to draw his gun. He didn't doubt that Ryford-Croft knew that. 'What do you want?'

'What do all spooks want? Information.' Ryford-Croft gave him a humourless smile. 'I'll provide a *quid pro quo*, don't worry. But I'll ask my questions first. Agreed?'

The watchers were now moving, keeping pace. One ahead, two behind. Maxwell noted their positions, then nodded.

'Very well, I'll get straight to the point.' Ryford-Croft paused to let some passers-by leave earshot. 'Has SC9 killed several Russian agents recently?'

Maxwell took a moment to answer. 'I have no knowledge of operations in which I'm not directly involved,' he lied. 'But even if I did, I wouldn't comment.'

Ryford-Croft gave him an odd look. Sharp, yet somehow almost pitying. 'Loyalty to one's superior is admirable,' he said. 'But loyalty to one's *country* is essential. The latter always supersedes the former. Wouldn't you agree?'

'I would, yes.'

'Good. Now, you topped Simon's shortlist to take over SC9 when he retires. At least, you did – until the Reeve affair dented your standing.'

Maxwell's mouth went dry. None of this should have been known outside SC9. 'I don't know what you mean.'

Ryford-Croft chuckled. 'Oh, come now. Grant us some credit. SC9 may be deniable, but it's not invisible. Whenever you make demands of us, we don't simply kowtow to master. We like to know why you're using – or misusing – our resources.'

'Then I guess we need to tighten up our procedures.'

'I'm sure you'll do a fine job.' Maxwell looked quizzically at him. 'We can help you restore your tarnished lustre. Put you back at the top of the list.'

'We?'

'The agencies that support SC9. Your financiers, as it were.'

'I don't see how,' Maxwell said cautiously.

Ryford-Croft's voice became lecturing. 'SC9 is not Simon's personal fiefdom. He depends upon us to operate. For intelligence, logistics, finance. Regrettably, he seems to have forgotten that. Thirty years in the same chair have made him lose sight of the wider picture. It may be for the best if he were to retire sooner than he intends. In which case, someone would have to be ready to replace him. Tony – may I call you Tony?' Maxwell replied with a noncommittal shrug. 'By all accounts, you've been an excellent senior Operative. I'm sure you would fit the role perfectly.'

'Thank you for your confidence,' said Maxwell, with a faintly sardonic smile.

'Oh, you would have it. As long as SC9 remembers where our true enemies are to be found.' He halted, facing Maxwell directly. 'We're all playing the same game, Tony. We don't need one of our own knocking over our pieces. Or placing them where they can be taken by the other side.' Ryford-

Croft smiled, with all the warmth of a crocodile. 'Do you understand?'

Maxwell nodded. 'I do.'

'Splendid. So if we were to give our support, would you return the favour?'

'I'll think about it.'

Somehow, the smile became even colder. 'Prevarication is not a good leadership quality, Tony. Think quickly.' He looked at his watch. 'Well, I'd better be heading back. I'll be in touch again. Soon.' With that, he started back along the riverside.

Only one watcher went with him. The others were still tracking the man he'd met. Maxwell eyed them, then continued northwards.

His calm face betrayed none of the frenzied workings of the mind behind it. Ryford-Croft had taken a risk by meeting him. Even more of a risk in tipping his hand about his knowledge of SC9's workings. How would Scott react to the realisation that his agency had been compromised? He regarded any threat to SC9 as a target to be eliminated.

But Ryford-Croft's implication was clear. Declaring war on Russian intelligence had been a step too far. Had SC9's involvement been proven, the other agencies would be taking action against Scott. Maybe even the agency as a whole.

And Maxwell with it.

It came down to a simple test of loyalty. To his superior, or . . .

He didn't need to think about the decision. He had already made it.

CHAPTER 23

Reeve spent Friday shadowing his father again. Finch's routine was a reduced version of the previous day's. Only a handful of collections, the rest of his time spent at home. Reeve had to fend off boredom as he watched the house.

His father's girlfriend returned. An hour later, she and Finch drove off in the Range Rover. Reeve followed on the bike. He wasn't surprised when they ended up at the Copper Kettle.

The Friday evening atmosphere was busier and louder. Reeve had to sit farther from his target. Finch was at the same table, with a larger coterie than the previous evening. A couple more women were amongst the group, girlfriends or wives of Finch's hangers-on. There was a shift in the power balance, though. An older man had also joined the gathering. His and Reeve's father's interactions were easy, yet slightly guarded. They were equals, but probably in business rather than socially.

Reeve sipped his drink, the movement nudging the gun inside his jacket. Despite its presence, he didn't plan to confront his father tonight. He was still gathering intel. The more he knew about his target's habits, the better. In the SRR, he had sometimes spent weeks observing his quarry. Determining the perfect time and place to strike.

The massage parlour was already a promising prospect. The car park behind the building was out of view of the street. There was a CCTV camera, but it only covered the stairs. He could lurk beyond its line of sight, waiting for his father to emerge—

His attention snapped to movement at the table.

It was only small, subtle. Most people wouldn't even have noticed. But it stood out to Reeve as if lit by a spotlight. The older man and Finch were talking. Finch's girlfriend spoke to him, not getting a response. She repeated herself, louder. He turned sharply towards her, one hand raised . . .

And she cringed.

Reeve knew instantly what that meant. It was a fear response, a Pavlovian flinch drilled in by painful experience. She was expecting to be hit.

His mother had the same reaction to any sudden movements by her husband.

Anger surged within him. His father was still the same monster he had always been. A violent, angry, tyrannical bully, hurting anyone weaker because he could.

No more.

He kept watching, feeling the gun's weight. Waiting for the right moment. The analytical part of his mind warned he was making a mistake. He argued it down. All that had changed about his plan was the timing. He had always meant to face his father. It drove his decision to fly to Manchester rather than London.

Besides, his father was no longer the same threat as when Reeve was thirteen. The gun was just insurance. He could take him down.

He would take him down.

Before long, Finch and his peer drained their glasses. Finch stood and confirmed the other man's order, then – as an afterthought – asked his girlfriend. Nodding at her reply, he headed for the bar.

Reeve followed him through the crowd. People who knew Finch either acknowledged him or moved out of his way. Those who didn't were bulldozed aside. Some harsh looks, but nobody challenged the big man.

A space opened at the bar. Finch pushed into it. Reeve edged in alongside him. He caught the scent of his father's aftershave. Time hadn't changed his tastes. The smell's associations provoked another gut-level knot. Weekend nights, loud, drunken homecomings. The best place to be was well out of the way.

Reeve forced down the fear. When he last faced his father, he'd been over a foot shorter. Now the difference was minimal. And he was trained to fight, to kill: his father was just a thug.

He *would* take him down.

Finch was looking away from him, trying to catch the barman's eye. Reeve took the opportunity to assess him at close range. Expensive Rolex watch, in gold. Scars on his jaw, the back of his head. He'd been hit by something, maybe a bottle. Reeve hoped it had hurt. He was squinting slightly, eyes narrowed. At his age he probably needed glasses, but refused to admit any physical weakness.

The same man as always, just older. Now living a high life he hadn't earned. Released from prison, his sentence quashed. A free man. While his wife – Reeve's mother –

lay cold and still in a grave . . .

Reeve realised his fists had clenched. He forced them open, took a breath. Prepared his words.

And spoke.

'You've done all right for yourself.'

Finch had been about to summon the barman when he realised someone was addressing him. His eyes locked on to Reeve's, who stared unblinkingly back. Hostility at the implied challenge – then he frowned. He knew the younger man, but wasn't sure from where . . .

'Since you got out of prison, I mean,' Reeve continued. 'You should still be there for what you did.'

'You what?' Finch rumbled, with clear menace. 'Who the fucking hell are . . .' Recognition finally flared in his eyes. 'It's you.'

'Yeah. It's me. *Dad*.' The word had a lifetime of loathing behind it.

'What do you want?'

'Justice. For Mum. For me.'

Finch said nothing for a moment, then drew back from the bar. 'Outside. Let's talk.' He started towards the pub's entrance.

Reeve followed. A glance at Finch's companions. A few saw him go. Questioning looks, one man starting to stand. Finch waved him down as he continued.

They went outside. Night had come, the ground glistening with drizzle. Finch led the way around the building, stopping near the outbuilding. He turned towards his son, right hand reaching into his jacket. 'All right, what—'

He froze. Reeve had anticipated the move. The revolver

186

was half-drawn from his jacket. 'Don't.'

Finch carefully lowered his arm. 'So,' he said, 'you're back. What do you want?'

'I want to put you where you belong,' Reeve replied, anger edging into his voice. 'Either back in prison – or in the ground.'

'Ooh, fucking scary,' was the sarcastic reply. But his eyes never left the gun. 'I spent sixteen years in Strangeways with some of the hardest bastards in the country. But I'm still standing. You think *you* can fucking threaten me?'

Reeve controlled his breathing as his inner fury grew. *Calm, stay calm. Don't let him get to you* . . . 'It's not a threat. It's a promise.'

'Is that right?' Finch's gaze finally moved, looking over his son. 'Big man now, are you? You know, they told me about you when I got out. Said you'd been in the army. Probably think you're a proper tough guy. Well, you were soft as shit as a kid. Doesn't look like that's changed.'

Still the same. Mocking, taunting, trying to provoke a reaction. Any excuse to respond with far greater force. The gun wasn't scaring him – which meant he didn't believe his son would use it. Reeve felt his control of the situation slipping away. He had to put himself decisively in charge. 'Think what you like,' he said. 'But you need to go to the police and confess to murdering Mum.' His father had denied it throughout the entire trial. 'Because the only place I won't come and kill you is in prison.' He drew the gun for emphasis, fixing it on Finch's face.

Despite himself, Finch drew back with a sharp breath. Then his mouth twisted into a sneering half-smile. 'There's a

187

saying. Never draw a gun unless you're prepared to use it.'

'I know it,' Reeve replied. The revolver remained fixed on its target, unwavering. Finch was about to say more, but then caught his son's look. It was as steady and cold as the gun. 'I'll give you a few days,' Reeve went on. 'If you haven't turned yourself in by then . . . I'll find you. But nobody else will.'

He backed away, keeping the gun raised until he reached the building's corner. Then he was gone.

Finch stayed still, glaring after him with rising rage – and calculation.

CHAPTER 24

Maxwell was up early, typing notes on the German job, when his phone rang. Scott's ringtone. 'Sir?'

'Maxwell, you need to bring your team back immediately,' said his superior, voice urgent. Something important had happened. 'Reeve is in England.'

That qualified. 'Is that confirmed?' Maxwell replied, surprised.

'GCHQ had a standing tap for us on Jude Finch's communications – Reeve's father.' Maxwell knew who he was, but said nothing. 'Automated; they've become very resistant to assigning actual human beings to our operations. And damn them for it, because a human would have told us this hours ago. Finch called someone last night to tell them he'd met his son.'

'Finch was living in Manchester. Alex has gone back home?'

'So it seems. Apparently he threatened his father. "Confess to the murder or I'll kill you," something like that. He wants Finch either back in prison, or dead.'

'Can't say he wouldn't deserve either.' Jude Finch was a nasty piece of work, from everything Maxwell had read. 'Would a confession do that? His sentence was quashed.'

'He never admitted guilt, so it would presumably open up a new inquiry. But that's not important. Reeve was face to face with his father less than ten hours ago. From what he said, he intends to be so again. So get everyone back from Italy. We'll set up a full watch on Finch. The moment Reeve meets him, we'll have him.'

'I'll call everyone right now. And I'll head up there to run the operation.' An internal sigh: he'd been looking forward to watching the Fulham match that afternoon . . .

'No, you stay in London,' Scott said firmly. 'I'll oversee this myself.'

Maxwell was taken aback. Scott hadn't directly run an operation for decades. 'Are you sure about that, sir?'

'Of course I'm sure,' came the snappish reply. 'Right now, eliminating Alex Reeve is SC9's top priority. This Russian's involvement is extremely concerning. If Reeve gives him the stolen files, Moscow *will* use them to harm this country. I will employ every means at my disposal to prevent that.'

'I completely understand, sir. But it'd still be *advisable*,' he chose the word carefully, 'to have me there coordinating.'

'Operative 55 will handle that.'

More surprise. 'Luke Wagner?'

'Yes, I've already spoken to him. He'll work comms and tracking from here. You'd agree he's up to the task, wouldn't you? After all, you did train him.'

'Yes, he's very good.' Maxwell decided to push his luck. 'But it does seem that I'm being . . . sidelined on this.'

A sound of annoyance from Scott. 'That's my decision to make, not yours. Frankly, I'm not happy with your results. Your people missed Reeve twice in Italy, with you directing them both times. That's not good enough.'

Maxwell controlled his anger. 'Sir, I still think I should be involved directly. The more Operatives we have on the ground, the better—'

Scott cut him off. 'You will continue with the German operation, Maxwell. That's your assignment; that's where I need you. Understood?'

'Yes, sir.' The reply was emotionless – on the surface.

'Good. Now get your team back. They have a target to kill.' Scott rang off without another word.

'Fuck,' Maxwell growled. He *was* being sidelined. Why? Had Scott found out about his meeting with Ryford-Croft? Or was he just taking out his frustration over Reeve on the easiest target?

Either way, it put Maxwell at a disadvantage. He wanted – needed – to be in the loop on the hunt for his former student. Both to cover his own arse, and to find out what was really happening. Reeve surely hadn't come back home *just* to seek revenge on his father. The risk was too great. He was here for another reason. But what?

First things first. He picked up the phone again and began to call his Operatives back from Italy.

Reeve also had a phone in his hand. But he wasn't making a call.

He'd made an excursion from the hotel to a nearby supermarket. His purchases seemed ordinary. Food, and food wrapping – plastic sandwich bags and aluminium foil. But the latter two items were being put to a less mundane use.

He took one bag and slipped Parker's phone inside it. It fitted with room to spare. Then he wrapped a neat layer of foil around it. That, he carefully slid into another bag. It took a little persuasion to fit, but the plastic was soft and slick. Things got trickier with the *third* layers of bag and foil. Finally came one last bag to cover everything.

He had made a Faraday cage: an electromagnetic blockade. He needed to charge the phone to access the stolen files. The layers of conductive metal and nonconductive plastic would stop it from receiving signals. Or, more importantly, sending them. He could carry it, charged, in the bag without revealing his location.

Charging it would be a problem. Any opening in a Faraday cage caused some signal leakage. The charger cable itself would act as an antenna. He couldn't power it up here; it would draw his enemies to him.

That problem was solved fifteen minutes later. He sat in a McDonald's at Manchester's Piccadilly Gardens. A baseball cap shielded his face from the ever-present CCTV. The restaurant offered free Wi-Fi, but he was only interested in its charging ports. He plugged in the phone. Black tape covered all its cameras. The best he could do to the microphone was muffle it.

The phone started up. He ate a burger as he watched the charge percentage rise. His tension rose with it. The phone was betraying him, hidden Russian malware covertly leeching power. The SVR would know where he was.

They weren't a major concern, though. The phone would soon be shielded again. He doubted they could reach him quickly enough. SC9 were a far bigger worry. Until now, he could have been anywhere in the world. Now, they knew to within metres. Operatives would be sent to Manchester after him . . .

The charge level read four per cent. That would have to be enough. Reeve unplugged the phone and slipped it into his Faraday bag. All signals in and out were now blocked.

His next destination was the pedestrian precinct near Manchester's town hall. It was busy on a Saturday morning. A public place, lots of people to provide cover – and protection. Even SC9 would hesitate to risk civilian deaths on home soil. At least, in theory. Some Operatives wouldn't care.

But he would only be here for a few minutes. Sheltering under a tree, he took out the phone. He accessed the files, looking for one in particular.

BARRIER STRATOS: the Nigerian union organiser. Operative: Tony Maxwell. He scrolled through the file, taking screen captures of every page. The moment he was done, the phone went back in the bag. Reeve left the precinct at pace, feeling paranoid. He took a weaving route through nearby streets. Only when he was sure he was safe did he start for his last destination.

It was a supermarket all the way across the city's centre. It had a photo-printing shop. He connected the phone and uploaded the grabs. Once done, he started recording video at full screen brightness. The same trick he'd used in Florence, to drain the battery. The phone went back into the bag. Then he went to the counter to pay and collect his pictures. The young woman serving him didn't even glance at them.

He exited the supermarket. A check for potential watchers.

There were none. But he still took a long route back through the centre. After thirty minutes, he risked checking the phone. It was dead. Nevertheless, he kept it wrapped securely in its electromagnetic isolation chamber.

Reeve headed for a tram stop. He now needed to catch a train to London. But there was someone he had to see first.

'Mr Maxwell?'

'Here,' Maxwell replied. The caller was Imogen Corwin at GCHQ, one of his contacts handling the Reeve operation. Not that she knew who he really was. She believed he worked for MI6.

'Morning. Got something urgent for you. The phone we're tracking went live in Manchester.'

'Whereabouts?'

'We picked it up in three different locations, but only briefly. A McDonald's, a square by the town hall, and a supermarket. We think he's shielding the phone – contact was lost very abruptly.'

'I see.' Reeve had probably made a Faraday cage. Something he'd been taught by Maxwell himself. 'What was he doing?'

'Not sure. He didn't make any calls or access the internet, though.'

'Any CCTV in the square?'

'Looking into it now. I'll let you know.'

'Okay, thanks.' He ended the call.

Interesting. What was Reeve up to? Probably nothing good. The only reason to power up the phone would be to look at its contents. But why for such short periods?

Not knowing made him wary. Reeve didn't take any actions without a reason. But hopefully the CCTV would reveal his current appearance. That would give the incoming Operatives something to use.

He checked the time. Still morning; hours before kick-off. He returned to his laptop, trying to focus on his current assignment.

But the same worrying thought kept returning: what was Alex Reeve doing?

CHAPTER 25

Reeve knocked on the door. 'Mummy! Someone here!' came a little voice beyond.

'Coming, coming.' Ally opened the door. She wore fleecy pyjamas and fluffy slippers. 'Oh! Dominic, hi. You're back.'

'I'm back,' he replied.

'Coming in? Or do you just want directions to another rough pub?'

They both grinned. 'I can come in for a bit, thanks,' he said.

'Only a bit?'

'Got a train to catch. But I wanted to see you first.'

Ally smiled. 'Come in, then.' She ushered him inside.

The house was much as he remembered from his childhood. Similar to his own home, but slightly larger. The walls had been repainted, but otherwise the living room hadn't changed. Even some of the furniture was the same. Daisy sat before the television, watching a children's show. 'Cup of tea?' she asked.

'Yes, thanks.'

She went through a door to the kitchen. 'So where are you going?'

'London.'

Ally filled the kettle. 'Ooh, nice. Doing anything fun?'

'Just business. But I wondered if you could do me a favour while I'm gone.'

'Sure. What?'

'Look after something for me. I don't want to take it with me. But I don't want to leave it at my hotel either.'

'No problem. Although – it's not anything that wouldn't be safe for Daisy, is it?'

'No, of course not. It's just a phone.'

'Why aren't you taking it?'

'I've got another one.'

'What, one for each ear?'

Reeve laughed. 'It's not mine. I'm holding it for someone else.' He took out the bagged phone.

Ally eyed the layers of plastic and foil. 'I think you'll find that's a sandwich.' He laughed again. 'Why do you want me to look after it?'

'The only other person I know in town is Mickey. I trust you to look after a thousand-pound smartphone more than him. A *lot* more.'

She smiled. 'Yeah. If it *was* a sandwich, Mickey'd eat it. Then tell you a dog stole it.' The kettle clicked off. 'You trust me with something that expensive, just because we dated as kids?'

'Yes.'

'I could have changed a lot since then, you know.'

Reeve watched as she made tea. 'You were a good person back then. I can tell *that* hasn't changed.'

Her smile was accompanied by a faint blush. 'Well, I try. It can be hard sometimes. But . . . I need to set a good example now I'm a mum.' Ally brought in the mugs. She nodded for Reeve to sit on the sofa, taking the spot right beside him. 'Here.'

'Thanks.' He sipped his tea, then noticed her amused look. 'What?'

'It's just funny. The two of us, back on this sofa together after all this time.'

'Yeah, it's been a while.'

'I've . . .' Her expression changed, becoming pensive. 'I've been thinking about you, you know. What it would have been like if we'd stayed together. If things had been different.'

'If my dad hadn't murdered my mum, you mean.' It came out more bluntly than he'd intended. She reacted in surprise. Luckily, Daisy didn't seem to have heard. 'Sorry.'

'It's okay. I can't even imagine . . .' It was not a topic she wanted to discuss in front of her daughter. 'Do you think we would have ended up together?'

'I don't know.' It was the only answer he could give. 'But I would've been a totally different person to who I am now. You might not have *wanted* to be with me.'

'It would've been my choice, though.'

'It would, yeah.'

Her smile returned. 'That's something I liked about you. If I *hadn't* chosen you as my boyfriend, you would have accepted it. Mickey, though, some other people . . . they wouldn't take no for an answer.' As quickly as it came, the smile faded.

'That sounds like you've had some . . .' He picked his words carefully, aware of the little girl. 'Bad experiences.'

She didn't respond for a moment, miles away. Then: 'But

I made it through them. And I'm still looking for someone. What about you?'

Before he could answer, Daisy came to her mother. 'Mummy, play with us!' she demanded, holding up a doll and a toy teacup.

Ally's reply had the barely contained exasperation of all parents of young children. 'I'm talking to my friend, lovey.'

'It's okay,' said Reeve. He pretended to examine the doll. 'So who's this?'

'She's called Sally!' Daisy proclaimed proudly.

'Do you both drink tea?'

'We drink mint tea. *Only* mint tea. Mummy's tea is horrid.' She pulled a face.

Ally huffed. 'Thanks, kid.'

Reeve moved his cup towards Daisy. 'Would you like some?'

'No!' She hurried away.

'Nicely done,' said Ally, laughing. 'Interaction, then distraction. You'd make a good dad. You ever considered it?'

'We've talked about it a few times. But it's not on the radar at the moment.'

'We? You're with someone?'

'Yes.'

'Oh.' Her face started to fall – then she caught it. 'Good for you. What's her name?'

'Connie.'

'Connie? What does she do?'

'She's a nurse.'

'Oh, good, that's good. How long have you been together?'

'Getting on for a year.' He changed the subject, leery of

giving too much away even to a friend. 'I can't stay much longer. I need to catch my train.'

Her disappointment returned. 'That's a shame.'

'I've got time to finish my tea, though. Whatever Daisy thinks, I like it.'

Ally managed a small smile. 'So, you still trust me to look after this phone after you rejected me?'

'That's not what I – oh.' A crooked grin. 'You're taking the mick.'

She chuckled. 'You finally managed to realise it before looking daft! No, I'm glad you've found someone. Everyone should have somebody who cares about them.'

'Yeah. You'll find someone too. I know you will.'

The flush returned to her cheeks. 'Thanks, Dominic.' A faintly awkward pause followed. 'Well,' she said at last, 'you'd better give me this phone, then.'

He handed it to her. 'You'll need to keep it in the bag to protect it. Don't charge it up, either. It needs to be repaired.'

'Don't worry. I won't poke around on it. Or sell it, either.'

'I know. Like I said, you're a good person.'

Ally's smile was wide, and genuine. 'That's the nicest thing anyone's said to me in ages.' She stood and put the phone in a drawer. 'When will you be back?'

'Hopefully Monday, but it might be longer.'

'Okay. Well, have a good time down there.'

'I'd love to, but . . .' A sigh. 'I know for a fact it'll be all business.'

CHAPTER 26

Morozov sat outside a café in Florence, gazing thoughtfully at the sunlit Duomo.

His mind was on the events of four days prior. The defeat still stung. His target had escaped with the phone, and he hadn't even killed the two Operatives. Now he was stuck in a holding pattern, awaiting new intelligence. He doubted Reeve or the SC9 agents were still here – but where had they gone?

He sipped his coffee. Perhaps he should return to Rome and finish his original assignment . . .

His phone rang. 'Yes?'

'Hey, Garald.' Pervak. He sounded upbeat. 'I hope you've got an umbrella. You're going to England.'

'You found Reeve?'

'The phone went active this morning, in the city of Manchester. Not for long, though. And Reeve's smart; he's covered the cameras, blocked the microphone. He's also shielding it somehow, probably an improvised Faraday cage. We can't track him. But it confirms he went home.'

'Why?'

'No idea. But you can ask him yourself. We've booked a flight for you this afternoon, to Frankfurt. First class, you lucky dog. Ustrashkin will meet you there.'

'Good choice.' *Ovcharka*, as he was nicknamed, was every agent's ideal backup. Not the most imaginative man, but as dependable, loyal and dogged as his wolfhound namesake. That Ustrashkin was a tough, conscienceless killer was a bonus.

'It gets better. We're arranging a private jet to take you both to England.'

'Really? I like the idea, but it'll draw attention.'

'You'll be flagged on entry no matter what. Ever since Salisbury, the Brits keep a close eye on all Russians. But there's one big advantage to a private jet.'

'Which is?'

'You can bring Reeve back on it without other passengers asking questions. You can't exactly claim a restrained prisoner is your carry-on luggage.'

A half-smile. 'You've convinced me. All right. I'll get to the airport.'

'If we pick him up again, we'll tell you at once. Enjoy your trip.' Pervak rang off.

Morozov finished his coffee. So Reeve had gone to Manchester rather than London? According to Parker, that was his home city. Why go there? To find shelter with someone from his past, perhaps?

The reason wasn't important. All that mattered was tracking him down.

And this time, Morozov would not let him escape.

The final whistle blew. Maxwell joined his fellow Fulham supporters in a mass groan of defeat. Losing four goals to nothing, at home, to Leeds? The goalie might as well have stayed in the dressing room.

He joined the dejected crowd filing from the stadium. On top of everything else, it was still raining. He turned south down Stevenage Road, heading for the Tube station at Putney Bridge. The fans streamed into the park beyond the ground; he followed. On a whim, he took the slightly less direct route along the riverside. The Thames was grey, gloomy. Maybe it supported Fulham too—

'Hello, Tony.'

Maxwell froze. He recognised the voice behind him instantly.

'Over to the wall,' the unseen man continued. 'Hands where I can see them.'

Maxwell sidestepped to the park's edge, already plotting potential courses of action. *Run, dive into the river, attack . . .*

He rejected them all. Right now, there was only one thing he could do. Only one thing he *wanted* to do: talk. He slowly turned.

Alex Reeve stood before him. His hair had changed colour since their last meeting, back to its natural brown. Slightly lighter than before; the rogue Operative was also tanned. Summer in Italy had agreed with him.

His appearance wasn't foremost on Maxwell's mind, though. Reeve's right hand was in his coat pocket. Whatever he held within looked enough like a gun to convince him it was. Maxwell, meanwhile, was unarmed. He'd neither expected nor wanted trouble at the football match.

His first words to Reeve in eighteen months were not a

greeting, or a threat. Just a statement of fact. 'You got careless, Alex. We found you.'

'You got careless too,' Reeve replied. 'I found you here once before. You should have changed your routine.'

'Once a Fulham fan, always a Fulham fan. For better or worse. Worse, today.' A half-hearted smile, then his face hardened. 'What do you want?'

'I want SC9 to leave me and Connie alone. Permanently.'

'That's our end goal.'

'Funny.' Reeve wasn't smiling. 'I've got Parker's phone.'

'I know. That's how we found you. Like I said, you got careless.'

'I've also cracked its password. I've got the files he stole from SC9. All of them.'

Maxwell kept his expression neutral, but inside he felt dismay. 'Can you prove that?'

Reeve produced some photographs from another pocket. He put them on the wall. 'There.'

Maxwell collected them. Another surge of concern. Pictures of documents; an SC9 operational file. His own name stood out on the first page as if emblazoned in neon. 'You've read them all?'

'I've read enough. That was the first I found involving you. But I also saw files on Michael Pierce, James West, Susan King . . .'

All were other Operatives. Reeve wasn't lying. 'It'd be extremely damaging to the country if these ever reached the media.'

'I know. So I'm giving you a chance to make sure they don't.'

'You're going to hand over the phone?'

Reeve let out a mocking laugh. 'I'd be dead five seconds later.'

'You know me. You can *trust* me, Alex. I let you go, for God's sake. We can make a deal – and I'll honour it.'

'You don't make the deals, though, do you? Scott does. I'm assuming he's still in charge.'

Maxwell nodded. 'He is.'

'Which is why I came to you. You helped me find him before. You can do it again.'

The older man's eyes widened at Reeve's sheer bravura. 'You want to blackmail Sir Simon Scott – in person?'

'I'm not going to die to protect SC9's secrets,' came the sharp reply. 'And I'm not going to let them kill Connie either. Tony, you know I'm not a traitor,' Reeve said, imploring. 'But Scott thinks I am, and nothing'll change his mind. So if I can't persuade him, I have to *threaten* him. If he doesn't call off the Operatives, I'll release Parker's files to the media. Unencrypted. Everyone will be able to read them.'

'*Would* you release them?'

'I'm not a traitor,' Reeve repeated.

'So it's a bluff. What makes you think I won't tell Scott?'

The younger man's gaze became penetrating in a way Maxwell had never seen before. 'Because you've got your own agenda. You let me go after I killed Parker. I was more useful to you alive than dead. And I don't think that situation has changed.'

An almost approving nod. 'You always were more insightful than most people gave you credit for, Alex. And yes, you're right. Scott is due to retire soon. I was top of the shortlist to replace him. At least . . . until you were declared Fox Red.'

'And you failed to kill me.'

A wry shake of Maxwell's head. 'That didn't help, no. It's actually why I'm here, instead of teaching a new batch of recruits in Scotland. Having a third of my graduates turn against SC9 didn't go down well.'

'Sorry for the inconvenience,' was the tart reply.

'At least I won't be eaten by midges. But,' he became serious again, 'your being alive puts pressure on Scott. People under pressure make mistakes. And heads of covert assassination agencies who make mistakes are removed from their posts.'

'We can help each other, then,' Reeve said. 'You tell me how to find Scott – how to find SC9. I'll give him my ultimatum: leave us alone or I release the files. Will he accept it?'

'I don't think he'll have a choice.'

'Which will put him under more pressure than ever. And if it somehow got out that he *had* been blackmailed . . .'

'He'd have to step down,' Maxwell finished for him. 'I'm impressed, Alex. I never thought Machiavellian plotting was your thing. Top marks.'

'So you'll help me?'

'I will. A little,' he quickly added. 'If I do too much, it'll expose my involvement. I can tell you where to find SC9. But that's all. Beyond that, it's up to you.'

Reeve regarded him closely, trying to judge his truthfulness. Finally, he nodded. 'Okay. Where do I go?'

'Walk with me.' Maxwell pocketed the pictures, then started along the path. Still holding the gun inside his coat,

Reeve followed. 'Officially, as you know, SC9 doesn't exist. But even non-existent agencies need secure facilities. SC9's is in the Office for Interdepartmental Communications, in Pimlico.'

'Never heard of it.'

'Most people haven't. It's one of those make-work departments that keep mediocre civil servants off the dole. You get put there, you can't cause any harm. At least, in theory.'

'So SC9's hidden inside it? Nobody looks there because it's too boring?'

'Pretty much. Now, I can't help you get into OfIC. You'll have to figure that out for yourself. But that's what we trained you to do. Once you're inside, you'll realise how to find SC9's office.'

Reeve frowned. 'You can't just *tell* me?'

'If you can't work it out, you don't deserve to know. Besides, there's a certain humour to it. It made me smile when I realised.'

'I'm glad I'll get some amusement while my life's in danger.'

'I have confidence in you, Alex. I always did. Which was why you were so bloody troublesome, I suppose.' Maxwell stopped, turning to face his companion. Reeve kept the concealed gun fixed upon him. He ignored it. 'I'll give you one piece of help. To get into SC9's office, tell them you're bringing the red files from Yardley. They'll let you in.'

Reeve was instantly suspicious. 'And how do I know that's not a warning code?'

'If SC9 capture you and you give me up, I'm fucked as

well. If you're going to do this, I want it done properly. We have a deal, remember? I get Scott's job; you get a nice, long, untroubled life. As long as those files are buried . . . you and Connie won't be.'

The two men stared at each other. 'Okay. I'll trust you,' Reeve eventually said. 'For now.'

'Just don't screw it up, Alex,' Maxwell replied. 'Both our lives could be on the line for this. Connie's, too.'

'I'll bear that in mind.' Reeve looked ahead. 'You'd better get moving. You don't want to miss your Tube.'

Maxwell gave him a small smile, then set off. He walked for fifty metres before looking back. When he did, Reeve was gone.

He let out a relieved breath. The encounter had been completely unexpected, but he'd turned it to his advantage.

Now he could only wait – to see if Reeve was as good as he believed.

CHAPTER 27

So this was Manchester? Morozov looked around as he emerged from the Gulfstream G550. A city couldn't be judged by its airport, of course, but he was unimpressed. Grey concrete on a grey landscape, shrouded in grey drizzle. But then, Britain as a whole was always disappointing. He had been here many times, under numerous names. It invariably felt . . . *cramped*. And damp. Russia got cold, but you could wrap up to keep warm. Here, the wetness seeped into your clothing. That explained why every Brit he'd ever met was so *miserable*. Italy, he loved. England? He wouldn't miss it if it were to vanish from the world.

Which was his goal, if only metaphorically. If he found Reeve and obtained the SC9 files, it could happen. Russia's eternal adversary in the Great Game would finally be removed from the board.

A minibus took Morozov and Ustrashkin to a terminal building. Morozov steeled himself for the inevitable drudge of the customs checks. Britain only welcomed Russians if they arrived with millions of roubles to buy property. Others were greeted with suspicion, lengthy paperwork checks, searches. He wasn't concerned. He carried nothing illicit, and had a cover story. The two men were guided to passport control.

The line was not long, but moved slowly. Morozov endured the tedium. Finally, he reached the booth. The Border Force officer inside regarded him with disinterest. 'Can I have your passport, please?'

Morozov handed it over. The man checked it, saw his nationality. 'And your visa.' The relevant papers were produced as well. They were forged. He wasn't worried about the deception being spotted. The SVR knew what they were doing.

The time to check his documents felt unnecessarily long. Morozov stayed calm. It was standard practice in Russia, too: make them wait, make them worry. People with something to hide often became visibly nervous. His only expression, though, was boredom. Finally the officer spoke again. 'What's the purpose of your visit, Mr Belov?'

'Business,' Morozov replied. 'We here to buy machine tools.' He spoke English fluently, but deliberately mangled the grammar. He fumbled in a pocket. 'I have letter here from head of Manchester company.'

'That won't be necessary.' Another few mundane questions, then the Russian's documents were returned. 'Welcome to the UK.' The greeting sounded almost sarcastic.

'Thank you.' Morozov passed through the gate. He kept any relief from his face. There were cameras everywhere. He moved on, taking the green *nothing to declare* channel through customs. If he were stopped, it would be here . . .

But he walked through without incident. He waited for Ustrashkin, who caught up a few minutes later. Both men headed away through the concourse.

*

Another Border Force officer, a woman, sat in a windowless room. Images of the two Russians glowed on her monitor. Their passport photos had been scanned, but she also had CCTV images of the pair.

Something about them bothered her. Their visa applications were months old, but from different dates. However, their flight to the UK had been arranged at short notice. That wasn't itself unusual; people who could afford private jets often flew on a whim. But neither fitted the stereotype of the rich Russian. Their clothing, she noted sniffily, was definitely economy-class. So why – and how – had they paid for a private flight?

There was nothing on file demanding their detention and questioning, though. And none of her observations were enough to warrant a red flag. There were, however, standard procedures regarding visitors from Russia. She filled in an electronic form, attaching the photos, then clicked send.

The record of the two men's arrival had been sent to MI5.

Reeve glanced up at the Office for Interdepartmental Communications. The building across the street was an anonymous post-war block, ten storeys high. From the front it looked like a single broad slab. He knew from online research it was actually T-shaped, with three distinct wings. That was the only interesting thing about the structure itself. Other, equally uninspiring towers stood close behind it.

The building's occupants sounded as dull as their environs. Reeve had looked up OfIC on a computer for guests at his hotel. Even their own official government website struggled to appear enthusiastic. 'Facilitating cross-department workflow and interoperability' was the buzzword stew that stuck in his mind. It *sounded* as if it meant something, but . . .

He wasn't here to apply for a job, though.

Somewhere inside were SC9's headquarters. Nothing stood out from the front, however. No panes of armoured glass, no anti-observation blinds. But he couldn't stop for a proper look. It would draw attention to him. Even on a Sunday, security staff would be on duty.

He carried on. He would return in an hour, wearing a different coat. In the meantime, he would survey the surrounding area.

Once he got into SC9's building, he needed to know every possible way *out*.

It had been a whirlwind few days for John Blake. Right now, he and Locke were supposed to be lying low in a safehouse. That was the rule after a mission on home soil.

But then, he'd been reactivated and yo-yoed across Europe in pursuit of Alex Reeve. Now, Manchester replaced Milan. A brief curl of his lip. To Blake, anywhere beyond the Home Counties was the province of barbarians.

He pulsed his Audi's wipers to sweep rain from the windscreen. Jude Finch's house resolved itself, fifty metres down the road. Surveilling Finch was a dull task, but one Blake had taken on himself. He was sure it would pay off. Reeve had threatened his father's life. He wasn't the type for bluster or hollow machismo. And, judging from his past, he had every reason to seek revenge.

He would come after his father. Blake was certain of that. Hopefully sooner rather than later. Another sweep of the wipers. He hadn't even had a chance to tail his subject to relieve the boredom. Reeve's father hadn't left the house since he began surveillance. Blake had used binoculars to glimpse what he was doing through a window. An eye roll: watching football on television. He didn't know who was playing; he suspected Finch didn't care. Men were kicking a ball about, and that was all that mattered. A shot of contempt towards the Mancunian. He regularly put his life on the line to protect these people. How many of them appreciated it? How many even *deserved* it?

But his disdain was only a fraction of that aimed at Finch's son. Alex Reeve had betrayed SC9 – betrayed the country. *That* was why Blake was sitting out here on this dull, wet evening. If it would help capture Reeve, then he would do it.

And then the traitor would suffer the consequences of his actions. Blake hoped to deliver that suffering personally. The mere thought of the rogue Operative's betrayal stoked anger within him—

His phone rang. He composed himself. 'Blake. Go.'

'Corwin here, at GCHQ,' came the reply. 'Jude Finch just mentioned your subject in another phone call.'

Blake sat upright. 'Has he made contact again?'

'No. He only mentioned him in passing, talking to Robert Burton.' Some criminal associate of Finch's. 'They were mostly talking about a drug deal.'

'I'm not interested in drug deals,' snapped Blake, annoyed. 'I only want *concrete* information about Reeve.'

'The standing orders your people gave us were to notify about *all* mentions.' Corwin sounded snippy, defensive. 'And if I can point something out? What we've heard would be more than enough to have Finch arrested. He's openly discussed drug sales with—'

'I don't want him arrested,' Blake cut in. 'I'm not interested in the sins of the father. Only the son.'

CHAPTER 28

Monday morning in London, and Reeve already felt the capital's energy rising.

The streets around the OfIC building had been quiet the previous day. Now they were bustling as people came to work. He moved amongst them, getting a feel for who they were.

Government drones, for the most part. Predominantly middle-aged, staid, colourful ties the limit of individuality. Maxwell's claim that OfIC was a civil service dumping ground seemed accurate. Nobody appeared thrilled to be working there. Individuals exchanged cheery greetings on seeing friends, but then approached the entrance almost with resignation.

He peered inside as the doors opened. A security turnstile lay beyond. The staff used ID cards worn on lanyards to swipe themselves through. Only one visible guard, a uniformed man behind a reception counter. There was probably another deeper within, but Reeve couldn't see him.

Minimal security. Enough to stop people from wandering in off the street, but no more. Was SC9 *really* inside? Without Maxwell, he wouldn't even have imagined it. But maybe that was exactly why Scott had chosen it. Who would think to look for a covert assassination bureau here?

The rest of the day was dull, an exercise in resource-gathering and time-passing. Reeve bought appropriate clothing and a pair of reading glasses. The lenses were promptly popped out and discarded; he only needed the frames. The thick tortoiseshell plastic would break up his features. He had his hair dyed black. Then, the Tube into central London to visit a stage makeup shop. As the working day neared its end, he returned to Pimlico. One last stop, and he got changed.

He regarded his reflection in a window as he emerged. He now wore a cheap grey suit and black shoes. White shirt, dorky glasses, burgundy tie. A mournful moustache matched his hair. A briefcase completed the look. Just another junior-level civil servant, stuck in a dead-end job.

There was one more thing he needed. It wasn't something he could buy, though. He would have to acquire it by other means.

He had earlier located the pubs in OfIC's vicinity. The closest was at the end of the street. Now, as it reached five o'clock, he waited nearby. He wasn't surprised when some of those exiting the government offices went into it. Even on a Monday, a drink was needed to mark the end of work. He let the place fill up for ten minutes, then entered.

The interior was dark but homely, divided into smaller sections. Reeve imagined that different cliques would roost in each. He moved through them, looking for a suitable candidate. They didn't have to exactly match his current appearance, just be similar . . .

Potentials presented themselves. A huddle of men near the

bar, drinking pints. Where were their ID cards? Some still wore their lanyards. Others had removed them, wanting to discard their work accoutrements in the outside world.

He bought a drink, then surreptitiously observed the group. One man's lanyard dangled a few inches out of his trouser pocket. Reeve assessed him. Older, late thirties, and considerably heavier around the gut. But he had glasses, and a moustache . . .

He approached them with drink at chest-height, briefcase dangling from two hooked fingers. His other hand was at his side. The target listened as one of his friends enthused about something. Reeve slowed, watching the speaker. He was becoming more animated, about to reach his story's climax—

'I went outside – and there was a *donkey* in the car park!' the man proclaimed. His companions all laughed. Reeve's target leaned back as he joined in – and bumped against him.

Reeve made a show of trying not to spill his pint. 'Whoa, whoops!' He twisted to move the drink clear – snagging the man's lanyard with his free hand.

'Oh, sorry, sorry,' said the overweight man, drawing away. The movement popped the ID card from his pocket as the lanyard pulled taut. Had he noticed, Reeve would have let it drop to the floor. It would have simply seemed to have fallen out. But the man instead turned back to his friends. Reeve quickly flicked the card up into his hand.

He headed for the toilets. A quick check of the ID's picture. The moustachioed man stared owlishly back at him. It would do.

In the toilets, he donned the lanyard. A splash of water on

his hands, which he then rubbed on his face. His reflection in the mirror looked sweaty, harried.

Perfect.

He headed out, avoiding the group of men. Once outside, he hurried down the street through the drizzle. People were still leaving the OfIC building. 'Sorry, 'scuse me, sorry!' he called as he weaved between them into the lobby.

The reception desk and turnstiles stood before him. Farther back was the arch of a metal detector. A guard perched on a stool beside it. It was a good thing he hadn't brought the gun.

The man at the desk looked up as Reeve passed, tie flapping. He flashed the ID badge in his direction. 'Forgot my keys, forgot my *keys*!' he gasped, feigning breathlessness. He swiped the ID through the turnstile's card reader. 'Train goes in ten minutes!'

Both guards were now watching him. If he wasn't recognised, if they challenged him . . .

'You'll be lucky, mate,' said the man at the desk with a mocking smile. A building the size of OfIC probably housed over a thousand employees. One unfamiliar face didn't stand out.

Green light above the scanner. Reeve pushed through the turnstile. 'Thanks,' he replied with equal sarcasm. He scurried to the metal detector, slapping the contents of his pockets into a tray. The lack of keys added believability to his story. He walked through the archway.

A buzzer shrilled—

The other guard gave him a pitying look. 'Your briefcase?'

'Oh, God!' Reeve cried. 'Sorry, sorry. I'm in such a mad rush.' He handed the case to him and stepped back. This time, no alarms sounded.

The guard gestured for him to come back through. 'Can I see inside—'

'Yeah, yeah, sure.' Reeve hurriedly opened the briefcase. He had earlier kicked it across some tarmac to scuff its new surface. It contained folders, an A4 notebook, pens – and empty crisp and chocolate packets.

That last detail convinced the guard he belonged there. 'Okay. Hope you make it.'

'Thanks.' Reeve smiled, then headed quickly for the lobby's rear.

He was in. Now where the hell was he supposed to go?

Maxwell had said he would realise how to find SC9 once inside. That suggested its name appeared somewhere. He reached the bank of lifts. There was a directory beside it. The floors were listed by letters, not numbers; the ground floor was K. A was the top floor, I skipped to avoid confusion with the digit 1. Three wings, East, West and South—

Reeve almost laughed. Individual rooms were listed by wing, floor and number, in that order.

South wing, floor C, room 9.

SC9.

If Maxwell had set him up, he at least had a sense of humour about it. But it made sense. In France, Scott had told him he'd created what *would become* SC9. The agency hadn't even had a name at first. So it adopted the most anonymous title possible – the room where it was based.

A lift soon arrived, late workers spilling forth. He took

their place. The doors briefly stayed open. Last chance to back out . . .

Reeve remained still. The doors closed with a metallic bang.

The elevator took him to floor C: the eighth storey. He was on full alert before it stopped. If SC9 knew he was coming, they would confront him here. He backed against the side wall, leaning forward to peer through the opening doors . . .

The corridor beyond was empty.

He listened. The only noise was a muffled mechanical clacking. A photocopier, somewhere to his left. A sign told him the west wing was in that direction. The south wing was straight ahead, at the building's rear.

Reeve left the lift and looked around. Drab, dated décor, the floor a hard-wearing linoleum speckled to hide dirt. The copier continued its thumping beat. He started down the passage ahead. The noise quickly faded behind him.

He passed several rooms. SC4, SC5. Small signs revealed they were storage and utility areas. SC9 didn't want any neighbours. He kept going. A camera was mounted on the ceiling above the last door. Anyone inside would know he was coming. But would they recognise him?

He would know soon enough.

SC8. The door bore warning signs. *Danger, high voltage; No admittance, authorised personnel only.* Slatted grilles provided ventilation. A server room? Maybe it contained the machines hacked by Parker. He continued to the final door.

SC9. This was it.

An intercom panel was beside the entrance. He pushed the

call button. A warbling bell sounded. He waited. No answer. Seconds passed, a steel spring tightening inside him—

'Yes?' A woman's voice from the intercom.

'I've brought the red files from Yardley,' said Reeve, trying to sound nonchalant. If Maxwell *had* given him an alert code, he would be dead in moments . . .

'Come in.' A buzz, and the door's lock clacked. He stepped through.

He hadn't known what to expect. Part of him felt almost disappointed. Hollywood had conditioned him to imagine an elite covert agency's headquarters as dark, high-tech. What he found instead was mundane, cut-price, bureaucratic. *British*. The space was mostly open-plan, with some private rooms at the far end. One had a door of dark, polished hardwood; he guessed it was Scott's office. A red light shone above the entrance. The only evidence that this was an intelligence facility was the windows. Green, gauzy blinds hung over them. They had two layers; the tiny holes in each formed an interference pattern. Daylight could leak through, but it was almost impossible to see in from outside.

The reverse was also true. The office would rarely see direct natural light. It had a gloomy, pallid air, lit by screens and fluorescent tubes. The computers were a few generations behind the state-of-the-art. There were desks for around ten people.

Only one was occupied. A woman in her fifties, hair in a bun, sat near the door. She looked up at him, expectant, impatient. No recognition in her eyes – yet. 'Just leave the files here,' she said, tapping a varnished fingernail on her desk.

Reeve put down his briefcase in front of her. 'Is Sir Simon here?'

The woman gave him a sharp look. She didn't know him, so how did he know the boss's identity? 'He's in his office. But the red light's on – he's occupied.' Rising caution, then suspicion, on her face. 'Can I have your name?'

Reeve started towards Scott's door. 'I just need a quick word.'

She jumped up to intercept him. 'You can't go in there.'

'It's important.' He pushed past her—

She grabbed his arm.

Reeve reacted to her move a split-second before she secured her hold. He twisted free as she tried to throw him. Even so, he staggered as he broke loose. She snapped up her clenched fists in a combat stance, facing him.

She was no ordinary secretary. She was also an Operative.

CHAPTER 29

Reeve hesitated. Operative or not, the woman was old enough to be his mother—

Chivalry was almost his undoing. She darted forwards, a fist lancing at his head. He jerked back to dodge it. The woman changed targets mid-strike and swept down at his chest. She was an expert fighter, maintaining almost all her momentum. Her knuckles pounded against his sternum. He staggered, grunting in pain.

She pressed her attack, winding up to deliver a kick—

No more qualms about hitting a woman. Reeve twisted and lunged as she lashed out. Her foot caught him hard on his hip – but missed his groin, its intended target. He chopped at her throat. She brought her head down just in time. The edge of his hand struck her mouth. Blood spurted. The woman careered backwards against her desk.

Reeve advanced. He had to take her down before Scott raised the alarm—

She snatched a large pair of scissors from a desk organiser. A snap of her hand and the blades opened. She gripped the hinge to hold them in place – and launched herself at Reeve.

He knocked the steel points away from his chest, but one blade slashed his arm. A burning sting as his skin tore. He pulled back, sending a punch at her head. Her other arm whipped up to intercept the blow. She gasped as his fist pounded her forearm, but kept coming. The scissors swiped at his eyes.

Reeve backed up beside another desk. He snatched items from it and flung them at the woman's face. Pens, a coffee mug, a large stapler. She swatted at them with her free hand. The last breached her defences, hitting her upper cheek. She flinched, eyes instinctively closing—

He grabbed her wrist. She tried to jab the scissors at him, but his hold was too strong. He dug his thumb into her tendons to force her to drop her makeshift weapon. She gasped – then hopped back to deliver another kick.

He twisted again, but this time the strike was closer to its target. Her heel hit his lower abdomen just above his groin. A fraction lower and it would have put him down. It was still a sickening blow. Reeve stumbled backwards—

Pulling her with him.

She was caught off-balance, reeling. There was an open laptop on the desk. He grabbed it – and swung it at her. The machine smashed against her head. She cried out.

Reeve didn't relent. He dug his thumb down harder. The scissors clattered to the floor. The broken laptop followed them. The woman was stunned, face bloodied.

He charged at her, hauling her off her feet. She recovered and tried to kick him. Reeve lifted her higher, still running—

And body-slammed her down on her desk.

It collapsed under her. She shrieked in pain. Reeve released her – then drove a brutal punch into her throat. The woman slumped, writhing as she strained to breathe.

Reeve stood, then turned to run across the office. The wooden door was opening—

He reached it just as Sir Simon Scott looked out.

The head of SC9 had come to investigate the noise. Shock, then fear on his face as he saw Reeve. He retreated, trying to slam the door.

Reeve kicked it wide. It was heavy, a security barrier. If it had closed, he might not have been able to open it again. Scott's office was also a sanctum, a panic room.

It was filled with panic now. The older man scurried around his desk, reaching for a drawer—

Reeve vaulted the desk and kicked him in the chest with both feet. Scott flew backwards, falling over his chair. Reeve pulled him up and slammed him down on his desk. Framed photos fell over. Not Scott's family, but Labradors. Reeve gripped his throat. 'You should have left us alone.'

Even terrified, Scott was unwilling to surrender his authority. 'That was – never going to happen,' he gasped. 'You're Fox Red, a threat to SC9. To the country. There's only one outcome for traitors.'

'Parker was the traitor, not me!' Reeve snarled. He clenched Scott's throat more tightly. The other man's face turned red as he struggled in vain to break free. 'He was the one working with the Russians. I stopped him from exposing SC9. You *know* that!'

'Doesn't – matter,' was the rasped reply. 'That you're here at all proves you're a security risk. You found me – you found *us*. You tell the Russians, they find us too.'

'I'm not going to tell the fucking Russians.'

Scott's eyes were bulging, but they still fixed him with a

cold glare. 'They won't give you a choice.'

Reeve saw a letter opener amongst the overturned items on the desk. He grabbed it and raised the sharp blade threateningly over Scott's face. Scott cringed. 'I've got Parker's phone, with the stolen SC9 files,' he said. 'And I've got the password to decrypt those files. If anything happens to me, or anyone I care about, the password gets released. It goes out to the worldwide media just like the encrypted files did. They'll be able to unlock them immediately. And you, and SC9, will. Be. *Fucked*.' He practically spat that last word into Scott's face.

'And you say you're not a traitor.' Scott was trembling in both fury and fear.

'You ordered the assassination of a Member of Parliament. We both know who the *real* traitor is. But this is the deal. You leave me alone, and I'll leave you alone.'

A mocking sneer. 'You're proposing *détente*?'

'Or mutual assured destruction. It's up to you. But if you really want to protect Britain, I've told you what to do.' Reeve brought the letter opener's tip almost to his prisoner's eye. Scott's breath hissed through his teeth as his terror rose. 'I've found you twice now. If I do it a third time . . . it'll be to kill you. Your choice.'

Scott said nothing. Reeve considered cutting him to make his point when he heard movement in the outer room. The secretary was recovering. He stabbed the opener into the desk beside Scott's ear. The other man let out a frightened shriek. Reeve dragged him upright. Before Scott could react, he twisted his arm up behind his back. Then he forced him to the door – using him as a human shield.

It was the right move. The woman now had a gun. She locked it on to the pair as Reeve advanced, pushing Scott before him. 'Sir,' she gasped through bloodied lips. 'I can probably hit him, but there's a good chance I'd hit you as well. Is that an acceptable risk?'

'No, it bloody well is not!' Scott shot back.

Reeve maintained his tight grip, continuing his measured walk towards the exit. 'Try anything and I'll kill him,' he said. 'Move back.' He forced Scott's trapped arm higher, straining muscle and sinew.

Scott let out a strained groan. 'Do it!' The secretary reluctantly backed clear. Her gun remained fixed upon them.

Reeve kept moving. He gradually turned as he went, keeping Scott directly between himself and the secretary. By the time he passed her smashed desk he was walking backwards. Just a couple of metres to the door. Once he was through, he would have to abandon his shield. Scott would slow him down. But how far could he get before the secretary retargeted him—

A noise. Outside. Metallic clicks, electronic bleeps in response.

Someone was putting their entry code into the keypad.

Reeve sidestepped as the door opened, pulling Scott with him. A fair-haired man in a suit entered. He carried a Pret A Manger bag in one hand, a coffee in the other. He froze in momentary surprise at the scene—

Reeve kicked Scott towards the woman, blocking her line of fire. Before the new arrival could react, Reeve spun and ploughed his elbow into his chest. The man fell back against the wall with a choked cry. Reeve ran, grabbing the door's

227

outer handle. It slammed behind him as he sprinted down the corridor.

The storerooms flicked past. Ahead were the lifts. He heard the door open again. The secretary—

He reached the end of the passage and dived around the corner. A gunshot echoed down the corridor. The bullet struck a lift door with a clank.

Reeve was already back on his feet. There was a stairwell beside the elevator banks. He ran to it. Stairs led up and down—

A bell clamoured. SC9 had raised the alarm. The guards in the lobby would be warned of a dangerous intruder. Police would soon reach the building.

But Reeve had never intended to go back downstairs.

Instead he pounded up the steps. B floor, then A. He had closely examined online aerial imagery of the building. There appeared to be roof access. To his relief, he was right. The stairs continued upwards.

A fire door at the top. Zip-ties secured the opening bar. Multiple no smoking signs told him what OfIC staff did on the roof. He slammed down the bar as he shoulder-barged the door itself. Plastic snapped, the barrier flying open. He barrelled through.

Drizzle hit him. He ran across the flat roof, puddles splashing under his cheap shoes. A neighbouring tower came into view. It was a floor lower than the OfIC building, more modern. The windows were taller, extending to the ceiling of each storey.

Reeve reached the edge and looked down. The two towers dropped away to grubby concrete below. Shit! He'd misjudged the distance between them. On screen, he'd estimated them to be five metres apart. The reality was more like seven, almost twenty-five feet. Barely within his reach as a running jump – on the flat. The three-metre drop would help him gain distance. But it would also make his landing more dangerous. One mistake, and he could break an ankle.

And then he would be dead. Operatives were surely pursuing already. If he fell, he would be a helpless target.

He backed up, readying himself—

A *bang* from behind as the stairwell door was kicked open.

Reeve ran—

And jumped.

CHAPTER 30

Empty space below – then the other roof rushed at Reeve. He would make it – just. Legs bent to absorb the impact, arms out for balance. The void was replaced by concrete—

Hard landing. His left leg took the brunt, pain erupting in his ankle. He dropped and rolled to spread the impact. Dirty water splashed his face. He shook it off as he leapt back up. His leg still hurt, but he could run on it.

The new building's stairwell access adjoined the machinery block for its lifts. He ran towards it, looking back. The fair-haired man reached the edge of the OfIC building. He spotted Reeve.

His gun came up.

Reeve reached the door and pulled the handle—

It didn't open.

It too was sealed from inside to deter smokers. Probably also only by zip-ties – but he couldn't get enough leverage to break them.

He didn't try. Instead he ran. A bullet struck the door behind him.

He raced around the blockhouse. Two more shots, one catching the brickwork close enough for flying dust to sting him. Then he was behind the structure.

A moment's reprieve; he didn't know if the Operative would risk jumping to follow him. But he had to get out of the new building. The dragnet would quickly close around it.

No other doors. So how—

He remembered his view of the exterior from the other rooftop. An idea formed. He hurried to the roof's edge, using the blockhouse for cover. A low parapet wall was topped by a safety railing. Reeve leaned over it. The top floor's window began a metre and a half below. He held the rail as he lowered himself, then gripped the parapet's lip. Fingers straining, he eased himself downwards.

His toes rubbed against concrete and brick – then found smooth glass. He kept going until he was hanging at full stretch. A look down. The window started at his waist. He kicked it. A loud bang, but the reinforced glass didn't break. He struck harder. The window made a deep ringing sound. Both feet into the attack, kicking outwards before swinging back. A second gonging note – but sharper, more brittle. Was it cracking? He battered at it, becoming desperate. He was running out of time—

The window broke.

Reeve felt one foot go through. He hurriedly pulled it back. A falling shard clipped his ankle. Another kick, and a larger piece broke away. Shouts of alarm from inside the building as he kept up his assault. 'Oh, my God!' cried a woman. 'What're you doing?'

'Help me get inside!' Reeve yelled back. He put a note of panic into his voice. It wasn't wholly fake. 'I'm going to fall!'

No response for a moment – then someone below took the initiative. The base of an office chair smashed away more glass. Pieces shattered on the ground far below. Luckily they were landing at the building's rear, rather than on the street. 'Okay, we're coming!' a man called. 'Let me get hold of you. Ian, hang on to me.'

Someone held Reeve's legs. 'You got me?' he called. The reply was positive. 'Okay, I'm letting go!'

He opened his hands.

A moment of sickening unsteadiness as he tipped backwards – then the man pulled him in. Someone else clutched his jacket. 'Careful, careful,' somebody said as he was lowered. 'Watch out for the glass.'

Reeve ducked his head under a knife-like hanging shard. Several people regarded him in wide-eyed astonishment. The two men supporting him carefully brought him into the room. 'I'm okay, I'm okay,' he said. 'Thank you.' He made a show of checking for cuts to shake off his rescuers.

'Jesus,' gasped the woman. 'What happened? What were you—'

'Sorry, got to go,' Reeve interrupted. Before anyone could respond, he ran for the exit. 'Thanks again!' He rushed from the office, leaving the startled workers behind.

The lifts were to his right. He sprinted for them. His ankle throbbed with each step. Reeve forced himself to ignore it. He had to get clear before the cops sealed off the area.

He'd intended to take the stairs, but one of the lifts was just closing. This was the top floor; it could only go down. He rushed in, turning sideways to fit through the gap. The occupants flinched back in surprise. Reeve nodded at them as casually as he could, catching his breath. He realised he had a bloodied arm and his clothing was wet and dirty. He

232

considered making a joke like 'Tough budget meeting,' but decided to stay silent.

Ground floor. He wasn't surprised when the other passengers let him exit first. More people were leaving the building. He headed out with them.

He had reconnoitred the road outside the previous day. OfIC was one street back; anyone coming from it would have to round the block. Even at a sprint, it would take a minute. He had time to get clear. Not much, but it would be enough.

Reeve turned northwest, moving quickly. The street was fairly busy as workers left other offices. His destination was a few minutes away. If he reached it unseen, he would change his clothes, alter his appearance—

A siren. Behind him, muted by buildings. The police had gone to OfIC in response to the alarm. Now, they'd been told their suspect had jumped to another rooftop. They were coming around the block after him.

He increased his pace. A look back. No sign of the police car – yet. He needed to cross the road. A pedestrian crossing was ahead, but he might not have time to reach it. He found a gap in the traffic and ran across. The siren grew louder. Another glance back—

He saw a police vehicle – a Discovery. Had they seen him? Yes.

The siren's note changed, harsh electronic screeches warning other drivers to get out of the way. They hurriedly complied. The SUV swung out to overtake them.

Reeve ran. He had plotted two routes to his destination. The easiest, a zig-zag course through different streets, was no longer an option. The cops would catch up. He needed to lose them.

Which was where the second route came in.

He turned down an alley. Grubby brick walls hemmed him in on both sides, forming an inescapable channel. If the cops caught him here—

But he was through by the time they turned into the alley. He entered a dirty concrete yard, lined with wheelie bins and piled trash bags.

Dead end. Walled in.

No escape.

Reeve stopped, turning to face his pursuers. The police saw he was trapped. Their vehicle skidded to a halt in front of him. The two men inside started to pile out—

He ran again – straight at the Discovery.

A vault brought him on to its bonnet. He kept going, leaping on to the roof. One cop shouted a warning. Reeve ignored it. He maintained his momentum, making a running jump off the SUV's rear corner. Arms outstretched, fingers clutching for the top of the wall—

They caught it. He pulled himself higher, swinging his legs upwards. A heel hooked over the wall's top. He levered himself on to it. Both cops were now out of the Discovery. One fumbled for a Taser. Reeve rolled over the wall – and dropped.

He landed with a bang on another wheelie bin. The cover buckled under his weight. He grimaced; his hip and thigh would be bruised. But right now, his only concern was escape.

His landing site was an enclosed yard behind some shops.

There was a gate to the street, but it was closed. Probably locked. He could climb it with some effort, but it wasn't his planned route.

Instead he went to the back of the building. The stores all had rear service entrances. He'd gambled that at least one would be open. It paid off. A sign by the nearest ajar door told him it was a clothing chain. Cigarette butts were strewn over the wet ground around it. He went in, peeling off his fake moustache and discarding the glasses.

Inside was a temporary storage area for newly-delivered stock, cardboard boxes piled high. Cheap plasterboard walls divided the remaining space into storerooms and offices. He strode through it. A doorway to one side led into a staff room. Coats and jackets hung along one wall. He ducked in and snatched a blue hoodie. He'd meant to take a new overgarment from the shop itself. This, though, wouldn't trigger alarms at the door. Reeve dumped his ruined jacket and donned its stolen replacement.

He opened the door to the shop floor. Bright lights beyond, piped pop music playing. The store was quite busy, catching the post-work trade. The street exit was at the far end. He marched out. A young woman in staff colours reacted with surprise, not recognising him. But by the time she summoned the courage to challenge him, he was past her. 'Ah – excuse me,' she called plaintively. 'Sir, excuse me!'

Reeve ignored her. A bored-looking guard stood at the exit. But he was more interested in checking out the female customers than the man striding past. Through the security detectors, and out.

A shopping street. He turned left, pulling up the hood. In

the incessant drizzle, the act didn't make him stand out. More sirens, not far away. He remained alert as he continued. Before long, a police car rounded a corner ahead. The officers inside scrutinised the pedestrians, looking for anyone matching the fugitive's description. Reeve watched them sidelong as they passed. The car didn't stop.

He kept walking. Before long, another police car tore past. Reeve saw a bright yellow dot in its rear window: an Armed Response unit. Other sirens wailed nearby as the state's reaction escalated. But his change of appearance had thrown them off.

It would soon change even more.

Reeve's destination finally came into view. The Queen Mother Sports Centre. He went to the changing rooms, opening his locker. His belongings were still safely inside. He took everything into a cubicle. When he emerged, he looked very different. He now wore jeans and an untucked casual shirt with trainers. A blond wig from the costume shop covered his hair, a baseball cap over it. The discarded items were inside a small rucksack. He donned a light weatherproof jacket, then headed out.

He had barely been on the street for thirty seconds before a police van passed. It was in a hurry, lights flashing, siren on. He glimpsed several officers inside it. None paid him any attention. The van continued into Pimlico.

The nearest Tube was at Victoria station. Reeve bypassed it: the police would be watching the busy terminus. He instead headed north on foot, head down to block CCTV facial recognition. In the rain, he was far from the only one with a lowered gaze. Past Buckingham Palace, slipping through the milling tourists. Across St James's Park. Along the Mall, then through Trafalgar Square to the Underground station at Charing Cross.

He rode a crowded Northern Line train to Euston. Another danger area, but it was across the capital from Victoria. The hunt was centred around Pimlico. Police at Euston would have been notified about him, but wouldn't be on full alert.

That was Reeve's hope, at least. An enraged Scott might have thrown all caution to the wind. If his capture were declared a national security priority . . .

But that didn't seem to have happened. Law enforcement was high-visibility at the station, but it always was. He maintained a discreet distance from the patrolling officers. None appeared to be actively searching for him.

He bought a ticket for a later train and waited for the evening crush to subside. The time was spent in a burger restaurant on the balcony level, overlooking the concourse. No sign of heightened police activity below. Eventually it was time to leave. He headed down to platform level. If he'd been spotted, the police would move in now . . .

They didn't. All the same, he kept checking behind as he went to the platform. Nobody seemed to be tracking him. He entered the train near the front, then moved back through it. A tail would either have to follow him, standing out, or come face to face.

But no warning bells were triggered. Confidence rising, he found a seat. The train set off. He waited a few minutes, then moved to a different carriage. No one did likewise.

He was clear.

He'd made his case to Scott in no uncertain terms. Now, he had to wait and see if his bluff had been believed. If it had, and SC9 ended their hunt for him . . . he and Connie were free.

For now, though, he had unfinished business back in Manchester.

'He did *what*?' snapped Blake. The tedium of observing Reeve's father had been abruptly ended by a phone call.

'He got into SC9's HQ and confronted the boss,' Maxwell repeated.

'How the hell did he manage that? *I* don't know where SC9's HQ is!'

'Either he's done some incredible detective work, or there's been a security leak. But we'll have to figure that out later. Right now, the boss wants all Operatives back in London searching for him. Get down here as quickly as you can.'

Blake said nothing for a moment, weighing up his options. Then: 'No.'

Maxwell's response was calm, even – yet threatening. 'Excuse me?'

'Reeve *will* come back here. I'm certain of it.'

'You realise this isn't just a direct order from me? It came straight from the boss.'

'I'm aware of that. And under normal circumstances, I'd obey an order from him without question. But this time . . . Tony, you *know* I'm right. You've said before, you know Reeve better than the rest of us. And you know how his mind works. He's like a computer – once his program starts running, it goes through to the end. Well, he issued an ultimatum to his father. Finch has no intention of obeying it. So Reeve will come back to make good on his threat. I'm one hundred per cent sure of that. And when he does . . . we'll have him.'

A long silence from the other end of the line. Finally, Maxwell spoke again. 'Understand this *very* clearly, John. I ordered you to return to London. You told me you were on the way. As far as I know, you are. If the boss asks why Operative 62 isn't here, that is on you. You take any and all consequences for disobeying orders. Agreed?'

'Agreed,' Blake replied.

'Good. Then get on with it.' The call ended.

Blake let out a breath. Maxwell was starting to grate on him. In theory, all Operatives were equals. However, the older man had been granted authority in the hunt for Reeve. That was becoming a source of resentment for Operative 62. Reeve wouldn't have escaped *once*, never mind multiple times, had he been in charge . . .

But now he could prove himself. The traitor *would* return to face his father, Blake was certain.

And he would be waiting.

CHAPTER 31

Reeve woke in his Manchester hotel room, feeling good.

It was too early to tell if he had won the war. But he'd definitely won yesterday's battle. He'd shown SC9 it was not impregnable, its boss not untouchable. Scott *surely* wouldn't risk continuing his vendetta. He believed the former Operative 66 was a traitor. So he would also believe Reeve was entirely willing to release the stolen files. That was what Parker, the real traitor, had intended to do. Reeve, in Scott's mind, would do the same – given reason . . .

As Scott said, however sneeringly, it was a state of détente. Or indeed Reeve's counter-suggestion of mutual assured destruction. The files were a figurative Sword of Damocles suspended above Scott's head. And Reeve could cut the thread.

If he chose to. He wouldn't. But Scott didn't know that. He only would if Tony Maxwell told him. And Maxwell had his own agenda, eyes on Scott's job. It benefited him to remain silent.

Scott would cave in, call off the hunt. He *had* to.

Reeve smiled. He'd won. He was safe. *Connie* was safe. He considered calling her with the good news. Too soon, he reluctantly decided. He should wait until he was out of the country, beyond SC9's immediate reach. Beyond regular law enforcement's reach, for that matter. He was still a wanted man. Perjury was a serious offence.

Even if the man he had perjured against was guilty.

Reeve's mood rapidly darkened at the thought of his father. Would he have turned himself in? Unlikely. Jude Finch never admitted error, nor guilt. As for doing what he was ordered by his son . . .

Then he would face the consequences. Reeve had spelled out his father's options. He'd rejected one. Which left the other.

Reeve retrieved his purloined gun from its hiding place. He'd warned his father he would kill him if he didn't confess.

It was not an empty threat.

Part of his mind raised strident objections. For some reason, they came in Connie's voice. *You can't really mean to kill your own father? It'd be cold-blooded murder!*

'It's justice,' he said out loud. Jude Finch was a murderer himself – one who had never owned up to the truth. Who had now been freed, exonerated – *rewarded*. His anger rose, evaporating the last traces of his good feelings. The British legal system had failed, then been corrupted. So if his father refused to do the right thing, there was only one other course.

Justice would be done. Violently.

Could he kill his father? Could he actually pull the trigger?

Reeve was sure he could.

It was a scenario played out in his head since childhood. Even before his mother's murder. *Kill the monster.* Poison him, run him over, stab him, bludgeon him. The more brutal the means, the more intense the image. Shoot him, again and again and again.

He could do it. He *would* do it. Today.

It could destroy his relationship with Connie. If she ever found out, she would be horrified, disgusted. She'd believed in him, thought him better than that. She would be crushed.

So he wouldn't tell her. Simple.

You hypocrite, said Connie's voice. He ignored it. Only the real Connie mattered. And he would see her again soon enough. Just one more thing to do in England.

The gun was a Colt Detective Special. He'd examined it with an expert eye after its acquisition. It needed cleaning, but the barrel was unobstructed, the cylinder turning easily. He tipped out the six .38 rounds and tested the trigger. The hammer drew back smoothly, clicking down as he completed the pull. Everything was working.

Ready to go.

Reeve reloaded the pistol, then slipped it inside his jacket. He had arrived at the hotel as a fugitive. He left it as an assassin.

'You're back,' said Mickey Rowland. Reeve had found him at Crispy's Chicken.

'Yeah, I'm back,' Reeve replied. 'Why, didn't you think I would be?'

'Well, you've got your job, business meetings to go to . . .' Mickey affected a shrug. 'Bigger things on your mind than your old mate.'

Had he developed an attitude since they last spoke? 'I've still got some stuff to take care of,' said Reeve. 'Wanted to see you again first, though. Actually, you might be able to help me out.'

'Yeah?'

'Yeah. If you see my dad around anywhere today, can you let me know where he is? Give me a call if you do.'

'I *tried* calling you. That number you gave me? It was wrong.' Mickey's tone turned truculent. 'Got some Welsh bloke. Might almost have thought you didn't want me to call you. But you wouldn't do that, would you?'

That explained the attitude. Reeve put on a concerned frown. 'What? No, course I wouldn't. Did you put it in right?' He recited the burner phone's number – the real one. He'd meant to 'check' their swapped numbers anyway, so Mickey could contact him.

Mickey took out his own phone. 'I've got five-four at the end.'

'It's definitely four-five.'

His childhood friend regarded him suspiciously. But the look gradually faded against Reeve's studiously maintained innocence. 'Maybe I typed it wrong.'

'No biggie. You've got it now.'

Mickey edited the number. 'Okay. If I see him while I'm out, I'll let you know.'

'Any chance you could *look* for him?'

'What do you mean?'

Reeve drew out a wad of cash. Mickey's eyes widened hungrily. 'You know his usual haunts, don't you? If you could ride by and see if he's at any of them . . .' He peeled away several notes. 'Two hundred quid?'

His friend was torn. 'I'm supposed to be working today.'

More notes joined the first batch. 'Three hundred? Must be more than you'd normally make.'

Mickey clenched his jaw . . . then nodded. 'Yeah. Okay. But why don't you do it yourself?'

'Like I said, got some stuff going on today.' In reality, Reeve had already ridden to his father's house. Neither car was there. He didn't want to risk being spotted while checking other possible locations. 'It'd be a massive help if you can track him down. I really want to see him.' He felt the revolver against his body as he spoke.

'That's good, you wanting to make up,' said Mickey, nodding. His eyes hadn't left the money. 'Yeah, I'll do that for you. I mean,' he finally looked back at Reeve, 'we're mates. If you can't do a favour for an old friend . . .'

Reeve held out the money. It was practically snatched from his hand. 'So you let me know if you find him, right? Oh,' he added as if an afterthought, 'tell me if he's with his own friends. I want to meet him on his own.'

'No problem.' The notes were already in Mickey's pocket. 'I'll call you if I see him.'

'Thanks.'

Reeve left. He knew Mickey might just keep the money and do nothing. It was a chance he had to take. Otherwise he would have to confront Finch at his home – with his girlfriend present. He didn't want any witnesses. He *definitely* didn't want to have to harm any witnesses to protect himself.

This would be entirely between himself and his father.

CHAPTER 32

The call Reeve had been waiting for finally came that evening.

'Hey, Dommo!' said Mickey with great enthusiasm. 'How're you doing?' He continued before Reeve had a chance to reply. 'Listen, I know where your dad is. There's a place called Vixen's, claims to be a massage parlour.' He gave its location. 'It's really a knocking-shop. I saw him go in there.'

'How long ago?'

'Couple of minutes.'

It was the same place Reeve had seen his father visit. He could reach it in ten minutes. But was his target there for business, or pleasure? 'I'm on my way. Can you keep an eye on it until I get there? If my dad leaves, call me again.'

'Yeah, no problem. There's a chippy up the street. I'll wait outside.'

Reeve rang off. He'd spent a dull day wandering eastern Manchester, passing time in shops and coffee houses. It was a relief to be moving with purpose.

Even if that purpose was to eliminate his father.

Murder, you mean, came Connie's voice. Deep down, he knew that was what it was. But it was justified. An eye for an eye, a life for a life. And then it would finally be over. He could leave the country – leave his entire past. Everything from then on would be about the future. A future with Connie. Longing rose at the mere thought of her name. He missed her. He wanted to be back with her.

Not long now. Just one more thing to do.

The gun kept nudging against him as he rode through the rain. Before long, he reached the fish and chip shop. Mickey was outside. 'Hi, mate.'

'Dommo!' Mickey greeted him with a broad grin. 'You came.'

'Course I did. Where's my dad?'

He gestured at the building housing the massage parlour. 'His car hasn't come out, so he must still be in there.'

'That's great.' Reeve drew out more banknotes. 'Here. You've been a big help. Thanks.'

Mickey regarded them with surprise, then took them. 'No problem. You, ah . . . you take care, okay? Hope everything works out with your dad.' He now sounded more subdued.

'I'm sure it will. See you later, Mickey. Thanks.' He shook his friend's hand, then got back on the bike. A glance behind as he rejoined the road. Mickey was already pedalling in the other direction.

Reeve rode into the car park behind the building. His father's Range Rover was there. He dismounted in a dark corner and waited. Again, the thought of his father's casual betrayal of his girlfriend filled him with disgust. There was nobody he wouldn't hurt to fulfil his own selfish desires.

He waited, fuming. Finally, the door at the top of the metal stairs opened. A figure clanked down them.

Jude Finch.

Reeve waited until he was almost at the Range Rover

before stepping from the shadows. 'Hello, Dad.'

Finch reacted with a start at the unexpected encounter. He recovered quickly, fumbling in his coat—

Reeve's gun was already fixed on its target. 'Uh-uh. Take the gun out with your other hand. Slowly.'

His father sneered at him. 'What, or you'll shoot me?'

'Yes.'

A pause, Finch assessing his son – then he did as instructed. He groped in a pocket. The revolver remained locked upon him. He finally produced the weapon. 'Throw it over that,' said Reeve. He indicated the wall bordering the car park's rear.

Finch reluctantly tossed the pistol over it. It landed beyond with a crackle of vegetation. He raised his hands. 'So what do you want, *Dominic*?' Deep disdain in his voice.

'I told you what to do,' Reeve replied. 'Confess Mum's murder to the police.' His jaw muscles tightened. 'Doesn't look like you've done that.'

'Why would I confess to something I didn't do?'

'You—' His sheer arrogance made Reeve's fury flare again. 'So she just *fell into* that pit where you made me see her body?'

'Don't know what you're talking about.'

His father assumed he was recording the discussion, he realised. 'I'm not taping this. I'm not trying to trick you into making a confession. You know why I'm here. So don't you *dare* fucking lie to me.'

'Oh, are we talking about lies, Dominic?' Angry sarcasm filled Finch's voice. 'What about the lie you told in court? The one that put me in prison?' A shrill, child-like tone. '"I watched my dad kill my mum." No, you fucking well did not. Well, you finally got found out. And now I'm free. I'm not a murderer – and that's official. Got a letter of apology and everything. So now, they can find the *real* killer.'

Reeve stepped closer, aiming the gun directly at his father's face. 'You *are* the real fucking killer!'

Finch twitched, but held his ground. 'You do *not* raise your fucking voice at me, Dominic,' he snarled.

'Or what? You'll beat me up like you used to?' Reeve lowered the gun back to Finch's chest. 'Try it. I'm not a scared kid any more. I'm not afraid of you.'

'You're not afraid of me? Then you're more stupid than I remember.' Finch's hands clenched into fists. 'You think I'm scared 'cause you've got a gun? I was put in the prison hospital *eight times* after people tried to kill me! But I made it. And guess what?' His tone abruptly became mocking. 'I'm out, and I'm doing *juuuuust* fine. I'm better than ever. I made friends in there, connections. Got an education in the tricks of the trade. *And* I got over a million pounds in compensation!' He gave Reeve a nasty smile. 'That's right, your dad's a millionaire. Bet you never expected that when you lied in court to send me down.' The smile remained in place, but there was a resurgent anger behind the words. 'So don't you try to fucking threaten me, Dominic.'

Reeve struggled to contain a volcanic rage. The urge to put a bullet in his father's head was almost overwhelming. He resisted, barely. 'Take out your phone. You're going to confess to the police about killing Mum, right now. If you don't, I'll kill *you*.'

'You don't tell me what to do, Dominic,' growled Finch.

'You want to shoot me? Then fucking shoot me. You're already wanted for perjury. You're going to add murder as well?' A dismissive snort. 'The pigs won't need Sherlock fucking Holmes to know it was you.'

'Nobody's seen me with you.'

'People know you've been asking about me. Like your mate Mickey.'

Cold concern suddenly rose within Reeve, damping the heat of his anger. Why would his father bring up Mickey—

Finch continued before he could complete the thought. 'Let me tell you what to do, Dominic. Fuck off back to wherever you've been hiding, while you still can.' A sudden sound from around the building's corner, footsteps on rough asphalt. The older man smiled. 'Oops. Too late.'

CHAPTER 33

Two men darted out from the car park's entrance. One held a crowbar, the other a flick-knife. Reeve snapped the gun at them—

Another sound – behind him. Someone jumping down from the wall. 'Fucking drop it!'

He looked back. One of his father's clique, the vain scally. Aiming an automatic at Reeve.

He instantly knew he couldn't turn to fire fast enough before being shot himself. Instead he slowly lowered his own gun.

'You heard him,' said Finch as his friends approached. 'He *will* shoot you. Wouldn't be the first time he's put a bullet in someone.'

Nothing about the scally's attitude suggested he was lying. With deep reluctance, Reeve tossed away the revolver.

Finch relaxed, lowering his hands. 'Nice one, Trick. Thanks.' The young man closed upon Reeve, weapon still aimed at him. 'You didn't see my gun over that wall, did you?'

Trick shook his head. 'Sorry, Jude.'

Finch made an annoyed sound, then reached into his pocket again. He produced a small black device. 'Seen one of these before, Dominic? They didn't exist when I got sent down. It's like a pager, except it's an emergency alarm. Uses GPS to send a text through your phone, telling people exactly where you are. My lads here,' he indicated the trio, 'have been keeping an eye on me. Waiting for you. Mickey told me you were back in town.'

'Mickey?' said Reeve, feeling the sudden sickening jolt of betrayal.

'He works for me, doesn't he? One of my delivery boys. It's not just food that goes out with the takeaway orders. He knows which side his bread's buttered. Came to my house saying you'd asked him to find me. I told him to send you here.' He turned to the bodybuilder. 'Skels, give me that.'

Skels handed him the crowbar. Finch hefted it. 'It's been sixteen years since I last gave you what you deserved, Dominic. When I'm done, you'll wish I'd fucking killed you as a kid.' He advanced on his son.

Reeve's gaze flicked between the four men. Trick, the gunman, was the greatest threat. He stood to Reeve's left, gun readied, out of reach. The bodybuilder was behind Finch. The wiry man with a moustache, holding the knife, was off to Reeve's right. Between them, they had cut off all escape routes.

Nowhere to run. So he had to fight.

Reeve was ready.

His gaze came back to his father as he closed in. Finch slapped the crowbar against his palm, turning it to put the claw foremost. 'This is what I had to teach people in prison. Fuck around with Jude Finch, and you get—' He swung, grunting out a last word. '—*hurt!*'

The crowbar blurred at Reeve's head—

And stopped short.

Reeve arrested the blow, lightning-fast hands catching Finch's wrist. His father was taken by surprise. He hadn't expected his son to have such speed or such strength—

Both were used against him an instant later. Reeve twisted his arm to force it downwards. Right elbow hard against Finch's forearm – then he turned his whole body. His father's elbow bent back to its limit, cartilage crackling. Finch cried out. Reeve kept turning. Finch fell to the wet ground, his shoulder now taking the wrenching punishment. Reeve released his wrist and whipped up his hands – snatching the crowbar.

The entire move took less than a second. None of the other men even had time to react.

Reeve spun, arm lancing out. He threw the crowbar. It smashed against Trick's outstretched wrist. The thunk of metal was joined by a crack of bone. The automatic flew from Trick's suddenly paralysed hand. He let out an agonised shriek.

Reeve finished his turn, going after the gun—

The knifeman rushed to intercept him. The blade stabbed out. Reeve jumped back. Another strike. He tried to grab and disarm his opponent. But the twitchy man was *fast*, reacting to the movement. The knife's tip caught Reeve's sleeve. He hurriedly pulled away.

'Fucking stab him, Boyzie!' yelled Finch as he got up. 'Skels, grab him!'

The bodybuilder came out of his stunned freeze and rushed at Reeve. Boyzie continued his own jittery attack.

Reeve managed to jerk clear of the knife, only to see Skels charging at him—

He dodged. Not quickly enough. Skels caught his shoulder a glancing blow as he barrelled past. Reeve staggered – and Boyzie's foot swung at his groin. He threw himself sideways. The blow caught his left thigh. He stumbled again, barely keeping his balance.

But now Skels had come about. The big man's fist drew back for a punch.

And Finch was upright. He faced his son . . .

Then turned.

Reeve knew he was going for the gun. He tried to follow, but Boyzie blocked him. The blade sliced at his throat. He jumped back, the knife's tip flashing centimetres from his neck.

Skels's punch came. Reeve twisted to avoid it – then slammed his elbow into his attacker's face. A muffled crack as the other man's nose broke. Skels screeched and reeled away.

Reeve looked at the others. Where was his father – and where was the gun?

Finch was searching in the shadows. He spotted something, darting towards it—

Boyzie lunged at Reeve. He scrambled to avoid the knife, then retreated towards the wall. The wiry man followed.

Finch grabbed something from the ground. Reeve knew what it was. His father's words came back to him. *Don't draw a gun unless you mean to use it.* Jude Finch had murdered his wife. Now he intended to do the same to his son.

He had to get away, *now*. But how—

Boyzie struck again. This time Reeve couldn't avoid it.

Sharp pain as the blade jabbed into his forearm. A strained cry escaped through clenched teeth. The twitchy man yanked out the knife, about to stab him again—

Reeve grabbed him – and pulled him sharply closer.

He delivered a brutal headbutt. A *crack* of impact, and fireworks of impossible colour burst in his vision. The blow hurt – but Boyzie came off worse. He wobbled back, dizzied.

Behind him, Finch brought the gun to bear – then hesitated. His friend was in the way—

Reeve sent a flying kick hard into Boyzie's chest. The other man flew backwards. Finch jumped aside to avoid a collision.

It was only a moment of distraction. But Reeve took it, twisting in mid-air as he used Boyzie like a springboard. He grabbed the wall's top and threw himself over it. Dark wasteland lay beyond. He crashed down into vegetation below. The sharp bark of a gunshot followed a second later. The bullet shattered a brick, fragments hailing over him.

Reeve scrabbled up and ran. More buildings were silhouetted against streetlights across the derelict plot. He raced towards them.

The ground underfoot was uneven, hidden by darkness. He almost tripped a couple of times. Finch shouted behind: 'Go after him in the car!'

But he was being hunted on foot as well. A figure clambered over the wall. His father. Boyzie followed him. They would harry him towards the next road, where the driver would cut him off.

Or try. Reeve was confident he could outrun his pursuers. Neither looked to have his combination of speed and stamina.

He needed to reach somewhere the car couldn't follow. Somewhere he could weave through narrow spaces to keep his father from taking aim.

He'd grown up around here. The streets and alleys and industrial yards had been his playground. He knew where to go.

He neared the buildings. A gap between them led to the street. He rushed out on to a pavement.

The road was quiet. Headlights approaching from his right, but the pursuing car would come from the left. He sprinted right. Across the street were some commercial properties. Behind them was a housing estate. If he entered, he could cut through to any of several exits, losing the car. His father was now the main threat, but the gap was already opening up. Hitting a moving target at night was extremely hard for an untrained shooter. He doubted it was a skill Finch had picked up in prison. Keep running, keep weaving, and he wouldn't get a shot.

Reeve angled across the street, cutting ahead of the oncoming car, an Audi—

A roar from its engine as it speeded up – and swerved to track him.

Shocked, Reeve leapt out of its path. Its nose swept past centimetres behind him.

The driver's door flew open.

The broad panel slammed into him. His weight knocked it back, but the impact pounded him off his feet. He hit the road hard, tumbling over and over.

His head cracked against the kerb.

It felt like a spike driving into his skull. More pain in his right arm and shoulder from the collision. A wet rasp of tyres as the Audi braked hard. Reeve turned his head to look for it. The movement brought dizziness, nausea. He tried to get up, but his muscles had liquefied, all strength gone.

The car stopped. The driver's door was dented, window cracked. It swung open. Someone got out.

Blake.

Reeve dragged himself on to the pavement. Just that short movement felt like running a marathon. Blake strode towards him, drawing his sidearm. Beyond, Finch and his companion reached the road, headlights flaring behind them. Reeve saw his father's gun come up—

Blake had already spun to face them. 'Armed police!' he barked, his own weapon raised. 'Leave *now*, or I will use lethal force.'

The running men halted. Finch glared at Reeve, then hurriedly pocketed his gun and retreated. Their car slithered to a stop. They got in, and it turned and sped away.

Blake turned back to his prey. Reeve struggled in vain to stand as the Operative stepped closer. Polished black shoes filled his blurring vision. He picked out tiny droplets on the smooth leather, dazed mind fixating on odd details. A painful look up. Blake towered over him, face filled with contempt.

The shoe rushed at his face. A crack, pain exploding.

Then darkness.

CHAPTER 34

Consciousness returned slowly, unwillingly. Part of Reeve's mind desperately resisted waking up.

It didn't want to face what was waiting.

Pain had taken root throughout his body. His arm, his side. His head. The spike had been removed, replaced by a dull, pulsing throb. But his face now hurt as well. He probed with his tongue, wincing as it met swollen, tender lips.

Other, lesser discomforts made themselves known. He was cold. His shoulder muscles felt strained, legs aching. He tried to move—

He couldn't. He was tied. Sitting position, wrists bound behind him. He was on a chair, ankles secured to its legs. He subtly shifted, testing his bonds. Could he work his arms loose? No. Not enough play . . .

A sound nearby. Approaching footsteps. Memory returned. Blake. Reeve froze, feigning unconsciousness. Had Blake seen the small movement? The footsteps stopped. A few metres away, Reeve estimated, at his two o'clock position. He opened his left eye a fraction. If he could survey his surroundings before Blake realised he was awake—

Freezing water burst over Reeve's body.

He gasped, thrashing helplessly against the ropes. He was

naked. Filthy liquid sluiced off him. His surroundings were dark. The only illumination was a cold white glow from one side. He turned his head. An LED hand torch was propped on a piece of corroded machinery.

Blake stood beside it, a dented bucket in his hands. He dropped it with a clang. 'Hello, Reeve,' he said. 'Welcome home.'

Reeve shook water from his eyes. A wave of sickening dizziness rolled over him. He let it pass, trying to assess his situation. He was in a derelict factory or warehouse. Night sky was visible through holes in the roof, rain spattering the concrete floor. How long had he been knocked out? Long enough for Blake to bring him here, strip and bind him.

Why hadn't he just killed him? Those were his orders. Reeve was still Fox Red: targeted for immediate termination. Blake had something else in mind . . .

The other man spoke again. 'Nice tan. I see Italy treated you well.' Then, almost casually: 'How's Connie?'

Cold horror flowed through Reeve. *That* was what Blake wanted. Not just to eliminate him, but Connie as well. Anger joined fear, disguising it. 'Safe,' he growled. He tried to move his arms again. Still no joy. His seat was a battered office chair. His wrists were bound to the base of its raised back.

'Not for long,' Blake replied. 'We can't have her running around. She knows too much.'

'She doesn't know anything.'

'She knows we exist. That's enough. We'll find her.' He moved to stand in front of Reeve. '*I'll* find her. With your help. Whether you want to give it or not.'

'Fuck you.'

Blake smiled. 'Grown attached, have you? It's funny; I never pictured you as the type to settle into domesticity. You always struck me as cold, emotionless, all about the job. But Connie was a nurse, wasn't she? She patched you up, and you fell in love with her. And she fell in love with you in return. Florence Nightingale Syndrome, how sweet.' Mockery was replaced by smugness. 'It made you careless, though. That's how I caught you. You let your emotions overcome your judgement.'

Reeve said nothing. Blake slowly circled him. 'You love Connie . . . and you hate your father,' he went on. 'You hate him enough to come to Manchester to kill him. Poor choice, Reeve. Bad motivation, bad planning. Not worthy of an Operative.'

'I'm not an Operative any more,' Reeve replied.

'Oh, but you are. Once you're in SC9, you're in for life. However it happens to end.' He continued his circuit, sneering condescendingly at Reeve as he passed. 'GCHQ were monitoring your father's phone. We heard you'd threatened him. Then you went to London – but I knew you'd come back. That's something about you that hasn't changed. You don't leave business unfinished. So I stayed here to keep an eye on him. And sure enough, back you came. Then bang – I had you.'

He stopped before Reeve again, leaning closer with a hint of a cruel smile. 'A secure van's coming to take you to London for interrogation. You're going to tell us where to find Connie. And the phone with all the stolen SC9 files. I don't suppose you'd care to tell me now? No? Oh, well. You will soon enough. Then . . .' The smile took on full malevolent form. 'You'll get what all traitors deserve.'

Reeve fixed him with an angry glare. 'I'm not a traitor.'

'Really? Because an interesting visitor arrived in Manchester on Sunday. A Russian. Two Russians, actually, but one in particular caught our attention. Border Force sent his picture to MI5; standard procedure. He was on file. They passed it on to us. Stone and Flynn recognised him at once.' He straightened. 'Your friend from Florence. Garald Morozov.'

'Morozov?' Reeve echoed. Memory finally clicked; it was the name Parker had told him. His control, the man who provided the software used to hack SC9's servers.

Blake misinterpreted his reaction. 'Yes. He's come to whisk you to safety in exchange for the phone, hasn't he? He has a private jet waiting at Manchester airport.' His face became harder. 'But that's a flight you're never going to take.'

'I'm not working with the Russians,' Reeve insisted. 'Parker framed me. He was going to murder Elektra Curtis and expose SC9. He was your fucking traitor, not me. I stopped him!'

'The boss ordered Curtis's removal,' Blake pointed out. 'SC9 was going to kill her anyway. Just more subtly.' He started to circle the bound man again. 'Stopping one traitor doesn't absolve you of treason yourself. You turned against us. You turned against your country. *My* country.' He came back around. 'And that is a crime I will *not* let stand.'

Blake stopped. His fists clenched. Reeve knew what was about to happen. But he was powerless to prevent it. All he could do was endure . . .

The first punch was to his stomach. Reeve convulsed, winded, but couldn't even curl up. The next blow hit his head. As did the third. A kick to the chest, the chair almost toppling over. Then punch after punch after punch—

Blackness finally, thankfully, swallowed him once more.

CHAPTER 35

The sound of a car's engine stirred Reeve from unconsciousness. He painfully rose from the dark void. The sharp tang of blood filled his mouth. He'd lost a tooth, a brutal blow to his cheek tearing out a molar. The gap in his gum was still oozing. He spat, feeling the red slurry land on his bare thighs.

Still bound. The assault hadn't loosened the ropes. Blake had been careful to avoid that. His one kick had strained the chair's legs as it tipped. The act hadn't been repeated.

Reeve opened his eyes. One was bruised, swollen. Blake's back was to him. Reeve took advantage of his moment unobserved to jolt in the chair. If he could weaken it further—

'Don't try anything stupid, Reeve,' said Blake in a bored tone. He moved his arm to reveal he was holding his SIG Sauer P320 Compact. Reeve stopped.

A door slammed. Someone was coming. A figure stepped through a doorway.

Blake's gun fixed upon the new arrival. A moment, then he holstered the weapon. 'I was expecting the transport team. I thought you were in London?'

'I was.' Reeve knew the voice instantly. Tony Maxwell. 'I drove up as quickly as I could.'

'Why? We're about to bring him back down there. It would have saved you a journey.'

Maxwell approached, feet crunching over detritus on the floor. He looked past Blake at Reeve. 'This bastard's caused me a lot of trouble. I wanted to see him myself, before he disappears into some hole.' He reached Blake and stopped, regarding the bound man coldly. A twitch of his eyebrows as he took in Reeve's punished face. 'I see you started early.'

'Consider it my bonus for capturing him. I *told* you he'd come back to challenge his father, Tony.' Blake sounded pleased with himself to the point of gloating.

Maxwell was unimpressed. 'I hope he can still speak, otherwise interrogation might be a bit of a problem.'

A shrug from the other Operative. 'I'm sure he can hold a pen.'

Maxwell stepped up to Reeve. '*Can* you speak, Alex?'

Reeve considered staying silent, but knew it would gain him nothing except more pain. 'Yeah,' he croaked.

'Good. Because I have some questions.' Maxwell folded his arms. 'You and Craig Parker – two moles in one intake. We did a serious review of our recruitment procedures after that. Luckily, it wasn't my department. But I blame myself for not spotting you sooner. I should have been suspicious of you during training. When you told me how much you hated the British class system? That should have been a red flag.'

It took all Reeve's effort not to show surprise. His former tutor knew he'd never said any such thing. Parker had hacked his file, attributing his own actions to another. Maxwell told him he'd only discovered the change after Reeve was declared Fox Red.

Was it a covert signal? Blake wouldn't know about Reeve's altered file. Was Maxwell somehow trying to help him?

'You slipped,' Maxwell continued, 'and I slipped by not picking up on it. But now I want to know what other damage you did. Was Garald Morozov your contact? Deirdre and Mark identified him, and we know he's in town. Were you planning to give him the phone?'

Reeve picked his next words carefully. If he accidentally revealed that Maxwell had aided him, they were both dead. 'I told you when I caught you on the Tube, I'm not a Russian spy. Parker set me up. He hacked into your files to pin everything he did on to me. You know that!' That last came out with unintended desperation. He still wasn't sure of Maxwell's intentions. Was this some excuse to silence him?

The older man's face revealed nothing. He stared at Reeve for a long moment, then started to slowly circle him. 'You're still saying you're innocent? That you were Craig's patsy?'

'Yes!'

'And yet you were flagged for other things during training.'

'What things?'

'For starters, your attitude problem.'

That cemented it for Reeve. Maxwell *was* trying to assist him. His mentor had told him he'd considered him an exemplary recruit. 'An attitude problem doesn't make me a traitor.'

Maxwell stopped behind him. 'Great oaks from little acorns grow, as the saying goes. I should have done something about it.' He leaned closer to Reeve's ear. 'I would have given you one chance to put your hand out for help.'

A faint emphasis in his words. *Put your hand out.* Reeve's body blocked Blake's line of sight—

His uppermost bound hand opened. A moment passed – then something dropped into it. Reeve closed his fingers again. The object was cold, damp. Metal. Some piece of scrap Maxwell had picked up outside.

One edge was sharp.

'Maybe you would have taken it,' Maxwell continued, straightening. 'Or maybe you were already in too deep with the Russians.' He stepped back from the chair. 'It doesn't matter. We'll get the truth. Someone'll put their interrogation training to good use.' He moved back around Reeve, regarding his bruised face. 'The brute-force approach doesn't seem to have worked so far.'

'Oh, don't worry, Tony,' said Blake. 'If I'd been attempting an interrogation, I would have got results. That was just . . . catharsis.' His faux-amiability vanished. 'Giving the traitor what he deserves.'

'Luckily, you didn't beat him to death,' Maxwell replied cuttingly. Blake frowned. 'I need to update the boss.' Maxwell took out his phone, turning away from the other Operative.

Reeve could still see the screen, though. Maxwell wasn't accessing his contacts; it looked more like the notes app. He tapped at it, then brought the phone to his ear. 'Sir? Yes, it's me.'

Reeve could still glimpse the notepad. A fake call—

Maxwell listened, then spoke again. 'John Blake's here. Yes, it looks like he disobeyed the order to return to London.' He gave Blake an unblinking stare as he spoke. The other man looked distinctly uncomfortable. 'But what's important is that we captured Reeve.' Another silence as he pretended to take in Scott's words. 'Sir, I don't think that— Yes, sir. Understood. I'm on my way back.' He lowered the phone.

Blake eyed him. 'You're leaving?'

'The boss wants me back in London, so . . .' A resigned shrug.

'Long way to come for a ten-minute chat.'

'Call it karma for my sending you to Italy.' Both men shared half-smiles. Maxwell raised the phone again. This time, Reeve saw, he was making a genuine call. 'Mike, it's Tony. How long before you collect Reeve?' He listened, nodding – with a glance at the prisoner. 'Twenty minutes, okay. I was going to be here, but I have to get back to London. Call me once you've delivered him.' He disconnected. 'Okay, John. I'll see you later.' He departed. Blake watched him go.

While he was distracted, Reeve felt the object Maxwell had dropped into his hand. The piece of metal was about ten centimetres long, one end pointed. Its long edge was rusty, ragged. Enough to cut his bonds?

If it wasn't, his life would soon end. And Connie's would follow. Maxwell had given him a chance. He had to take it.

He fumbled the shard's edge towards the rope. A moment of fear as it slipped. If he dropped it—

He caught it. An involuntary gasp. More carefully, he gripped the metal piece again.

His noise caught Blake's attention. The black-haired man turned back to him. He smiled. 'Well,' he said, raising a fist, 'it seems we have a little time on our hands.'

CHAPTER 36

Reeve froze, clutching the shard tightly as the Operative approached. If Blake started beating him again, he might drop it. That would end his chances of escape – and expose Maxwell. Nobody else could have given it to him . . .

But Blake stopped short. 'Now, I could spend it giving you more of what you deserve. But, unlike Locke and Stone, I'm not a sadist. And I'd prefer you not to die before a proper interrogation. That's not to say—' His fist slammed against Reeve's jaw, snapping his head back. '—that I'm finished with you. But we'll see how things go, shall we?'

Breathing heavily, Reeve lifted his head. His whole body had flinched with the impact, almost jolting the shard from his grip. He secured it again, finding the edge. A twist of his wrist brought it against the rope. He began a small but firm sawing motion, back and forth against the strands.

The action was minor enough for Blake not to notice. He was more concerned with his own words. 'I always had my suspicions about you,' he said, regarding Reeve with disdain. 'You could never put your hand on your heart when it came to the country. You managed platitudes, but there was never any conviction behind them. Myself, though?' He turned slightly away, looking towards some unseen horizon. 'I'm not afraid to say I love my country. I would die to protect it. That's why I joined SC9. I might die in the line of duty, but . . . at least the gloves are off. No need to pussyfoot around with our enemies.'

He looked back at his prisoner as if expecting a response. Reeve locked eyes to show he was listening, but said nothing. All his concentration was on his makeshift saw. Back and forth, back and forth. He felt the rough edge catching on the rope. Was it cutting the strands? He had no way to check. All he could do was keep working.

Again, Blake was more interested in expressing his superiority. 'Everyone correctly guessed during training that I was in the Royal Navy. It was hardly a secret; I'm proud of it. My family have served in the navy for over three hundred years. One of my ancestors captained a ship in Nelson's fleet at Trafalgar. My father commanded another ship in the Gulf.' A sneer twisted his face. 'Remind me what *your* father did again? Oh, yes – he's a drunk, and a drug dealer, and a murderer. Worthless, utterly worthless. And the apple didn't fall far from the tree.'

His expectant look suggested he hoped to provoke an angry response. Reeve didn't take the bait. He had definitely cut through the rope's outer skin. There was still a long way to go to sever it, though.

Blake appeared irked at the lack of a reaction. 'You weren't ever the chatty sort, were you?' His fist clenched again. Reeve barely braced himself before the blow landed. He spat out blood and saliva, glaring at his attacker. Blake smirked. 'I never did see what drove you to join SC9,' he continued, stepping back. 'You always came across as . . .

empty. Hollow inside. I'd thought that if they ever invented androids, they'd probably act just like you. Of course,' he added, 'now it all makes sense. You were hiding your true intentions. You were a saboteur, a mole. A traitor.'

This time, the incoming punch was more telegraphed. That didn't make it hurt any less. Reeve couldn't contain a snarl of tormented fury. 'Mother*fucker*!'

'So there *is* some emotion in there after all,' mocked Blake. He kneaded his fingers. 'Even if it is only hatred. For me – for Britain. But that explains why you joined SC9, I suppose. To attack us from within. Now for *me*, it was duty. Pure and simple.'

He stepped back, again almost addressing an imaginary audience. 'I was a commander in the navy. I could have taken the easy route and pursued promotions. My own ship; eventually a place at the Admiralty. But I wanted . . . something more. I wanted to be *hands-on*.' Another glance at Reeve, as if to check he still had his attention. Reeve briefly paused in his task, shooting a nasty look back at him.

That was apparently enough. 'You see,' Blake went on, 'in the navy, you're trained to kill. But it's impersonal, abstracted. You kill ships, submarines, aircraft, shore targets. That there are people inside them is not really dwelled upon. And modern warships have very few windows. You could be in a pitched naval battle and never once see your enemy. It's almost unreal, like a game – blips on a screen. Over time, I realised I prefer something more human. To see your opponent. Man on man.' His jaw tightened. Reeve readied himself for another punch. It arrived a moment later. 'To make it *personal*.'

'So you joined SC9,' Reeve hissed.

'Not immediately,' Blake replied. He seemed almost pleased to have expanded his talk into a dialogue, however limited. 'I actually went to SIS. I imagined that would give me what I wanted. The James Bond fantasy version of MI6, I suppose. But it didn't take long to become disillusioned there as well. The place is hidebound, unbearably cliquey. And most of the work was done on computers. Monumentally tedious stuff. Even as a field officer, I spent most of my time indoors. But when I actually *got* into the field . . . my work caught SC9's attention.'

'You were good at killing.' The shard started to make faint rasping sounds as it cut. Reeve spoke more to cover the noise than to engage his captor. He could now feel the tear in the rope . . .

Blake nodded. 'As were we all. But it's where I learned my motto: "Always confirm the kill." It stood me in good stead at SIS – and it brought me to SC9.' Something elsewhere caught his attention. From outside came the clatter of a diesel engine.

More Operatives had arrived to collect their prize.

Blake gave Reeve a small, cruel smile. 'It's something I'll be doing to you soon enough. And then, on to your girlfriend. We have one thing in common: we both see the job through to the end. As I said, I always confirm the kill.' He moved towards the chair again, fists balling.

Reeve strained to pull his wrists apart. He felt the rope give, but not enough. No choice but to saw harder, even if Blake saw the motion. Three more strokes, the rusty blade rasping, but now Blake was on him—

270

Another punch landed. Reeve cried out. The sound was as much distraction as pain, drawing attention from his hands. Blake struck again. Blood gushed from Reeve's nose. He blew through his nostrils to clear them, red bubbles swelling. He twisted his wrists. Faint snaps from the rope as strands tore.

He rubbed the shard harder against his bonds. Blake drew his arm back once more—

A vehicle's door slammed outside. The Operative looked around. The new arrivals weren't yet in sight.

One last frantic slash – and Reeve put all his remaining strength into his arms. A shuddering roar of exertion escaped his mouth. Blake turned back to him—

The rope broke.

CHAPTER 37

Reeve's hand whipped up with snakelike speed. He plunged the shard's point into his captor's neck. Blake lurched back. Blood ran on to his collar.

Reeve seized his coat with his other hand. He pulled Blake sharply towards him. The Operative stumbled, toppling over Reeve's shoulder. Reeve grabbed him as he went. The overbalanced chair tipped backwards.

Both men fell. Blake hit the grimy concrete face-first. Reeve landed heavily on top of him. Metal cracked, the chair breaking apart. Reeve kicked. One leg came free. He rolled off the broken seat. The dazed Blake writhed beneath him. Reeve slammed an elbow against the back of his head. A solid *crack* as Blake's face struck the floor again.

A chair leg was still tied to Reeve's ankle. He yanked it free and hit Blake with it, then hurriedly rooted through his coat. His fingertips found leather: a shoulder holster. He snatched out Blake's gun.

Confirm the kill. He thumbed off the safety and brought the P320 to Blake's head—

'Blake?'

A voice from the entrance. Reeve whirled. A man came in—

Reeve fired. The initial snapshot narrowly missed his target. The second found it. The new arrival fell.

A second man was right behind him. He darted back behind cover.

Reeve jumped up, muscles trembling from cold and abuse. There was another doorway off to his left. He sent several suppressing shots at the entrance as he ran for it. The rounds smacked against brickwork, but did their job. The other Operative stayed out of sight. He reached the doorway, the air moving over his wet, naked body making him shiver.

The room beyond was dark, but broken windows let in the city's night-time glow. A workshop, long benches rotting away. He hurried past them. Grit and sharp debris on the floor stabbed at his feet. Behind, he heard a growled shout from Blake. 'I'm okay! Get after him!'

Reeve cursed at not having killed him, but escape was his priority. How to get out of the building?

An opening ahead where a door had been partly broken from its hinges. He ran to it. Glass crunched underfoot. He gasped, gritting his teeth. The gap wasn't wide enough to get through. He barged at it with his shoulder. One hit, two, and the wood splintered. He squeezed out into the open.

The long yard of the derelict works. Wind-blown drizzle washed over him. Reeve forced his trembling muscles back under control. He had to keep moving.

Streetlights beyond a crumbling wall fifty metres to his left. He ran towards it. Pain shot through both feet. Glass and splinters had embedded in his soles. He gasped, struggling to maintain pace—

An engine started. He looked back. Lights flared around

the building's corner. The Operative had returned to his vehicle rather than chasing him through the workshop.

Reeve knew he wouldn't reach the wall in time. Several battered metal drums stood nearby. He angled to them, ducking down.

The van, a long wheelbase Ford Transit, tore around the corner. Reeve peered between the barrels. The driver had his window down, gun arm out. Searching for his prey. He turned, headlights sweeping the yard. Nobody in sight. He accelerated, heading down the factory's length—

Reeve sprang up and fired all his remaining rounds at the windscreen.

Multiple bullets hit the driver. His outstretched arm flailed, the gun flying from his hand. The van veered towards the barrels. Reeve threw himself out of its path. It crashed into the empty containers and slewed to a stop.

Reeve ran to it. The driver, a large man in his late forties, was slumped in his seat. One cheek had been blasted gruesomely open, teeth and eye socket exposed. If he was still alive, he wouldn't be for long. Reeve clambered in and shoved him on to the passenger side. The rear compartment was separated from the cab by panelling. He guessed it was soundproofed: this was a covert prisoner transport vehicle. The engine had stalled. He restarted it. Into gear, and he swung the van back the way it had come.

He rounded the factory's corner. There was the gate – but Blake had emerged from the factory. One hand clutched his bloodied throat. The other held the first dead Operative's gun—

Reeve spun the wheel as Blake fired. The round punched

through the van's side just behind him. He kept turning to head directly away from the other man – then braked hard. The Transit skidded to a stop. Another bullet hit the rear door. It thunked against the panelling behind Reeve. The soundproofing was dense enough to catch the incoming fire.

He checked the mirrors. Blake's Audi was outside the building's entrance. Blake himself was running towards him. The rear compartment might be shielded, but the cab wasn't—

Reeve slammed the van into reverse. Foot down, hard. It lurched backwards. He kept his eyes on the mirrors. Blake jinked out of his path. Reeve turned to track him. The Operative was forced to dive clear as the Transit roared past.

Another course change. The Audi filled the mirrors. Reeve braced himself—

The Transit slammed into the car's front wing. The impact sent the Audi spinning. The larger, heavier van reeled to a standstill.

Reeve shoved the gear lever into first. Where was Blake?

Already recovering. His gun rose again—

Reeve ducked. The bullet-riddled windscreen finally shattered. Glinting little cubes of safety glass sprayed him. He stayed low as he accelerated, turning for the gate. More shots. One penetrated the passenger door, hitting the dead man with a wet thump. The van bounded over the potholed surface, then found smoother tarmac beyond the exit.

Reeve raised his head. A glance at the mirror told him he'd smashed Blake's front wheel. The Operative wouldn't be following. One last round caught the Transit's tail, then he was clear.

He couldn't keep driving the van for long. Houses ahead;

someone would have heard the gunfire. But he needed to get beyond Blake's reach. He kept going, taking turns at random. Where he was, he had no idea. The van had a satnav screen, but it was switched off. Another turn, thirty seconds more along the new road, then he risked pulling over.

First things first. He was freezing. The grim task of stripping the corpse's outer clothing took a minute. The Operative was about his size, slightly broader; the jacket and trousers fitted. He plucked glass from both feet, then tried the shoes. They were tight, but would have to do. Then he checked the dead man's belongings. Wallet, phone, a set of keys. He only took the first. The phone could be tracked; he expected the van could too. A look inside the wallet. Cards; useless, as again they could be traced. About five hundred pounds in cash – far more valuable. He pocketed the banknotes. Various IDs naming the driver as Jack Fraser. Reeve remembered seeing the name in Parker's stolen files. One of SC9's longer-serving Operatives. Perhaps retired from frontline missions, but still active in support roles like kidnapping and interrogation.

Not any more. Reeve drew back from the body and switched on the satnav. He was roughly two miles from Clayton. Reachable on foot, even with his injuries. He just had to avoid the police.

But he was trained to do exactly that. He wiped away any fingerprints as best he could, then got out. Even with shoes on, his feet hurt as they took his full weight. Ignoring the pain, he set off.

A siren sounded in the distance. But by the time the police found the bullet-pocked van, Reeve was gone.

CHAPTER 38

It took Reeve longer than expected to reach Ally's home. Part of the reason was that he took a circuitous route to avoid the cops.

The rest was that his whole body hurt. His arms and legs from being tightly bound, head and chest from Blake's beatings. The adrenalin of his escape had now burned out. He was left weak, aching, cold. His single layer of clothing did little to keep out the damp chill.

It was well after one o'clock when he arrived. The house was dark. He didn't want to wake Ally or Daisy, but had no choice. He rapped on the door.

No answer. He waited, then tried again, louder. A light came on inside. 'Who is it?' Ally demanded. 'I've got my phone – I can call 999 in two seconds.'

'It's me. Dominic,' Reeve replied.

'Dominic?' A rattle of chains and deadbolts, and the door opened. Ally flinched in shock when she saw his bloodied face. 'Oh, my God!'

'Can I come in, please?' he said.

'Yeah, yes. Oh, Jesus!' She quickly ushered him inside and locked the door. 'What happened to you?'

'Had a run-in with my dad and his mates.' It wasn't technically a lie.

'Jesus,' she repeated. Then she remembered she was holding her phone. 'I'll call an ambulance.'

'No, no.' Reeve put his hand on hers. 'If I go to hospital, they'll find me.' The cover story came easily. It was more or less what he'd said to Connie when he first met her.

'Then call the police.'

'I can't. They'd arrest me rather than him.'

She eyed him. 'Because of what you said in court to put your dad in prison?'

So she *had* known the full story. 'Yeah. Doesn't matter that I was only a kid. There's no statute of limitations on perjury.'

Ally regarded him uncertainly – then shook her head. 'Come on, into the bathroom.'

She led him up the stairs. Reeve was relieved that his arrival hadn't woken Daisy. His appearance would probably have terrified her. They entered the bathroom, Ally taking a large first-aid kit from a cabinet. She opened the box; it was well-stocked. 'You have to be ready for anything when you have a child,' she said. 'Although this wasn't what I expected.'

Reeve lowered the toilet seat and sat upon it. He managed a faint, fat-lipped smile. 'Me neither.'

She shook her head, more exasperated than amused. 'All right. I'll try to clean you up.'

The process was drawn-out and painful. Ally was horrified to find he'd lost a tooth. He used a wad of gauze to soak up blood from his gum. There were also numerous cuts: hands, arms, feet. Tweezers picked out glass fragments, stinging antiseptic cream applied. But eventually the work was done. She held up a mirror for Reeve to see himself. Even with the blood and dirt removed, he was a mess. One eye was puffed and blackened, his lips split, nose swollen and tender.

Ally regarded him with sympathetic sorrow. 'I did my best, but . . . that must really hurt.'

'Yeah.' Even with the gauze, he still had blood on his teeth as he spoke. 'Still, at least it wasn't a gunshot wound this time.'

'This time?'

'That's how I met Connie. I'd been shot.'

'You'd been—' Ally gasped. 'God. I'd wondered what this was.' He had taken off the coat, leaving himself topless while she worked. The scar of a bullet wound on his left arm was clearly visible. 'I thought you sold paper towels! Why did someone shoot you?'

'Dissatisfied customer.'

She let out an involuntary laugh. 'Idiot.' Her hand rose as if to swat his face, but she thought better of it. 'So that's not really what you do?'

'No. I *was* in the army, like I told you, then I joined special forces.' Another technical truth. 'Ran into some bad people.'

'But you're not in special forces now?'

'Not any more, no. I left. Moved away with Connie.'

'Oh.' Ally was briefly silent, lips pursed. 'She . . . she must be somebody special.'

Reeve nodded. 'She is.'

'Where is she?'

'In Italy. That's where we've been living.'

'She didn't come with you?'

279

'I told her to stay there so she'd be safe.' He indicated his face. 'So this wouldn't happen to her.'

She narrowed her eyes thoughtfully. 'You came back to see your dad, didn't you?'

'Not specifically. I really did have some business in London. But . . . yeah,' he admitted. 'That was part of why I came here.'

'Right.' Her emotions were unreadable, though Reeve suspected disappointment was strong amongst them. 'It's late,' she went on, changing the subject. 'You need to get some rest.'

'I'll sleep on the sofa,' he offered.

'Don't be ridiculous. You go in my bed. I'll sleep in Mum and Dad's.'

'Are you sure?'

A hint of her old humour. 'You should know better than to argue with me, Dominic Finch. I always win. Come on.'

She led him along the landing. 'Daisy's in there, so try not to wake her up,' she said, indicating one door. She opened another. 'Here.'

'Thanks, Ally,' he said, managing a smile.

She returned it. 'See you in the morning, Dominic.' She turned, giving him a last glance over her shoulder, then walked away. Reeve watched her go, then entered her bedroom. He was asleep within moments of lying down.

A noise woke him. A door opening? He raised his head, exhausted, confused. An unfamiliar room, morning half-light seeping through the curtains. His whole body hurt. Movement – someone climbing on to the bed. He sat up sharply—

A high-pitched scream made his ears ring.

Reeve jerked back as Daisy shrieked in terror. She leapt from the bed and ran out. 'Mummy! *Mummy!* There's a man in your bed, a scary man! Mummy!'

'No, no, Daisy, it's okay!' Reeve cried after her. A moment later, Ally also offered frantic reassurance. He hurriedly pulled on his trousers.

'It's okay, lovie, it's okay,' said Ally, emerging on to the landing. 'Dominic?'

'I'm here,' he said, peering around the door. Daisy was hiding behind her mother. 'Sorry, sorry.'

'That's all right,' Ally said, blowing out a sharp breath. 'Wow. That woke me up.'

'Me too.' He looked at the little girl, who shrank back. 'Sorry I scared you. I . . . had an accident. Your mummy let me stay the night.'

It was apparently enough of an explanation. 'That's why your face is all purple?' Daisy looked more closely at him, then tugged at Ally's pyjamas. 'Mummy, find my colouring book.'

'In a minute, lovie.' Ally gave Reeve a joking shrug of helplessness. 'How are you feeling?'

He decided the truth was best not said in front of a three-year-old. 'Fine,' he said, making it clear that was far from the whole truth.

She nodded. 'Let me sort things out with Daisy, then I'll get you breakfast. I'll find you some clothes too. My dad might have something.'

'I've got more clothes at my hotel.'

'You can't go out in just trousers and a coat,' she insisted.

'You don't even have any socks. You look like a tramp. I mean, you never were super-stylish, but . . .'

'Funny,' said Reeve, acknowledging that she was winding him up. Ally smiled again, then went with her daughter.

She returned a few minutes later with a baggy green jumper. 'Dad never wears this, so I doubt he'll miss it,' she said. 'I got you some socks as well.'

He took them. 'Thanks.'

'No underpants, though. That would have felt . . . weird. And you were in the army, so you're probably used to going commando.'

'No, we always wore pants.' He kept his expression deadpan, pretending not to have understood her joke.

Not deadpan enough. 'Are you trying to wind *me* up?' she said after a moment of suspicion.

'Yes.'

She smiled. 'I guess Connie's been a good influence. Okay, you get dressed while I do breakfast.'

Reeve joined her downstairs a few minutes later. Bread was in the toaster, and she was frying eggs. Daisy gave him a wary look as he sat opposite, but kept drawing. Ally soon brought him a plate of food. 'Thanks,' he said.

'My pleasure,' she replied. She watched as he started to eat. He winced. 'Oh – are you all right?'

'Just got some hot egg right in my missing tooth.'

She cringed. 'How do you feel? In general, I mean.'

'I'm okay.' It was a gross exaggeration. His swollen eye and lips had started to go down, but still hurt. 'Amazingly, I've felt worse.'

'Like when you got shot?'

Reeve's eyes flicked to Daisy, but the little girl was more interested in her colouring book. 'Yeah. That wasn't much fun.'

'And Connie fixed you up?' asked Ally. 'You said she was a nurse.' He nodded. 'How did you end up in Italy?'

'Her mum was Italian. So she qualified for an Italian passport, which meant she was an EU citizen again. We travelled around Europe for a while before staying in Italy.' It was a potted, and sanitised, version of events. He didn't want to give away any specifics, even to someone he trusted. Not after what happened with Mickey.

'How did you manage it, though? You're not an EU citizen.'

'I stayed a bit under the radar.'

A look of sly amusement. 'I'm shocked. Not. But,' Ally became serious again, 'why did you come back here?'

'Like I said, I had some business in London. But it was connected to my dad.'

'About him getting out of prison?'

He nodded. 'I . . . I know seeing him was a mistake. A painful one, as well.' He indicated his wounded face. 'Connie didn't want me to come, and she was right. But I couldn't let him get away with what he did to Mum. I just *couldn't*.'

'So you made Connie stay in Italy – to protect her?'

'Yes. I didn't want her to get hurt. I won't *let* her get hurt.'

'Do you love her?'

The directness of the question caught him by surprise. 'Yes,' he replied, without thinking.

Ally smiled again – with a hint of sadness, he thought. But it was quickly hidden. 'I'm really happy for you, Dominic.

283

I'm glad you found someone.' An attempt at insouciance. 'Would have been nice if it'd been me, but . . .'

'You wouldn't have had Daisy,' Reeve reminded her.

'I wouldn't, no. So things worked out in that respect.'

'You'll find someone too,' he assured her. 'Things happen when you least expect them.'

Her old cheekiness returned. 'Maybe I should get someone to shoot me.'

'I absolutely would *not* recommend it.'

They both laughed. 'I did find someone, a couple of times,' Ally went on. 'One of them ran a mile the moment I told him I was pregnant. The other one, well . . .' Her eyes didn't leave his. 'He couldn't stay. That was a long time ago, though.'

'I'm sorry.'

'It wasn't your fault. Not at all.' Another smile, this one wistful. 'Go back to her, Dominic. Make the most of love. Sometimes it lasts for ever, like my mum and dad. They've been married over fifty years! Other times, though . . . you have to enjoy what you have. While it lasts.'

'I will.' He reached over to hold her hand, giving her a warm look. 'Thanks, Ally. For everything.'

'No problem.' They sat still for a long moment, his hand still on hers. Finally, she spoke again. 'Are you going back to Italy?'

'Not just yet. I'll see you again before I go.'

'Good.' She gently squeezed his fingers, then slowly withdrew. 'Is there anything else you need?'

Reeve shook his head. 'Just that phone.'

CHAPTER 39

Reeve returned to his hotel. He'd booked it for several days, wanting a base of operations. There had been nothing on him when he was captured to lead SC9 to it. He'd paid in cash, the key always left at the front desk.

Despite that, he was wary as he approached his room. The receptionist had been shocked at the sight of him. 'I got mugged,' was his explanation. Had anyone left a message or asked to see him? No on both counts. Her answers seemed genuine. But there was still doubt, justifiable paranoia . . .

It *was* only paranoia, though. Nobody was waiting for him. The room had been cleaned, but his belongings seemed untouched. He checked them just in case. Certain items in his bag had been carefully positioned against each other. They hadn't moved.

SC9 hadn't found his bolt-hole.

They would soon. But he would no longer be in it.

He put down the items he'd just bought. All were mundane – but would be essential. After leaving Ally, he spent the morning devising a plan. Two plans, actually. One regarding SC9; the other, his father. They were, however, interlinked.

They also both involved considerable risk. There was a

chance he wouldn't see either through alive. All he could do was minimise the danger.

The most immediate threat was one he had to face. He needed to power up Parker's phone. That would draw SC9 to his location. But it would catch the attention of others as well.

He was counting on it.

He was *depending* on it.

Reeve took the phone from the Faraday bag. A pensive breath, then he plugged in the charger.

The screen lit up, battery starting to charge. He peeled the tape from the cameras and microphone. How long before the Russians could access them? More Operatives would surely have joined Blake. They could be close by. If they reached the hotel before he left, he was dead.

The phone's boot-up sequence began. Reeve sat on the bed, listening for speeding vehicles, running footsteps . . .

The grid of icons. The phone was now active. He had to hope the Russian spyware was too. He waited another thirty seconds, using the time to switch on his remaining burner phone. Then he spoke.

'This is Alex Reeve,' he said – in fluent Russian. Another language learned during SC9's training. 'I know you can hear me. I'm willing to offer you a deal. You get me safely out of this country and back to Italy. In return, I'll give you this phone – and all the files on it. If you're interested, call me.' He recited the burner's number. 'But be quick. SC9 will already be tracking me. So if you want Parker's phone, we need to talk, *right now*.'

He waited. How long dare he stay? Even five minutes was

dangerous. Three? Two? GCHQ's computers would have detected the phone by now. That information would be passed on to SC9. Operatives could already be coming—

A sharp trill echoed around the room. The burner phone was ringing.

A moment's hesitation – then Reeve answered.

Later that day, he was back in Clayton.

The phone call had been brief, his terms prepared. As soon as they were accepted, he rebagged Parker's phone and left. Now he had to see if the Russians were as good as their word.

Reeve followed an evasive route to his former home. There were no signs of pursuit. He was still being cautious, though, not wanting to draw attention. Luckily, the miserable weather kept other people's minds on their own affairs.

He needed to be careful now, however. His old house might be boarded up, but it had neighbours. He walked down the street, glancing through the windows of the adjoining properties. One was occupied, a television on in the living room. The other was dark. He went around the block, doubling back along the alley behind the terrace. Again, no lights in the second house. Was anyone watching from other windows? Nobody in sight.

He reached his back gate. It was chained shut. But the wall was low enough to scale easily. Another glance around. Still nobody visible. He hoisted his belongings on to the wall's top, then swiftly climbed over.

The yard beyond was overgrown, paving cracked. Rubbish was strewn everywhere. Momentary disquiet: his mother had always tried to keep it tidy. He went to the back door. Like the front, it was boarded up. Someone had attempted to break in, the wood damaged. They'd done part of his work for him. A crowbar was amongst his new possessions. He set to work on the barrier. It soon gave way.

The door behind it brought back memories. Rippled glass, now smashed; blue paint, scabbed and faded. Quick effort forced it open. He went inside.

His entrance left him even more unnerved. The kitchen was exactly as he remembered – in form. But everything was filthy, broken. A mug on a counter was covered in cobwebs, filled with mould. The logo of Manchester City football team was visible under the dirt. His father's.

He took out another purchase, a torch, and moved deeper into the house. The beam revealed the dining room. Stairs led upwards. A tray sat on the table. Again, it was familiar. He'd chosen it on a shopping trip with his mother. It bore a cheery picture of colourful birds. They were now almost lost beneath dust and grime.

Reeve moved through a door into the living room. The front door, barred by planks, was in the far corner. Dim light oozed around the boards covering the windows, picking out furniture. The sofa, now decayed by damp. His father's armchair. The television it had faced was gone, probably stolen.

His torch picked out one wall. Marks were visible beneath the peeling paper: dents. He felt a sickening chill. His father had made them when he kicked Reeve's pet cat to death. One of his many drunken rages. Reeve and his mother had also been on the receiving end. His jaw tightened in resurgent anger. Again and again, Jude Finch had got away with monstrous acts.

Not this time. Reeve took a breath, then started his preparations.

Mickey Rowland hurried out of the takeaway's kitchen, cargo in hand. He quickly put the delivery box on his back. One of the shop's 'special orders'. A pot of sauce hid something extra: three wraps of heroin. That was the reason for his haste. People who received their drugs and food in good time usually tipped well.

He unchained his bike and made a rolling start. His destination was a mile away. If the early evening traffic was with him, he could be there in five minutes. That should be good for at least a tenner.

He rode through the car park, rounding the building's corner—

Someone's arm swung at his head.

It was as solid as a tree branch. It hit Mickey square in his face, knocking him backwards off his ride. The delivery box collapsed under him, contents crushed.

Dazed, nose pulsing with pain, Mickey looked up—

The man he knew as Dominic Finch gazed stonily down at him. His face was bruised. 'Mickeyyyy,' he said. There was no friendliness in his voice.

'Oh, shit, shit!' Mickey gasped, scrambling back. 'Dommo, it – it wasn't my fault! Your dad made me set you up!'

'Right,' came the unimpressed reply. 'And I'm sure he didn't pay you thirty pieces of silver to do it.'

A moment of incomprehension. 'No, two hundred quid,'

was the confused admission. 'But I had to tell him, or he would've beaten the shit out of me.'

'And you think I won't?' Reeve stepped closer.

Mickey frantically waved his hands as if to ward him off. 'You don't understand. When I was sent down, Jude – your dad was in the same prison. He knew me. He – he didn't exactly look after me, that's not what he's like.'

'Yeah. I know.'

'But I started doing stuff for him. I was on his team. That meant other people who would've tried to fuck with me left me alone. I – I *owed* him, Dommo. Even though I know what he's like, how scary he is. That's why I'm doing this now.' He gestured at the overturned bike. 'Your dad's in charge of the drug stuff. I'm still working for him.' His voice became pleading. 'I *had* to tell him about you. If I hadn't, he would have found out anyway.'

Reeve took another step. Mickey cringed. Then: 'I *should* beat the shit out of you, Mickey. But I won't. You don't need to be scared of my dad any more – he's going back to prison.'

A mixture of confusion, relief and worry in Mickey's eyes. 'How come?'

'I've got proof he murdered my mum. He won't be able to deny it this time. So if you stay out of prison, he can't hurt you.' He glanced at the broken box. 'I'd start by getting out of the drug delivery business.'

'I was planning to, Dommo, honest,' said Mickey, nodding vigorously. 'How're you going to put him back in prison? I thought you couldn't be tried for the same thing twice.'

'You can if there's new evidence. Which I've got.'

'What is it?'

Reeve stepped back. 'I'm sure it'll be in the news after he's arrested. I'm going to give it to the police tomorrow.'

'Tomorrow? Why don't you do it now?'

'Got some stuff to take care of first. I need to make sure everything's totally watertight. I don't want that bastard getting off on some technicality.'

Mickey shook his head. 'No, no. You don't.' His gaze fixed more solidly upon Reeve, becoming thoughtful. 'You need any help from me?'

'No, I'm sorted. Although,' he added, 'I could use some hot food. I can't cook anything – I'm hiding out in my old house.'

'What're you doing there?' Mickey asked, surprised.

'It's the last place anyone'd think to look for me.' He indicated his face. 'I don't want my dad or his mates finding me again.'

'Yeah, that'd be bad.' A faint, stressed laugh. 'I can fix that for you. Least I can do. I'll bring you some chicken round tonight. What time?'

'About nine o'clock; I'll be there all night. Oh, and come to the back door. I've opened it up. You'll have to climb the wall, though – the gate's locked.'

'Back door. Right.' Mickey took mental notes. 'I'm really sorry about what happened, Dommo. I was just scared of your dad. Everyone is.'

'Not for much longer.' Reeve held out a hand. 'You'd better get moving. That food's going cold.'

Mickey took it and pulled himself up. He fumbled the box from his back and looked inside. 'Don't think they'll accept this lot. It's a bit fucked. I'll have to get more made. I'll tell 'em I got knocked off the bike. Which . . . I actually was.' Another small, humourless laugh.

Reeve nodded. 'Yeah. See you later, Mickey.' He walked away.

Mickey watched him go, then retrieved his bike and turned back. He stopped short of the kitchen entrance, though. Instead he glanced warily over his shoulder before using his phone. 'Mr Finch?' he whispered, on getting an answer. 'It's Mickey. Mickey Rowland.' Another nervous look back. His childhood friend was not in sight. 'Listen. I need to see you again. It's about Dominic.' He clenched his lips together, then: 'I know where he is.'

CHAPTER 40

The night-time streets were quiet. Mid-week, in the rain, few people were out.

Which suited Jude Finch perfectly. The fewer people who saw him, the better.

Skels was driving, guiding his lowered Peugeot 208 GTi through Clayton. It wasn't the most inconspicuous car, being a lurid green. Finch thought it was hideous. But it would still stand out less in the neighbourhood than his Range Rover.

'Down here,' he said as they neared a corner.

'Thought your old place was further on,' said Skels. The nickname was short for 'skeleton'. He'd been on the skinny side before becoming obsessed with bodybuilding.

'It is,' Finch shot back. 'That's why we're not fucking parking there. You don't leave your own car outside where you're going to beat someone up.'

'Beat someone up, yeah,' echoed Boyzie from the back seat. The wiry man was one of Finch's oldest, most trusted friends. He recognised the faint sarcasm in the words. They both knew that beating up Finch's son was only the beginning.

They were going to kill him.

Skels pulled up. 'Okay, everyone ready?' Finch asked. Boyzie produced his flick-knife, the blade popping out with a sharp *tchack*. Skels, meanwhile, drew what had been Reeve's revolver. Finch checked his own – formerly Trick's – weapon. 'Let's go.'

They got out and continued on to the alley behind Finch's old home. Finch surveyed the windows overlooking it. Almost all had their curtains closed. As he'd expected. With the dwellings so close together, privacy was at a premium.

They reached the house. Finch paused. This was the first time he'd been here in sixteen years. The sight produced no nostalgia, no feelings, good or bad. It was just somewhere he'd lived. The ground floor windows were boarded up. A closer look at the back door. The wood covering it had been forced open.

'Let's have a look,' he said. 'Keep quiet.'

He clambered into the overgrown yard. Skels and Boyzie followed. Glass and debris crunched underfoot. Finch scowled. Would they be heard? He signalled for them to stop, then listened. No activity inside. More carefully, they advanced again.

Finch went to the dining room window. He peered around the board's edge. The gap was too narrow to reveal any details . . .

But there was a glow inside.

His son was here.

'There's a light on – he's in there,' he whispered. 'Get that board out of the way. Quietly.' Boyzie and Skels went to the door and manoeuvred the wooden panel clear.

Finch glanced at the houses overlooking the yard. Nobody was watching. 'Skels, go in and check the kitchen.' He drew his gun and thumbed off the safety as Skels cautiously stepped through the doorway. Boyzie took out his knife and followed the bodybuilder inside.

'It's empty,' Skels whispered.

Finch entered. The kitchen was dark, lit only by spill from elsewhere. Skels crept towards the doorway. 'He must be in the front room,' he muttered. 'There's a lamp or someth—'

He crossed the threshold – and something hit him so hard that bone cracked.

Skels flew backwards, almost knocking Boyzie down. He fell at Finch's feet, dropping the revolver and clutching his chest. An animalistic squeal of pain escaped through clenched teeth. 'God, oh, God!' he gasped. 'I can't – I can't fucking breathe!'

Finch whipped his gun up at the doorway. The object that had hit Skels was silhouetted across it. A plank, still juddering from its forceful swing. A large metal bracket was gaffer-taped to its end. Its blunt edge had caught Skels squarely in the chest. A length of string ran from it across the dining room.

Boyzie looked nervously through the doorway. 'It's a fucking booby-trap. Maybe he's not here. Jude, we should fuckin' leave.'

'He's here,' Finch said firmly. The string was the trigger – and someone had pulled it.

'Fuck, oh, God!' Skels cried, writhing in agony. 'It's broken my fucking ribs! Get an ambulance!'

Boyzie looked to Finch for confirmation. 'Don't you fucking dare,' the big man growled. 'The cops'll come as well. Skels, get up. Get up!' He glared at Boyzie. 'Fucking help him, you idiot.'

The other man's mouth pinched at the insult, but he crouched to lift his friend. Skels screeched as he staggered upright. Finch had no sympathy. 'Got your phone?' he asked. Skels managed to nod. 'Go back to your car before you call nine-nine-nine. Do *not* tell anyone you were with me. Understand?' Another nod. 'Right. Get moving.'

'How'm I going to climb over the wall?' Skels whined.

'I don't fucking care, as long as you do it quietly.' The injured man staggered out into the yard.

Finch gestured for Boyzie to collect the dropped gun and follow him. 'Dominic?' he called as he warily ducked under the plank. 'Your dad's home. Come on out.'

The only light came from the living room. Finch checked under the table. No one there. But his son had been in here when he triggered the trap. He'd either gone into the front room, or up the stairs. Where was he hiding?

The thought triggered a memory. There was a cupboard by the front door. It contained the electricity meter, and had been used to store coats and shoes. Dominic once tried to hide from him inside it. He might still fit . . .

He took out his phone and switched on its torch. A brief sweep of the stairs. They were clear. Only two bedrooms and the bathroom on the upper floor. They offered few hiding places even for a child, never mind a grown man. 'I'm going into the front. Boyzie, see if he's up there.'

Boyzie snorted. 'What, on me own?'

'You want me to hold your fucking hand? You've got a gun now. If you see him, shoot him.' The wiry man begrudgingly used his own phone to light the way upstairs.

Finch moved to the living-room entrance. The light came

from an LED lantern on the floor. Bags revealed his son had set up camp. He cautiously pushed the door fully open. The hinges creaked, but no traps were sprung.

One foot placed to block the door if it suddenly swung back, he entered. The cold light made the once-familiar room seem alien. The front door was in the far corner, barred by planks. Dominic couldn't have escaped that way. The mouldering furniture cast black shadows against the walls. He shone his torch into them. His son wasn't there.

That left only one place he could be.

He heard footsteps overhead. 'Boyzie?' he called. 'You seen him?'

'Not yet,' came the reply. 'Front bedroom's empty. Going to check the back rooms.'

The bathroom was small, with no possible hiding places. That just left the boy's bedroom. A small wardrobe and beneath the bed itself were the only options for concealment. They were cramped, awkward. If Dominic was in either, he wouldn't be able to get out in a hurry. He would be vulnerable.

Finch was sure his son knew that. But the front door cupboard was easier to get into – and out of. He advanced on it, gun ready. 'Dominic,' he said, mocking confidence returning to his voice. 'Playing hide and seek, are you? You've forgotten something – I always found you.' He pocketed his phone and brought his free hand towards the cupboard's handle. 'Coming, ready or not . . .'

He yanked open the door—

The cupboard was empty.

CHAPTER 41

Upstairs, Boyzie checked the bathroom. It was so cramped he could have touched both sides at once. Nowhere to hide.

That left the back bedroom.

Gun raised, he shoved the door open. It banged against the wall. No one behind it. He raised his phone's light. A single bed, mattress damp and torn. He crouched to peer under it. The torch beam reached unobstructed to the wall beyond. Clear.

That left the wardrobe. Finger tight on the trigger, he opened it—

Nothing inside but coat hangers. Boyzie shrugged, a little relieved. 'Not up here,' he announced, returning to the landing.

The room fell back into darkness. Stillness for a moment . . .

Then the mattress began to rise.

'What do you mean, he's not up there?' Finch demanded from below. 'He must be!'

Boyzie halted at the top of the stairs. 'I checked all the rooms.'

'Then check 'em again! He's definitely not down here.'

'There a loft?'

'No. Did you check the airing cupboard in the front bedroom?'

'Course I bloody did,' he said, but under his breath. All the same, he went for another look.

Nothing had changed in the last minute. He squatted to check beneath the bedframe again. Just dirt under it. The wardrobe's doors were missing, only an empty carcass remaining. That left the cupboard . . .

Its door was open. The upper half was wooden shelves, a few rotten towels on them. Below was the hot water tank, lagging jacket torn. Thieves had stolen all the copper piping. The tank itself was wedged in too tightly to remove without tearing out a wall. No room to fit a person either.

Jude couldn't accuse him of not checking properly. He stared at the tank for a last moment—

A hand clamped hard over his face.

Reeve had hurried upstairs in the confusion after springing the booby-trap. There was only one place he'd ever successfully hidden from his father. Not under his bed; under his *mattress*. It was supported by strong elasticated straps rather than wooden cross-beams. There was enough give in the straps to let him slide beneath the mattress unnoticed. From above, it looked flat, with no giveaway bumps. The bedframe's side panels were deep enough to conceal him.

It had worked for him as a kid. It still did.

He silently pushed the mattress away, then rolled off the bed. The wiry man was talking on the landing. He heard

Finch order him to check the main bedroom again. Footsteps as the man entered the room.

Reeve followed him. His target was examining the airing cupboard. He moved up behind him – then struck.

His hand locked solidly over Boyzie's mouth and nostrils. His other fist slammed with brutal force into his kidneys. The man convulsed, a cry choked in his throat. Reeve hit him again. Then he seized him around the neck in a choke-hold. His opponent struggled, squirming helplessly . . . then went limp. His gun clunked to the mouldering carpet.

Reeve laid him quietly on the floor and pocketed the weapon. Then he headed downstairs.

Now for his father.

Finch shoved the old sofa aside. His anger grew: Dominic wasn't behind it. So where the fuck *was* he?

Footsteps on the stairs. Boyzie returning. He went to the doorway. 'Have you found him? He's got to—'

He expected to see his friend. His son was there instead.

Finch's gun was at his side. He whipped it up – but Reeve intercepted it.

One hand clamped around his wrist, the other the gun itself. It was twisted from his grip, bending his index finger backwards. Finch instinctively jerked away in pain. He recovered – to find the automatic pointed at him. 'Shit,' he gasped, backing up.

Reeve followed him into the room. 'I knew Mickey'd tell you I was here,' he said. 'So I lied to him about having evidence against you. Going to kill me to protect yourself, were you?'

Finch's gaze darted between the gun's muzzle and his son's eyes. Both were equally threatening. His heart raced as the gun rose towards his face—

Then Reeve thumbed the magazine eject. It clunked to the floor. He tugged back the slide. The chambered round spun across the room. He tossed the empty gun behind the sofa.

Finch glanced briefly after it. 'Not going to shoot me?'

'I should have done. But it'd be too quick.' Reeve raised his fists, taking up a boxing stance.

Finch's exhalation was part relief, part mockery. His son was going to *fight* him? Even fully grown, he was still shorter and lighter. 'That's big talk, from a little shit,' he said with a sneer. He brought up his own fists. 'I'm not fucking scared of you, Dominic.'

'You should be. Before I'm done, you'll be as scared as Mum was when you killed her.'

A sarcastic laugh. 'That bitch. She fucking ruined my life! Getting pregnant, wanting to get married. And I fucking gave in to her! I should've made her have an abortion.' His voice dropped to a malevolent growl. 'And if she hadn't done it . . . I should have fucking kicked you out of her.'

Reeve stared at him, emotion slowly breaking through his cold mask—

Then he charged at his father with a roar of fury.

One fist rushed at Finch's head. The bigger man was nearly caught off-guard by the sudden attack. He jerked backwards. Reeve's knuckles slammed against his cheek. The blow jarred his senses. Before he could recover, another punch struck his stomach.

It would have bent most men double. But Finch hadn't spent sixteen years sitting idle in his prison cell. In a dog-eat-dog environment, the fittest dog got the meat. And he'd never gone hungry. He was stronger in his fifties, muscles more solid, than in his thirties. The strike hurt – but he took it.

Then he hit back.

An angry sweep of his arm caught Reeve's chest, knocking him away. Finch turned to follow. A left jab at his head. Reeve deflected it, catching a bruising blow to his forearm.

Finch pressed his attack. Another jab, again deflected – but he followed with a rapid right hook. This got through, scoring a ringing strike on Reeve's ear. He staggered, hurriedly retreating. 'You've grown up,' Finch scoffed, 'but you still hit like a fucking pansy.'

He closed again—

Reeve jinked to avoid his next jab – then ducked under his arm. His own hook pounded Finch's unprotected side. A breathy grunt exploded from the older man's mouth.

'Not as much fun when they hit back, is it?' Reeve snarled. 'Not like when you murdered Mum!'

His father didn't reply. He'd underestimated his son. That wouldn't happen again. He advanced, both hands raised. His right fist lanced at his opponent's face. Reeve pulled back from the jab. Another strike, this a swinging left hook – aimed lower, at his liver. Reeve snapped his right arm down to block it. Before he could pull away, Finch drove another opportunistic jab at him. It caught Reeve's chin, snapping his head back. He spat out blood.

'Fucking right you should have shot me,' growled Finch. 'You wouldn't be getting hurt so much, would you, *Dominic*?'

The name was said with venom. He swung again, a murderous right cross aimed at his son's face—

Reeve caught it.

One hand clapped tightly around Finch's fist, the other seizing his wrist. He twisted his upper body, forcing his left elbow against his father's forearm. A hard shove would bend his arm back the wrong way, breaking it—

Finch knew what he was trying to do. He lunged, using his weight advantage to shove the younger man backwards.

Reeve lost his hold – then retaliated. His left arm whipped up. Finch pulled his head back – but Reeve's fist still clipped his jaw. He lowered his arm, about to grab his father's throat—

Finch dropped his chin – and bit him.

'Jesus!' Reeve gasped. He jerked sharply away. The bigger man drew back his arm for another strike.

Reeve was quicker. His fingers stabbed at Finch's eyes. Finch ducked to protect his sight. The movement threw off his punch. It only grazed Reeve's cheekbone.

But now his hand was in his son's face. Finch took advantage, savagely hooking his thumb into Reeve's mouth. He pulled hard, exposing his son's teeth in a grotesque grimace. Reeve tried to pull clear. Finch gouged at his eyes—

Reeve's arm swept up at Finch's forearm. The blow knocked his hand away from Reeve's face. But it also left Reeve open as he regained his balance.

Finch swung again. His elbow pounded into Reeve's chest. The younger man stumbled backwards through the dining room doorway.

He recovered. Finch expected him to run—

Instead he returned to the living room.

A mistake, and Finch would make him pay for it. He tackled Reeve against the wall. Plaster and lath crunched beneath the damp wallpaper. Both men fell to the floor – Finch on top.

Finch punched Reeve's face, then clamped a hand around his throat. He squeezed, pushing down with his full weight. Reeve flailed at him, but couldn't score a solid strike. Finch gave him a sadistic, snarling smile. 'It's funny – this is where I killed your mum,' he crowed. 'This is *how* I killed your mum! That fucking bitch. She was going to leave! She was going to walk out on me. Nobody fucking walks out on Jude Finch!'

He levered himself higher. Reeve's blows became weaker, more desperate. 'So I put her in the ground, on the moors,' Finch went on. 'Where I should have fucking put you too. But now I'll do it right. And nobody'll find the hole this time. You're *dead*, you little piece of shit!'

His hand clenched even tighter. Reeve's straining face turned red, choking, dying—

A phone rang.

The sound startled Finch. It wasn't his. Somewhere behind him, high up. He looked around. The noise came from above the boarded front window. A black rectangle was taped to the curtain track—

Reeve's fist slammed up at his jaw like a steel piston.

The punch's force cracked a tooth. Finch's head snapped back. Dizzied, he thumped against the wall. His weight shifted off Reeve's body. His son immediately kneed him in the groin. Finch convulsed. He felt Reeve slide out from beneath him, but could do nothing to stop his escape.

His son stood over him – then kicked him, hard. Again, and again. And again. Reeve roared, louder with each strike. It was a scream of pure, incoherent fury, decades of pent-up rage finally unleashed.

One final blow – down on to his helpless father's knee. Bone snapped. The breathless Finch's only response was a choked rasp of agony.

Reeve stepped back. Fists clenched, panting, he turned to face the phone. 'Did you get that?' he gasped.

The ringing stopped.

Reeve stared at the phone, struggling to control his breathing. His entire body trembled with exertion, pain, anger – and relief.

He'd done it.

The call was from the Russians. Confirmation that they had what he needed. They'd been watching, listening – recording. His father had finally confessed to his mother's murder. And they had it on video.

That was the deal he'd made. *Put my father back in prison, and you get Parker's phone.* Not that he trusted them; nor, he was sure, did they trust him. He limped to the window and painfully stretched up to collect the phone. The makeshift Faraday bag was amongst his belongings. He slipped the phone back inside. It had been connected to a battery pack, charging up until needed. Now he needed it to run down again. It had a long journey ahead; he couldn't risk its being tracked en route.

He'd taken a huge risk letting it be tracked at all. Both the

Russians and SC9 now knew where it was. They were probably already on the way. He'd only taken the device from its shielding when his father entered the back yard. Reeve was ready for him, Mickey's betrayal as inevitable as nightfall. All part of the plan.

A plan that could have meant his death. In his attempt to goad his father into confessing, he'd pulled his punches. But Finch was trying to kill him. It took all his willpower not to do the same in return.

He quickly collected the few items he needed. Then he stared down at his father. Finch was starting to recover his breath. 'You little . . . fucking . . .' he wheezed.

Reeve didn't reply. He had nothing else to say to him. Instead, he took out the burner phone and dialled 999. 'Ambulance,' he told the operator brusquely. When a despatcher came on, he gave the address. 'There are two men here. They've been beaten up. One's got a broken knee. Oh, and they broke into the property. Send the police as well.'

He ended the call by pulling out the phone's battery. Then he went to the doorway. His father flinched as he stopped beside him, expecting another attack. Projection, Reeve knew; it was what Finch himself would have done. But all he gave him was a cold, unreadable stare. Then he left.

Back alleys and secret routes from childhood got him clear of his former home. Finally satisfied that his enemies weren't following, Reeve disappeared into the night.

Blake drove quickly through Clayton. Parker's phone had unexpectedly gone live minutes earlier. Its location, start-lingly, was Reeve's old house. Was he hiding out there?

If he were, it wouldn't be for long. Blake had just been updated by GCHQ. The phone had disappeared again. Reeve was probably about to move. One chance to catch him—

Was gone.

He turned on to the street – and braked hard. The blue strobes of an ambulance and police car lit the little terraced houses.

Blake cautiously drove past Reeve's home. The boarded-up front door had been forced open. Paramedics brought someone out. Blake's hand went to his gun—

It wasn't Reeve. His father lay on the stretcher, yelling at an officer. 'I'm not a fucking burglar!' he bellowed. 'It's my fucking house!' Blake drove on, anger simmering.

The traitor had escaped SC9 again.

CHAPTER 42

A police car was parked near the entrance to Manchester Royal Infirmary. Reeve kept watch from beyond railings, pretending to wait for a bus. Earlier that morning, he'd told reception his father had been brought in. The staff helpfully gave him a room number. He investigated; a police officer was stationed outside. He then left the building and waited.

It might take some time, but he was patient. He wanted to be sure the Russians had done as he asked. His demand was for them to send Finch's confession to the authorities. The police, the Crown Prosecution Service – and also the press. If they had, and if it was acted upon, his father would be arrested. Broken leg or no, he would be taken for questioning. At the very least, there would be an assault charge. At most . . .

Eventually, a police van arrived. Two more officers went into the hospital. More time passed, then finally they returned.

Jude Finch was with them – in a wheelchair, one leg splinted. Both wrists were cuffed to the chair's arms. The reason quickly became clear. Finch was red with fury, bellowing abuse. 'Cunts! Fucking pigs! I'm the fucking victim! Why are you arresting me? Get your fucking hands off me!'

His threats were ignored. The cops hauled the chair and its struggling occupant into the van.

Reeve was already moving, taking a large bouquet of flowers from a bag. He held it high to conceal his face.

'Jude,' he said as he passed the van. Finch looked around sharply at the sound of his name.

He saw the card attached to the flowers. Two words in large block letters.

For Mum.

Finch's eyes went wide as he realised who was holding the bouquet. 'Hey! *Hey!* That's my son, that's fucking him! Arrest him! He broke my leg – he's wanted for perjury! Fucking arrest him, you useless fucking—'

The van's doors slammed shut, cutting him off.

One officer turned to see who the prisoner was ranting about. But Reeve was already gone.

Other tasks occupied the rest of Reeve's day. The last was to send a small parcel from a FedEx station. It was some way from Manchester's centre, but trams ran close by. He filled out the paperwork. Express delivery, to be collected from another FedEx station near Rome's Leonardo da Vinci airport. He was assured it would be there tomorrow. He paid in cash, then left. All his tasks were completed.

No. Not quite. There were other things he needed to do. Not for his mission: for himself.

'I got your text.'

Reeve looked up from the grave. Ally stood before him, carrying a sleepy Daisy. 'I'd hoped you'd come,' he said.

'So you're going?'

'Yes. I wanted to say goodbye first, though. And thank you.'

'For what?'

'Keeping me out of hospital. Keeping me out of a police cell. That kind of thing.'

She stepped closer, seeing the new bruises on his face. 'Oh, my God,' she said, shocked. 'What happened?'

'Had another run-in with my dad. Don't worry, though. He's going back to prison. I got him to confess.'

'To your mum's . . .' She trailed off, not wanting to mention murder with Daisy there. Instead, her eyes flicked to the grave. The name inscribed upon it was *Nicola Abigail Finch*. 'How?'

'I set things up so I could record him. Then I got him mad enough to admit it.' A beat, then: 'While he was trying to strangle me.'

Ally shook her head. 'You . . . oh, you bloody idiot, Dominic. You *let* him beat you up? What if he'd . . .' her voice dropped to a whisper, '*killed* you?'

'He didn't. And the police've got the video. They arrested him this morning. That's all that matters.'

'Will a video be enough in court? I mean, you can't go and give evidence. They'd arrest *you*.'

'It'd better be enough,' Reeve said firmly. 'I don't want to have to come back here.'

Ally's face fell. 'You're not coming back?' she said.

'I – I don't know.' He'd meant the statement to be about his father. It hadn't even occurred that she might interpret it differently. 'Not for a while, at least. I've got to get back to Italy.'

310

'To Connie.' She couldn't quite meet his eyes.

'Yeah.'

Now her gaze went to the damp ground. 'Of course, yes. Silly of me.'

'Ally . . .' He came to her, unsure what to say. 'I'm sorry.'

She looked back at him. 'For what?' she said, with exaggerated brightness. 'It's not your fault. You moved away, you grew up, you made your own life. You found someone you love. That's what counts.' A smile, but with regret behind it.

Reeve still didn't know what to say. He settled instead for hugging her. She reacted initially with surprise, before wrapping her free arm around his waist. 'Sorry,' she said. 'I'd use both hands, but I'm juggling a kid.'

'That's okay,' he replied. 'I'm glad I met you again.'

'Me too.' She kissed his cheek. He returned it. She squeezed him more tightly. Then: 'But . . . you've got to go. Right?'

He gently eased back. 'Afraid so. I wanted to say bye to Mum as well. Let her know that . . .' He drew in a deep, slow breath. 'Dad didn't get away with it. I wouldn't *let* him get away with it.' Another glum look at his mother's headstone. He hadn't been here since childhood. Even then, it had been for her funeral – with his father. His poisonous presence had been inescapable. 'Just hope he goes back for good this time.'

'So do I,' said Ally, with sympathy. 'He's hurt you enough.'

He nodded. 'Yes.' Another kiss to her cheek. 'Bye, Ally. Thank you. 'And it was nice meeting you, Daisy.' Her only response was a look of mild annoyance.

'Kids,' Ally said with a laugh. 'They don't know what

they've got.' Before Reeve could retreat, she kissed him again – on the lips. 'Goodbye, Dominic. I hope I see you again.'

'Me too.' They both knew they never would. A last shared look, then he walked away through the wet graveyard.

CHAPTER 43

Reeve watched the waiting car for five minutes before approaching. It had stopped in the centre of a supermarket's car park on Manchester's southern outskirts. Pre-dawn, the roads were quiet, the parking lot deserted. That would make it easy to spot anyone following the man he'd come to meet. There was nobody.

He strode to the car. Both front doors opened. He didn't recognise the driver, a big, thuggish man.

He knew his companion, though. 'Morozov,' he said, regarding the man he'd last seen in Florence.

Morozov covered his surprise. 'You know my name?'

'Parker mentioned you. It took me a while to remember.' No point revealing that Blake had told him. That might make Morozov suspect a trap by SC9. Right now, he depended on him to get out of the country. 'Is the deal still on?'

'We did our part,' the Russian replied. 'Now it is your turn. Where is the phone?'

'I sent it by courier to Rome.' He'd already told them he was sending the phone ahead, but not to where. 'It'll be ready to collect today. You can have it – if you fly me there. You'll need to get me out of England. But I'm sure you can manage that.'

'I am sure we can.' Morozov regarded him with clear suspicion. 'We have a jet standing by. But first . . .'

He nodded to his companion, who quickly and rather forcefully searched Reeve and his bag. A menacing glare as he found the revolver. He took the gun, but found nothing else of note.

'Happy now?' said Reeve. He opened the car's rear door and climbed in. 'Then let's get started.'

Maxwell's phone rang. Scott's ringtone. 'Sir?'

'Maxwell.' Scott sounded agitated. SC9 had already been thrown into turmoil by Reeve's appearance at its headquarters. Security compromised, the organisation hurriedly decamped to a backup location. Whatever Scott had to tell him was apparently of equal urgency. 'I just received a report from MI5. The Russian who came into Manchester, Morozov, and his friend? The two of them arrived in a private jet. It left an hour ago – with *three* men aboard.'

'Reeve was the third man?' A guess, but the obvious one.

'We're relying on some poor-quality CCTV, but so it seems. He got through security without a passport check.'

'Was he being coerced?' Had the Russians captured him? 'It didn't look like it.'

Maxwell felt a sudden concern. Reeve had been adamant he wasn't a traitor. So why would he now work with Morozov? He covered his worry. 'Either the Russians have an inside man, or somebody got a nice bribe. Has Five started an investigation?'

'Yes, but that's not important.' Scott's tone became even

more intense. 'We know where the jet's going. The flightplan is filed for Rome – da Vinci airport. Assemble a team, immediately. We've got to pick up his trail.'

'How many Operatives?' Maxwell asked.

'Everyone available. Is Blake fit for service?'

'Reeve did a number on him, but he's fine. Sir, I should point out that we don't currently have any Operatives in Italy. He'll have a big head start. Morozov could take him anywhere in that time.'

'I'm aware of that,' said Scott coldly. 'I'm going to contact Six right now. They must have someone available who can reach the airport before Reeve arrives. Their officer can tail him until the Operatives catch up.'

'You're relying on MI6?'

'We don't have a choice until we get our own people out there.'

'I assume you're not authorising their man to take action.'

'Of course not. Some SIS errand boy, versus an Operative? And then there are the Russians as well.' An angry huff. 'I knew Reeve was involved with them. This confirms it. Those bastards have gone too far, Maxwell. I'm taking the gloves off – I want Morozov and his associates eliminated along with Reeve.'

'That would be . . . quite an escalation, sir,' Maxwell said, alarmed. SC9's reprisals against Russia had, in his view, already gone too far. The blowback from a mass killing could threaten all of British intelligence.

'They infiltrated two agents into SC9,' Scott snapped. 'Now they're helping a traitor escape. I will *not* allow that to go unpunished. So get the Operatives to Rome. I want Reeve,

Morozov and anyone with them dead. And recover that damn phone.' The call ended.

Maxwell's mind raced. What was Reeve doing? He couldn't accept that after everything, his former student would suddenly turn traitor. Was he just using Morozov as a way to escape the country? The Russian would surely expect deceit on Reeve's part. Trust was a rare treasure in this business.

Yet Maxwell trusted Reeve to be true to his word, insofar as he trusted anyone. And Reeve seemed to trust him. He'd set out his stall clearly enough: *leave me alone, and I'll leave you alone.* Maxwell was, for now, willing to take that offer. Scott, on the other hand . . .

But he was still in charge of SC9. Which meant his orders had to be followed. Maxwell made the first of several calls.

For the tenth time in five minutes, Archie Swaine checked his phone. It was running a flight-tracking app, showing all aircraft around Rome. One in particular was highlighted. A Gulfstream G550, which had left Manchester two and a half hours prior. It was now on final approach to da Vinci airport.

Who was on it, the young Secret Intelligence Service officer didn't know. He also didn't know why its occupants were of interest to MI6. He'd been given his unexpected assignment barely an hour earlier. Wait for the plane, confirm one passenger's identity, follow him. Discreetly – under no circumstances approach or engage. Continue observation until relieved.

Swaine was glad of the chance to get out of the field office. It was a pleasant – even exciting – change from endless paperwork. He wasn't sure why he'd been chosen for the job, though. He had the distinct feeling it was because he was still 'the new guy'. At twenty-three, he was very much the office junior. Or, the cynical part of his mind noted, expendable.

He shrugged off the unwelcome thought. If the target were dangerous, surely more than one inexperienced officer would have been assigned. Mind you, he'd got the impression his superior knew little more than he did. That perhaps meant the tail request had come from outside MI6. Maybe another agency had been caught on the hop by their subject's departure. Leaving the country in a private jet was a pretty big middle finger.

The icon representing his target neared one of the four runways. Swaine had found a seat by the windows in a terminal's café. He looked out across the airport. There was the jet, a white dart in the blue morning sky. He raised the SLR camera he'd been issued. Its lens had a decent amount of zoom; he tracked the plane down. The tail number matched the one he'd been given.

Swaine stood. He'd been trained in surveillance and tailing techniques; now to use them for real. Even on the ground, the Gulfstream's position was shown in his app. He would see which terminal it was using. Passengers on private flights still had to pass through customs. He could pick them up as they exited, confirming his target's identity.

And then follow him wherever he went.

CHAPTER 44

The customs check was a tense moment for Reeve. He was using another fake passport: French, the name in it Philippe Jaulin. Morozov had paid a contact at Manchester to log 'Jaulin' on to the flight. Whether his ID would be accepted on arrival in Italy was another matter . . .

But there were no problems. The checks were quick, courteous. A few brief questions, but no apparent suspicion. The passport had been worth the money. Which was good; he'd burned through his other false identities.

Hopefully he wouldn't need any more. Once he found Connie, he could return to hiding.

After he got rid of the Russians.

Morozov and his companion, the hulking Ustrashkin, weren't EU citizens. As such, they faced more stringent entry procedures. Reeve cleared the customs area before them. He could have run, but knew Morozov would have anticipated the possibility. There was surely a reception committee. He waited outside the exit gate. Sure enough, when Morozov emerged, two large men came to meet them. One, Reeve had spotted watching him, but the other had remained incognito. The first man had been deliberately visible. Intimidation was a standard Russian tactic.

Someone else had set Reeve's internal radar twitching. A man in his early twenties, whose face and demeanour screamed *British public school*. That was of more concern than the Russians. MI6? The intelligence services knew about Morozov. His departure would have been noted. Were they seeing who was with him?

It was entirely possible that SC9 had requested the observer. After Reeve surfaced in England, Scott would have recalled any Operatives in Italy. SC9 were now hours behind him, having to rely on MI6's resources. The young officer probably hadn't even been given his target's name. Scott wouldn't want it known that the rogue Operative had slipped away yet again.

That hopefully meant MI6 had no idea who they were tailing. Reeve put the young man to the bottom of his threat list. The Russians topped it.

He had to be ready for any opportunity to deal with them.

'So,' said Morozov, after speaking to the other two men, 'where do we go?'

'The FedEx station at Viale Alexandre Gustave Eiffel,' Reeve replied.

The Russian entered the address into his phone. 'Not far from here. Let's go.'

The group headed out of the terminal. Reeve glanced back as they reached the exit.

The young man was following them.

The Russians' car, a Mercedes E-Class sedan, was in the short-term parking area. Morozov took the front passenger seat, one of the reception committee the wheel. Reeve was unsurprised to be assigned the centre rear seat. The two other men flanked him on each side. Even in the large car, it was a tight fit.

Morozov opened the glove box. Almost casually, he took out a pair of handguns and shoulder holsters. One set went to Ustrashkin. He kept the other. Both quickly shed their jackets, donned the holsters, then dressed again. The guns were slipped inside their clothing.

'Don't you have one for me?' Reeve asked.

Morozov chuckled sarcastically. 'It is always take, take, take with the British.' He gestured to the men beside Reeve. The man on his right drew a gun of his own. He pushed it against the Englishman's side. Ustrashkin, however, found doing the same far more awkward. He was right-handed, and couldn't bring his weapon to bear in the confined space. He gave Morozov an apologetic look. His superior frowned. 'Just watch him,' he ordered. Ustrashkin holstered his gun and stared balefully at Reeve, fists balled.

The car set off. Its destination was a few kilometres away, in a commercial estate off the autostrada. The drive took only ten minutes. Morozov got out, signalling for Reeve to follow. Ustrashkin slid from the car so he could exit. The trio went into the FedEx office. 'Stay with him,' Morozov told Ustrashkin as Reeve went to the counter. 'I'll report in.'

He watched Reeve as he made a phone call. Pervak answered. 'Where are you, Garald?'

'At a FedEx office,' Morozov replied. 'Reeve is collecting the phone.'

'Good. Grishin wants to talk to you.'

A pause while the call was rerouted, then: 'Garald

Kazimirovich,' said Grishin. 'Do you have the phone?'

Reeve spoke to the man at the counter. The FedEx employee checked his passport, then went into a back room. 'We're collecting it right now,' said Morozov.

'Excellent. Now.' A shift in his superior's tone. 'Once you confirm it is the real phone, kill the Englishman.' The command was issued without emotion. 'I have changed my mind about interrogating him. Exposing SC9 to the world will destroy it more effectively than we could. The British government will burn it to the ground to protect themselves.'

Morozov suppressed a smile. 'I'd thought the same thing, sir. I was going to kill him anyway.'

A faint, grunting laugh. 'You always did take the initiative. But do nothing until you have the phone. We must have the files. And their password.'

The FedEx employee emerged with a small parcel. 'You'll have everything soon,' Morozov assured Grishin. 'I'll report back when it's done.'

He ended the call. Reeve collected his item, then came to Morozov, Ustrashkin following. 'Got it.'

'Outside,' Morozov ordered. They left the building. 'Show me.'

Reeve opened the parcel and took out a transparent plastic bag. Foil lined it. 'A Faraday cage,' he explained. 'So nobody could track it.'

Morozov nodded. 'Let me see it.'

Layers of plastic and metal were peeled away. Reeve took out their contents. A phone. It was the make and model Morozov had expected, but . . . 'Switch it on.'

'The battery's flat. You'll have to charge it yourself.' Reeve gave him the device. 'Take me into Rome, like we agreed, then the deal's done.'

'Once we know it is the real phone,' Morozov replied. 'Get into the car.'

Reeve regarded both Russians, then climbed back into the Mercedes.

Swaine's anonymous Fiat Tipo was parked farther down the street. He hadn't been specifically ordered to report on events, but felt this warranted it. 'They've just come out of a FedEx office,' he told his superior by phone. 'The primary collected a parcel. He gave something to one of the other men from the plane.'

'Did you see what it was?'

'No, I'm too far away.' He remembered too late the camera's zoom lens, and silently cursed his inexperience. 'It was small, maybe a book or a phone. Oh – they're getting back into their car.'

'Stay with them. I still haven't heard when you'll be relieved. Or by whom, for that matter. Which makes me think it won't be anyone from SIS.'

Swaine was puzzled. 'Who else has authority to act outside Britain?'

A laugh without humour. 'A bit of career advice, Swaine. If you ever find yourself thinking about asking that question? Don't ask that question. Especially not of anyone senior.'

'Ah . . . understood,' the young man replied nervously. Some black-ops thing, then. His boss was right; best not to know. 'They're setting off. I'll stay with them.'

The Mercedes pulled away. He waited several seconds, then followed.

Morozov's driver brought the car towards the A91 autostrada. It led into Rome, but before then met another motorway orbiting the city. Other routes radiated outwards to the rest of the country.

The intersection was only a few kilometres away. Reeve hoped his chance would come before they reached it. It would give him more opportunities for escape. But the man to his right still had a gun pressed against his side. He couldn't do anything without a distraction . . .

Morozov took a charger cable from the glove box. He connected the phone to one of the car's USB ports. After a moment, its screen displayed the 'battery low' icon. He propped it in the centre console, then took out his own phone.

'Who are you calling?' Reeve asked.

'Directorate S,' came the reply. 'They will tell me if this is the real phone. If it is, when it has enough power it will start streaming video and audio. If it is not . . .' Morozov glanced at the gun covering Reeve.

'You don't trust me?'

'If you trusted *us*, you would have given us the phone in England. Now, quiet.' He spoke to the person answering his call.

Reeve sat still, observing the men with him. The driver merged on to the autostrada, flat farmland rolling by. He brought the car to the 90kph speed limit and activated the cruise control. Italy's speed camera network, the much-hated

Sistema Tutor, was effective and merciless. The Russian didn't want to bring any attention – or fines – upon the SVR's cover organisation. Covert espionage groups couldn't claim diplomatic immunity.

Ustrashkin's attention had wandered, curious about Morozov's task. The armed man on Reeve's right was less distracted, but still glanced at the phone. Morozov himself kept talking. His voice was deliberately low; Reeve couldn't tell what he was saying.

He looked back at the phone. It still displayed the battery warning. But surely not for much longer . . .

As he completed the thought, the screen glowed more brightly. The phone began its boot-up sequence. Morozov reported this to his contact. Reeve watched his reactions intently. He didn't think the spyware would activate until the operating system was fully running. But he could be wrong . . .

Morozov's expression remained one of expectant impatience. He stared at the screen. Finally, the grid of apps appeared. Another report. Both Reeve's guards now watched with interest. But he could still feel the gun's muzzle against his side.

Morozov picked up Reeve's phone, looking into its selfie camera. 'Can you see me?' he asked. 'Can you hear anything?'

Reeve readied himself. Any moment—

The person on the other end of the line spoke. Morozov's jaw clenched . . .

Then his head snapped around, eyes locking accusingly on to Reeve. 'It's a fake!' he barked. 'Kill him!'

CHAPTER 45

Reeve was already moving.

His right hand flashed out, forcing his guard's gun away from his body. His left hand also lanced at the weapon. He stabbed his index finger into the trigger guard.

And drove the Russian's own finger back.

The gun went off. The retort was almost deafening. Muzzle flash scorched his clothing. But the bullet missed him—

It hit the driver's shoulder. The car lurched as his hands jerked the wheel. Reeve clawed at the gun. If he didn't get a weapon, he would be dead. Morozov was already reaching for his own automatic.

And Ustrashkin, to his left, was fumbling for his gun too. It didn't matter if he had to shoot with his off-hand. At point-blank range, he couldn't miss.

Reeve hauled the other guard's hand higher – and pushed the trigger back again.

The bullet hit the back of the driver's skull. Gore erupted across the windscreen. He flopped sideways on to the centre console. The car swerved out of its lane.

Morozov swung his gun at Reeve—

Only Reeve had seen the car in the neighbouring lane. He braced himself. The Mercedes slammed into its rear quarter. The impact was hard enough to trigger the airbags. Morozov had twisted around; the large passenger-side bag punched his right shoulder. The blow jarred the gun from his hand. It glanced off the corpse and clattered into the driver's-side footwell.

Reeve was first to recover from the collision. He swung his left arm back, hard. His elbow smashed into Ustrashkin's face. The Russian's nose collapsed in a burst of blood. He shrieked, blinded by pain.

The car veered back across the carriageway. The first minder clamped his left hand around his gun's grip. He forced the weapon towards Reeve's torso—

The motorway's barriers swept into view through the windscreen. Morozov desperately grabbed the wheel, trying to turn the Mercedes away from them. But the car was still doing over seventy—

It hit the steel barrier at an angle. The impact spun it around. Everyone inside was thrown to the right. The man fighting Reeve was flung against the door. His head struck the window hard enough to crack the glass.

His hold on the gun suddenly slackened. Reeve tore it from his grip and shot him twice in the chest.

The E-Class slewed to a stop. Ustrashkin, lower face running red, raised his head. Fury overcame pain as he saw Reeve with the gun. His own weapon came back up. Reeve twisted towards him, but the Russian was already aiming—

Colour rushed at him – and another car ploughed into the Mercedes' left side.

The rear door caved in, window exploding. Torn metal speared into Ustrashkin's side as he was driven sideways into Reeve. He in turn slammed against the dead guard, meat in a painful sandwich. The car spun again, almost flipping over before crashing back on to all four wheels.

Reeve had just barely raised an arm to shield his face. He lowered it, glass fragments cascading off. Ustrashkin squirmed in agony, leg and hip impaled by the wrecked door. He had lost his gun. No threat. That left Morozov—

The Russian leader was slumped against his door, unmoving. Reeve couldn't tell if he was alive or dead. *Shoot him to make sure*, the ruthless – or pragmatic – part of his mind ordered. But he could smell leaking petrol. Escape took priority.

His seatbelt was still fastened. He shoved his hand between himself and the dead man, searching for the button. The smell of fuel grew stronger. Outside, he heard tyres shrill and the crunching bang of another collision. *Get out, get out*—

His fingertip found the release. The belt popped free. Reeve lunged to grab the decoy phone. His other hand reached across the Russian's corpse to open the door. He clambered over the body and fell out on to the autostrada.

The stricken Mercedes blocked two lanes. A shunt as a driver tried to avoid it had closed the third. Traffic was already building up behind. A few cars ahead had stopped, a Renault Megane reversing to provide help. Reeve rose clumsily to his feet. He had to get clear, fast. He held the gun behind his back and hurried to the approaching Renault. It stopped and a man got out, regarding the crash scene in alarm. 'Are you okay?' he called.

'I'm fine,' Reeve replied. 'Sorry, but I need your car.' He brought up the gun. The Italian backed away. Reeve entered the Megane—

Metal creaked behind. He glanced back.

Morozov's door swung open. The Russian started to slide out – then saw Reeve. He immediately leaned back into the cabin, groping for his gun.

Reeve grabbed the gear lever – and shoved it into reverse. Foot down. The car surged backwards. He hunched lower, using the wing mirror for guidance. The battered E-Class filled it. Morozov sat back up. The gun was in his hand. He fired, shots striking the Megane's rear. The rear windscreen blew apart. Reeve ducked—

The Renault hit the Mercedes, slamming the driver's door shut. Morozov pulled back. Not fast enough. The door's edge caught his gun – and hand. The Russian screamed as his fingers were crushed.

Reeve jammed his car into first. The Merc's mangled door was wrenched back open as the vehicles tore apart. Morozov dropped the gun, clutching his wounded hand. Reeve accelerated past the horrified Italian and tore away down the autostrada.

He was clear.

The phone in his pocket had been bought second-hand in Manchester the previous morning. Parker's identical handset was elsewhere in Italy. The decoy had been shipped to Rome by FedEx. The genuine article had gone to Venice by DHL. Both deliveries had been paid for in cash, leaving no trail. Reeve was confident the ruse would have thrown off both the Russians – and SC9.

Now he had to get to the *real* phone . . . and Connie.

Swaine threw caution to the wind and got out of his car. He ran between the vehicles that had stopped behind the crash. The Mercedes lay wrecked across the carriageway. Blood was splattered over the inside of the windscreen. A man in the back seat writhed and moaned in pain.

His surveillance subject was gone, tearing away in another car. 'Oh, shit,' Swaine gasped, staring after it. This would not look good in his report. A simple tailing errand had suddenly become a bloodbath . . .

Someone struggled from the Merc's front seat. One of the other men from the plane, the apparent leader. Swaine briefly lost sight of him as he crouched behind the car. Then he rose again – holding a gun.

The young MI6 officer hurriedly retreated. *Do not engage* had been a firm rule of his mission. He was now more than ever committed to not breaking it. He scurried back to his Fiat, hoping he hadn't been noticed.

To his relief, the Russian had other priorities.

Morozov, panting in pain, glared after the retreating Renault. He had to pursue. Chase Reeve, stop him – *kill* him.

He turned back to the Mercedes. Smashed. He needed another car. What about his men?

He already knew the driver, Velkov, was dead. Half his brain was dripping from the windshield. He looked into the rear. Lemkov was also gone, two oozing bullet wounds in his chest. Ustrashkin was still alive. But Morozov could see he was badly hurt. Torn metal from the caved-in door had been driven into his side. No time to free him.

But Morozov couldn't let him be captured by the Italian authorities. A live prisoner might talk in his delirium. A corpse left only fake IDs, and mysteries. 'Ovcharka,' he said. The moaning man looked up at him. 'You've served the motherland well. I'm sorry.'

Ustrashkin opened his mouth in fearful protest—

Morozov shot him in the face. The pale cream cabin lining abruptly turned red and grey and black.

The Russian straightened. People in the nearest stationary cars had witnessed the killing. Unable to back up, several jumped from their vehicles and fled. That suited him well. Head down to shield his face from any dashcams, he went to the empty cars. With his right hand smashed, he needed an automatic. A BMW 5-Series, still idling, fitted the bill. He got in and put it into drive, left hand taking the wheel. The Mercedes blocked his way. Only briefly – he revved hard to shove it aside, then drove off.

A look ahead. Reeve's stolen car was out of sight. A sign told Morozov he was nearing an exit to another autostrada. Which way had the Englishman gone? Into Rome, or north or south on the other motorway?

A one-in-three chance of picking the right route. Less; there were probably other exits nearby. Reeve could be anywhere.

Morozov let out a snarl of anger. He had lost. Worse than that, he'd been *tricked*. The humiliation hurt almost as much as his crushed fingers. He spat out a curse, aimed at the late Craig Parker. His mole had underestimated Reeve, costing him his life. And his error had just been repeated by his paymaster. Reeve was smarter – more dangerous – than he had been credited.

It was a mistake that would not be repeated.

Morozov's immediate priority was evading the Italian police. Get off the autostrada, change cars, reach the SVR safehouse in Rome. Have his wounds treated, leave the country. Then . . .

However long it took, Morozov vowed, he would hunt Reeve down.

And make him beg for death.

CHAPTER 46

After contacting all available Operatives, Maxwell joined Scott at SC9's backup facility. Its new home was even less appealing than the Office for Interdepartmental Communications. An old warehouse in south London served as a government storage facility. Outdated, unclassified paperwork was kept there. Not because it might be needed – more just to get it out of the way. Civil servants never disposed of anything. Unless, Maxwell thought wryly, it potentially embarrassed anyone important. Then it couldn't suffer 'water damage' quickly enough.

The endless ranks of shelves and filing cabinets were not what he had come to see. His destination was a stairwell in one corner, leading underground. The door at the bottom bore several no entry signs. The numerous security cameras were more discreet. A heavy, old-fashioned lock plate was fitted to the door. No key for it existed. Maxwell instead swung it upwards. A keypad was concealed behind. He entered the code. Seconds passed – then heavy locks clunked.

He opened the door and went through. It swung shut with a bang; it was heavy steel. A short concrete passage led to another door. This too was metal, but not locked. Beyond were SC9's new headquarters. The grim, windowless space was painted institutional green. Maxwell guessed it had been some kind of wartime bunker.

The people inside, despite their professionalism, looked less than thrilled to be there. Maxwell went to the desk closest to the entrance. 'Morning, Susan. The boss in?'

Susan King was a woman in her fifties. Her face was bruised: remnants of her fight with Alex Reeve. Operative 8 had been with SC9 since its founding three decades earlier. She was retired from active duty, but still skilled and capable. Just not up to the more recent recruit's level. 'Tony,' she replied with a polite nod. 'Yes, in the back.' She gestured to a door in the far wall.

He headed for it. The five others present were also Operatives. Four no longer took on field assignments, through injury or – in one case – international infamy. The fifth was somewhat younger. Luke Wagner, Operative 55, was another of Maxwell's former students. 'Luke,' he said. 'How're you doing?'

'Fine, thanks, Tony,' came the reply. Wagner had encountered Reeve at OfIC. 'Bit bruised, that's all.'

'How's the new assignment?'

'You mean, working directly with the boss?' Wagner's forced smile said it all. Maxwell grinned and continued to the door.

'Come in,' Scott called when he knocked. 'Ah, Maxwell. Good timing. We had an update on Reeve a few minutes ago. Six's man is tailing him and Morozov from the airport. They stopped at a courier firm to collect a parcel.'

'Parker's phone?'

'Presumably. I'm waiting for more on where they're

going.' Scott leaned back in his chair. 'Where are your team?'

'On their way to Heathrow.' He shook his head. 'It's a two-and-a-half hour flight. They'll be a long way behind Alex. And MI6 only put one man on him?'

Scott bristled. That had clearly been his decision. 'Reeve is *ours*, Maxwell. I don't want anyone else getting involved. They don't even know who they're tailing. They can locate him – but we'll take him down.'

'And what about Morozov? If he's already got the phone—'

He broke off as the desk phone rang. Scott snatched up the receiver. 'Yes? Good. Hold on.' He put the phone on speaker. 'Go ahead.'

'Our officer reported in,' said the man at the other end of the line. He did not sound positive. 'There's been an . . . incident.'

Scott and Maxwell exchanged looks. 'What kind of incident?' demanded the former.

'It seems the primary subject had a dispute with the lead secondary. Their car crashed on the autostrada heading for Rome. There was an exchange of fire; at least two of the other secondaries dead. The lead secondary was injured.'

Scott's face was fixed. 'And where is the primary?'

'Escaped. The road was blocked by the crash; our man couldn't follow.'

Silence for a moment. Then: 'I see. Well. Get a complete written report to my inbox as soon as possible. I want every detail of this *screw-up*.' That last almost spat from his mouth. He banged the handset down. 'Unbelievable! Who the hell did they assign, the tea-boy?'

Maxwell ignored his boss's anger. Even that truncated report had plenty to say. 'Alex and Morozov had a "dispute",' he said, thinking out loud. 'About what?' The answer came almost immediately. 'The phone,' he realised, looking at Scott.

'You think Reeve tried to renege on handing it over?'

'I don't think he ever *intended* to hand it over. Alex needed to leave the country. He made a deal with Morozov – a flight out in return for the phone. Except . . . he didn't give him the *real* phone. It was a decoy. Morozov checked it in the car, but Alex was ready.'

Scott was unconvinced. 'And why wouldn't he hand over the real phone? He's a traitor – that was his plan all along.'

Maxwell couldn't reveal why he believed otherwise. However, he did have other arguments. 'Why didn't he hand it over eighteen months ago, right after killing Parker? Or at any other time between then and now? If he gave it to the Russians, that would cause massive diplomatic damage to Britain. But if he held on to it . . . it gives him leverage against *us*. Against SC9. We leave him alone, he leaves us alone. He just wants to disappear.'

'The only place he'll disappear to is six feet beneath the ground,' Scott snapped. 'He's a threat, plain and simple. And our job is to eliminate threats.'

'Then we have to find him. Do that, and we also find the real phone – and the stolen files.'

'And how do you propose we do so?'

Maxwell's mind whirled into overdrive. 'He sent the phone by courier. Do you know which company?'

'FedEx, I believe.'

'And he probably sent it from Manchester. So – we get GCHQ to dig into international courier firms with offices around the city. Not just FedEx, all of them. Alex wouldn't have used the same company to send the real phone. Check the records of all packages going out within a certain time window. From when the phone went live at his house to when Morozov's plane took off. Anything going from Manchester to Italy in that window is suspect. Anything paid for in *cash* is top priority.'

Scott's anger was replaced by a ruthless optimism. 'Yes . . . yes. That makes sense. I'll get GCHQ on it.'

He made a call. 'This is Sir Simon Scott,' he said imperiously. 'I need to speak to Michael Barwell. A matter of extreme urgency.' He waited with rising impatience for a minute. When he was finally connected, any politeness and courtesy were as brittle as dried grass. He made his demands; the response was predictably resistant. 'I'm entirely aware this will require a lot of resources, Michael,' he replied. 'I'm also entirely aware of the potential for political blowback. Frankly, I don't care. No,' he added as more objections were raised, 'there will not *be* any warrants. You know full well how SC9 works. And you also know I do not make such requests on a whim. This is of utmost importance to national security. On such matters, SC9 has absolute priority. So break into those systems, access those records, and get the information we need. *Immediately*, Michael.' He hung up without a further word.

Maxwell drew in a breath through his teeth. 'Was that wise, sir? Treating the head of GCHQ like a kid, I mean. We need his cooperation.'

Scott glowered at him. 'We already *have* his cooperation, Maxwell. SC9's charter ensures it – *demands* it. Whether he's happy about it is not my problem. I don't have time to waste mollycoddling anyone's feelings.' As if in illustration, he waved a dismissive hand towards the door. 'Now, work with Wagner and the others. As soon as GCHQ's files start coming in, go through them.' His voice rose to a bark. 'Find that phone!'

CHAPTER 47

Reeve left the Megane at Roma Aurelia railway station on Rome's outskirts. He assessed his latest injuries as he waited for a train into the city proper. Only bruises. He'd been lucky.

The train to Roma Termini station soon arrived. The journey took just under half an hour. He was on alert the whole way, but saw no indication of danger. The only person who'd seen his face was the Renault's owner. Even then, he'd probably been too shocked to remember details. The Megane would soon be found, but Reeve had wiped it down. All the same, he needed to leave Italy as soon as possible.

To that end, he bought a ticket for an Italo high-speed train to Venice. Roughly a three-and-a-half-hour journey; he would arrive mid-afternoon. He also bought a new cable and SIM for the decoy phone. The train had USB sockets at every seat, so he could charge it. Neither SC9 nor the Russians knew its number. They wouldn't be able to track it. It would give him a map – and he could also use it to call Connie.

Not yet, though, as impatient as he was to speak to her again. For his safety – and hers. He wanted to be sure he wasn't being tracked by the Italian authorities.

Or anyone else.

But he felt increasingly confident. Morozov's crew had

probably represented most of SVR's muscle in Rome. With them out of action, the Russians would have few resources available to hunt him. They couldn't predict where he intended to go. The odds of their finding him again were slim.

As for SC9 . . .

They almost certainly knew he'd returned to Italy. MI5 would have noted Morozov's departure from Manchester. The young public-school guy at the airport was probably MI6. But Scott hadn't managed to send Operatives to intercept him. That implied two things. There weren't any Operatives in-country; and MI6 had been kept in the dark. If they were working directly with SC9, they would have sent more men. *Armed* men. An ambush would probably have come outside the FedEx office.

Reeve didn't feel fully safe, though. SC9 still posed a threat. But a manageable one. Like the Russians, they didn't know where he was going. In an hour, he would be two hundred kilometres from his last known position. Tomorrow, he would be in another country entirely.

He boarded the red-and-black bullet train shortly before departure. Nobody followed him. All the same, he kept his hand near the gun. But it wasn't needed. The train set off on time. He was clear.

Seven stops, and he would reach his destination. Then, at last, he could speak to Connie again. Once he collected the real phone, they would be safe.

'Sir!' Maxwell called out. 'I think we've got him.'

Scott hurried from his office to join Maxwell and Wagner. 'Look at this,' Maxwell continued, pointing out one particular item on Wagner's screen. GCHQ had surreptitiously – illegally – extracted data from courier firms around Manchester. 'This parcel was sent to Rome by FedEx yesterday. Payment was in cash – no credit or debit card recorded. The packet was the size you'd need to send a smartphone.' Scott's eyes lit up at the revelation. 'And this . . . go back, Luke.' Another entry appeared. 'This was sent to Venice by DHL, about an hour earlier. Same size packet, also paid in cash. Both items were scheduled to arrive this morning, for pickup at regional offices. The name of the recipient is the same. Philippe Jaulin.'

'A fake identity for Reeve?' asked Scott.

'I'd say so, yes.'

'Then that's it. We've got him! He's going to Venice – so his girlfriend's there too. How soon could he get there from Rome?'

'By car? At least five and a half hours. He'd need to change vehicle, as well. The police will be looking for the one he stole. It'd be quicker by train, but still getting on for four hours.'

'We can beat him there.'

Maxwell's brow creased in confusion. 'I don't think so, sir. We'd have to get our people on to different flights, at zero notice—'

'I don't mean commercial flights,' Scott interrupted. 'This is an emergency. I'll authorise a private flight. The Operatives are already at Heathrow. It'll take under two and a half hours to reach Venice.' He straightened. 'Come with me. You want my job, Maxwell? Then see how to do it properly.'

He strode back to his office, Maxwell following. Scott had

plucked the phone's receiver from its cradle before even sitting down. Another call went out, this to Aubrey Ryford-Croft, Chief of MI6. Perfunctory greetings, then: 'Now listen, Aubrey,' said Scott. 'You have a mobile command van in Milan. I need it in Venice immediately. No, my people will man it. We also need transport.' He looked up at Maxwell. 'How many Operatives have you rounded up?'

'Seven,' Maxwell told him. 'Eight, including me.'

Scott nodded. 'At least four vehicles,' he continued. 'Fully equipped.'

He listened to Ryford-Croft's reply. Maxwell could tell it wasn't to his liking. 'No, you may not,' Scott finally said. 'This is a national security emergency. SC9 needs to deal with it immediately. That's all you need to know.'

The objection was so forceful that Maxwell heard it from several feet away. Scott's response was cold. 'I'm well aware of the potential risks from an operation in an allied nation. I will not have you challenging me at a critical moment. Schedule one of your bloody meetings for next week, if you must. But I need this equipment, and I need it *now*. Have it ready for us at Venice airport. That will be all.' He banged the phone down. 'Obstructive little bastard. He used to work for me at Six, you know.'

Maxwell hadn't known. 'He did?'

'God knows how he climbed to the top of the greasy pole. Must have got chummy with someone on the political side. But,' Scott became businesslike again, 'he'll do what he's told.'

'Are you sure, sir?'

'I know him, and I know his type. They resist and complain – but always give in when faced with the rules. And the rules are clear-cut here. SC9 gets whatever it needs. Now, I've got to ring GCHQ again. If Reeve's meeting his girlfriend, he'll almost certainly phone her. We need to catch that call.'

He began a second conversation with Michael Barwell. His demands were even greater than before. All phone calls in the region of Venice were to be scanned. Keywords to be flagged included *Alex*, *Connie*, *SC9*, *Scott*, *Morozov*, *phone*, *Manchester* . . . The list continued. Barwell was predictably unhappy. 'No, the checks can't be limited to calls in English,' Scott replied impatiently. 'No other restrictions, either. Both subjects speak Italian. And they may well have phones with Italian SIMs. They might even use a landline; we don't know. That's why I need the broadest possible sweep.' His irritation grew as he listened to further objections. 'I was under the impression that GCHQ owns multiple supercomputers for exactly this purpose, Michael. So put them to good use. If our subjects make any phone calls, we need to know.' This call ended with the same force as the previous one.

Scott took a breath, then looked back at Maxwell. 'That's how it's done. When push comes to shove, SC9 is top of the intelligence pile. Sometimes, the other heads need to be reminded of their place. Be firm. Be resolute. Be ruthless. That's how you get what you want.'

'I'll remember that,' Maxwell assured him.

'Good. Now, let's arrange a plane. I want to be in Venice before Reeve.'

Maxwell's eyebrows rose. 'You're coming, sir?'

'Absolutely. I'm taking personal command of this operation.' Chilling determination in his gaze. 'Alex Reeve is *not* getting away this time. I want to see his body for myself.'

CHAPTER 48

Muggy afternoon heat smothered Reeve as he left the train. He'd disembarked at Venezia Mestre station, one stop before Venice proper. It was closer to the DHL pickup point. After collecting Parker's phone, he would continue on to the island city.

He'd used the decoy phone to plan his route. A bus went to a shopping mall near his destination. He headed for the stop. A short wait, and he boarded. The journey would take forty minutes.

He waited until he was ten minutes out. Then he finally made the call he'd been longing to make. The number was entered from memory. A ringing tone started. And kept going. Five rings, six. Reeve started to become concerned. Seven. Why wasn't she answering? Eight—

'Hello?'

Connie's voice. At last. He hadn't heard it for over a week. 'It's me,' he said, relieved.

'Alex!' Pure delight in the word. 'Oh, thank God, you're okay!'

'Yeah, I'm fine. What about you? Have you had any trouble?'

'No, none. I'm good. Well, apart from spending the last

ten days totally paranoid. It would have been a *lovely* holiday if not for that.' Reeve smiled. He'd missed her. 'Where are you?'

'I'm back in Italy. I'll be in Venice in about an hour.'

'What happened in England? Did you . . . do what you needed to do?'

'I did. Hopefully we won't have any more trouble.'

'You spoke to Scott? What, in person?'

'I'll tell you about it when I see you. Where do you want to meet?'

He expected her to suggest some Venetian landmark. 'I found a really amazing restaurant,' she said instead. 'Right on the waterfront past the Doge's Palace. It has the best gelatos I've ever tasted. I've eaten way too many of them.' She laughed. 'I had to do *something* to occupy myself.'

'I'll help you work them off.'

'I'll hold you to that,' she said suggestively. 'The place is called Falconi's, on the Riva degli Schiavoni. Will you be able to find it?'

'Yeah, I will.'

'Great. Okay, I'll meet you there. About an hour, you said?'

'I don't know exactly. Just wait for me, and I'll be there as soon as I can.'

'All right. God, Alex. You have *no* idea how happy I am to hear your voice again. I can't wait to see you.'

Reeve couldn't help but smile. 'I can't either. Oh, don't forget to get rid of the burner phone.'

'I know the rules,' she said, with joking testiness. 'I love you. See you soon.'

'See you soon,' he echoed, ending the call. His smile didn't fade until the bus reached his stop.

He got out opposite the large Valecenter mall. The DHL office was half a kilometre farther along the road. He dropped the phone into a bin, then started walking.

In the heat, he soon wished he'd brought some water. There was an Aldi supermarket ahead. Go in and buy a drink? On the way back, he decided. His priority was collecting Parker's phone.

He crossed the road at an intersection and continued onwards to a roundabout. No pavement beyond it, only a white line separating pedestrians from oncoming traffic. He rounded some parked cars, almost having to go into the road to clear them. A man in a black Discovery SUV glanced up from his phone as he passed.

His destination was on a side road, past a restaurant. He cut a corner through its parking. A woman sat in a car, door open as she talked on her phone. She didn't seem used to the heat, wiping away sweat.

He went along the road. Little houses and flats on one side, industrial units on the other. He saw a large yellow DHL sign ahead. The street led to the courier firm's car park. Other vehicles sat along the kerbside.

One was a Range Rover Evoque. Someone was inside it.

Reeve had already become wary. An old saying came to his mind. Was it a quote of Churchill's? He couldn't remember. *Once is happenstance. Twice is coincidence. Three times . . .*

Enemy action.

The man in the Evoque watched his approach in the wing

345

mirror. The moment he realised Reeve was looking back, his attention snapped to his phone.

The man in the Discovery; the woman in the car; now this. No fat on their faces, lean and strong. None looked Italian. All were in their thirties. The right age for a previous intake of Operatives . . .

Despite the heat, he felt a chill. Had SC9 found him? He'd taken every precaution he could think of. But was that enough against the entire intelligence apparatus of the British state? If he'd unwittingly left a trail, they might find it—

He realised his mistake.

Both phones, real and decoy, had been in padded envelopes. Same size, same weight. The courier companies would have recorded the information. If GCHQ had hacked their computer networks, they would have spotted the correlation. He should have put one in a larger box . . .

Too late for self-recrimination now. Survival took priority—

Connie. His inner cold deepened. GCHQ could also be scanning phone calls. Even in another country, it was well within their capabilities. She had used his name, and Scott's.

And said where she would be.

He instinctively reached for the phone, before remembering he'd discarded it. Not that it mattered. She would have done the same. A security measure – which was now working against them. He had no way to warn her.

Reeve passed the Evoque. He didn't look back, but listened intently. His hand went towards his gun. If he heard the SUV's door open . . .

The sound didn't come. He reached the car park's entrance. A glance down the street as he turned towards the building. The man in the Range Rover was still watching him.

Three Operatives, along the only route out. Probably more nearby. But they would all come for him when he left the building.

His eyes swept across the car park. Vehicles flashed past beyond its edge; it was beside an autostrada. A bridge led over the motorway. He burned his surroundings into memory, analysing them for escape routes.

'Lost sight of him,' the man in the Evoque warned. He wore an earpiece and concealed microphone. 'He's gone into DHL.'

'Good,' replied Maxwell. 'Tell us the moment he comes back out. Everyone get ready to move once he's in the box.'

'Will do.' The man, Operative 59, was called Spurr. He took every assignment seriously, but this had gained extra importance. The boss himself was overseeing it – in person. The flight from London was the first time Spurr had ever met him. He had until then been almost a mythical figure, imposing, threatening. The reality was nearly a let-down. But Spurr was still determined not to disappoint him.

The plan was straightforward enough. There was only one road from the DHL depot. Other Operatives were already moving into position at the far end. Once Reeve re-emerged and passed Spurr, he would be boxed in. No escape.

Spurr drew his gun and waited. A few minutes passed –

then the building's door opened. 'He's coming out,' he announced. 'Starting towards—'

His target looked around – then ran for the autostrada.

Reeve's parcel had been waiting for him. He opened it. The phone was inside its Faraday bag. He pocketed it and left the building.

The man in the Evoque was still there. His head rose in alertness when he saw him. That nailed it. Reeve turned and sprinted across the car park, drawing his weapon.

The clunk of a car door being flung open, behind him. Reeve swung the gun around and fired. The shot went high, but it didn't matter. The man threw himself back into the cabin. If the Evoque was MI6's, it was probably at least bullet-resistant, if not bulletproofed.

Reeve quickly reached the car park's edge. A low fence marked the boundary. He hurdled it, landing in tall grass beyond. At the top of a short slope were the autostrada's crash barriers. There was a gap between them to give access to maintenance workers. He raced through on to the narrow shoulder. Cars and trucks hurtled past barely a metre away, displaced air blasting him.

The man ran through the car park in pursuit. Reeve sent another round at him. He dropped behind a car. A silver Discovery powered into the lot, tyres shrilling as it made a hard turn. Two people inside.

Two Operatives.

Reeve raced under the bridge. He used a concrete support for cover as he aimed back at his hunters. The 4x4 stopped, passenger door opening. A familiar figure jumped out:

Deirdre Flynn, gun in hand. Reeve fired. The bullet hit the window beside her head. It crazed, but didn't break. It was indeed bullet-resistant. Flynn ducked back behind the door.

Reeve turned and ran. The slipstreams of passing vehicles pounded his face. Out from beneath the bridge, and on. More grey industrial blocks to his left, then the rear of a multiplex cinema. He vaulted the crash barrier, angling down a grassy embankment. A petrol station and car wash lay ahead. The mall was visible beyond them. He pounded through the forecourt. Where were his pursuers? He looked back. The watcher from the Evoque jumped over the barrier after him. No sign of Flynn, or anyone else.

Tyre squeals warned that others were coming, though. Off to the left, from the main road. He glanced that way as he raced towards the mall. The first Discovery he'd passed was speeding towards him. He glimpsed the silver one's roof flashing above parked cars farther back. Ahead of it, a dark Audi shot across an intersection. It was almost certainly involved in the chase.

If the woman outside the restaurant was also an Operative, that made four cars. At least. Operatives usually worked alone, maybe in pairs. There were five – or more – hunting him. Scott was pulling out all the stops.

He wanted him dead. At any cost.

Reeve made it across the road and jumped over a low hedge. A McDonald's drive-through was in front of him, the mall rising behind it. He stayed close to the building to block the oncoming Discovery's line of fire. There was the mall's entrance, a colourful Valecenter sign past a round red structure. He ran towards it. Shoppers milled in and out of the complex. Civilians might deter his pursuers from shooting at him.

Or they might not.

Another howl of tortured rubber as the black Discovery powered around the drive-through. It stopped at the end of the road just as Reeve reached the mall's doors. Beyond it, the running man barrelled past the McDonald's. Two Operatives behind him – but where were the others?

Reeve rushed into the building. Air-conditioned cool hit him like a dry wave. He had no idea of the interior's layout. Which way?

Right, on instinct. Roughly southwards. He passed lifts and escalators to reach the mall's central aisle. The place was busy, but not enough to obstruct him. He raced past the shops at top speed.

Behind him, the two Operatives entered the mall.

Maxwell was with Scott and Wagner, listening to their team's incoming reports. From outside, the MI6 mobile command centre looked like an anonymous Mercedes Sprinter van. Inside, the long-wheelbase vehicle was packed with computers and communications equipment. It had room for four officers to oversee the agency's covert operations.

Only one person was handling that role for SC9, though. Even with Maxwell's assistance, Wagner struggled to keep up with events. 'Harris and Spurr just entered the mall from the northwest,' he reported. 'Colt, Flynn and Stone are heading for the east side. Ah . . . Locke is on the way, behind them.' His gaze flicked over screens. The Operatives' positions were overlaid on maps, but the updates weren't quite in real-time.

Scott jabbed a finger at one marker. It had bypassed the mall, speeding along the main road. 'Where the hell's Blake going?'

'John, where are you going?' Maxwell demanded on his behalf. 'I read you as heading south.'

'I'm going to overtake and cut him off,' came the reply. From his tone, a sarcastic *obviously* was the unspoken suffix.

Wagner looked back at the map. Valecenter had four main access points: west, northeast, east and south. Reeve had used the western entrance. 'Colt, Stone, keep going – there's an entrance halfway along the main building. Locke, when you get there, go to the northeast door.'

'Ewan, how far ahead is Reeve?' asked Maxwell.

The reply came between heavy breaths; Harris was running at full pelt. 'About thirty metres. Lots of civilians. Shall I take a shot?'

Maxwell looked sharply at Scott as he reached for his microphone toggle. His superior was about to approve. 'It's a *very* public place,' he warned. 'It'll have blanket CCTV, security guards. Any Operative who starts shooting in there will be identifiable – compromised. We'd have to disavow them.'

'That's what they're trained to accept,' Scott replied angrily. But he didn't answer Harris's question.

The running Operative asked again: 'I repeat: do I take a shot?'

'Negative,' said Maxwell. Scott gave him a stern look, but

said nothing. 'Wait till he's clear of civilians. We need to drive him into the open.'

He checked the other Operatives' positions. Locke had just arrived at the northeastern entrance. Harris and Spurr were running down the building's length. Colt in one vehicle, Flynn and Stone another, neared the eastern door. Blake was looping around the complex's southern end to enter the car park.

Reeve was in the middle of the closing net.

They had him.

CHAPTER 49

Reeve hared through the mall. Stalls selling phones, chocolates and perfumes were dotted along its main aisle. He weaved past them to block his pursuers' line of sight.

But the Operatives hadn't fired since entering the building. Their controller – Maxwell? – was being cautious, prudent. Gunfire would bring the police, in force. Having multiple Operatives arrested or killed would be a huge blow to SC9.

A respite, however brief. But he still had to escape. He needed a car. A broad passage branched left off the main aisle. A green sign told him there was an exit in that direction. He raced around the corner. More shops and stalls ahead. Beyond them, glass doors to the car park—

Two running figures silhouetted against it. Flynn and the woman from the restaurant were already inside.

Reeve instantly swung back into the main aisle. The two male Operatives had gained ground.

'He's turned back from us,' Flynn reported over the radio. 'Heading south.'

Maxwell and Scott regarded the map intently, watching the markers update. Flynn's companion, Colt – Operative 60

– also called in. 'Civvies are light here. I can get clear line of fire.'

'I repeat,' said Maxwell, 'hold fire and keep weapons concealed until he's outside. We can't—'

Scott pushed his microphone toggle. 'Ignore that instruction.' Maxwell stared at him in surprise. 'This is a direct order to all Operatives. Shoot Reeve, then escape the area.' He looked back at Maxwell, releasing the button. 'This has gone on long enough.'

'Sir,' Maxwell said, 'with respect: that's a bad idea.' Scott's eyes flared at the direct challenge to his authority.

Flynn spoke again. 'Tony, contradictory orders received. Confirm rules of engagement.'

'That's a high-risk strategy,' Locke chipped in. 'It would mean sacrificing several Operatives to eliminate a single target.'

Scott's reply was clipped, angry. 'That is your *function*. You have your orders. Carry them out.'

'Hold fire,' Maxwell countermanded. 'At least until—'

'Carry out my orders!' his superior barked, standing face to face with him. 'Or I will remove you from duty.' A brief standoff, neither man moving. Then Maxwell reluctantly stepped back.

'Good.' Scott activated his mic again. 'Kill Reeve! *Now!*'

Reeve heard sudden shouts of alarm from behind. There was only one possible cause. The Operatives had drawn their guns.

Which meant they intended to use them.

Too many civilians around. He swerved between kiosks.

If he could deter them from shooting—

Gunfire echoed through the mall.

An advertising screen shattered beside him. He ducked. More panicked cries. Another shot. A woman spun and fell as a wound burst open in her shoulder. The child with her, no older than four, screamed.

Reeve could do nothing but run by. There was a supermarket to his right, the aisle's side open to provide access. He swerved behind the metal-clad support pillars for cover. Another round struck one just behind him. Shoppers fled, trolleys toppling and spilling their contents.

More daylight ahead, past escalators to the upper level. The southern exit. Reeve pounded towards it—

Someone barged people aside as he sprinted through the doors.

Blake.

He saw Reeve. His gun snapped up.

Reeve made a hard turn and dived for the escalators. Blake fired. The round cracked over Reeve. He scrambled up the moving staircase. No choice but to return fire: he would be exposed on the ascent. He snatched out his gun and sent two shots back at the pursuing Operatives. The pair split up, darting into cover. Further back, he saw Flynn and the other woman still coming.

Reeve reached the upper level. It led left, then angled back along the building's length. A glance down the escalator as he ran. Blake had reached its foot. The two male Operatives were moving again, not far behind him. The woman sprinted after them.

Flynn, though, had turned back. Reeve remembered there

were more escalators near the eastern entrance. She might try to cut him off there.

The four Operatives chasing him were his most immediate problem. The upper floor was less crowded. He raced along the corridor, rounding the corner to head back north.

Blake reached the escalator's top behind him.

Flynn hurried back through the mall. Security guards ran the other way. She kept her gun hidden, blending into the panicking crowd.

A familiar face ahead: Locke. His weapon was also still concealed. They met at the intersection where she'd first spotted Reeve. 'Where is he?' the blond man asked.

'Upstairs,' Flynn replied. 'But there didn't look to be any exits from the top floor. He's got to come back down somewhere.'

'There are lifts and escalators back there,' said Locke, indicating the way he had come. 'I'll cover them.'

They separated without another word. Locke reversed course, Flynn running down the side corridor to her entry point. More escalators were ahead.

If Reeve descended them, *then* she would draw her gun.

And use it.

'Get out of the way! Move!' Reeve shouted as he raced through the upper level. Shoppers here were more confused than frightened, unsure what was happening. The ones who saw his gun hurriedly cleared his path.

Those who didn't paid the price. He ran past an oblivious young man wearing ostentatiously large headphones. A bullet hit the youth in the back a moment later. *Now* everyone realised the danger as more gunfire erupted. An older man fell as a round blew open his temple.

Reeve saw more escalators ahead, off to his right. The main corridor continued past them. Go down, or keep going? Down. It would block his pursuers' line of fire. He swerved right. Another shot cracked past behind him. A shop window burst into a waterfall of glass.

He reached the escalators. The one descending was clogged with fleeing people. The other was clear, the stairs moving upwards. There was an emergency button at the base of the black rubber handrail. He shoved through the crowd and stamped on it. The up escalator abruptly stopped, an alarm trilling.

Reeve ran down the steps two at a time. Below, shoppers stampeded towards the exits—

Flynn was amongst them.

She looked up at the escalators – and saw him. Her hand whipped into her clothing—

Reeve vaulted over the escalator's side. The drop was three metres. He plunged downwards – hitting Flynn feet-first.

The collision sent him painfully to the floor. But Flynn took the worst of the impact. She was pounded flat, knocked breathless. Her gun skidded away across the polished tile. Before she could recover, someone tripped over her and fell. Another man right behind also stumbled, landing on them.

Reeve managed to get up before suffering the same fate. A woman reeled into him; he shoved her away and ran.

The exit was before him. It was a choke point, people

battling to get through the sliding doors. He checked behind. Flynn was somewhere under the human logjam. Blake had just reached the top of the escalators.

Reeve knew he was about to be targeted. If he tried to squeeze through the doors, he would be a sitting duck. Instead he ran to the exit's side. His gun came up – and fired. The window ahead of him burst apart. He jumped through the new opening without breaking stride.

Out into the car park. He needed a car, any car—

A woman was getting into a small red-and-black hatchback nearby. He ran to it and pulled her out. She screamed. '*Scusate*,' Reeve said in apology as he snatched her keys. A rapid check that there wasn't a child in the car, then he jumped in. The woman yelled for help. He slammed the door. Key in the ignition. He started the engine.

The shrill sound as he revved it warned him not to expect supercar performance. It was a Lancia Ypsilon, last surviving model of a once-proud marque. He didn't know the engine's displacement or horsepower. He doubted the latter came anywhere close to three figures.

It was all he had. He threw it into reverse and backed out of the parking bay, fast. The woman shrieked abuse at him. A sharp jerk of the wheel and the Ypsilon skidded around. Into first. He had to get to Venice, to Connie. The autostrada ran right past the mall. There must be a way on to it . . .

Foot down. The little car sped away. A glance in the mirror. Blake pushed through the scattering crowd. Gun up. Reeve ducked. Shots struck the Lancia's tailgate.

He turned right at the car park's edge. A circulation lane orbited it. He realised too late he was going against the traffic. All he could do was keep moving. He swerved to avoid an oncoming car, left wheels bounding over a kerb. Back down, and he accelerated.

The car park's exit – technically, entrance – was ahead. He dodged another car, then reached the road beyond, searching for the autostrada.

CHAPTER 50

Maxwell and Scott watched the screens as confusing radio chatter came in. The Operatives had been converging; now they were dispersing again. 'What's happening?' Scott demanded. 'Did they get him? Is Reeve dead?'

Wagner struggled to make sense of the overlapping messages. 'I don't think so – no. He's mobile, he's in a car.'

Scott jabbed an angry finger at the map. 'Then get them after it!'

'I'm at my vehicle,' Locke announced. His marker was back outside the mall's northeastern corner. 'Starting pursuit.'

Flynn cut in. 'I need pickup! Stone, where are you?'

'Coming around the car park,' the Londoner replied. His leg wound had relegated him to driving duties. 'I'm on my way.'

Maxwell saw that Stone was indeed looping back towards Flynn's position. Where were the other Operatives? Blake was running south outside the mall, presumably back to his car. Harris was heading through the mall to his own vehicle. That left Colt and Spurr—

'I'm mobile,' Spurr announced. He'd spotted a man in an Abarth 124 Spider convertible sports car. A quick, brutal pistol-whipping, and the Spider was his. He dumped the unconscious owner and set off. 'What am I looking for?'

'Black and red Lancia Ypsilon,' Blake said through his earpiece. 'Heading south.'

Spurr made an amused sound. 'This'll be a short chase.'

He swept the Spider on to the circulation lane alongside the mall. Blake was running along the pavement ahead. To his left, he glimpsed Colt acquiring transport of her own. A young man was riding a Suzuki SV650 motorbike. She delivered a flying kick to his chest as he passed. He tumbled from his ride. The bike crashed to the ground. Colt hauled it back up and jumped on, twisting the throttle. She caught up with Spurr in moments.

'Nice job,' he called. A smile in reply, then she powered away.

They both passed Blake as he rounded the mall's end. His Audi A6 was on the pavement outside the south entrance. He cut through fleeing shoppers and got in, starting up. A sharp squall from the tyres and he was away.

All seven Operatives were now pursuing Reeve.

Reeve's wrong-way departure brought him to a roundabout. More traffic came at him around it. He turned hard to the right, thumping over the roundabout's inner kerb on to grass. The Lancia lost grip and slewed around. He spun the wheel to counter it, then slammed back on the road, orbiting anticlockwise. The manoeuvre had cost him a few seconds. But at least he wouldn't risk any more head-on collisions.

Green signs at the exit ahead. The autostrada. He swept towards it. Mirror. Someone tore out of the car park behind him. The Operatives were already on his tail.

He raced up an incline, a bridge spanning the motorway. A slip road dropped away to the right. Another green sign pointed down it: *Trieste*. That way led northeast – away from Venice. He needed to get to the other side—

The car's satnav finally came to life. It revealed a problem. There was another roundabout on the bridge's far side. Farther away than the one he had just exited. By the time he circled it, the Operatives would be over the bridge. They would shoot him – or ram him – before he reached the autostrada's westbound slip.

Options flashed through his mind. A handbrake turn when he reached the slip road. Or—

Instinct made the decision for him. He jerked the wheel, crossing the white line and swerving left.

Through no entry signs – on to the eastbound autostrada's *exit* slip.

So much for no more head-on collisions, mocked an inner voice. He ignored it, concentrating totally on the road. This gamble made the Operatives less likely to follow him. Over the incline's brow, then down towards the motorway—

A surge of fear at the sight of a car rushing at him. He swung the Ypsilon left, hoping the other driver would avoid him. She did – just. The two vehicles whipped past mere centimetres apart. Metal shrilled as the Lancia scraped the crash barrier. He checked the mirror. The other car caught the opposite barrier harder and veered back across the road. It skidded to a stop, blocking the lane. His gamble had paid off. His pursuers wouldn't be able to follow.

Reeve looked ahead again. Another car headed towards him, but its driver pulled out of the Lancia's way.

The autostrada was ahead. Reeve swept on to it . . .

And realised he'd made a potentially fatal error.

Three lanes. No hard shoulder. Head-on into traffic. Which was charging towards him at 130 kilometres per hour.

The Operatives wouldn't need to kill him. He had just done it for them.

Colt led the pursuit on the SV650. She swept around the roundabout and powered up the incline. Reeve had gone left – on to the wrong side of the motorway. She turned to follow, then saw a car lurch to a halt on the slip road. There was room to pass it, but instead she swerved back towards the bridge. She wasn't wearing a helmet, or even riding leathers. With zero protection, chasing someone into oncoming traffic was suicide.

She saw she'd made the right decision as she crossed the bridge. A glance revealed Reeve facing three lanes of speeding traffic. 'He's heading west – on the eastbound motorway!' she yelled through the wind into her microphone. 'The lunatic's going to kill himself before we catch him!'

'Stay with him, Emma,' Maxwell ordered in her earpiece. 'Don't underestimate him.'

'We need to confirm the kill,' someone else added. It took a moment to identify the voice. Blake, she remembered from the flight. Smooth, suave . . . smug. She hadn't liked him.

'Will do, Tony,' she replied. Maxwell had been her tutor. 'I'm following.'

She crossed the bridge. The slip down to the westbound

autostrada was to her left. She braked hard and cut sharply across the other lane to zip down it. A few seconds and she was up to speed, squinting into the blasting wind. She glanced over the central barrier.

Somehow, her target was still alive.

Not for long. She pulled into the outer lane and reached for her gun.

Reeve's heart pounded as vehicles shot past, a terrifying meteor storm of steel. And he was driving straight into it.

The autostrada's lanes were just wide enough for him to pass between cars. But anything larger meant *he* had to move. He swerved clear of an approaching truck. Its horn blared, dopplering away as it thundered past.

The move put another car directly in his path. The driver was stunned by the sight of someone coming straight at him. Reeve swung back into the truck's wake. The car whipped by, veering as its driver panicked. A flat *bang* of crushing metal and breaking glass fell away behind.

He'd only been on the autostrada for thirty seconds. But that was already his fifth near-miss. His luck couldn't hold for ever. A couple of trucks side-by-side would finish him. He had to get off this road.

A split-second glance at the satnav. It showed other routes ahead, a complex rat's-nest of curving lines. Reeve looked up again. A sign on the other carriageway revealed an approaching exit. All destinations were backed by green: this autostrada met another motorway.

How far? Half a kilometre, less. If he could survive another thirty seconds, he could make it . . .

Another swerve took him up to the central divider. He was almost matching the speed of the westbound traffic beyond it—

Something in his peripheral vision triggered a warning. He glanced at the wing mirror. A motorbike on the other carriageway, closing.

The rider wore no helmet. A dark-haired woman – the Operative.

Gun in her hand—

Reeve hunched low, sweeping back across the lanes. A car clipped the Lancia's rear quarter, making the wheel jolt in his hands. He recovered. The impact was minor. Where was the woman?

The front passenger window exploded.

Reeve winced as the rush of incoming wind sprayed glass fragments over him. He nipped between two more cars. The Operative was gone from the mirror. Where—

She had drawn almost level. The gun tried to track him, jostled by the hundred-knot-plus wind. Another shot. This landed behind the passenger door, striking metal. The woman adjusted her aim. Reeve braked. She suddenly rushed ahead, then also slowed. He accelerated again as they passed under a bridge. Another crossing over the autostrada beyond, larger. The other motorway. The inner lane peeled away, becoming a slip road.

He waited until the last moment to let another vehicle pass – then swerved on to it.

The Ypsilon's tyres screeched, fighting for grip. He braked and wrestled with the wheel. The little hatchback rolled, then steadied.

Another shot from his right. This one missed. He accelerated. The road split again, one leg continuing straight while the other curved left. He took the latter. Too fast – centrifugal force threw the car against the barrier. The screech of metal assaulted his ears, sparks flying outside the windows. This slip road was narrower than the others. If a car came down it, they would clip each other. Anything bigger than a car . . .

Luck was on his side. Nothing ahead. He looked back at the main autostrada. The woman disappeared beneath a bridge, still heading west.

He slowed and stabbed at the satnav, zooming out. Where was he? This road led off the A57 – the autostrada to Venice's Marco Polo airport. It would take him away from Venice proper. The airport was on the mainland, well north of the city. He could follow another road along the Venetian Lagoon's edge, but it would be slower. He needed to reach Connie as soon as possible. The quickest route to the long bridge across the water was . . .

Back on to the autostrada he'd just left. Then take the SR14 highway. It met the only road into Venice.

He couldn't risk going against the traffic again. He'd barely survived a kilometre of it; the intersection was twice as far away. He needed to get on to the westbound lane. That meant risking another encounter with the Operative on the bike. But she'd seen him turn south, towards the airport. She might direct her companions after him, but wouldn't expect him to come back . . .

The slip road met another. Reeve zoomed the satnav in. The road curved around – to join the westbound autostrada. It would take him exactly where he needed to go.

He braked hard, yanking the handbrake. A sharp spin of the wheel sent the Ypsilon's tail screeching around. It came to rest pointing along the new road. He accelerated again.

Colt looked to her left. No sign of Reeve's car on the swooping tangle of slip roads. She'd lost him.

No, wait – another slip merged on to the autostrada ahead. It was at the end of the route her target had taken. He would still be going against traffic. That would slow, even stop him. She could catch up—

No sooner had the thought formed than she braked. Across the lanes, still slowing – then down through the gears. Hard on the front brake, weight shifting off the back wheel. Right foot down – and a sharp turn, releasing the clutch. The rear tyre shrieked as it laid a black arc on the asphalt. Colt expertly swept the Suzuki around, opening the throttle as she straightened. She jinked to avoid a car coming down the slip, roaring past it. Brakes screeched behind.

She accelerated. The road forked; she went right. The route would take her under the other autostrada, then back over the first. How long before she caught up with Reeve? Her gaze followed the road—

The Lancia was heading towards her.

CHAPTER 51

Reeve forced the Ypsilon back up to speed. He could hardly have picked a worse car for his escape. Its acceleration was painfully slow, the speedo's 200kph claimed top speed ludicrously optimistic. He glanced back along the autostrada as he crossed over it. A sports car was overtaking slower vehicles on the inside. The black Discovery was farther back, also speeding.

The Operatives. Could he stay ahead of them? Maybe he should have taken the airport route after all—

He looked back at the road ahead – and saw the woman on the bike.

Coming straight at him.

Her hand snapped up. *Gun*—

Reeve ducked as she fired. Rounds struck the car's front . . .

The windscreen blew apart.

A tsunami of shattered safety glass hit him. He closed his eyes, feeling thousands of tiny crystals scour his face. Then open again, despite the risk to his sight. He needed to see his enemy. She was still coming. Another shot hit the headrest just above him.

He'd instinctively lifted his right foot when he shut his

eyes. He stamped it down again. The Lancia's engine shrilled. He aimed the car at the Operative, gripping the handbrake. She would swerve to avoid him. Which way? Left or right?

Right—

He spun the wheel hard to the left – and yanked the handbrake. The Ypsilon's back end slewed around again, tyres shrieking. The rear bumper clipped the crash barrier . . .

Closing the Operative's path.

She braked. Too late. The Suzuki slammed into the Ypsilon's rear quarter. Colt was flung over its roof. She cartwheeled through the air – and hit a bridge support.

Reeve sat up, shaking off glass fragments. A burst of bright blood on grey concrete told him the Operative's fate. Her broken body was wrapped around the pillar's base.

The Lancia had stalled. He restarted it and straightened out. Through the gears, gaining speed. Too slowly. He'd barely reached a hundred when he rejoined the autostrada.

The wind through the broken windscreen blasted his face. He had to squint to see. The speedo's needle finally passed 130: the autostrada's limit. He kept his foot down, sweeping the car through gaps in the traffic. Mirror. Where were his pursuers?

He glimpsed the sports car as it swerved between lanes. A Fiat 124 – no, the black bonnet meant it was an Abarth. Tuned, more powerful, faster. The Discovery was visible some way behind it. Both were catching up. The needle reached 150 and hovered there, straining.

The Abarth grew in the mirror. He could see the driver now – the man outside the DHL depot. He'd abandoned his Evoque and stolen something faster.

The man's gun hand rose. Reeve swept into the lane ahead of the Spider. The Operative would have to blow out his own windscreen to shoot at him. But his pursuer simply pulled to the right, gun arm across his chest. The Fiat was still gaining. He would have line of fire in moments.

Reeve went left to overtake a van. The outside lane was blocked by another car. He charged up behind it, flashing his headlights. It didn't give way. Where was the Operative? He looked back. The Spider's driver would have a clear shot in seconds—

He braked and swung back across the motorway. His car was now a weapon, trying to ram the SC9 agent.

His opponent saw him coming. The Spider dropped back. Reeve found himself veering into empty space. He straightened, again directly in front of his opponent.

The Operative pulled himself higher, aiming over the windscreen's top. Reeve heard the shot even through the wind. A hole exploded in the rear windscreen. He weaved between lanes. Green signs on an overhead gantry. He was nearing a junction – the exit to Venice. If he could trick his adversary into thinking he was continuing straight on—

Reeve pulled into the outside lane to pass a car. The exit was coming up fast. He held his course until the last possible moment – then threw the Lancia to the right.

The car he'd just overtaken braked hard and spun out. The Ypsilon lunged across all three lanes. It cut in front of an SUV heading for the slip. Reeve gritted his teeth as he aimed through the narrowing gap. A yellow-painted crash barrier marked where the road split. His car scraped against it. Then he was through. He checked the mirror.

His pursuer hadn't been fooled. He'd also taken the exit lane, considerably less dangerously. The SUV Reeve had cut up was between them. That situation didn't last. The Operative moved almost against the barrier and blasted his horn. The other driver realised he was coming through no matter what, and slid over. The Spider powered through the gap.

Reeve looked ahead. Barriers hemmed him in as the road curved to the right. And he was coming up behind a truck. Not quite enough room to squeeze past it. The Abarth closed. The gun rose again—

Reeve braced himself – and aimed the Lancia into the gap to the truck's left.

It wasn't big enough. But he had nowhere else to go.

The car hit the barrier and the end of the trailer's rear safety bar simultaneously. The latter caused far more damage. It sheared away the right end of the Ypsilon's plastic front bumper. The debris fell under the now-exposed front wheel, briefly kicking the Lancia off the ground. Reeve fought to hold his vehicle straight as its left flank ground against the barrier. The safety bar was meant to stop cars from ploughing fatally beneath the trailer. But he was now alongside it – and it threatened to shred his front tyre. The Operative was right behind him. If he stopped, he was dead.

He might be dead anyway. The man rose in his seat again, lining up a shot—

The road snaked to the left. The truck driver hadn't yet reacted to events behind him. His vehicle eased rightwards as it rounded the bend . . .

Opening a space.

Reeve took it. Down two gears, and he accelerated. The

Lancia pulled clear of the trailer's rear. It skipped off the barrier as it overtook – and rebounded back to the right. The Ypsilon sideswiped the trailer's side underrun bar. The rear passenger-side window smashed with the impact.

Now the trucker realised something was wrong. Reeve glimpsed his startled face in the cab's mirror. The man braked, instinctively swinging his rig away from the car.

Too far. He hit the barrier on the other side of the confined slip road. The trailer rocked violently, threatening to tip over.

The barrier inside the curve ended, open grass replacing metal. Reeve swerved around the skidding prime mover. Behind, the Operative sent the Abarth snarling into the newly opened gap—

The truck reeled back into the slip lane. The trailer's left rear wheels were off the ground, still teetering on the brink. They pounded against the Spider's rear wing.

The blow knocked the sports car's nose around. It swerved helplessly to the right . . .

The trailer toppled back down on top of it.

The underrun bar fell like a guillotine blade. Spurr screamed as the trailer's entire weight pounded down on to him.

Reeve looked back. The truck lurched to a stop just past the end of the inner barrier. The trapped Abarth's driver was pinned – crushed – beneath the trailer.

Another threat removed.

He belatedly realised he'd been holding his breath. A gasp, then he turned back to the road. A blue sign told him he was nearing a roundabout. Left was the SR14: Venezia.

Where Connie was waiting. He increased speed, determined to reach her before SC9.

*

'Christ,' muttered Blake as he threaded his Audi past the stationary truck. Harris's Discovery was already through. The Spider was a mangled wreck, its occupant ditto. 'Spurr's had it. He went under a lorry.'

'Where's Reeve?' Scott demanded over the radio.

'Out of sight, but he can't be far ahead. We'll soon catch up. And we know where he's going.' He cleared the obstruction and accelerated again.

'I'm caught in a tailback,' said Locke. He was trailing the others, still on the autostrada. 'Traffic's stopped – I can't get through.'

'Mark, where are you and Deirdre?' asked Maxwell.

'On the slip road,' said Stone. 'I can see the crashed truck. Some cars in front of me, but I'll shove past 'em if they don't move.'

'Okay. Everyone stay on him. But be careful – we've lost two Operatives now. I don't want to lose any more.'

'He's just one man,' Scott cut in. 'How the hell have you not killed him by now?' His voice rose to a shout. 'I want him dead! At any cost! Do you understand?'

A grim smile formed on Blake's face. 'Absolutely, sir,' he said.

In the van, Maxwell stared silently at Scott. He knew what needed to be done – but it could end his career.

Or more.

A moment of thought, weighing his options . . . then he spoke. 'All Operatives – stand down. I repeat, stand down.' Wagner looked up at him in surprise. 'Regroup at location alpha. This has got out of control. There are only a limited number of ways out of Venice. We'll reacquire Reeve later.'

Scott's expression went from outrage to contained, dangerous fury. 'I beg your pardon?' he said slowly. No politeness behind the words: they were an undisguised threat. 'You do *not* countermand my direct orders, Maxwell.'

'Sir, we've got two dead Operatives already. We've engaged in a firefight in a public place, with civilian casualties. This has gone too far – it'll expose SC9. It's too risky.'

'*I* decide what the risks are!' Scott roared. Even though the older man was considerably shorter, Maxwell still flinched. Scott activated his mic. 'All Operatives, ignore that last message. Maxwell, you're relieved of duty. My orders still stand. Kill Alex Reeve!'

Shock hit Maxwell like ice water. 'Sir, you can't relieve—'

Scott jabbed a finger at his face. 'One more word, and I'll declare you Fox Red. Reeve is a threat to SC9, and must be eliminated at all costs. At all costs! Now, get out.' The finger stabbed towards the van's door.

Wagner looked between his two superiors in disbelief. Maxwell held position, eyes locked on to Scott's . . .

Then he turned away. Without a word, he exited.

The Italian warmth swept over him as he stepped out. A similar heat rose inside him.

He controlled it. Now, more than ever, he needed to stay calm. Everything depended on what happened in the next few minutes.

He took out his phone and made a call. It was quickly answered. 'Sir,' he said. 'We have a problem.'

CHAPTER 52

The SR14 was a two-lane dual carriageway. For the first kilometre, Reeve made rapid progress. Anyone in his way quickly moved over when he flashed his lights. His car's smashed front delivered an unsubtle message: *I'm not stopping for anything*.

But then he saw traffic lights ahead. They turned red, cars halting at the intersection. He couldn't do the same. The black Discovery had reappeared in his mirrors – only to be overtaken by an Audi.

Three lanes at the lights. The leftmost was empty, feeding the road crossing the junction. Vehicles trundled through the crossroads. Reeve charged towards it, judging speeds, distances – gaps. Could he make it through the traffic?

He would *have* to. There was now no way to stop in time. A car crossed in front of him, another not far behind. He reached the intersection, aiming for the space he hoped was still there—

The second car's driver saw him coming and braked. The gap opened up – just enough for the battered Lancia to whip through. Reeve cringed. He was doing over a hundred and twenty, with mere centimetres of space.

Where was the Audi? He checked the mirror—

Another vehicle rear-ended the car that had stopped. It bounded forwards – closing the gap.

Blake powered after Reeve. His prey had made it through the gauntlet; now, so would he—

The stationary car suddenly lurched forward, rammed from behind. It crossed Blake's path. He responded with pure reflex, jerking the wheel to the left and braking. The Audi swerved in front of the other car, missing by inches.

His evasive move took him on to the wrong side of the central barrier. Traffic waited in all three lanes behind the lights. Heel harder on the brake, spinning the wheel. The Audi's rear end swung out. Flick the wheel back to counter the spin, toe applying more power—

He already knew a collision was inevitable. He braced himself. The A6 squealed around, its tail swiping the car in the rightmost lane. The other vehicle was thrown sideways. Smashed glass and plastic showered the road. Both cars spun to a stop.

Blake straightened, pain rippling through his neck muscles. The airbag hadn't fired, to his relief. He heard Harris in his earpiece. 'Blake is out. He's crashed.'

'Like hell I have,' he growled. Harris's Discovery went more cautiously through the intersection. 'I'm still in the chase. Resuming pursuit.'

He swung the car around to bring it back on to the southbound carriageway. Before he reached it, another Discovery overtook him. 'Oi!' snapped Stone through his earpiece. 'Get out of my fucking way.'

Blake swore under his breath. He followed the Land

Rover out of the crossroads, then pointedly surged past it. He was as angry at himself as Reeve; he knew he was the better driver. He shouldn't have been caught out like that.

It wouldn't happen again. The next time he got that close to Reeve . . . it would be to kill him.

Maxwell waited with both anxiety and impatience for the man he'd called to speak. He'd explained the situation; there was surely only one possible course of action. But he wasn't going to take it unilaterally. That would be a death sentence. Scott had loyalists within SC9; they would kill him in retaliation. Unless he had support. *Official* support . . .

It finally came. 'I agree,' said Aubrey Ryford-Croft. Maxwell's call had been to the Chief of MI6. 'This operation has gone out of control. And I believe you're correct; it does risk exposing SC9. Which means that Sir Simon Scott . . .' A long, heavy breath before the sentence was completed. 'Has become a threat to the country.'

That was what Maxwell had been waiting for. But he wanted to hear Ryford-Croft say his next words unequivocally. GCHQ would be recording the call, as per Scott's own demand. He needed that proof to be somewhere in the system, to cover his own arse. To cover his own *neck*. 'So what should I do, sir?'

'You're a senior Operative of SC9,' Ryford-Croft replied. He knew exactly what game Maxwell was playing. 'You know what has to be done. Remove the threat.'

'Yes, sir.' Maxwell ended the call. A moment of stillness . . . then he turned back to the van.

*

Reeve cut through traffic, swerving between lanes to find every gap. The Operatives did the same. The black Discovery led them, bullying other motorists aside.

Farmland gave way to low urban sprawl. The chase was entering the outskirts of mainland Venice. The road dropped into an underpass, the lanes more confined than ever. Reeve was forced to slow as a BMW SUV overtook a van. No room to pass, and his Ypsilon was too small to shove either vehicle aside. The Discovery expanded in his mirrors. The BMW finally drew clear, a gap opening. Reeve took it.

So did the Land Rover. It followed him through, just metres behind. Was the Operative going to ram him, or—

The Discovery pulled out, engine roaring as it surged alongside him. Reeve glanced at it. The passenger-side window slid down. The driver reached into his jacket.

Out of the underpass. The Discovery held position, a metal wall to his left. A slower car was in Reeve's lane a few hundred metres ahead. The Lancia couldn't go any faster.

He was about to be boxed in.

The Operative's gun came up. Reeve braked a split-second before he fired. Two rounds clanked into the Ypsilon's bonnet. The Discovery slowed, falling back into place alongside him. More shots. Reeve shielded his face with his arm as the driver's side window blew out. He heard – *felt* – the whipcrack as a bullet passed right in front of his face. The slower car was only a hundred metres away. He braked again, dropping down the gears. The Operative matched his speed. A round hit the steering wheel, shredding the padding between his hands—

Now!

Reeve jammed his right foot to the floor. The little Lancia sprang forward. The Operative took a moment to react – by which time Reeve was past. He turned hard to the left, narrowly missing the slower car as he overtook.

But now the Discovery was right behind him.

It lunged, ramming the Ypsilon. Reeve fought to keep control as the damaged wheel squirmed in his hands. Another impact. This time, the Land Rover didn't fall back. It kept accelerating, pushing him with it.

The speedometer needle passed its previous high. Reeve felt panic rise. The Operative would either plough him into another vehicle, or spin him out. Both would be fatal – if not instantly, then very soon after. The wing mirror revealed the Audi and second Discovery coming up from astern.

The inside lane was clear. But if he turned into it while being pushed, he would spin – or flip over. He tried to coax more power from the Lancia. If he could pull away, just for a moment . . .

But it had nothing more to give. He was a helpless passenger, the Discovery a locomotive driving him to his doom. A glance at the rear-view mirror. Even through the bulletproof windscreen, the Operative's face was alight with impending triumph—

Not bulletproof. Bullet-*resistant*.

Fully protected MI6 vehicles couldn't lower their windows. The glass was too thick and heavy, the doors lined with armour. This one, though . . .

If the side windows were only bullet-resistant, the windscreen would be too.

He snatched out his gun and twisted in his seat. The

Operative reacted in surprise as the weapon swung at him—

Reeve fired. The first round hit the strengthened glass, creating an opaque spiderweb. The next landed almost precisely upon the same spot. The ragged white lines spread outwards. He kept firing with near machine-gun speed. The windscreen buckled, fractured . . .

Broke.

His final round punched a hole through the cracked window. It hit the Operative in his chest. He jerked back in his seat, arms spasming—

The Discovery abruptly swerved away. It almost dragged the Lancia with it, bumpers grinding. Reeve dropped the empty gun, sawing at the wheel to hold a straight line. Then the SUV swung clear. Another terrifying shimmy, barely caught.

Behind, the Discovery careered across the carriageway. It hit the low barrier, flipping into a corkscrew roll along the roadside. Two tumbles, three, demolishing road signs – then it hit a gantry's support. The Land Rover folded around it, debris flying.

Breathing heavily, Reeve regained full control. He flashed through traffic lights – these luckily at green. The Operatives were forced to slow to avoid the wrecked Discovery's strewn remains.

Respite. But only brief. He checked the satnav. A couple more kilometres to the road into Venice.

Whether he could reach the city itself was another matter. His pursuers had only been slowed, not stopped.

They would soon catch up.

*

Maxwell re-entered the van. He immediately knew the situation had worsened. 'Harris is down,' Wagner told Scott, dismayed. 'His vehicle's destroyed. Flynn says he looks dead.'

'I heard her,' Scott growled. He looked around as he realised Maxwell had returned. 'I told you to get out.'

'Sir,' Maxwell said. This was the moment that would decide his future. And how long it would be. 'I'm ordering you to stand down the pursuit.'

Wagner's eyes went wide. Beside him, Scott slowly straightened. 'You are . . . *ordering*?' His gaze fixed piercingly upon Maxwell. 'You have no authority, Maxwell. You're finished.'

Maxwell took a deep breath. *Be firm. Be resolute. Be ruthless.* 'SC9 is empowered to eliminate threats to British national security, by any means necessary. Your current actions constitute such a threat, by risking its exposure to a foreign power. On the orders of the UK intelligence chiefs, I am assuming command of the agency.' He drew his gun.

Scott stared at it in momentary disbelief. Then his face flushed with anger. 'On the *orders* of the intelligence chiefs? They don't have authority over SC9. And nor do you. I *am* SC9! I decide who is a threat – and you just qualified!' He turned to Wagner. 'I'm declaring Tony Maxwell as Fox Red. You know what that means. Kill him!'

The younger man looked helplessly between his two superiors. Then he swallowed, before speaking again – to Scott. 'Sir, he . . . he has a point. We've now lost three Operatives, very publicly. The Italians are already responding.' He nodded towards a radio scanner, LEDs flickering as it intercepted police transmissions. 'I agree with Tony. We need to stand down.'

Scott's fury only grew. 'This is treason. Treason! You're both Fox Red. You're dead.' He reached for the microphone's toggle to alert the other Operatives—

Maxwell's gun rose higher, pointing directly at his face. 'Don't.'

Scott froze. His expression changed, calculation, deduction behind the anger. 'This is what you wanted all along, isn't it? My job – control of SC9. And you'd do anything to make sure you got it.' Resurgent rage as a new thought came to him. '*You* helped Reeve, didn't you? *You* told him how to find me in France – and in London. He knew how to get into SC9's headquarters. You told him!'

Maxwell kept his own face carefully blank even as he felt a chill. It was a long-standing fear, the realisation that he'd been found out . . . 'I'm acting to protect British interests, sir,' he said, pretending to ignore the accusation. 'As I always have. My loyalties are to SC9, and the country. I will do whatever's necessary to protect them.'

Scott looked between the gun and the man behind it. He breathed faster: fear? Or was he about to try something? Maxwell didn't move, maintaining his cold mask . . .

When Scott finally spoke again, it was with a tremble. Resignation – or acceptance. 'What . . . what about my dogs?'

'They'll be looked after,' Maxwell told him. Scott gave him the slightest nod, exhaling—

Maxwell pulled the trigger. At almost point-blank range, the shot was instantly lethal. It punched a hole the thickness of a little finger through Scott's forehead. The exit wound was far larger. Blood and brain matter sprayed over the empty workstations. Scott's eyes rolled upwards, and he collapsed nervelessly to the floor.

All Operatives had killed before being recruited to SC9. Even so, Wagner reacted in shock. 'Jesus Christ, Tony!' he gasped. 'Shit!' He looked up at Maxwell, as if afraid he would be next.

Maxwell merely holstered his gun and retrieved his headset. 'All Operatives, attention,' he said. 'This is Tony Maxwell. I've assumed command of SC9. I have the full authority and backing of the UK intelligence chiefs. Stand down pursuit, immediately. Change your cars' plates at the first safe opportunity, then regroup at location alpha. We'll catch Alex another time. For now, protecting SC9 has priority. Acknowledge receipt of orders.'

The end of the road was approaching, fast. But Reeve knew he wouldn't reach it.

His remaining hunters jockeyed for position, competing to kill him. Blake was in the Audi, Stone driving the Discovery with Flynn beside him. Blake had led, until a car pulling out to overtake another forced him to brake. Stone used his larger, heavier SUV to ram the slower vehicle aside. He swept past Blake on the inside. The other Operative angrily dropped his Audi in behind him.

The highway ended at a roundabout. Reeve needed to go left to reach Venice. Too many cars coming towards him to cut the wrong way. He had to orbit it – which meant slowing down or risk losing control.

But either would kill him. Flynn leaned from the Discovery's passenger window, gun raised. Reeve ducked as low as he could as she lined up her sights on him—

He jinked the Lancia sideways. The round cracked past. But she was already readying her next shot.

They reached the roundabout. He had to brake as he rushed into it. The Discovery followed, right behind him—

It suddenly peeled off, taking the first exit.

For a moment Reeve thought the SUV had gone out of control. But it swept around the corner, carrying Flynn and Stone away.

There was only one possible reason for the hunt's sudden abandonment. They had been ordered to stand down. Maybe three dead Operatives was too high a price for Scott to pay.

But Blake's Audi was still in pursuit.

CHAPTER 53

'John,' said Maxwell in Blake's earpiece. 'The tracker shows you're still heading for Venice. I repeat: stand down. End pursuit.'

'I received clear orders,' Blake replied, powering after Reeve. He didn't know what had happened, but doubted it had gone well for Scott. There was no way he would meekly stand down for Maxwell. And SC9 was meant to be completely independent from the other intelligence agencies. If Maxwell was taking orders from them, SC9's integrity had been compromised. 'The boss said to kill Reeve, whatever the cost. I intend to carry out those orders.'

'John, *I'm* giving you a direct order. Stand down! I'm—'

He tore out the earpiece. Screw Maxwell. Blake had always regarded his former trainer with vague disdain. He was a glorified drill instructor with ideas above his station, nothing more.

And now he'd killed the boss to take his place? What was this, some banana republic? A power play, backed by rival intelligence heads: that was it. A grubby, cowardly attempt to defang and control SC9. To Blake, that was a threat to the country as a whole. SC9 was vital to national security, the sharpest of all its spears. Blunting it – or breaking it – was madness. Borderline treason. When this was over, he would take a very close look at the plot's backers. There were other Operatives who would join him. Perhaps it was time to clean house . . .

First things first. A blue sign: *Venezia 6*. Less than four miles, and Reeve would literally run out of road.

Not that Blake intended to let him get there. It was now a straight race. A straight *fight*: man on man, hunter versus hunted.

No matter what, he would kill the traitor.

Reeve weaved through traffic as he headed for Venice. A new, unexpected obstacle appeared. He'd registered an odd single rail set into one lane as he left the roundabout. Now he saw what it was. A tram stood at a stop ahead. Cars had slowed and pulled out to pass it. He was forced to join them: there was no way around. Blake's Audi was a few cars back, also hemmed in. He overtook the tram. The single rail was explained; it had pneumatic tyres, the steel line just a guide.

The cars spaced out beyond the obstruction. He swung around them. Horns blasted in his wake. Another roundabout ahead. The road to Venice was reduced to one lane at the exit. It crossed a bridge over a waterway. Oncoming vehicles were dotted along the other side of the road.

Reeve followed the traffic on to the bridge approach. He regarded the approaching string of cars, dropped into second – then pulled out.

The Ypsilon's engine felt more pitiful than ever, straining on the incline. A car ahead flashed its headlights in warning.

Reeve ignored it, rapidly closing the gap. The other driver panicked and braked. That gave Reeve the extra few metres he needed. Engine screaming, he cut back in centimetres ahead of the car he'd overtaken.

The Audi was stymied by other cars on the confined road. Reeve pulled out again to round a second vehicle. The bridge ended; back on land. He glanced at the satnav. How much further to the Venice road?

Not much. Over another river, then he would merge on to it. Behind, Blake overtook one car, making up lost ground. The road forked ahead. Reeve followed the tram line. The route dropped downwards, straightening. *Venezia 4*. Only the bridge to cross now . . .

And then he had to find Connie. Before Blake did.

Roads merged – and he was at last on the SR11 highway. It led directly to the Venetian islands. A large brown sign on a gantry greeted him. *Welcome – Willkommen – Bienvenue: Venezia*.

He was finally in the city limits proper. But he was still on the mainland. The bridge started ahead. The speed limit was 70kph. He'd already exceeded that before reaching the waterline.

The lagoon opened out around him. A bright red high-speed train headed for land; the bridge took road and rail. The two-lane dual carriageway ahead shrank to a distant vanishing point. Reeve saw the towers of Venice rising beyond it.

But the Audi was closing. Would he make it? He *had* to. He had to reach Connie. He kept his foot hard down.

Left, right, left, snaking through more traffic. Most of the other cars were doing seventy, holding at the limit. Nobody wanted a speeding fine. He whipped past them, wind scouring his face. Blake's car was a constant presence in the mirror, growing ever larger.

Reeve was at full throttle, such as it was. He passed more vehicles. So did Blake. The Operative's hand came out of the side window, light catching gunmetal. He fired. The shot went wide. But Reeve knew it was only a sighter. Blake was judging how much the wind affected his aim. Too much at this range.

So he would get closer.

There was nothing Reeve could do to open the gap. All he could do was maintain it. He made harder turns as he overtook other drivers, trying to scare them into braking. If he blocked both lanes—

They were already blocked. But not for Blake. For him.

A coach filled the inside lane, a tourist bus on its way into Venice. An Opel Astra matched its speed alongside. There was no room to squeeze between them. Reeve came up behind the Astra, flashing his lights. But the driver refused to move.

Reeve forced the issue. He bumped the other car. Too hard an impact and the Astra would lose control and crash. The Ypsilon pushed at it, engine straining.

But rather than speed up, the Opel's brake lights came on. Reeve dropped a gear and revved hard. The Lancia jolted, but couldn't make headway against the larger car. Behind, Blake's Audi closed on its prey. His arm came out of the window again—

Reeve ducked sideways. A gunshot cracked behind him.

The bullet went over his shoulder – and through the smashed windscreen.

It hit the Astra's rear window. Glass shattered. The driver jumped in fright – then the brake lights went off. The car pulled sharply away.

Reeve followed it. The coach slid past to his right. The Opel swung in front of the bus to get clear. He overtook it. Blake was still on him. A second shot struck the Lancia's rear window pillar.

Venice swelled on the horizon. Reeve could now see the bridge's end, curving rightwards to meet the island. He swung around another car. Blake followed. A bullet thunked against the Ypsilon's tailgate. Reeve darted back to the right to limit Blake's firing angle. He would have to draw alongside him to shoot—

Blake withdrew his gun and accelerated. But he didn't aim the weapon through his passenger-side window. Instead he turned his entire car into a projectile. The A6 slammed side-on against the Lancia. The smaller car hit the barrier. Metal screamed as it ground against it.

Reeve tried to steer away. No use. The Ypsilon was pinned by the bigger, heavier Audi. Hammer-blows pounded at him through the steering. The right-front wheel had been left exposed when the bumper was sheared away. Whenever he turned the steering wheel, the tyre hit the corrugated metal. If it burst, he was doomed—

Blake suddenly pulled clear. Reeve immediately swerved away from the road's edge. But the Operative had only retreated so he could make a more powerful attack.

The Audi surged forward – then smashed back into him.

The Lancia slammed against the barrier—

And bounded on top of it.

The front wheel, spinning fast, rode up and over the obstacle with a bang. Reeve was thrown against the door as the car tilted. He hauled frantically at the steering wheel. Nothing happened. Both front wheels were off the ground. The Audi was forcing him along.

Blake braked – then dropped in behind the Ypsilon and accelerated again.

The collision flung Reeve against the wheel. The Lancia swung around, grinding along the barrier's top. It was now moving sideways, the Audi's nose hard against the passenger door. Blake stared at Reeve with an expression of impending victory.

Horror filled Reeve as he realised why. The rear of a tram filled the lane ahead. Blake was going to plough him into it. Nowhere to go.

He braced—

The Lancia hit the tram.

The impact threw it over the barrier, spinning on to a pedestrian walkway. The safety railing was demolished by a tonne of flying metal. The wrecked vehicle bowled over the bridge's edge . . .

And plunged into the lagoon below.

Reeve yelled as he fell – then was silenced as seawater exploded into the cabin.

With its windows blown out, the car sank like an anchor. Choking, blinded, panic almost overcame him. He fought back his fear. His seatbelt was still fastened, trapping him. He fumbled for the release. The Lancia kept sinking, bubbles swirling around him. His hand found the button. It depressed – but didn't click. He was upside-down, his weight straining the mechanism. He swung his legs up and pushed against the dash. Come on, release—

The metal tongue popped from the buckle. He dropped free – as the inverted car hit the bottom of the lagoon.

The Lancia's roof collapsed beneath him with an echoing boom. His head struck it. He almost cried out, but clamped his mouth firmly shut. His jacket swirled around him as he tried to turn in the confined space. Something slipped from a pocket, bumping his arm—

Parker's phone.

His leverage – his lifeline. His protection against SC9. He grabbed for it. But it was already gone. He forced his eyes open. Grey-green murk filled the cabin. Sediment had been kicked up when the car landed, roiling through the broken windows. Reeve could barely see his hands, never mind anything beyond them. He groped at the roof, but found nothing. The phone was lost.

Immediate survival trumped longer-term concerns. He pulled himself through the driver's window. The bug-out bag's strap snagged on something. He squirmed loose, leaving it behind, and swam out. Light shimmered above. He kicked away from the wreck. The pressure in his lungs, the urge to breathe, was rising—

Icicles stabbed down at him.

Not icicles. Bubbles, cavitation trails. The wake of bullets fired into the water.

Blake.

*

The Audi whirled to a stop behind the tram. The car's front end was caved in, steering damaged by the crash. Blake didn't care. It had done its job.

Now he had to finish his.

He clambered out and vaulted the damaged barrier. The Lancia had ripped a six-metre length of railing from the walkway's edge. He went to the gap. A frothing bullseye marked where Reeve's car had hit the water.

A grey rectangular shape was barely visible beneath. Had Reeve survived? He aimed his gun at what he thought was the driver's side and opened fire. Another car had stopped, its occupant getting out; they hurriedly retreated. Blake emptied the magazine, smoothly slotting in a replacement.

No sign of movement beneath the waves. But that didn't mean Reeve was dead. The Lancia's windows were broken, so water pressure wouldn't have trapped him inside. If he stayed deep as he swam, the churned surface would hide him.

A muttered obscenity. He couldn't confirm the kill.

Blake withdrew with a frown. He couldn't stay any longer. The police would have been alerted. A glance along the bridge. He was only a few hundred metres from land. The road led into Venice.

Where Reeve's girlfriend would be waiting.

The kill wasn't confirmed – yet. But he knew where she would be. Where Reeve would go. If he arrived, Blake could get both targets at the same time.

If he didn't . . . a threat to SC9 would still have been eliminated.

He ran along the walkway. The tram had stopped fifty metres on, its rear smashed. There were casualties, bloodied passengers staggering out. Blake ignored them. All that mattered was completing the mission.

Alex Reeve and Connie Jones had to die.

CHAPTER 54

Reeve swam along the lagoon's floor, heading towards darkness. The bridge's shadow. It would shield him from Blake. He stayed underwater until the fire in his lungs forced him to the surface.

He broke though the rippling waves and gasped for air. The burning in his chest gradually subsided. He was beneath a brick archway. Boats bobbed at their moorings ahead of him. He looked back. The froth of his car's impact with the water was fading.

Other boats were coming to investigate the crash. The nearest approached from the island side of the bridge. Reeve waved, then waited for it to reach him.

The boat was a working craft, carrying several wooden crates. Venice's canals were not merely tourist attractions: they were vital arteries for residents and businesses. Reeve grabbed its side. The pilot stepped carefully around his cargo and pulled him up. Reeve flopped gratefully on to the flat deck.

'Are you all right?' said the boatman. 'I saw your car go into the water! What happened?'

'Someone crashed into me,' Reeve replied wearily. Despite his exhaustion, he summoned his reserves of strength. He would need them. 'I'm sorry.'

'For what?'

'For this.' Before his rescuer could react, Reeve shoved him over the side. The man crashed on his back in the water.

Reeve hurried to the stern and squeezed the outboard's throttle to full. The engine roared, pushing the craft out into the open. Reeve looked up at the bridge. No sign of Blake. The boatman surfaced, bellowing abuse after him.

Where was he? Reeve only knew Venice's layout from tourist maps. Somewhere at the city's western end. Connie's meeting place was on the eastern side, beyond the Doge's Palace. That meant it was along the Grand Canal. He was in a boat – going by water was probably the quickest way there.

But which route? Circling the islands? That would take him the long way, rounding the cruise and container ports. Along the Grand Canal itself? Not a direct route either. It twisted and coiled back on itself as it bisected the city. The police also patrolled it; he doubted his boat could outrun them.

But Venice was criss-crossed by smaller canals. As long as he headed roughly southeast, he should reach St Mark's. And the police presence would be lower in the lesser waterways.

He hoped.

Strings of boats headed under other arches of the road bridge. A lot of traffic – a major route. Perhaps even the entrance to the Grand Canal itself. He brought his craft to full speed, following them.

Blake reached land. He heard an approaching siren and immediately slowed to a brisk walk. His jacket was reversible, the inside a much stronger colour. He quickly flicked it inside-out and redonned it. Seconds later, a police car appeared ahead. He kept his hand near his gun. But the cops raced past, heading for the bridge.

He continued until he could leave the main road. Once out of sight, he brought up his phone's map. GCHQ's blanket surveillance had told SC9 where the Jones woman would be. He entered the Riva degli Schiavoni as his destination. Route options appeared. He frowned. At least thirty-four minutes, on foot? And the shortest choice required a ferry crossing. No telling how long he might have to wait. Unacceptable. If Reeve wasn't dead, he would also head to Jones. Most likely by boat. All he had to do was mug any Good Samaritan who picked him up. Blake would have done the same thing.

So he needed a boat himself. A new search. Numerous water-taxi stops popped up on the map. The nearest were only a short distance away. He hurried for them.

Reeve brought his boat past a rank of water-taxis, large and small. To his left was Venice's railway terminus; ahead, a sweeping steel and glass bridge. The number of tourist vessels suggested he was already on the Grand Canal. Which meant he needed to get off it.

Beyond the bridge was a smaller, older one crossing a canal to the right. The Grand Canal curved away leftwards, heading north. He turned down the minor route. A sign warned that the speed limit was five knots. He ignored it, heading south as fast as his boat could go.

*

Blake reached the Grand Canal. He was directly across the water from the railway station. According to his map, the water-taxis should be to his right.

They were. Plenty to choose from, large and small. The biggest was a *vaporetto* – more water bus than water-taxi, carrying dozens. Like a bus, though, it would only go to specific stops. He needed something to take him to an exact spot.

Some of the smaller boats were traditional in design, made from polished dark wood. They were the official, licensed craft serving the city's visitors. Others, however, were ordinary, unremarkable motorboats – waterborne gypsy cabs. Unlicensed, possibly even illegal. Their pilots sat up with predatory attention as he approached.

'Hey, *inglese*?' Blake called to the nearest man. Italian had not been one of his priority languages during training. He knew enough to scrape by, but didn't want to waste time.

'*Sì*, yeah,' the pilot replied. 'You want a ride?'

'Can you take me to the Riva degli Schiavoni? Fast?'

'Yeah, yeah. No problem. Get in.' He moved to untie the boat as Blake clambered aboard. 'Okay. Ride's gonna be . . . two-fifty euros.'

The Operative eyed him coldly. 'Two *hundred* and fifty?'

The man shrugged. 'You want fast, it costs. If the cops stop me, I got to pay the fine, yeah?'

Blake didn't have time to argue. Besides, he could afford it. SC9 had provided a decent amount of contingency money. 'Okay, fine. Let's go.'

The pilot's only movement was to hold out his open hand. 'You pay first, okay?'

An even colder look, then: 'Here.' He counted out notes and slapped them into the man's hand. 'Now get moving.'

He sat as the pilot went to the wheel. The knowledge that he was being ripped off rankled. But he needed to cross Venice quickly.

Besides, he could always kill his driver and take the money back.

The boat pulled out and began its journey. It passed under the long arching footbridge – and turned north, following the Grand Canal. The fading wake of another speeding craft briefly rocked it, unnoticed, as it powered away.

CHAPTER 55

Reeve guided his stolen vessel southwards. Irate shouts came from behind. He looked back, seeing other boats rolling wildly in his wake. He was barely doing twenty-five kilometres per hour, but that was enough to bring chaos.

Ahead, the canal split. One route continued south, the other turning southeast. Which way? He took the latter purely because it was wider. The buildings lining it were modern, as out of place as an alien spacecraft. He was off the tourist route, somewhere Venice's citizens actually lived and worked. It felt oddly as if he was peeking behind the curtain.

A crossroads. Straight on, or right? Neither route offered any apparent advantage. He continued ahead. Older, traditional buildings surrounded him again. A woman on a balcony shouted angrily. He saw why as he passed. His wake splashed against a doorway slightly above water level. He had probably just flooded her hall. 'Sorry,' he called back. The apology was not well-received.

He passed under a bridge. The canal narrowed. Two boats were coming the other way. He turned between them – only for the rearmost to swing in front of him. The pilot was trying to get out of *his* way. Panic in the other man's eyes as he realised Reeve was on a collision course. The Englishman cut his engine, shoving the tiller. His boat curved back towards the canal's side. Not quickly enough—

The two boats thumped against each other. One of the crates slid off the deck into the water. The other man clutched his gunwales for support, then yelled at him. 'Serves you right, moron! Slow down and watch where you're going!'

Reeve gave him a half-hearted shrug and resumed his journey. A thought occurred, and he threw the other crates overboard. Reducing the load let the boat go slightly faster.

Another, wider waterway ahead. He headed out into it – realising he had rejoined the Grand Canal. His shortcut had sliced a large chunk out of the journey to Connie.

He turned south. The Grand Canal was busy, dozens of boats going in both directions. Several *vaporetti* clustered ahead. He soon saw why. They were slowing to let tourists photograph the famous Ponte dell'Accademia bridge. He cut left so as not to pass between them—

A new noise over the burble of diesel engines. A siren. Reeve looked between the water buses. A blue-and-white speedboat was powering in his direction. Police. Looking for a stolen, speeding boat.

Even without cargo, his craft wasn't making close to thirty kilometres per hour. The oncoming speedboat was easily exceeding that. He couldn't outrun it.

He had to get ashore. But where?

The boat passed under the bridge. A large ochre building stood on the waterfront to his left. There was a gap between it and the structure beyond. A side canal? He turned towards it. The approaching cops did the same. They'd seen him.

A sign told him he was entering the Rio de l'Orso. He

swept into it, the boat's side scraping a wall. The narrow new waterway was a dead end, gondolas moored along it. The memory of a thriller Reeve had once read popped into his mind. The hero's boat had swept up a ramp at the end of a Venetian canal. That wouldn't work here. Brick and stone formed a decisive, vertical end. Instead he kept going for as long as he dared, then cut the engine. The boat glided on. Reeve stood as the gondolas slipped past. Ready, time it just right—

Jump.

He leapt into a gondola. It rocked violently, but he grabbed the quayside to steady it. His own boat continued onwards – then hit the wall at the canal's end. The bow caved in with a bang.

Reeve scrambled up to the pavement above. He was at the southern end of a long piazza. Tourists looked around in surprise at the noise. He raised his hands to say *nothing to worry about*, then ran, wet clothes flapping.

Connie's meeting place was to the east. He needed to head parallel to the Grand Canal. A street led from the piazza in that direction. He raced down it. Another square opened out ahead—

Shit! The space was totally enclosed by buildings. Gates and doorways led off it, but he had no idea to where. He couldn't risk getting caught in a maze, not with the police closing. He ran back into the piazza. The siren echoed from the narrow canal. He sprinted northwards. Buildings blocked his way east. How the hell was he supposed to reach Connie?

There. A narrow alley, crowded with people in shorts and

sunglasses. A yellow sign with an arrow beside it: *Per S. Marco*. St Mark's. Reeve shoved into the confined passage. Like it or not, he would have to follow the tourist routes. He weaved around visitors, beginning his desperate race east.

Blake sat impatiently as the boat cruised under the Rialto bridge. Under normal circumstances, he would have taken the time to admire the landmark. He wasn't in Venice to play tourist, though. 'Hey,' he called to his driver. 'I paid you a lot of money to go fast. So go fast.'

'I'm going fast,' the boatman replied insolently. 'You want to go faster? Buy a speedboat.'

Blake considered shooting him and taking the controls himself. Instead, he took out another hundred euro note. 'Will this help?'

The man hesitated, then took it. 'Yeah. Okay. Hold on.'

The boat picked up speed. Other canal users shouted abuse as its wake rocked their craft. Even so, Blake estimated it was only making twenty knots. Over twice the limit on the Grand Canal, but still frustratingly slow—

The engine note fell again. He glared at the driver. 'What are you doing?'

The Italian gestured ahead. 'Police, look.'

Blake saw a blue-and-white speedboat back out of a side canal, strobe lights flashing. 'I thought you were willing to pay the speeding fine.'

The boatman snorted. 'No, I'm not stupid.'

Blake again overcame the urge to kill him. He settled irritably back into his seat.

*

Reeve ran through the narrow streets, following the signs for St Mark's. The route was inevitably crammed with tourists. Several times, he had to physically force his way through crowds.

But his path was at least relatively straight. There were some stretches where he'd even reached a good speed. Not for the first time, he was glad he'd kept training while in hiding.

He pounded over a bridge into a square. An ornate white marble church stood before him. He glanced at the nearby shops as he raced past. Versace, Prada, Cartier. Pricey brands – he was nearing the city's touristic heart.

Bulgari. Jimmy Choo. Chanel. Through a dark, bustling passageway – and the Piazza San Marco opened out before him. The marble and red-brick tower of the Campanile rose directly ahead. He was nearing the rendezvous with Connie. The thought of her spurred him on.

Past the great domed Basilica, painted frescoes aglow in the afternoon sun. Southwards towards the lagoon, around the Doge's Palace. He was back at the Grand Canal. The waterfront was packed with people gazing at the church on the island opposite. He couldn't remember its name. It didn't matter. All that did was reaching Connie.

He weaved through the crowd, heading east over a bridge beyond the palace. Connie had said to meet at somewhere called Falconi's. He couldn't see it yet, but spotted awnings ahead. Another bridge, and he reached a row of restaurants.

His destination was just beyond an alley running. Ranks of tables outside, large square marquees providing shade. His gaze darted over the seats. Connie wasn't there. Maybe inside. He hurried to the café's entrance. No sign of her. 'Connie!'

People looked around at the shout. None were her. She wasn't here.

He darted back outside, looking frantically back and forth. Still nothing. Fear rose within him.

Had SC9 reached her first?

CHAPTER 56

Connie checked her watch as she strolled towards the Grand Canal. Still a while before Alex was due to arrive. And he would probably be late. By now, she knew how long it took to get around Venice. The place was a maze, and crowded at that. It was always worth adding at least ten minutes to any estimated journey time.

That was assuming you were heading straight to your destination. The problem with Venice was that there were so many interesting things to delay you. She couldn't wait to share her discoveries with Alex. Every winding street contained some unique shop, fascinating museum or beautiful architecture. The city was everything she'd hoped.

She only wished she'd been able to enjoy it more. The first few days had been fearful, paranoid – and lonely. It took some time before she overcame her anxieties. She'd stayed at four different hotels and hostels, picked at random. She had made a point of being friendly to the staff. In return, they'd confirmed nobody had asked about her. SC9 hadn't found her yet.

And, she gradually came to accept: why would they? Nobody knew she'd come to Venice. She'd followed Alex's instructions. All her transport and accommodation had been paid for in cash. She hadn't made any phone calls. Web use had been limited, and only from public computers in internet cafés. After the first week, she began to feel safe – as safe as she could, anyway.

Then, finally . . . the phone she always had with her rang.

Her relief at hearing Alex's voice again was almost overwhelming. He was alive – and safe. No duress code. Thank God. So now she was on her way to meet him, filled with growing excitement. More than that – joy. The man she loved had survived his self-appointed mission. Had he actually forced SC9 to back down? *Oh please, let it be true . . .*

She crossed a bridge, glancing down the canal. A section had been closed off by steel dams at each end, the water drained. She'd been this way before, appreciating the rare glimpse into Venice's hidden underpinnings. The thick wooden pilings supporting a museum's foundations were being replaced. A barge was grounded in the exposed mud, a small excavator sitting incongruously atop it. The workers were knocking off, a last man climbing scaffolding to exit the canal.

Connie continued on, rounding the museum itself. It was somewhere she wanted to visit. Not today, though: the elderly custodian was ushering visitors out. Maybe tomorrow, with Alex. She didn't know what he thought of historic Venetian carnival masks and costumes. But after what she'd endured, he could bloody well *pretend* to be interested . . .

More cramped streets led to a small piazza. A local station for the Carabinieri was at its south end. Beyond, an alley led to the Riva degli Schiavoni. The restaurant was right beside its end. She blinked as bright sunlight hit her. A pair of youthful cops standing nearby gave her approving looks as she emerged. She suppressed a smile at the attention.

No sign of Alex outside the restaurant, but she wasn't surprised. She took a seat and waited for him to arrive.

Connie could approach the rendezvous from four possible directions. West or east along the waterfront, or two alleys to the north. Reeve hurried eastwards, neck craned in the hope of spotting her over the crowds. He got as far as the crest of a bridge sixty metres on, then stopped. If she was coming his way, he couldn't see her.

He turned around. All he could do was keep searching. Back to the other bridge, then check each alley, before returning. Sooner or later he would find her.

If Blake didn't find her first.

Blake's boat bumped to a stop against the quayside. Gondolas were moored along it; his driver squeezed between them. From the gondoliers' scowls, he wasn't meant to be there. 'This is it,' announced the boatman. 'Riva degli Schiavoni.'

'About time,' said Blake, clambering ashore.

The Italian had his hand out again. 'Hey. A tip?'

The tip of a nine-millimetre round, delivered at high velocity, was Blake's immediate thought. But he'd already noticed some police officers along the waterfront. He settled for venting his annoyance verbally. 'You want a tip? Don't rip off your passengers, or you may end up face-down in a canal.' The man muttered an insult.

The Operative ignored it, looking around. The arched white façade of the Doge's Palace was beyond a bridge to his left. No cafés or restaurants on the stretch where he'd landed. He turned right. Crowds, tourist stalls, then another bridge. Canopies extended from the buildings beyond it.

Reeve's meeting place had to be amongst them. He set off through the milling tourists.

The hunt had resumed.

Reeve pushed through the throngs on the waterfront. Falconi's was ahead. He would quickly check it again, then continue to the next bridge—

No need. Connie sat at a table outside. He recognised her even though she'd dyed her hair much darker. Not one of his instructions; she'd changed her appearance on her own initiative. He felt a brief moment of pride in her.

But it was overpowered by other, conflicting feelings. Relief and happiness at seeing her again – versus concern and fear. She was in plain sight. Anyone coming along the Riva degli Schiavoni could spot her.

He broke into a run, elbowing people aside. 'Connie!' he cried. 'Connie!'

Her head turned – and she saw him. Delight blossomed on her face. 'Alex!' she replied, standing.

Someone else reacted to her call. Reeve saw a head in the crowds beyond the café snap towards her. A man, tall, black-haired.

Blake.

Thirty metres away. His hand darted into his jacket—

It paused. Two uniformed carabinieri stood near the

alley's entrance. Blake lowered his arm, then marched towards the restaurant.

Reeve reached it first. 'Connie, move! We've got to go.'

Connie's smile vanished. 'What is it?'

'SC9, right there.' He glanced towards Blake. 'Come on.'

He took her arm and manoeuvred her between the tables. They emerged beside the alley. Blake was still coming, nearing the carabinieri. One of the cops caught the sudden movement at the restaurant. His eyes went to Connie – then the man with her.

Reeve knew from his change of expression the officer had been given his description. His wet clothes were the biggest giveaway. 'Run,' he snapped, pulling Connie with him into the passage.

The carabinieri turned to his comrade. 'It's the guy who stole the boat!' he said. 'Call it in – I'll catch him!' He raced after the couple.

The other officer hurriedly raised his radio to alert the nearby station. Blake ran behind him.

Reeve and Connie charged down the alley. A building with an Italian flag outside was, to Reeve's alarm, a police station. But they were past it before anyone inside responded to the alert.

They entered a square. 'Over there,' Connie said, pointing ahead and left. 'It's the only way out. My hotel's near here,' she added.

Reeve didn't question her local knowledge. They ran on, swerving past tourists—

Shots echoed around the piazza.

*

The carabinieri was a few metres ahead of Blake as both men pursued their targets. He was a problem, the Operative decided. The Italian authorities couldn't be allowed to arrest Reeve or his girlfriend. Too great a risk to SC9 if they talked. Without breaking stride, he drew his gun and shot the cop twice in the back. The young man tumbled, head striking the flagstones with a crack.

Blake leapt over him – realising too late he was passing a police station. He cursed. Nobody was coming out of it, but that would very soon change.

The piazza ahead was busy. The shots brought terror, screams rising. He hid his gun and joined the fleeing crowd, following his targets.

Reeve and Connie hared through the streets. 'Where are we going?' Connie gasped.

'I don't know.' Reeve's knowledge of the city was limited to its tourist landmarks. 'We've just got to lose him.' He glanced back. Blake rounded a corner twenty-five metres behind. But there were too many people between them for him to get a clear shot.

'Maybe we should split up?'

His reply was firm. 'I'm not leaving you again.'

She gave him a look of grim thanks – then pointed. 'Wait, I know where we are. Go right!'

They swerved down a side street. It twisted and jinked, blocking Blake's line of fire. 'There's a real maze this way,' Connie panted. 'I got lost in it once. If we can stay ahead of him—'

She broke off as they entered a small, bustling square. Several confined streets led out of it. A policeman barrelled down one, shouting for pedestrians to move. 'Not that way,' said Reeve.

'But that was where I was taking us!'

'We'll have to improvise.' He angled towards another exit—

'Alex, wait!' Connie pulled at his hand, leading him to the doorway of an old building. A sign read *Museo Carnevale*.

'We'll be trapped inside,' he warned.

'There's scaffolding at the back – we can get out that way.'

Again, he accepted that she knew Venice better than he did. They rushed in. Darkness swallowed them; the interior was dimly lit. Reeve blinked, eyes struggling to adjust. Connie tugged at him again. 'I think the back's this way—'

'Hey, you can't come in.' An old man holding a broom came from a side door. 'The museum's closed.'

Reeve glanced outside. The cop had reached the square. Whether Blake had too he didn't know, and had no intention of looking. 'Go,' he urged Connie. They hurried past a counter through a doorway marked *Ingresso*.

The custodian shouted angrily, banging his broom on the floor. 'Hey! *Hey!* Get out!'

Blake rushed into a small square – and slowed as he saw a running cop. Had his description reached the authorities? His hand crept towards his gun . . .

The officer passed him and disappeared the way Blake had come. The Operative relaxed, fractionally. He still had to reacquire his targets. Where had they gone?

Not up the street the cop had come from, obviously. That left three possibilities. He looked down each. No sign of them. Damn it! He'd been so close to catching Reeve . . .

A muffled commotion caught his attention. He turned towards an old building – a museum, from the sign. Shouted Italian came from within. He understood enough to know the speaker wanted somebody to leave.

Adrenalin surged. Reeve, it had to be. Hiding rather than running had served him well for a year and a half. He was falling back into old habits. *Flawed* habits. He'd been found. And now, it had happened again.

He went through the doorway. Low light in the hall beyond. He reached for his weapon; Reeve might try to attack as his eyes adapted.

But the traitor and his girlfriend weren't there, only a gesticulating old man. He turned, seeing the new arrival. '*Oh, e adesso?*' he protested. '*Vai fuori di qui! Il museo è chiuso!*'

Blake noted a set of large, old keys in the exterior door. He closed and locked it. The custodian reacted in offended surprise. 'You're quite right,' Blake told him, drawing his gun and firing. A single shot punched through the man's heart. He collapsed, twitching as blood pooled around him. 'The museum is indeed closed.'

CHAPTER 57

Reeve and Connie scurried through the dimly lit museum. Mannequins in elaborate costumes lined it, painted faces watching them pass with masked eyes. 'The scaffolding's through those windows,' said Connie as they entered a gallery.

The path through the exhibition doubled back around a divider bisecting the room. Several tall but narrow windows, shutters half-closed, were on the other side. Reeve hurried to check the openings—

A gunshot echoed through the building.

Blake. He'd realised where they'd gone, killed the custodian . . .

And now they were trapped inside with him. 'Reeve,' Blake called in smug triumph. 'I've locked the door. I rather doubt a place this old has a fire exit. You can't get out.'

Reeve went to the nearest window. Connie was right; there was scaffolding outside. The museum backed on to a drained section of canal. But it was far from an easy escape route. The poles and planks extended some way in both directions. 'He'd pick us off before we could climb along it,' he said.

Connie's face filled with resurgent fear. 'So what do we do?'

'I've got to take him down.'

'Do you have a gun?' His silence was answer enough. 'Shit.'

Reeve quickly surveyed the room. The only other exit led back towards the entrance hall. No escape that way. The exterior door was thick, old wood, and Blake had the keys.

More mannequins stood against the divider. They were a mix of male and female. Most of the latter wore elaborate dresses with long, sweeping hoop skirts. Reeve noted something on the floor beside him – then moved. 'Get behind the dummies,' he whispered, ushering Connie down the row of figures. He halted halfway along and pushed between a pair of splendidly attired women. 'Keep going, and stay low.'

She followed him into the shadows and crouched, slipping along behind the mannequins. Reeve went the other way, heading back towards the divider's end. He hunched low behind another female figure.

Footfalls on the old wooden floor. 'Playing hide and seek, are we?' said Blake as he entered the gallery. Switches clicked, and the lights came on. Reeve tensed, but the illumination level only marginally increased. It was kept low so the exhibits wouldn't fade. Blake continued his cautious advance. Fabric rustled as he pushed at a costumed dummy. 'You've had a good run, I'll give you that. But it's over. For you too, Connie. I know you're in here.'

Reeve glanced back, glimpsing Connie past the mannequins. Her eyes were wide in terror, hand to her mouth. He silently willed her to remain still.

Blake rounded the divider, then stopped. Reeve guessed he was peering behind the row of exhibits. But the figures were posed in various positions, denying him a clear view. He moved on . . .

And paused again.

Reeve knew what he'd seen. The light angling through the windows was catching something on the floor.

Damp footprints.

His clothing hadn't dried from his plunge into the lagoon, his shoes still wet. Leaving a trail. Faint by now – but enough for the Operative to notice.

Blake resumed his advance. Reeve waited, coiled. The Operative was only a couple of metres away, following his footprints. When he drew level, he would strike—

But Blake halted again. 'I always confirm the kill, Reeve,' he said, suspicion clear in his voice. 'You know that. But first, I have to *make* the kill. Or in this case, two. So—'

He fired.

The first bullet blew an arm off Reeve's cover just above his head. The next round transfixed the dummy beyond it. Its torso shattered, the costume collapsing in on itself. Blake kept shooting, sweeping along the row. The exhibits fell, toppling like dominoes—

Connie screamed.

A cry of pain, not fear. She'd been hit—

Reeve burst from cover, knocking down the wounded mannequin. Blake was too far away to reach in a single movement. He vaulted the falling dummy as the Operative spun towards him. Another shot. Searing pain as it clipped his torso.

The two men collided. Reeve swung, batting the gun away from him. Blake reflexively pulled the trigger as he was knocked back. The round hit a wall. Reeve kept up his charge. Blake slammed against a window—

And smashed through it.

Reeve tried to stop. But the Operative grabbed him as he toppled backwards – into the drained canal beyond.

The two men crashed on to a wooden walkway atop the scaffolding. The impact jolted planks loose. Blake bowled over the side and fell towards the mud below. Reeve, though, dropped straight downwards with the dislodged boards. He hit another tier beneath. Planks snapped under him. He clutched at the metal poles as he fell again, but couldn't find grip.

His next landing pounded him to a painful stop on more boards. He lay still for a moment – then heard something heavy shift above. A rope-bound bundle of spiked wooden pilings slid towards the broken hole—

Reeve threw himself over the side as the giant stakes plunged at him. They slammed down where he had just been. A couple jarred loose, falling after him. He hit the stony silt hard – but still managed to roll sideways. The pilings stabbed into the mud beside him. The rest of the bundle snagged on the scaffolding. Couplers broke as the makeshift structure shook. One of the vertical supports swayed outwards. Metal pieces clanged down around him.

Groaning, dizzied, he raised his head. High walls surrounded him. The canal's bottom was eight metres below the window. A grimy barge lay grounded in the sludge, a small excavator sitting on it. Rusty metal dams rose at each end of the drained section. They were not fully watertight. A large piece of machinery sat on one dam, hoses hanging from it. A pump, constantly drawing water from the pools in the mud. Repulsive slurping sounds came from a hose in the largest.

Blake lay near it. He had suffered a harder landing, not yet recovered. Reeve saw his gun in the mud beside him. He staggered upright. His side burned where the bullet had hit. A flesh wound, but it still hurt enough to slow him.

He started towards Blake, step by painful step. The other man stirred. His hand closed – around nothing. The realisation that he'd lost his gun sparked him to full alertness. He spotted the weapon and clawed for it—

Reeve kicked it from his hand. It splashed down in the pool of dirty water – near the hose. The powerful pump immediately sucked it up. It clanked against the wire mesh covering the nozzle's end.

Blake sat up. Reeve's foot hit his head and knocked him back down. Blood burst from Blake's nose. Reeve struck again, booting his chest. The Operative rolled over with a strained roar.

Reeve kept up his attack. He had Blake at his mercy.

And this time, he was going to kill him.

CHAPTER 58

Connie peered cautiously from the broken window, face tight with pain. The bullet had hit above her hip, carving straight through her flesh. Her left hand was pressed hard against the bloody entrance and exit wounds.

Below, Reeve and Blake fought. Her lover was winning. She felt brief retributive exhilaration as another kick hit the downed Operative.

But she couldn't influence the battle. Instead she searched for a way to reach safety. The top of the scaffolding was not far below. To her right, it ran along the museum's side to a wall. Could she climb over? The only other choice was a ladder on the scaffolding by the farthest dam. It rose to a closed-off footpath.

She chose the nearest escape route. The walkway directly beneath the window was damaged, planks missing. She would have to traverse the scaffolding itself for a couple of metres.

Another glance at the two men. Reeve was still laying into the assassin. Silently egging him on, Connie lowered herself over the windowsill. Burning coursed through her hip as she was forced to release her injury. She gritted her teeth and lowered her foot to the scaffold. It swayed under her weight.

Holding the window frame, she brought her other shoe down. Another unnerving shift beneath her. But it held.

Flat against the wall, she edged sideways. The gap in the walkway was quickly traversed, fear driving her. She found her footing on the remaining boards. The scaffolding's end was not far away. She started towards it—

The structure rocked, an unsecured vertical pole leaning outwards. She clutched at the museum's wall. Below her, the bundled pilings shuddered. Another of the thick three-metre poles broke loose. It plunged into the muck with a bang.

Reeve was about to stamp on Blake's head when the piling struck. He whipped his head around at the noise – and saw Connie on the swaying scaffold. A moment of alarm as she staggered, but she caught herself. Relief—

Blake rolled, one arm coming up. Reeve finished his move. Too late. The Operative deflected the blow. Reeve was momentarily unbalanced – and Blake took full advantage. He grabbed the other man's leg and twisted around. Reeve was pulled with him. He tripped over Blake's torso and fell into the mud.

Blake released him and rolled again, scrambling up. He splashed into the pool and groped at the pump's nozzle. Suction still held his gun against the filter. He pulled it free—

Reeve hurled himself bodily at his opponent. Blake was slammed down into the pool. The gun jarred from his grip, vanishing in the muddy water. Reeve pushed himself up – then grabbed the Operative's throat. He forced his head into the pool. Blake thrashed, clawing at Reeve's face. Reeve tipped his head back and squeezed harder. *Die, you bastard, just die—*

Connie shrieked.

Reeve looked up – and saw a section of scaffolding give way. Connecting couplers snapped, boards crashing down through the clanging metal forest. Connie staggered as she was swung away from the wall. A foot went over the edge. She fell—

One hand caught a metal pole. She clung to it, legs flailing several metres above the ground.

'Connie!' Reeve shouted. Her other hand tried to find grip on the scaffolding. Failed. She cried out again – in fear. The bundled pilings swung like a pendulum, rocking the weakening structure. She was going to fall—

Save her, or kill Blake. There was only one choice he could make.

One final savage thrust of both thumbs into Blake's throat, then he jumped up. What was the quickest way to her?

The barge. He ran to it and scrambled up to its deck, rounding the excavator. A ladder led part-way up the scaffolding. He scaled it, then pulled himself to the top level.

Connie saw him. 'Alex! Help!'

'I'm coming!' He moved as fast as he dared. Past the museum's broken window, vaulting the hole in the walkway. He saw her fingers straining, slipping. 'Hold on! I'm almost—'

She lost her grip.

Reeve dived and grabbed her wrist as she dropped. Her weight almost pulled him with her. Fire surged up his side as muscles strained around the bullet wound. He yelled, bracing one leg against a pole. The scaffolding reeled away from the wall. More couplers groaned and cracked under the stress, about to snap . . .

But he had her.

He gripped her clothing with his other hand. More pain as he lifted her. Her fingers hooked around the boards. The strain on his arms eased. He pulled harder, raising her up. She swung a knee on to the walkway. He rolled, hauling her alongside him.

The movement made Connie scream. There was blood around her left hip. Blake's bullet had gone through the flesh. 'Connie, I've got you,' he said. 'Can you walk?'

She looked at him, eyes narrowed by pain. 'Yeah.'

He stood. The scaffold rocked again. He looked along it. A wall past the museum was climbable. The dam with the pump was just beyond. He helped her up. 'You need to get to a hospital.'

Connie glanced into the canal. Blake was stirring, a hand to his throat. 'What about him?'

'We'll be gone before he can climb up.' He carefully led her along the unstable boards.

Blake strained to draw breath through his bruised airway. He'd almost passed out as Reeve choked him . . .

The thought of the traitorous Operative stoked the angry fire within him. He opened his eyes. The bright blue sky was briefly dazzling. Then he focused. Where was his target?

Targets, plural. They were both heading along the scaffolding. He sat up, searching for his weapon.

It was somewhere in the muddy pool. By the time he found

it, they could be gone. He would have to pursue unarmed. What was the fastest way up? The barge—

His eyes locked on to the excavator.

Purpose overcame pain. He hurried to the barge and clambered on to its deck. Reeve and the woman were still sidestepping along the scaffolding. Blake checked the little digger's cab. The keys were in the ignition. It wasn't as if anyone could steal it, stranded in the drained canal . . .

He started the engine.

Reeve looked back sharply at the raucous noise. Blake was in the excavator. What was he doing?

The answer became horribly clear a moment later.

The machine's arm extended – then its body rotated on its base. The toothed bucket swung at the scaffolding—

He pulled at Connie's arm. '*Run!*'

Too late.

The bucket smashed into the metal poles. A vertical standard broke loose with a shrill of disintegrating metal. Planks fell, tiers collapsing on to each other. Blake set the excavator into motion, bringing it to the barge's bow. The arm scraped behind more supports, knocking out a diagonal brace.

Then he turned the machine back around.

The bucket ripped out more standards. A whole section of scaffold peeled away from the wall. Plunging poles struck each other with deafening clangs, planks cartwheeling into the canal.

Reeve made a desperate lunge at the wall, grabbing it with one hand . . .

The walkway toppled beneath him.

Connie screamed again as she was carried with it. Reeve still had her arm. He could keep hold, or let go to save himself—

He caught her. For a moment.

Then his tenuous hold on the wall was torn away.

The scaffolding swept them back down towards the mud. Reeve made a desperate jump to bring them clear of the debris.

He lost his hold on Connie as they hit the stony sludge below. Wood and metal landed deafeningly behind them. A standard toppled like a tree – pounding down on Connie's back.

Another falling pole caught the pump's hoses. They tore from the boxy machine. More metal hit the dam itself. The rusty barrier shook, connecting plates straining. Bolts snapped. One plate burst free and spun out over the canal. It slammed into the mud near Reeve like a mortar shell.

Water erupted from the exposed gap. It kicked up silt from the dam's base, splattering the couple. The pools on the canal floor started to rise.

One swelled around Connie.

Reeve blearily sat up. Half the scaffold had collapsed. The remainder swayed, barely holding in place. A bundle of pilings still hung precariously from the damaged structure. The excavator had been knocked from the barge. He couldn't see Blake.

Frothing brown water gushed around him. The large hose's nozzle was close by, but it was no longer draining the canal. He crawled to Connie. She spluttered as the wave hit her face, trying to push herself up. The metal pole held her down at the waist. 'Alex!' she gasped. 'I'm stuck!'

Reeve tried to lift the fallen standard. It barely shifted. Wreckage covered its end, pinning her. 'Can you move?' If it had damaged her spine . . .

She squirmed, legs kicking frog-like in the mud. 'Yeah. I just—' Another cough as more water splashed into her face.

Several wooden pilings trapped the standard. Reeve grabbed one. The giant stake weighed as much as Connie herself. His feet slipped in the wet sludge as he hauled it clear. He moved to the next. 'Alex, help!' Connie cried. The last word was choked off. The rising pool was up to her mouth.

Reeve pulled hard at the piling. It rasped free of the cluttered debris. Another attempt to move the standard. It shifted a little more, but still not enough. He took hold of another length of wood—

A metal pole smashed down on his back.

Blake had recovered.

CHAPTER 59

The brutal blow dropped Reeve into the pool beside Connie. His face hit the water. He tried to get up—

Another strike pounded him into the submerged silt.

Blake leapt knees-first on to his back. Reeve's remaining breath exploded out in a rush of bubbles. He thrashed, snagging his attacker's jacket, and pulling. No leverage. Blake's entire weight was upon his upper body.

Blake spoke. Reeve couldn't hear him through the water. But the tone was victorious, gloating. He released Blake's clothing and groped in the pool. He needed a rock, a piece of wood – anything he could use as a weapon. Nothing was big or heavy enough. Blake shifted his weight. The pressure on Reeve's back grew more painful.

His hand closed around a stone. He batted it at Blake's side. No effect. Too light. The Operative retaliated by punching the back of his skull. Sludge squirmed disgustingly up Reeve's nostrils. He had no breath left to blow it out. Drop the stone. Need something bigger. A hissing roar grew louder in his ears. His fingers scraped through the silt. Stone, wood, unidentifiable trash, stone—

Metal. Solid, angular.

Blake's gun.

He clutched it, finding the grip, the trigger. His hand was weakening, fingers barely able to close. Every instinct, every nerve begged him to breathe. He tried to raise his arm from the water. It refused, muscles trembling. Just the hand, then. Lift your hand.

His body refused the order. His chest was on fire.

Turn your hand, or you're going to *die*—

He twisted his wrist – and pulled the trigger.

It felt like a bomb going off by his hip. The water took most of the round's explosive force. His ears were beneath the pool's surface, the noise deafening—

The weight on his back suddenly vanished.

Blake landed hard in the water beside him. Reeve dredged up a last scrap of energy and rolled sideways. His head broke the surface. He drew in a rasping breath. Air hit his lungs. Another breath, and another. He felt strength returning.

Connie—

Blake first. The Operative was still a potential threat. Reeve raised the gun – only to find the slide locked back. He tugged feebly at it, but it didn't release. Firing underwater had jammed the mechanism.

But the weapon had done its job. Blake lay curled on his side in the churning water. The bullet had hit his abdomen, red staining the rising brown. The Operative's face was contorted in agony. No exit wound; the bullet was still inside him. If it had shattered on impact, it would be like knives carving through his organs.

Reeve felt no sympathy. All he cared about was saving Connie. He tossed away the useless gun and crawled back to her.

Her head was underwater. She wasn't moving.

He gripped another piling. In his weakened state, it felt like moving a car. Wood scraped over metal – then splashed into the pool.

Reeve dropped to his knees beside Connie and strained at the standard pinning her. This time, it shifted. He pulled it higher, then used the piling to wedge it. Then he dragged her clear.

She didn't react even after her face cleared the pool. He turned her head to one side. Water ran from her mouth and nose. Tip her head to clear the airways. No breathing. A rapid check of her pulse. Nothing.

Fear and anguish threatened to overcome him. He drove the feelings back down, training defeating emotion. He could save her. He *had* to. He would do whatever it took to keep her alive.

Reeve sealed her nose and blew deep, forceful breaths into her mouth. Five in all, then he began CPR. Hands together on her chest, then firm, rapid compressions. The ringing in his ears faded as he worked. A glance at Blake. The Operative had barely moved. Repeat the process—

Connie suddenly convulsed, coughing and gasping. He drew back. 'Connie! Are you okay?'

It took several seconds before she could reply. 'I – I, oh, God! I don't know, I—' She coughed again, vomiting up foul, brackish water.

The pool was still rising. 'We've got to get out,' he said, unsteadily standing. The scaffold's collapse would draw attention. People on a bridge beyond the undamaged dam had stopped to see what was happening. The authorities

427

would be called – and the police weren't far away.

Connie tried to rise, but her legs buckled. 'I . . . I can't get up.'

Reeve hoisted her in a fireman's lift. The effort almost felled him, but he forced his protesting muscles to stand firm. How to get out? The scaffolding's far end was mostly intact. He spotted a ladder on it, near the other dam.

Another glance at Blake. He had curled more tightly, hands clutching his wound. He wouldn't be chasing them. Connie over his right shoulder, he lumbered towards the scaffold. The overturned excavator lay beside it. He skirted the vehicle, looking for a way up.

The broken metal skeleton creaked as the bundle of pilings swung from an overstressed coupler. Reeve's instinct was to stay well clear. But a partially collapsed walkway formed a ramp beneath it. One eye on the spikes above, he went to the wooden slope.

Every movement felt like a molten poker driving into Blake's guts. But remaining still was scarcely less excruciating. The rising water forced the issue. If he didn't move, he would drown.

He pushed himself up. The pain almost overwhelmed him. But he resisted. He was SC9, damn it! He could take it. He had a job to do.

A kill to confirm.

Two kills. Where were Reeve and the woman?

Escaping.

No! his mind roared. They couldn't get away, not now. But Reeve was carrying her up the wrecked scaffolding. He had to pursue. But merely moving was agony. Climbing would make him pass out.

Reeve had shot him with his own gun – but not finished him off. Where was the weapon? Had Reeve taken it, or—

The SIG lay in the mud near the barge, slide locked back. Blake knew the magazine wasn't empty – so firing from underwater had jammed it. Reeve wouldn't have discarded it if he'd been able to clear the problem. But he was wounded, weakened. The gun might still be useable . . .

He forced himself to his feet. Determination – anger – drove back the pain. Reeve was *not* going to escape.

His target was still ascending, looking up. The woman was draped limply over his shoulder. Blake followed, legs stiff, wooden. It didn't matter. Nothing did, except completing his mission. The traitor had to die. He reached the gun. More pain, a red-hot drill carving into his body as he bent down. *Ignore it*, he ordered himself. *Only the dead feel nothing.*

Make Reeve feel nothing.

He straightened, tipping the gun to drain water from it. Metal glinted within the ejection port. The empty cartridge had jammed inside. He took his other hand from the wound. Blood slopped out. His vision went dark. Then it cleared, revealing the world swaying around him. He battled to stay upright, then gripped the slide. A sharp tug. It rattled, but didn't move. He pulled harder, then pushed. Faint clinks as the cartridge was dislodged. Another pull – and the spent brass popped from the port.

Blake released the slide. It snapped smoothly into place – chambering a new round.

Palm back against the oozing wound, he staggered to the

scaffolding's base. His hand was shaking, accuracy compromised. And Reeve and the woman were partially obstructed by metalwork. He wanted as clear a shot as possible. There was a chance the gun was damaged; it might jam again. He had to make sure he didn't *need* a second shot. Jaw clenched, abdomen searing, he leaned back and raised the weapon. A step closer to remove some poles from his line of fire . . .

He had them.

Blake aligned the gunsight on Reeve's heart. Then he locked every muscle except his trigger finger. It tightened—

The woman raised her head – and saw him.

'*Alex!*'

Reeve reacted instantly to Connie's cry of alarm. There was only one possible cause.

Blake.

His head snapped around. The scene formed in an instant. Blake stood almost directly below. Gun raised.

The bundled pilings less than a metre away. Rope taut on a scaffolding coupler, its snapped bolt wedged against the standard—

Reeve whirled – and hit the coupler.

The impact drew blood, metal cutting his hand. But the strained connector broke. The rope instantly went slack—

And the pilings fell.

Blake fired. But too late. The bullet struck only falling wood.

The pilings slammed down before Blake, beside him—

On him.

A thick, spiked pole hit his chest. Blake was hammered to

the wet ground. The pointed end stabbed into the mud – through his back. Blood spouted from his mouth. A final strained gurgle of pain and defeat . . . then he fell limp.

Reeve stared down at the broken figure. 'Confirmed,' he murmured. Then he continued his climb.

He soon reached the intact section of walkway. 'Are you all right?' he asked as he brought Connie to the ladder.

'Yeah,' she said, voice weak. Then: 'You got that guy.'

He started to climb. 'Yes.'

'I . . . I thought we were both dead.'

'So did he.' He reached the top. 'Okay, I'm going to put you down. Can you stand?'

'I . . . I don't think so.'

Reeve carefully lowered her. Despite his best efforts, she let out another keening cry. 'Okay, I've got you,' he said, crouching to help her sit.

Connie looked at her wound. 'Oh, God. I've lost a lot of blood.'

'You'll be okay,' he assured her. More onlookers had clustered at the barrier closing the footpath. 'They'll get you straight to hospital.' He called out to the bystanders. '*Hey! Le hanno sparato – chiama i paramedici!*' A woman hurriedly raised her phone to call an ambulance. 'The cops'll be coming too,' he told Connie, holding her hand. 'I've got to go.'

'But you're hurt,' she protested.

'I can't risk being arrested. Not with SC9 so close.' A glance back at Blake's transfixed body. 'He wasn't the only one chasing me.'

'But – but they're trying to kill me too.' She squeezed his hand, fearful.

431

'Something's changed. I don't know what, but two of them almost had me – then backed off. I think they were ordered to stand down.' Another look towards the corpse below. 'I guess Blake refused. But this operation got out of control – and SC9 pulled the plug. I doubt they'll come looking for you right away. Not with so much police attention.' He stood, still holding her hand. 'If they have a chance to catch *me*, though . . .'

Connie sighed. 'I understand,' she said, reluctantly releasing him. 'Go. I won't tell them anything. I'll find you when I get out of hospital.' Reeve hesitated, not moving. She instantly realised something was wrong. 'What is it?'

'You . . .' He knew he shouldn't tell her anything. It would make things easier. *For her, or you?* the self-critical part of his mind asked scathingly.

Which was why he knew he had to do it. He owed it to Connie – to the woman he loved. 'You won't find me,' he finally said.

She stared at him, not comprehending. 'What do you mean?'

'I have to leave you,' he went on, fighting rising emotion. 'As long as you're with me, you're in danger. You'll . . . you'll be killed. It might be sooner, it might be later. But it *will* happen.' Connie's eyes went wide as she realised where he was leading. 'If it's not SC9, it'll be the Russians. They want me dead now just as much as Scott. I . . .' A pause, the admission hard to make. But he would do whatever it took to keep her alive. 'I can't protect you. But I can't let anything happen to you, either. Not because of me. So you've got to leave – you've got to hide. I have to go.'

'No, Alex,' Connie said. 'No, no.' She clutched at his hand again. He pulled away, anguished. She gasped. 'No! You can't go, you can't leave me!'

'I have to. I'm sorry.' His eyes filled with stinging tears; he blinked them away. 'I love you, Connie. I love you so much.' He stood, slowly backing away.

She tried to follow, but pain halted her. 'No, don't go,' she said instead. 'Please. Alex, don't leave me. Don't leave me!'

'I have to go.' His voice quavered. 'I love you.' Reeve turned away before emotion could change his mind. He rounded the barrier, pushing through the onlookers. Nobody dared try to stop him.

Then he was gone.

CHAPTER 60

Tony Maxwell walked along the Thames, taking in the Houses of Parliament across the river. Two days had passed since the events in Venice. He felt strangely ambivalent about how things had turned out.

It was in some ways a catastrophe for SC9. Four Operatives killed, others at risk of exposure. The mall shootout had been international news. Some of the action was caught on CCTV. A couple of faces were clear enough to identify. Luckily, they belonged to the dead agents. The false identities created by SC9 should block further investigation. If anyone from their past lives recognised them, further covers were in place. Altered records claimed they had left their former services with tarnished reputations. Bad apples, disgruntled, embittered.

Four such people all dying in the same vicinity was, of course, a problem. Smart and diligent investigators might make the connection. The one relief was that such investigators would be outside the UK. Post-Brexit, cooperation with European law enforcement had been reduced. Attempts to dig deeper could be stonewalled. Scott had still left him with a headache, though.

Scott . . .

His former boss was the cause of his ambivalence. SC9 had taken a major hit because of his actions. The hunt for Alex Reeve had driven Scott to take too many risks. He'd lost control of the situation. And paid for it with his life. The man who built the agency, created the Operatives, was dead.

But . . . as a result, Maxwell was now in charge of SC9. Which had been his goal all along. Britain's most lethal covert unit was his to command.

His promotion came with a price tag. By involving the other intelligence heads, he'd tacitly accepted a degree of their authority. He would have to tread carefully. Scott had been absolutely right to assert SC9's total independence. It would take time, and careful political manoeuvring, to re-establish it. But it would happen.

And then the *other* piper would come calling.

Maxwell had already spotted the man he was meeting. Both were walking in the same direction, his contact slightly faster. The other man drew alongside. He didn't look around as he quietly spoke. 'What's the situation?' His accent was not British.

'Scott's gone,' Maxwell replied. 'I'm now in charge of SC9.'

'Good. We'll contact you via dead drop when we have an assignment for you.' The man strode away.

Maxwell went to the wall at the river's edge and stopped, gazing at Parliament. The political heart of the United Kingdom. Yet not a single politician within knew what he did to protect them. Or that SC9, the agency he now controlled, even existed. Nor did they know the Faustian bargain he'd made to reach his new position.

He would do whatever was necessary to ensure they never did.

He already had tasks to handle as SC9's new head. The German job, for one. With Scott gone, his orders on how to approach it could be ignored. Better solutions found. Maxwell had considered it ideally suited to Locke's particular talents. That would be his first order of business, then.

The second was Alex Reeve. Four Operatives had died – pointlessly – while hunting him. Should more be sent to finish the job?

No, he decided. Not for now. Maxwell still believed his assessment of his former student was correct. Reeve wasn't a traitor; he *couldn't* bring himself to harm the country. He could have given Parker's phone to the Russians, but didn't. He could have released the stolen files' password to the media, but didn't. Even after an attempt on his life, he hadn't carried out his threat.

Leave him alone, Maxwell decided. Reeve had served his purpose; let him live in peace with his girlfriend. There was no reason to disturb the status quo.

Unless Reeve himself disturbed it . . .

He regarded the building across the water for another moment, then set off again. The man was no longer in sight. Maxwell continued onwards, disappearing into the capital's crowds.

San Giovanni e Paolo Hospital occupied a sprawl of buildings in Venice's Castello district. Modern facilities were artfully concealed behind its historic structures. The one housing the main entrance could be – and often was – mistaken for a church.

Reeve waited in the canalside piazza outside the hospital. He knew he was taking a risk by being there. He'd changed his clothing and hair colour, face hidden by sunglasses and baseball cap. The disguise had taken a chunk out of his meagre remaining money. But the Venetian authorities were still looking for him. He'd been caught on camera at the Valecenter mall. His link to the vehicular chaos, boat theft and Blake's death was obvious.

But he'd taken a greater risk the previous day by going into the hospital itself. Claiming to be Connie's brother, he learned her injuries were still being treated. She was expected to be released in twenty-four hours. As for the police . . .

Her room wasn't under guard, which was something. But he didn't dare try to see her. Not just in case someone – cops, Russians, SC9 – spotted him. He was afraid that if he did, he might never leave her.

Which would, eventually, cause her death. He was more certain than ever he'd done the right thing for her. However much it hurt them both. After the body-blow he'd inflicted, Scott would be even more determined to kill him. He'd lost Parker's phone, lost all leverage against SC9. All he could do was draw the Operatives away from Connie. He had to run.

Alone.

He kept up his watch as the day wore on, regularly changing position. Finally, Connie emerged. She descended the steps with a limp. No police escort; she'd convinced them she was an innocent caught up in events. That didn't mean she wouldn't face further questioning. But for now, she was being released without charge.

Connie stopped and surveyed her unfamiliar surroundings. He knew what she was thinking. Two thoughts: the first was, *What the hell am I going to do now?* She couldn't return to what had been her home – her life.

She continued to look around the piazza. Searching for someone. For *him*. Her second thought: *Where is Alex?* He had come to her out of nowhere once before, after she left England. Gare du Nord station, terminus of the train through the Channel Tunnel. After confirming she wasn't being followed, he'd revealed himself. Her delight at seeing him was a happy memory he would never forget.

But now, everything about her would be nothing but memories.

The thought made his throat clench with emotion. Sadness, despair, grief . . . loss. He loved her. And now, he had to leave her.

No choice.

Connie turned towards him. For just a moment, their eyes met. Then a gaggle of tourists passed between them.

They moved on. But Reeve was gone.

Have you discovered Andy McDermott's bestselling Wilde and Chase series?

  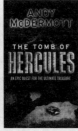 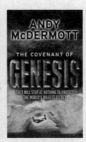 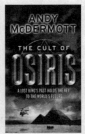

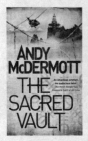 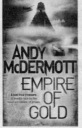  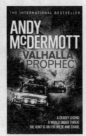 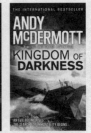

 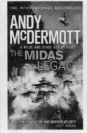 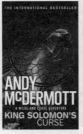 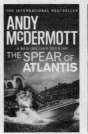 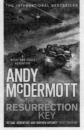

Available from Headline

THRILLINGLY GOOD BOOKS
FROM CRIMINALLY
GOOD WRITERS

CRIME FILES BRINGS YOU THE LATEST RELEASES FROM TOP CRIME AND THRILLER AUTHORS.

SIGN UP ONLINE FOR OUR MONTHLY NEWSLETTER AND BE THE FIRST TO KNOW ABOUT OUR COMPETITIONS, NEW BOOKS AND MORE.

VISIT OUR WEBSITE: WWW.CRIMEFILES.CO.UK
LIKE US ON FACEBOOK: FACEBOOK.COM/CRIMEFILES
FOLLOW US ON TWITTER: @CRIMEFILESBOOKS